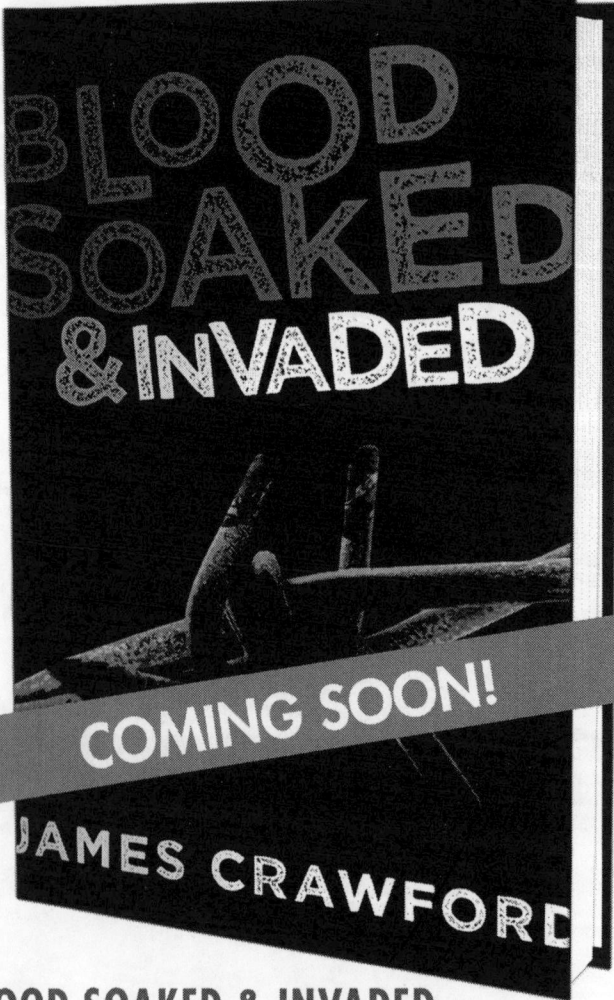

BLOOD SOAKED & CONTAGIOUS

JAMES CRAWFORD

Judy -
Don't worry, You
Still cum first in
an me.

A PERMUTED PRESS book

ISBN (trade paperback): 978-1-61868-106-5
ISBN (eBook): 978-1-61868-107-2

Blood Soaked and Contagious copyright © 2011, 2013
by James Crawford.
All Rights Reserved.
Cover design by Karen Fletcher

**PERMUTED
PRESS**

Chapter 1

Brain spattered on asphalt doesn't look very much like anything at all, especially if the asphalt is new. Older asphalt, gray and cracked from years in the sun, shows more of the fatty gelatinous smear but leeches away much of the color.

Standing there in the late morning sun outside the evacuated shell of what used to be one of the best bakeries in town, I couldn't help but feel a little sad. The headless body on the ground didn't feel anything at all. I strongly suspect that the head, after I'd spread it over fifteen feet of asphalt, didn't feel anything either. I suppose that's a good thing.

Really, if the zombie still felt anything after fighting with me, it would mean that I had not done my job very well. It would also mean the zombie had won.

A zombie winning the fight means you die.

In my case, thankfully, dying would get me out of his way. I'm an annoyance, rather than a possible food source, and that might mean that my transition from this world to the next would be somewhat uneventful. Depending on the personality of the victor, it could as easily mean that my final moments would be even more hideous than being eaten alive. An undead sadist is still a sadist.

The world of "Kill or Be Killed" has only one prize and only one type of fame. You're the one still alive. Pat yourself on the back!

I've been doing this gig, Freelance Zombie

Extermination, for just over a year and a half. My claim to fame is simple: "Hey! I'm still alive!" Better, I'm sure, than the other options.

The post-fatal menace that I had finished off outside the old bakery had been harassing a small community of squatters who had appropriated an office building two blocks away. One of my previous satisfied customers had told them about me and they had tracked me down, in the hopes that I'd be able to help them out before anyone else was brutalized.

My profession is not one that pays well, especially since the economy is mostly shot to Hell. All the same, this pleasant group of people offered me a good barbequed chicken lunch if I could make their unctuous bother disappear. Believe me, I don't usually work for so little, but they were quite kind and polite. I really didn't want to see them killed off one by one, so we made an appointment for me to drop by on the most likely day their local Trouble would be back and obnoxious. Apparently, he liked to stick to a schedule.

I'm anal about being punctual and keeping appointments, so two days later, I grabbed a few things after my morning coffee and took a walk. Walking served a couple of purposes. It gave me an opportunity to settle my thoughts and get my Zen on. Perhaps, even more importantly, it was a chance to survey the local landscape. The overall impression that I had, as usual, was that we were much better off than a large portion of the United States as a whole.

There is still a government, albeit at a reduced level; the nation's Capital needs to function. The city of Arlington, Virginia, depending on where you're standing, is within five miles of Washington, DC. Many of the people who live out here in the suburbs continue to commute into DC or work at companies that were nationalized in order to keep everything afloat. We have power more often than not, and even phone service. There are actual stores and restaurants that are struggling to provide services, unlike other parts of the country that look like Mad Max gone to Hell.

All and all, it was a pretty enjoyable walk, even if there were a lot of abandoned homes and businesses along the way. Most of the inhabitants had fallen victim to the epidemic in one way or another. My clients were squatters, but they had a certain established feel to them because they'd been in that office building for a goodly amount of time. They sounded like an interesting group of people and I had hoped to talk to them for a little bit after my hunt and reward luncheon, but that wasn't how it worked out.

At some point before my appointed time to come around, their friendly neighborhood zombie killed every single one of them. As near as I can tell, he got wind of my impending arrival, and decided to show off his creativity. The cold-blooded bastard did a brutal, methodical, and sadistic job of slaughtering innocent people.

It wasn't difficult to tell something was wrong when I arrived that day. He'd left me a trail of bloody parts to follow.

The job had changed from a paid gig into revenge — nice, uninfected people should not be killed, willy-nilly — it offends me on a primal level.

He was strong enough, smart enough, and far cleverer than he needed to be. In other words, he was not easy to kill, and he made the best of it by explaining to me everything he'd done in Technicolor detail. When I finally got the drop on him, I did not feel a single pang of remorse or twinge in my conscience as I decapitated him. I will admit that I went a bit overboard when I smashed his skull open.

I'm only human.

A few hours after being a complete scavenger, rooting over the things the poor squatters no longer needed, I knew I needed a break. Between the old bakery and my neighborhood, alongside empty storefronts and a burnt-out McDonalds, was an actual bar. Not just any bar, but a real, functioning drinking establishment that was still serving customers. A beer at that bar became the target of my desires, so I went forth.

It was barely a short walk, all things considered, and before you can say, "asshole," I was stepping inside Marvin's dystopian bar and grill. The owner and his wife greeted me with their characteristic warmth, which is to say their grunting was somewhat less bitter than what one would normally receive. There was a beer on the bar in front of my customary stool, so I knew the grunting was just for theatrical ambience.

No one has a beer waiting for you if they don't actually *like* you.

I was midway into my third beer when I noticed a new face at the bar. Anyone you'd never seen before, especially if they didn't look like one of the undead, was cause for pause. Being a gregarious soul, if a bit crusty around my rim, I decided to engage him on my favorite topic.

"It's like the whole Han Solo and Greedo thing. People are still slapping around whether it was the virus or zombies that showed up in the world first. They'll be debating it from now until... I guess, until human beings die out all the way, or we don't." I locked eyes with him and attempted to draw him into the conversation by force of will and two and a half beers.

"Regardless, there are zombies and there is a virus. There has to be a relationship, because wherever one appears, the other is soon to follow. Right? Some people are immune to the virus, and they're generally left alone by the zombies. If you contract the virus, sure as the sun rises, you're going to be zombie chow."

He stared back at me, this youngish scrawny fellow. What he did not do, however, was hold up his end of the conversational bargain. That's the social exchange in which I give you a piece of my mind and you give me a piece of yours back.

"You already know that the zombies will find you. They'll kill you. Killing someone their way generally involves eating the liver and kidneys and sucking the blood out of the victim's arteries like a copper-flavored milkshake. At some point, days or weeks later, the poor schlub will rise from whatever grave he ended up in and join in the bloody festivities." He just kept looking at me, almost as though he didn't speak any English, and he made no move to agree, disagree, or shush me. Emboldened, I continued.

"Now, say they get you... and with any luck, I mean this from the bottom of my heart, someone will bash your head in or set you on fire. One or the other would be sufficient, but it never hurts to be sure. For my personal preference, head bashing is best because you don't have to cope with a bacon-smelling fat candle that walks around, catching other things on fire before it finally falls over."

My brain rummaged around, grabbing at random things, in hopes of making a cogent point. Your average, motivated person could wreak all kinds of havoc on a zombie, and they'd do their damnedest to keep coming. The only real way to stop it is the classic way: destroy the cranium, pulverize the brain, and there will be one less walking horror in the world. Why? The brain appears to be the one thing the virus can't or won't regenerate when someone dies the first time. It certainly won't regenerate if there's nothing left to regenerate in the first place.

Anyone infected with the contagion will reanimate when they die. But if their brain is not intact, all you're left with is a body in a coffin that can't finish regenerating because there's no air for the body to breathe. Now, if a brainless body manages to come back to life prior to being interred, you have a critter that wants to hunt but can't really manage the proper sequence of movements.

All you have to do for them is round them up and burn them. Easy. Their cousins that reanimated with their gray matter intact, however, are a different story. Those have to be killed in a much more active fashion because they're willing and able to fight back.

It would also be simpler, of course, if they weren't so

personable.

I pulled myself out of the alcohol-induced reverie, and addressed my companion.

"Dude, I can't tell if you're getting any of this at all," I waggled a finger at him while I contemplated beer #3.

"Look, sit here with me in this dingy-ass suburban cantina and imagine this scenario. And I mean 'dingy' in the sweetest possible way, mind you! I think it will clue you into what I'm talking about." The owners nodded at me, but this dude just kept staring like I had slugs using my nose for a love hotel. I wasn't going to let him win this game of civil inattention.

"All right, say: your little sister comes back as a zombie. That's tragic, and I'm very sorry for your loss. Here's the 'but.' The creature that used to be your hot Lolita of a sibling still looks, talks, and acts very much like you would expect her to." I just kept right on going despite his lack of response, working toward my degree in dramatic monologues...

"She still knows where you hid your porn. That time at the carnival when you swallowed the goldfish she had just won? She remembers that, too. You'll find her memory has crystal clarity and her mouth has no internal editor whatsoever.

"Did I mention there's no expression in her eyes anymore, she's got a deathly pallor, she's incredibly strong, and her cute little fingernails are four inches longer and about 20 times thicker than before?

"Oh. Sorry...

"Well, Little Heidi, who now remembers everything down to the smallest detail thanks to the virus, as sure as the sun will rise, is now coming after you because you're infected, too. She's adorable, deadly, and will not stop until she's dined on your innards. Just to put the polish on that, she is absolutely willing to do and say anything that comes to her ravaged mind in order to manipulate you into being an easier target.

"Nice!

"'Tommy! These evil zombies are defiling my virginal, Aryan body! Ooo! Ack!,' she might scream from beneath your window some night.

"'And I bet you're up there yanking on your gristle because it gets you so hot. You're an evil, nasty big brother. Come down here and show me how nasty you are! Heidi wants your gooey drippings!'

"You're looking a little pale around the edges, my new friend. I didn't hit the nail on the head by accident, did I?" There was no way to know if I'd managed to pull something true from the fabric of uncertainty. That being the case, all I could figure was that my honesty was rippling around the recesses of his heart and giving him a nasty case of gas. I continued.

"You are so screwed! Take a few deep breaths. That's really the best thing you can do after someone has shared horrible truths with you. Good. Good.

"I should tell you, if you manage to cripple Little Heidi, you have to deliver the cootie grace as soon as you can after that. The reason is pretty simple. She's calling you every name in the book, tossing every secret you've ever had around as loud as she can, and is probably trying to seduce you at the same time.

"After all, her brain is intact and she knows every weakness you've got. I guarantee that she will exploit everything in order to keep you from finishing her off, because she has not lost sight of the original goal: kill my brother and eat him. All she wants to do is stay alive, even if she's been crippled by your attempts to save your own life. She won't heal super quickly or anything like that, but at least she'll be able to live until she can hunt again.

"God forbid that you have this little confrontation in public. Can you imagine how insane it would make you to have to listen to that for any length of time or to see the faces of other people as they listen to the litany of bizarre excess spewing from her mouth while you delay in finishing her off?

"Then again, it is possible that she'd take another route entirely. She could scream in a high-pitched, childlike voice. It's classic and might even work. How long do you want to listen to something like that?"

Apparently, he didn't want to listen to that at all, because he tossed his cookies all over the floor.

"That, my vomiting friend," I said, giving him a friendly pat on the shoulder, "is why you kill them as quickly as you possibly can."

I probably would have kept going even after he upchucked because beer (for some reason known only to God) pulls down the panties of my good sense. But Marvin, the bartender, gave me an ugly look and a gentle suggestion.

"Frank, get the fuck out before I slap you upside the head with a baseball bat."

He didn't get any sweeter when I gave him my "you've wounded my heart" pout. I suppose that's what you get from someone who used to be your landlord. Truth be told, that's probably why I didn't hang out in his place very often. He's a good soul, but we'd shared some really fucked up times together.

I got up and walked outside. A reasonable number of Coronas and being the bearer of bad news ruins the comfortable environment of any local watering hole. With any luck, Marvin and Shirley will let me come back in a few days. You have to let the memory of some things fade a little bit, but they know I will tell anyone and everyone The Way Things Are at the drop of a hat. Blunt, cynical commentary is a dying art.

Then again, I'm a wonderful customer to have, and that goes for any establishment. I pay my bill virtually every time, and I am always willing to take out a pesky zombie. Zombies, on the other hand, do not pay, ever, and tend to murder your clients in the most unfortunate ways.

I do have a certain gentle abrasiveness about me, but I like to think that is part of my overall personal charm. Then, like the Lolita Zombie Sister, I also have a tendency to say exactly what is on my mind without considering the possible consequences. Happily, no one to date has decided that it merited killing me, in or out of bars and restaurants.

My reputation for being Johnny-On-The-Spot for Undead Pest Removal does a lot to overcome my quirks in public places. No one wants a zombie farting around in their establishment if they can possibly avoid it. It isn't just the murdering and feasting—there's also the smell. The walking dead do not, as a rule, give a flying politician whether or not they've bathed since they came back from the Big Quiet.

Zombies call death "the Big Quiet." Some say they remember dying, the parts after the explosive agony of being eaten alive and bleeding out. They say there's nothing there, Out There, and that there is just this big quiet blackness that swallows you. If you can believe the walking dead have a religion, this is as close as it gets.

The scripture would be short.

"In the beginning, there was life and it was a random pattern of good events and bad events. In the middle, there was dying in a very nasty way, assisted by unfortunate mobs of undead cannibals. At the end of the middle came Death. Death was big, silent, and black. In the end, there is life after Death. That will also be nasty, because you have to eat your fellow man to stay alive."

Like I said, a very short scripture. Their idea of a worship service probably wouldn't be all that wonderful, if you consider that the only thing that really gets them going is eating people.

Chapter 2

I just wanted to stand there, drinking in the afternoon sun. This section of Route 29 in Arlington is quiet that time of day. At least, it has been since a good-sized chunk of the population started croaking, coming back to life, eating their neighbors, and somehow forgetting to show up for their fulfilling IT and government contracting jobs every day.

They declared martial law during the start of the Emergency, but much of the enforcement slacked off around non-critical areas. The suburbs, for the most part, were classified as non-critical. Even so, in this neck of the woods, you're more likely to see a stream of urban camo-painted vehicles, driven by various members of the Armed Forces, rather than morning commuters. When I was younger, we'd hang out on the way to school and beat the steaming poo out of one another while counting Volkswagens. These days, you shouldn't play games like "Punch Buggy" with military Humvees, because there are more of them moving around than commuter cars. That game nowadays always devolves into a fistfight and a kid gets his nose broken. And I dislike screaming children.

However, once in a while, the kid is screaming because Mom and Dad are about to force them into a corner and bite their ears off. Like today. I heard the noises before I decided to stroll up to the burnt-out McDonalds to confirm what I suspected.

Yeah.

Dad, I guess, had backed his son into a box of mostly

melted Happy Meal toys and was doing his level best to eat the kid alive. Shit.

"Pops! Back off the youngster!"

The man, covered with gore, looked up and out across the wilted plastic seats in the remains of the dining room and smiled at me.

"Don't you see, this is just a little family squabble—nothing to worry about. Fuck off, Chester."

I had a hard time believing that, watching the little boy writhing underneath his hands.

"My name isn't Chester, and I'm not going to let you munch on that kid."

Dad wasn't one to waste time. He stood up and hurled himself through the distance that separated us. I'll admit that, in retrospect, he had one of the best Angry Zombie Growls I've heard. What he didn't have was any clue about human body mechanics.

Faster. Meaner. Claws. But just as stupid.

Charging someone with your arms spread wide, foaming at the mouth, and at full speed is not smart and won't prepare you for someone who charges back at you.

I ran straight at him, popped the Man Scythe out of the Kydex rig across my back, and snapped the blade out as I moved. To his credit, Dad did not flinch, stop, or do anything else that would have made my day more unfortunate. He just kept coming like a pasty-white, scrawny, undead linebacker.

I planted my leading foot, which checked my forward motion, and collapsed to one knee while pivoting. His arm went right over my head. I came back to my feet, following his motion so that we faced the same direction. He was still in range.

Swing, batter!

The Man Scythe is a compact, folding, melee weapon that is based on a single-handed scythe design. If you're a martial arts fan, you've seen a kama before—it's a folding kama on steroids.

The frame is milled titanium, with a synthetic rubber grip for traction and shock absorption. The blade is three-quarters the length of the entire weapon, and it folds out into position with a flick of the wrist. A slot in the titanium forms a tongue that snaps into place under the blade, keeping it open for use and does a good bit to keep the blade from folding back in when you least want it.

I had this one made for me. No bullshit off-the-shelf models, as if anyone could mass-produce a thing of beauty like this. The blade is hand-forged, laminated steel, selectively hardened, with a hamaguri (clam) edge profile, as sharp and strong as a samurai sword. Don't ask me what it cost to have it made—I may never be able to erase that debt.

Dad's head popped off his shoulders, and the body kept going, spraying blood in a beautiful arc as it fell forward. I didn't even feel it when the scythe sheared his vertebrae. The blade is a testament to modern workmanship, executed by a Master of his craft.

The kid screamed—he was conscious enough to watch the show. Shit, again.

I figured that I'd cope with him as soon as I'd finished the necessary process. You have to open the skull to the air. You can either squish the brains around with your boot or hope for hungry animals of one kind or another to find it and consume it. In the light of day, with people milling about, animals are less likely, which means the first method is the one to use.

Boot.

The back of the scythe blade ends in a beveled spike. It was a thoughtful design decision on the part of the whackjob who came up with the idea. (That would be me. My self-deprecating sense of humor will be the death of me.) All you have to do is reverse your grip, spike forward, and give the decapitated head two or three love taps. By the time you're finished, either the brain will be exposed, or you will have sufficiently damaged the brain and won't have to stick your boot in.

The scythe came down with a positive sounding thunk, albeit a bit deeper than I had planned. I was about to put my foot on the cranium to pull the blade free when I heard the kid screaming "My daddy!" over and over again, right behind me.

I spun around, gave the child a complete dose of the "Hairy Eyeball," and was very disappointed when he didn't stop the noise.

"Kid! Shut the fuck up!" I bellowed at him, gesturing with both hands. "Your daddy was eating you!"

The little boy's eyes bugged straight out of his head, the remaining color drained from his face, and he passed out. I marveled at my success and was about ready to pat myself on the back for properly establishing my dominance and pointing out the reality of the situation, when I realized something.

I had never put the scythe down. I'd been flailing around in front of the kid with it still in my hand, flinging his father's head around in front of him like some kind of macabre magic wand. His short little life would be forever tainted by the image of a madman yelling while his own dad's bloody noggin danced in front of his face.

There have been times when I knew what I'd just done was a one-way ticket to Hell. In that instance, I was sure I'd just earned a table in the chef's kitchen in the club car to Hell.

"Aw." I was very earnest. "I'm really sorry, kid. I didn't mean to do that to you."

But he was out. Passed clean out—little psyche gone completely AWOL. That really did not help the situation because I really wanted to confess myself to this little fellow and have him forgive me for terrorizing him. That was no way to die.

I took a good look at his visible wounds and sighed. He wouldn't make it. Emergency medicine didn't exist for people who carry the virus. Ninety percent of the time, if a carrier is wounded, they wouldn't live long enough for an ambulance to arrive. The blood draws zombies from all around.

"Fuck me!" I stormed away from the little prone form on the concrete and proceeded to dash the head against the curb. Destroy the brain and get the damnable thing off the spike of my tool. That was about all the satisfaction I would be getting out of this.

Some moist minutes later, I cleaned off the blade with my shirttail and was just about ready to fold it down, stow it, and move on. Then I heard the little boy stir and start crying. It went way beyond pitiful and I knew that I wouldn't be able to leave him there to fend for himself. Tears get me every time and I know it.

It was Hard Lesson Time, and there was nothing I could do about it. I got down on my knees beside him and tried to keep a wary eye on our surroundings.

"Uh. Hey. Your dad was eating you because you're infected with the virus that makes zombies. You're hurt really bad." I realized that saying all of this was pointless, but I couldn't just let him die alone without someone. I kept talking to him.

"Kid. Do you have any family or anyone?"

He just shook his head at me.

"Nobody? No family? No nothing?"

Same shake of the head, tears flying left and right.

There was a chance that I could flag down a Humvee in a little bit and hand him off to the military if he lived long enough. It was an option. They'd take him to the local processing station and put him in the next convoy of infected people that they send to the Pens in Tennessee. They might even patch him up some.

The Pens had been set up to handle situations like these. An infected child who is orphaned with no family or means of support, the elderly, and anyone who cannot reasonably be expected to contribute to what remains of America's economic infrastructure were sent to the Pens. It was not a great solution, but it was better than nothing.

He'd live for a while in one of the heavily guarded tent cities that had been slapped together out there. Maybe, but not if the convoy was overrun or the Pens invaded. Then he would go back to being chow, only to join the ranks a little while later.

My choices were not fabulous. Toss the kid at a Humvee, leading to his likely death. Or leave the kid to fend for himself — infected and about to die.

The choices looked like: die; die; live for a little bit, terrified, hungry, no medical care, and *probably* die.

I should have just let his father do the dirty work, but for the fact that it would mean the boy would've died the most horrible way imaginable. Maybe I didn't do anything good for the kid after all.

We just held our places, staring at each other. Weepy Kid and Zombie-cide Man.

"Kid, how old are you?"

"I'm seven years old," he whispered, starting to wheeze a little bit. Not good.

"Okay." At that age, he really wouldn't get the complexity of the choice that I wanted to lay down in front of him. There was no doubt in my mind that choosing whether to die now or die later would be too much for any child to really grasp. But I had to give it a try, because I couldn't choose.

"Kid. I need you to think about something. I know you're really upset now, but you have to think about what I'm going to ask you. Can you do that?"

"Huh?"

Great. Just great.

"Do you want bad things to happen to you today, or do you want bad things to happen to you tomorrow or the next day?"

He looked at me with the glazed eyes of the utterly bereft. Tears had dried on his cheeks, and snot had trickled down his face. If it hadn't been for the expensively tasteful clothes, he could have been any tragic victim from any Third

World country you could name. He was the sort of child that gets plastered all over "Adopt Timmy from War-Torn Belize" advertisements.

"Bad things have already happened today," he whispered. "I don't want tomorrow to be bad, too."

I nodded at him. This reduced the options I was considering by one. Don't hand him to the military. Fuck. I was wasting time.

"Do you want bad things that happen fast and are over, or do you want bad things that might take a while before they stop?"

"Fast bad things." He didn't even pause before he answered. Bam. Clarity.

I couldn't leave him to fend for himself, be hunted, and then eaten. I also couldn't take him with me, because he'd just be a juicy worm on the fishing pole. They'd find him and me. Worse, the kid could infect me somehow.

I nodded at him again, and took a deep breath.

The boy said, "You killed my dad. Are you going to kill me, too?"

The breath rattled out of me, and I had trouble taking in another one. I don't know how this little boy knew, but he'd figured it out. Sure, I could just do it and never answer his question, but I knew that it would eat at me, strain my resolve, and give me more reason to hate myself for the things I had to do to survive.

"Yes." I said it.

"Why?"

"Because if I don't, things worse than your father will find you really soon. They'll eat you, just like he wanted to, and then you'll become just like them. You will go out and eat people." The words tumbled out of me in one breath.

"Oh," he replied in that small voice children use when something makes sense. "I don't want to eat people. It's bad and it hurts them."

His eyes started to glass over.

"You're right," I said, looking into his fading eyes. They

were a really warm brown. "Eating people does hurt them. I'm proud of you that you don't want to hurt people like that."

I still don't believe it, but he actually smiled. It was a good smile. I bet there were little kids like him who went to the guillotine, being brave like that.

"Hey," I said, "do you see that cloud over there? The one that looks like a duck?"

He turned away from me and looked up. It was the last conscious thing he ever did. Between the beats of my heart, this innocent little boy went rigid, relaxed, rattled deep in his tiny chest, and gave up the ghost. I'd waited too long.

Damn it. Damn it. Damn it.

I'm sorry. I'd hoped to do better for you than talk you to death, kid.

It is always the same story, a decent sort of person who didn't deserve to have their life tragically cut short. There was only one thing left to do: destroy the brain and then move on.

When it was done, I cleaned off the scythe, folded the blade back into the handle, and snapped it back into the rig. I wasn't seeing very clearly or breathing very easily. My face was wet.

All I could do was walk away from it. By the time I made it back to my place, my face was dry again.

Chapter 3

My home used to be a local hardware store. I like it because it is fairly easy to keep secure, as it had very few windows to begin with and only three sets of doors (two of them being steel). The best thing about it isn't the security aspect, which isn't as much of an issue as it would be if I were infected; it is the ready access to supplies. I need a nail, and all I have to do is walk down an aisle.

It is also a fantastic source of trade goods.

The virus and zombies appeared about two years ago, and roughly 40 percent of the North American population contracted the contagion or was in a position to return as a zombie. As I said, we don't really know what came first, just that they rolled out concurrently.

After six months of cannibalism, martial law, resurrection, and mayhem, modern society was starting to seriously break down. Goods and services were impacted, as well as delivery of the same. Zombies, you see, regardless of the fact that they retain their memories, do not really give a shit about the 9-to-5 workday. They are much more concerned with their nutritional intake.

Barter became a reasonable way to get things done, and many people adjusted to it with little effort. Of course, adjusting to that sort of economy is easier when you are capable of making a product yourself. Cheese, for example.

My neighbor, Yolanda, makes cheese. All she needed to live a comfortable life was a supply of raw material and time to scale up her operation. She found a dairy that could supply the milk and a willing neighbor (me) who could help her build cheese presses.

I've got cheese. I've got enough cheese that I could trade it, the hardware supplies, and my own semi-skilled manual labor, and also live a comfortable life. As you might imagine, a comfortable life where I didn't go out and kill zombies would probably be more satisfying. Sadly, you don't get that kind of choice when you need to defend your community from undead squatters. Worse, because we're all bartering and interdependent, we can't just kill someone who produces what we need if they contract the virus. We're in a position in which we actually have to try to keep them hidden, safe, and productive for as long as possible. The longest we were able to keep someone hidden was measurable in days, not months.

Mister Yan was a tailor. He had become our source for clothing repair and anything we made that needed more than hand sewing. Somehow, he got infected. It took only five hours after he was infected for a hungry visitor to find him.

Yolanda's husband, Omér, took care of that critter. Two hours later, Mister Yan had been moved into Shawn Cooper's basement. Two guards at all times, four-hour shifts. Neighborhood watch on similar shifts. Perimeter patrol duties assigned as well.

It kept every able-bodied adult in our community working an extra four hours a day on top of whatever they normally did. We did a good job, but we were not prepared for a direct focused assault.

There were 40 of them and were led by someone who had been a captain in one of the infantry battalions. We finished off most of them, but there were enough left to take Mister Yan from us. We also lost people in that fight.

The blessing for us is that our former neighbors did not come back from the dead. They had been victims of a sniper or someone else with good aim. A single large-caliber bullet to the head ended each of their lives.

Six months after that attack, we still feel the loss of those people every day. It makes you reevaluate the meaning of each human life, let me tell you.

I am seriously glad Shawn wasn't one of those we lost. He's our machinist, armorer, gunsmith, and metalworker. Without him, we'd all be dead.

The military wanted to be useful, and I'm absolutely sure the commanders, chiefs, and so on who were sequestered in the bowels of the Pentagon were attempting to help the common man. At least, I have to believe in that a little bit, or the rest of my sanity will give way to something less friendly. The sad reality of the matter is that the Armed Forces usually cause more damage and loss of life than they prevented.

When it came to neighborhood-to-neighborhood conflicts, the military kept their noses out of it. The only occasions in which they were called out to do anything besides protect the national critical infrastructure were situations where there was a direct threat to the government's status quo.

Two weeks ago, the Army assaulted Chain Bridge. For those of you who are not as intimately familiar with the Washington, DC area, let me give you a little framework to help it make sense.

Chain Bridge is a bridge. Clever name, don't you think? It stretches from what used to be an insanely ritzy enclave of Northern Virginia into the upper northwest side of Washington, DC. Trust me, it is a high-dollar area, with heavy commuting and lots of undead formerly rich people meandering around.

The bridge itself is the sort of structure that always seems to be under constant repair for one reason or another.

Another bright spot in that general area is Langley. The CIA. Smack in the middle of many people who are not keen on organic meats, artisan-baked breads, and superb wine cellars anymore. These days, they're immensely interested in foraging for two-legged, free-roaming people.

Having been human, spoiled rotten or not, these creatures are not stupid. Where are you most likely to find your meat animals in quantity, if those meat animals are still trying to live their lives and "make a living" by going to work every day?

Yes, you guessed it: high-traffic arterial roadways and intersections. Shopping centers. Houses of worship. Office complexes, and in the Washington, DC area that meant either federal government or government contractors.

The area around Chain Bridge was positively stuffed with the undead. They just waited for infected people to drive by or to stop at the traffic signal. That's when a dozen or so would block your car, break in, pull out whoever was infected, and then feast.

This caused quite a blockage of abandoned vehicles in that area. Again, these are not stupid creatures. Some former project management professional created a feeding schedule, and a car removal system based around a team of three Action Groups per day.

It worked like this. Action Group A, "Team Lobster Bisque," would intercept the vehicle, remove the occupant(s), and feed. Action Group B would drive the car back into town and park it in the grocery store lot. Action Group C follows Action Group B in a re-purposed school bus, picks them up, and brings them back to the Project Work Site.

Each team would rotate through. B eats, C drives, A retrieves, and so on. It was deadly efficiency.

It was also decimating a significant part of the workforce that keeps America at least partially operational, from a governance standpoint. That couldn't stand. The Powers That Be made a decision to cordon off the area, destroy all zombies, and maintain the area as a protected commuter zone.

Two major mistakes were made. The first being that the assault happened at night. The second, I feel, was the assumption that our former friends, family, and so on had come back from the dead with moron-level IQs.

Night vision equipment is not super effective in making creatures with low heat signatures visible in contrast to local foliage, automobiles, rocks... up in the trees behind you... sneaking, jumping, and generally flanking the living shit out of the poor sods who were assigned to this mission.

In the heat of the one-sided rout, some poor schmuck used a laser targeting system to "paint" a group of rushing vitality-challenged combatants. I believe I've mentioned they move a lot faster than normal humans do. That's absolutely the case.

By the time the artillery sergeant (two miles away in an armored fighting vehicle) got the order to fire, the zombies had already overrun the soldier who had targeted them while they were still on the bridge. Consequently, the missile hit the bridge, not a horde of critters.

I don't remember what the weight of TNT that weapon was compared to, but I do know it collapsed the bridge entirely.

Undead: low losses, had to relocate toward Route 29 in Arlington.

Army: 100 fatalities, 31 wounded, and a genuine, gold-plated dunce cap.

The backlash from this event was intensely personal. The zombies relocated to the major intersections near my home. I have new neighbors, and we will need to get rid of them.

Chapter 4

Prior to being dead, he was probably a stoner. Substantial, really dirty, blood-caked dreads draped around his head like a bead curtain made of wooly bear caterpillars. Thankfully, the caterpillars were dead, otherwise he would have been doing the Medusa thing, and that would have been far too much for me to handle. The fact that he was browsing around in my hardware store was just icing on the soufflé.

Yes, you don't put icing on soufflé. Think of it as nouvelle cuisine.

"Hey man," he said to me, clearly aware that I'd been watching him from the moment he'd walked up to the door. "Have you got any hatchets?"

"No."

"Axes?"

"I'm afraid not."

"Uh. Any kind of," he gestured, "choppy thing? Machete?"

"Nope. Not a thing. Got a few brooms," and I pointed toward that section of the wall.

"Yeah... I don't think brooms would do it. Got some stuff I need to cut up."

He turned toward me and smiled. It was a fairly horrible, full-of-teeth kind of smile. His gums had receded, making years of fine suburban orthodontic work look like a White Picket Fence of Doom. From the look of things, he'd been a zombie for a rather long time, maybe even an early conversion.

"So, dude," he continued as he began to approach the counter. "Is there any chance at all you'd, like, let me move in?"

"Marvelous," I remember thinking, "this one is going to try to fuck with me." Any moment, I imagined, he'd move forward at some insane speed and be sitting on the counter in front of me before I could blink. Again, just to fuck with me.

While dying and coming back does not make you stupid, it doesn't do a thing for increasing your IQ. He was stupid enough to be clever, stay alive, hook up with people smarter than he was, and be completely predictable to someone with a sufficiently cynical mind. Me.

Zoom! Plop! There he was, sitting cross-legged on the counter in front of me, his rank scent filling my nostrils. I guess he felt as though he'd invented the shit-eating grin.

If "shit-eating grin" was an Olympic competition, I think the stoic French judges would have allowed him a 7. The Russian judges, from behind their vodka bottles, would have been hard-pressed to offer him a 5.5. Your favorite American judge, me, gave him a 2.

A 2-pound sledgehammer.

Zombie testicles. Meet Mister Hammer. Aw! Did he upset your composure?

He didn't scream. All that came out of him was a long, whiny exhale of fetid air as he rolled backwards off the counter. There was a delightful thunk when his head met the concrete floor.

I took about four steps backward and vaulted over the counter, landing behind the body on the floor. He had not changed position at all; he was still cross-legged in a sitting position, just facing the floor instead of me.

I heard some mumbling.

"Speak up, Sonny Boy, this old fart can't hear ya!"

"You crushed my nuts. Why?" It came out as a breathy whisper.

"You offended my social sensibilities."

"I was just messing with you. You don't smell right. I wasn't going to eat you."

"Thanks for clearing that up. Just so you know, and we can have clear communication from this moment on: I do not give a flying gob of opossum semen why you're here or what you want."

"Man. That's nasty."

"How are your nuts?"

"Did you have to remind me?"

"I'm friendly that way," I said, and raised the sledge over my head. I have never had compunctions about hitting people from behind, or from the front.

"They don't look so goo —"

As much as I hate to cut people off in the middle of what they're saying, I decided to make an exception in his case. The hammer did exactly what I hoped it would, since his head was so conveniently resting on a hard surface and I put a solid amount of force behind the blow. His skull caved in and turned the rear of his brain into borscht.

Never turn down the opportunity to make a statement or use a symbol to express yourself when raw material throws itself into your lap. I took the head, a permanent marker, and an empty milk crate outside. The head sat on the upside-down crate to the right of my doors, and I wrote "Oops! Wrong Store!" on the forehead with the marker.

Smelly, but useful.

The only problem with beheading things in your store is that it makes a mess. Thankfully, this can be remedied as long as you're speedy about it with a mop and a bucket full of soapy bleach water. I hopped right to task after I set out my porch decoration. Of course, you are still left with the headless, bloodless body.

Our neighborhood had a very ecologically friendly approach to such things: drop the buggers into a 55-gallon plastic drum with a bag of quick lime. In three months, drain off the smelly goo, grind up the bones, mix it all back together, and trade it as fertilizer.

Let me tell you, it is the secret to award-winning heirloom tomatoes.

I admired my handiwork for a few minutes after I closed the door to the store and debated how long I would actually leave the head there. Dead things, even twice dead, do not smell good. Certainly, it wasn't an issue of being off-putting to my customers, because there really weren't any. Anyone worth speaking to would come to the back door in our little barter neighborhood.

I suppose my concern was for the overall ambience of our civilized enclave of craftspeople. I blinked a few times and realized I was starting to think like some sort of post-apocalyptic homeowners association director. Whether it was due to coming down off the endorphin high of having one of the enemy saunter into my home or because I really needed to eat something, I may never know.

Taking my train of thought and rumbling stomach as a warning, I locked the front door and went for a walk up the street. Bajali and his lovely bride, Jayashri, would probably have a pot of something tasty cooking, and they were the most generous hosts anyone could ever imagine. Of all the people I'd come to know during these months of upheaval, they were my favorite.

Baj had been a programmer for one of the large defense contractors before things went down the tubes. He was tall, smart, and gentlemanly, with a hint of British Raj accent that I enjoyed hearing, and one of the most intelligent people I had ever met. Five years ago, he had gone back home to Delhi to meet his future wife. He joked it was "positively countercultural" to do something so traditional in a modern world where traditions are rewritten every day.

I suspect that Jayashri knocked his composure to bits. To not use the word "brilliant" to describe her—everything about her—would be a travesty. Her voice was music. Even I fell a little in love with her; she matched his graciousness and added her own sublime beauty to it. Imagine a Disney

Princess brought to life in a glorious red-and-gold Indian sari with a smile that could melt the heart of every evil overlord in the galaxy, and you might have an idea of what she looked like. Unfortunately, such beauty might blind you to her other amazing attributes. The lady is brilliant and has a will of hardened steel. Fuck with her at your peril.

While I can't speak for the rest of the world, when you see two people who truly love one another, it ignites something inside. It might be a yearning to find your version of the love they share. On the other hand, it might inflame you with a sort of jealousy. For me, I found it made me want to protect them both. Something like finding a flower growing in the sewage.

I knocked on their door, and Baj opened it before I could put my arm down.

"Ha! I saw you walking down the street and thought to myself that you would be coming here," he reached out, put an arm around my shoulder and ushered me into his home, "and, as you can see, I was right!"

"One of these days, I'll surprise you, you know."

"Not bloody likely, and you know it!" His smile was more contagious than the common cold, and I could not help but smile with him. "You have come over for supper?"

"Yes," I answered, feeling a bit sheepish.

"What? Did Shawn forget to tell you that you I invited you as well?"

"I suppose he did. I've not spoken to him today."

"Ah hah. I will bet you he fell into tinkering with one thing or another and forgot. Seeing you here will remind him. Come! Let us teach him the error of his ways!"

We marched together, as jovially as you please, through the house to the dining room. Baj was right, and Shawn looked properly abashed when he saw me.

"Oh. Damn, I'm sorry man. I meant to come over and get you," Shawn blushed to the roots of his receding hairline and shrugged his elephantine shoulders, "but I got stuck on tricking out that M-50 I got last weekend."

"No worries. We all know how you are when there's a project on the bench." I slugged him on the shoulder and sat down in the chair next to him.

There isn't anyone I can punch affectionately like I can Shawn. He's built like a Hell's Angel crossed with a freight train. Rumor has it that two of his younger brothers made it into the NFL, after full-ride football scholarships in college. I don't know if it's true, but I could believe it if the rest of the family was built along the same lines.

I knew he had a kid sister. I found that idea both daunting as Hell and strangely erotic, all at the same time. No point pumping him for information, because he knows my piss-poor history with the opposite sex.

Jayashri brought the food to the table in quiet flutterings of her sari, sending the aroma of spices into the air around us. They were vegetarian, keeping with the particular Hindu traditions that they had grown up with, but did allow themselves cheese, cream, milk, and butter. I was immensely grateful that they weren't as strict with their religion as some people that I'd known in the past, because her paneer was painfully good.

Don't make me tell you about her cream sauces for pasta. If anything happens to Baj, she's mine. I'll fight you for her. I'll win.

The initial dinner conversation was light, and by unspoken agreement we didn't bring up our smelly new neighbors.

Shawn made conversational noises but was too busy savoring the cooking to really make a dent in the chatting. I knew his family was from rural Somewhere and that their idea of ethnic cuisine was pizza. Watching him eat and enjoy foods that had been alien to him just a year ago was amusing and oddly joyful.

It was so damned normal and we all loved it. That was a common thing we all felt: the absence of our normal lives. The three of us ate our food, and the conversation quietly faded in favor of sharing Shawn's delight in something that was so common to the rest of us.

"Shawn, you should try the raita with the curried daal," Jayashri said, spooning a bit of the yogurt sauce onto his plate.

"Thank you. I certainly will," and he did. His expressions were priceless. For someone as strong, solid, and intimidating as he was, he had no guile at all around people he cared about.

We watched him close his eyes in bliss, gently rolling the flavors around in his mouth.

I heard Jayashri sigh and looked at her out of the corner of my eye. She was crying noiselessly and immediately noticed that I'd seen her. She sniffed, rose quickly in a bustle of draped fabric, and floated over to my side of the table.

She kissed Shawn on the forehead, mussed my hair, and whispered, "I am so happy." A moment later, she was gone, but I heard the bathroom door close down the hall.

Baj looked a little misty himself. Shawn looked confused. Me? I don't know how I looked.

"Guys, did I just miss somethin'?"

"Ah, you know," Baj said, "women will be women sometimes."

I just chuckled to myself.

The wistful look on Baj's face slipped away and was replaced by something far more serious. I tensed up, immediately expecting bad news. Shawn's breathing changed.

"I wanted to talk to both of you for a number of reasons. Serious ones. Please don't feel as though I invited you both here under false pretenses, because Jaya and I very much wanted to see you," he said, ducking his head slightly. "What we have is an unfortunate confluence of events and data."

Shawn sighed, tore off a piece of naan, and began munching on it in a very thoughtful way.

"All right, Baj, what's going on?" I believe I actually asked the question, but it could have been either of us. The tension in the room was enough to inspire near-telepathic communication; empathic, at the very least.

"As you both know, I've been working on establishing some kind of reliable internet connection for the past month. Two days ago, I managed to do it. The news out there is not good. The zombies are even using the web to advertise."

Looking back, I'm still pleased that my mouth was both empty and dry at that moment. I would have probably ejected anything in my mouth after hearing such a thing.

"What are they doing? Telling people who are infected to come see them and get pumped full of anesthetic before they're eaten alive?" I couldn't keep the incredulity out of my voice.

"Yes, there is that. I also saw quite a lot of 'We are the Master Race' sorts of things. Disgusting, but not as disturbing as the news feeds."

"I guess you're going to tell us that things are worse than we imagined. Right?" Shawn asked.

"Oh yes. Africa is almost devoid of human life. South America is nearly as bad off, but there are pockets of civilization in Belize and Costa Rica. China is," he just shook his head, "very bad off. They bombed and gassed major population centers to destroy the zombie population but keep the industrial infrastructure."

"Good God Almighty. That is beyond insane." I couldn't find words, but Shawn's were eloquent enough for both of us.

"What about things here in the US?"

"Based on what I saw, we may be somewhat better off in terms of existing industry and services, but the rate of infection is increasing. DARPA and the NIH have confirmed the virus is passed human to human. Luckily, it has yet to go airborne."

"What is the," I needed to ask, "viral vector between people?"

"They are confident it is passed through sexual contact and non-sexual fluid exposure. There is some possibility it may even be passed in sweat and saliva."

"Any idea why the critters are eating the infected?" Shawn asked it quietly, but I heard his knuckles cracking as he squeezed his fists closed.

"Apparently, the virus starts to die within 24 to 48 hours outside of a living host. It provides the initial resurrection and subsequent maintenance of the zombie, actually repairing or replacing damaged tissues. However," he paused, "it begins to die off quickly. They attack living people to obtain fresher viral material to keep their bodies going. It isn't even a choice on the part of the zombie."

"The virus compels them to do it," I asked "or do they attack out of their own fear of dying a second time?"

"Everything seems to suggest that they are compelled by it, at least as far as pain is concerned. The viral die-off is complete and utter agony, coupled with fading cognitive and motor functions."

Shawn cut to the chase, "That's not the only bit of news. I mean, we sort of figured that the virus was keeping them alive. Sucks to know we can get it from touching other people and all. You've got something worse to tell us. Don't you?"

Jayashri reappeared behind Baj and put her hands on his shoulders. I began to pray, silently, that he wasn't going to tell us they were infected. Not only would we, in time, lose them to the enemy, but the chances of being infected by them scared the piss out of me.

"From my perspective, Shawn, I do have something worse to say. We had a visitor yesterday afternoon: the leader of the zombies that relocated to this area after Chain Bridge."

My stomach curled into a knot. I didn't really like the idea that a second intruder had made it inside our defenses. The dreadlocked dude was bad enough. I made a mental note to talk to Gina about more explosives in useful places.

"You see, my friends, I knew him when he was alive. His name was Warren Hightower, and he was the CEO of the company I worked for before things began to fall apart." Baj looked very upset. His long face seemed more compact, as if the weight of his emotions added 20 pounds to his brow, causing it to sink and shadow his eyes. Maybe it was that weight and the combined gravity of whatever else he needed to say that kept him silent for a few minutes.

"I love you, man," Shawn said, "but you have to finish the story. Why is Hightower a bad thing? We might be able to negotiate with a former businessman."

Baj sighed, and from where I sat, it looked like he had to force himself to go on.

"Warren is a genius. He was also a major player in the US involvement in the Middle East for a number of years. After that, he was recruited to lead Section 41, an extraordinarily secret intersection of DARPA and the NSA. Shortly after leaving that position, he started his own company, the one I worked for as a lead programmer."

"Correct me if I'm wrong, but this is starting to look bad for us," Shawn said, cracking his knuckles in irritation.

Bajali snorted. "Our business was computer modeling of airborne, weaponized particulates. We also did similar things for predicting the impact of terrorist attacks with a variety of scenarios, weapons, and locations. One particular branch of the company, my group, was also tasked with design, manufacture, and programming of nanomachine systems," he said before he paused, breathed deeply, and began again. "I strongly suspect that Hightower has access to everything we ever created. He inferred as much and offered to let us live if I would continue my work for him."

I felt the color drain from my face. Shawn didn't look much better. Things had taken a turn that we were absolutely unprepared to deal with.

Chapter 5

Baj told us he saw the man walking down the street before he even got close enough to knock on the front door. Apparently Warren Hightower has a swagger that is hard to miss once you've seen it. Then again, any well-dressed stranger is worth noting if you happen to be looking out your window at just the right time.

After getting his breathing under control, he called down to Jayashri and quickly detailed his plan to properly greet the Devil that was about to knock on the front door. She agreed, started the water boiling for tea, and adjusted her sari. For himself, Baj combed his hair, splashed some water on his face, and composed himself a tiny bit more.

There was a knock on the door, and he heard his wife attend to greeting their guest.

"Mister Hightower. Bajali has been expecting you for some time. Do come in," she said with a delightful lilt in her voice. "May I serve you tea?"

He heard them moving around the living room and how she gently suggested where their guest should sit. It was the chair with the clearest line of sight from the kitchen, and all Baj could think was that he had married an utterly irreplaceable woman.

"Mrs. Sharma, I would very much enjoy tea. Thank you for your hospitality."

"My pleasure. Please, sit. This is a very comfortable chair for our guests who have a more Western sense of how a seat should be. Bajali will be with you shortly. I am sure you know how difficult it is to pull him away from a project."

Hightower laughed gently. Bajali was well known for how deeply he could sink into any project that caught his attention, and he remembered the ribbing he had received from everyone.

"Yes, Bajali could ignore almost anything in favor of his work," the guest said, "except for you. Now that I've met you, I can understand why."

"You are too kind," she replied, "I will bring you tea. Do you take sugar and cream?"

"Yes. Thank you again."

Jayashri floated off into the kitchen, leaving Hightower alone in the living room, relaxing in an astoundingly comfortable easy chair. Bajali called down to his wife in the kitchen, speaking in Hindi. Then he walked downstairs and crossed into the room.

Hightower started to stand.

"No, Mister Hightower, there's no need to be so formal. Be at ease." Bajali sat in the chair opposite him, separated by a roughly hewn wood coffee table.

'Bajali, I can't tell you how nice it is to be greeted with something other than an armed response," he smiled that winning smile, made unfortunate only by how far his gums had receded, "and that dovetails so neatly into what I came to talk to you about."

Baj related the bill of goods Hightower attempted to sell him on. It sounded wonderful, if you were a zombie: a peaceful meeting of the minds where X percent of the population would be kept as cattle for the undead to feed upon, and the rest of mankind was left alone to pursue their lives. Better yet! Given time, the two societies might integrate again and build a new future for the entire planet!

I think we all rolled our eyes when we heard that. Shawn looked more like he wanted to hand back his dinner at a supersonic speed, but he managed to control the reflex with the sheer force of his willpower.

Our friend had more to share, and we swallowed our

disgust long enough to listen.

"I must tell you, Baj, I was uncertain of the welcome I would receive were I to visit you. I am moved, deeply moved, by your hospitality and warmth."

"Well, you know, Mister Hightower, greeting guests in a civilized manner has been practiced and refined for thousands of years in India." Baj reported this segment of the conversation with an insane, obsequious smile on his face, and I can only imagine what it had looked like during the original chat.

His guest complimented him on his superb hospitality for a final time, and urged him to pass the regards along to Mister and Mrs. Sharma, Senior, if ever the opportunity presented itself.

Bajali laughed heartily and replied, "It isn't that different in India, you know. I will tell them you spoke well of the results of their hard labor. I suspect they will be pleased."

At this point in the visitation, Jayashri brought in the tea, poured them both a cup, inquired about lumps of sugar and milk before deftly stirring each cup, and retreated softly into the kitchen. She added, to us, that she found the nearest firearm as soon as the tea service was safely settled on the countertop.

"She is... so graceful." Hightower sipped the tea, still smiling.

"She never ceases to amaze me. So, what brings you to my home? It has been quite a while since we last conversed. I believe you were on a flight to Baghdad at the time."

"Yes, I'd called you to get an update on the A-344 program. That's why I'm here now, as a matter of fact. I would like you to continue your work on that project for me."

"I hardly have the facilities for such a thing, with the world changing as it has," Bajali replied. As an aside to us, he explained that the mere mention of the A-344 program was enough to reveal how our neighbor planned to bring about his perfect world of coexistence.

Hightower nodded at him, "I know. I still have all the equipment, materials, and data in a new location. All you have to do is come on board and we can finish A-344."

"May I ask why you would be interested in such a thing," Bajali waved his hand idly in the air, "after you've gone through the change in your life?" The question was superfluous, really, because he knew full well what the answer would be. He simply wanted to soothe his soul over the truth, before he made the decision to try and kill his guest.

"Let me tell you why," and Hightower explained what was known about the virus, how it operates in the human host, and his plan to make a herd of human cattle for the zombie population.

"Ah." Bajali did not let his disgust show because he had predicted his work could be used in such a manner: selectively targeting and infecting a swath of the population. "I can see that you've given this the thought it deserves. Indeed, I can see how you have come to the conclusion this would bring stability to the situation, if not actual peace."

"I knew you would understand, Bajali. The big picture was never lost on you."

They sat quietly for some minutes, sipping tea.

Baj told us he had truly expected some sort of threat to be delivered during those tea-laden moments. He was aware that in certain circles there was an unspoken rule that you never threaten the family of a man from whom you need something. A family man would gladly force you to kill him, thereby saving his loved ones, rather than allow them to be harmed. Any threats had to be intensely personal and backed up by action, until the subject broke. Then you could threaten the family with impunity.

Surprisingly enough, no threat appeared. With no threat, there was less certainty that action was necessary, or so Bajali felt. Instead, he tried a delaying tactic in hopes it would give us more time to figure out a course of action.

"Warren? May I call you Warren?"

"Of course, Bajali."

"Warren, I would like to have a day or two to think this over. We are, after all, talking about altering the world as we have known it in a way that makes the fear of climate change look like small potatoes."

"Absolutely! I would not have it any other way. If two days will help you work with me, then I will gladly spend them."

"Thank you so much, Warren. I will discuss this with Jayashri, if you do not mind. She is, in so many ways, my better half."

"Please do. I tell you what, I'll drop by again in two days and we can review the details. Will that work for you?"

"I think that would be marvelous. May I pour you more tea?"

"I would, but I do have a schedule to keep, and I walked here. It will take a bit of time to get back to our staging area, and I'll have to refresh the virus when I arrive."

"Ah. In that case, don't let me keep you."

Bajali escorted his former employer to the front door. They shook hands with smiles and promises to speak again in two days. Hightower left and strolled down the street with a swing in his step.

Bajali closed the door, leaned up against it, and took a deep breath. There was a metallic click behind him, and he turned to see his wife standing in the doorway between rooms. She had just released the hammer on the .44 Magnum she was holding in her delicate hands.

"My love, did we not decide the 9mm fit your hand better than the .44?"

"Yes, my treasure, but we don't have soft, jacketed hollow points for the 9. I was also concerned about needing more than one round to destroy his skull with the smaller pistol."

At that point, he walked over to her, embraced her, kissed her on the forehead and said, "I am never disappointed when I trust your judgment. You are the finest part of my life."

Chapter 6

"Fuck me," Shawn said, blinked, and added, "Oh shit! I'm sorry for my rough language there, Jayashri!"

"Oh no, I'm not the least bit bothered. I have said many similar things about this situation; I just did it in Hindi at the top of my lungs."

"Is that what that was this afternoon? I thought the two of you were having a knockdown, drag-out fight or something," Shawn commented.

Baj and Jayashri laughed and shook their heads in an eerily coordinated movement. I'd seen them do things like that in the past and took it as a sign that their family matchmakers had really done an amazing job or that there were alien pods somewhere in the house. We already had zombies. We just don't need bug-eyed monsters at the same time.

"Not to interrupt this discussion about etiquette in the face of the apocalypse, but we need to have some sort of plan," I said.

"Well, that is why I called the two people I respect the most," Baj smiled, "over for dinner. You are an impressively cynical person, and Shawn is a walking repository of country common sense. Between the four of us, I can't imagine we won't think of something."

"Thanks, Baj," Shawn said, grinning like an idiot. "I have to say, it doesn't feel like I get much appreciation for anything other than 'Dude? Can ya fix that?' and it just warms my heart that you feel that way... "

I cut him off. "Shawn, okay. We all love you and think that not only does your shit not stink but you're our local Leo-fucking-nardo da Vinci. I'm not gonna hug you, but I would fuck your sister."

His eyes crossed and he may have turned a little green at the thought of me enjoying a carnal embrace with his sibling. Jayashri's eyes were a little wide, and Baj was coughing gently behind his hand.

"All right. Baj is the resident genius, which means he's already thought of a couple of ways to approach this." I continued, regardless of the facial expressions, "I'm betting he's thought of the old 'Go Along With It So I Can Sabotage The Project,' the 'Kill The Fucker Now,' and maybe even 'We Are Going To Flee And Hope He Doesn't Find Us.' Am I missing anything?"

"I had also considered going along with it in order to give the human race more time to fight and find some sort of cure or vaccine. To be honest, I also considered that suicide could be a valid option. Of course, the karma involved in any of these options is difficult to contemplate. I'd prefer not to be reincarnated as a weevil."

"Nobody dies, at least none of us at this table. Can we agree on that point," I asked, holding out my hands, expecting agreement.

Everyone made noises of assent or nodded at the very least. I wasn't worried they'd disagree. Really.

My esteemed country boy, mechanical genius, and sibling to my imaginary love interest, tossed out an excellent question.

"Is there any way to use the nanomachines to kill the virus in the zombies?"

"Based on what I understand, Shawn, it doesn't look possible," Bajali answered. "It might be, but making a change like that to the base programming would be obvious enough that Hightower or one of his minions would know something was amiss."

"Silly question, but if the virus can't be grown in the lab, how are you going to get enough of it to spread?" That part didn't make sense to me.

"Since the virus is healthiest in living humans, the particles would harvest the infectious material from people who already have it and spread it to the designated population within a 24-hour period."

I nodded my head and asked, "Would it be possible to use the nanos to strip all of the virus out of people who are infected and then self-destruct?"

"I had thought of that, but it becomes an issue of particle-to-virus density. If one nanomachine can destroy one infected blood cell, you have to manufacture enough particles so every infected cell is effectively targeted." He put his teacup in the middle of the table. "If you have enough infected cells to fill this teacup, then what will be destroyed is twice that because it is both the particles and the cells."

Shawn and I nodded, following along.

"Now, you have two tea cups of material. How should the particles destruct? Heat? Micro-explosions? A teacup of explosive material powerful enough to destroy two teacups completely is not a small detonation."

"Okay, yeah, but how much virus does one person have in them anyway?" Shawn asked.

"Have you ever had a bad cold, Shawn?" Bajali asked in response.

"Yeah, not too long ago."

"The mucus your body expels," Baj explained, "contains cells that have consumed the cold virus. About how much did you blow your nose when you had the cold?"

"A whole lot. Oh. I see. All the snot I had would be like the particles and the virus. Damn."

"Exactly. Let us imagine a teacup of infected cells as an estimate for someone experiencing a moderate level of infection." We nodded. "Imagine the explosion of a teacup-size bomb spread out through a human body."

Shawn and I had no trouble imagining it, based on how

we groaned at the thought.

He continued, "If it could be done, it would certainly erase the zombies from the planet, but there would be a huge amount of collateral damage from human being-sized bombs going off everywhere. The only other method would be to build nano-material that would strip the virus from infected cells and render the material inert. Unfortunately, there would still be apparent alterations to the particle design, to say nothing of the waste material that would be created."

I sipped my tea. It was wonderfully tasty cardamom-flavored tea that would, under the best circumstances, relax the Hell right out of me. At that moment, I was using it to swish around in my mouth to cudgel my brain into coming up with an idea that Baj hadn't.

The main problem was that Hightower, no matter what we did as far as Baj himself went, could keep right on moving toward that goal. Our friend doing the Hindu seppuku would make no difference in the grand scheme of things. At most, it would delay the use of those nano-thingies. Eventually, another qualified programmer/architect/mad genius would be found and work would continue.

Answer: improbable. Execution of answer: way out of our league. Possibility of wrangling help in 24 hours or less: equally, fucking unlikely.

"I know what we need to do," I spoke up, "but I don't think we can do it without major backup, evacuation, and the US Cavalry."

"All right, we are considering all the possible options here, even if they're immensely unlikely. Go on," Baj said and motioned for me to continue.

"We have to kill Hightower and massacre every single undead shithead that might have been taken into confidence about his Evil Plan." I enunciated those capital letters with great care.

"That's not all that outrageous," Shawn said. "We'd just

have to be more organized about things. Hit them at the right time. That kind of thing."

"I think I see what the problem is," Baj said from behind steepled fingers. "The most efficient way to do that, and you can correct me if I'm not following your lead, is to do it in a single massive strike. Something on the order of an atmosphere-ignition bomb."

"Bingo," I replied.

"Gentlemen, I am assuming that this weapon is not nuclear," said Jaya, with one graceful eyebrow arched in an expression both inquisitive and appalled. "I hope you are not talking about such a thing."

"No, Jaya," Shawn spoke up, "but it's got similar destructive power. I mean, right up under a nuke, but it isn't radioactive. Things like these ignite the oxygen in the air and make a fucking huge fireball out of acres of territory."

"Oh my."

"Yeah, I got to say though, it would sterilize the area," Shawn added, with no small amount of regret in this voice.

"True, but as it was mentioned, we do not have access to military ordnance of that kind or the means to evacuate all the living people from the blast zone without being seen." Baj's expression was looking more and more grim, and I can't say we all didn't feel the same. " It might be possible to assassinate Hightower when he returns tomorrow, but I am under no illusions; we are being observed. It would have to be Jayashri and I for that task."

I couldn't fault his logic, even if I wanted to. Hightower hadn't gotten where he had in life without good intel and planning. There would be fallback plans.

"Right. You two kill him. What happens next? They'll just overrun us." Shawn's frown was huge, weighed down with redneck gravitas. I didn't feel much better about it.

"They might not," I said. "It would take a little time for them to reorganize under someone else, unless that's already been planned out. Baj, you said he seemed completely at ease."

"Yes. Chatty, even."

"He didn't expect you to say no. The two of you treated him as if he were a normal human being, not the walking dead. He couldn't have been expecting that. By the time he left, I'm betting he was mostly convinced you'd be on board for it."

"You sure you're being properly cynical about this, man?" The redneck caveman creased his forehead at me. The ridges it created were so severe that I could have grated cheese on his face, if I had been so inclined.

"I think he might have a point. I listened to the conversation while I was in the kitchen, and the man spoke like a zealot. He is completely convinced this is the best way to do things," Jaya reported. "There was not enough tension in his tone of voice to make me feel as though he was anything less than optimistic about recruiting my husband."

"Well, it appears that we have two choices. Jayashri and I flee for our lives and hope we're never found again, or we kill him and see what the reprisal looks like. It is entirely possible that we would need to flee anyway, all of us."

Shawn reached out, tore off a piece of naan, and started to munch on it. The crease between his eyes shifted as he chewed, and it was all I could do to wipe the awful things I could say off my tongue before my mouth opened. I didn't want to make my hosts go into an apoplectic fit, or piss off my favorite human mountain. After all, he does have a sister.

Never piss off a guy who has a sister. At least, not when you're lonely like I am.

"Shawn, will you share your thoughts with us?" Jaya asked in her musical voice. Baj echoed with little agreement noises.

"We've forgotten one big thing. Maybe two. First one is, they're still watching us and I would bet money someone's bugged the house or has got a parabolic thingamagig trained on your front window." He pointed past my head at the big picture window to the left of their front door. "Second, he might be a zombie, but he ain't stupid. He's got a plan in case ya'll do something."

Baj and Jaya broke out into quiet tirades in Hindi that sounded like the way gangrene looks.

"I knew, I fahking knew I would forget something so fahking simple!"

"Dahling, we are already in cow shit up to our eyes. Do not be so harsh with yourself. If he wanted us dead, we would be dead already," Jayashri managed to comfort and chide her husband at the same time. I was just amused at how thick their accents became when they got vexed.

"That ass fucker don't want ya'll dead," Shawn joined in with foul language. "He needs you too goddamned bad to just drop a load of sheep cunts on ya'll."

The stress and intensity was getting to me, but Shawn's unique way of phrasing things pushed me right over the top. I started laughing like a complete loon and was joined by everyone at the table. We were not the only people laughing. There was a fifth voice with a different tonal range, laughing very quietly. It was coming from somewhere around the floor.

They didn't hear it, but I did. I let the laughter die down naturally, pulled my ever-present notebook and pen out of my pocket while everyone was catching their breath, and wrote, "There's a fifth person laughing." Everyone read it with wide eyes, but never changed their breathing.

I love working with people who know how to maintain an illusion.

"Boys, I do not know if any of this has left you in the mood for dessert, but I made Rasmalai and fresh ice cream."

We didn't have to fake the happy noises that came out of our mouths.

Baj borrowed my notebook and pen and, while he wrote, said, "My love, to turn down your Rasmalai would be doubly insane if this is the last chance we may have to enjoy it. Might I have some?" He wrote something entirely different.

"There are heat registers at floor level. Laughing person is not a pro. They're somewhere near other heat registers or in the basement. Maybe roof?"

Jayashri replied naturally, "I have crushed pistachio. Would you like that on your dessert, darling?"

"Oh, heavens, yes!"

"Jaya, I'd love some of your ice cream. If it is as good as what you made last spring, I'll be here all night!" Shawn wasn't a bad actor either.

Chapter 7

We ate our desserts and made small talk about the community. The notebook and pen slid around the table like a hot potato and none of us had thought to bring the sour cream and chives. We were in a bind; no one could get up from the table to do anything "unnatural" that might allow that person to scout around a little bit.

There were four of us. There was one someone observing us, at the very least. The fact that this stranger allowed him or herself to laugh while listening to us via the house's ductwork pointed towards inexperience. Our major unanswered question concerned the spying itself. Was this person transmitting or reporting to someone, or were they simply there to make sure that Baj and Jaya didn't leave?

We simply didn't know and wouldn't until something tipped the balance somewhere. It was Shawn who came up with the idea, and we were all pretty surprised with the simplicity of the solution. The whole thing hinged on the spy being an observer, not a reporter. Although Shawn did point out that if he's transmitting data, then we're all in worse trouble to begin with, and cornering this person would make little difference in the outcome of things.

The simple plan looked like this: Shawn and I would leave at about the same time, as though the evening had come to a pleasant end, having made no clear decisions on what the next meeting with Hightower would bring. Shawn would head to the backyard, and I'd wait somewhere out front. One way or another (unless this jackass could fly), he'd have to pass one of us if he was flushed out.

Jaya and Baj would have to do the bush beating to stimulate our little friend. With any luck, being made aware that his presence had been noted would be enough to make him bail.

We brought the conversation back around to Hightower.

"I don't think I can turn him down," Baj said, as he lowered his spoon to the table.

"That might mean the end of everything, man. I mean, I know it gives us time and a chance to fight back, but," Shawn should have been an actor, "*human cattle*?" His delivery of the last two words was so perfectly outraged and left me hoping that someone would start a community theater. The man needed to play Hamlet.

Jayashri chimed in, "As much as I hate to say it, I think there might be less wholesale slaughter that way. I know Bajali is concerned for the karma of this decision, but even livestock must be cared for. The infected would not have perfect or wonderful lives, but at least they would be alive and make the best of their situation."

I don't know. Jayashri had that even tone that could convince anyone of anything. I was nearly swayed then.

"Look. You two need to do what you need to do. I don't have to agree with it," I said, sounding carefully cynical and petulant, "but if I get infected, I will take out as many of those fuckers as I can before they cart me away. I have to go," and I did the best acting of my life, "but whatever you do, I'll miss you both."

Baj and Jaya made sad noises and rushed forward to embrace me. We were all doing a fabulous job of method acting and feeling the moment. When they released me, I walked out the front door, down the steps, and fucking sprinted to the hardware store.

When I got there, I snagged my .45 and the Man Scythe. I loaded up and sprinted back to the front porch of the vacant house next door to Baj and Jaya's home.

About the time I got my breath back, I heard Shawn

bellow something. I pulled the scythe but didn't open the blade and walked down the porch steps.

Running feet. Two sets. One sounded a little bit heavier than the other.

I had a sensei once tell me you could get away with having perfect timing if your technique was a little off, but you could never have perfect technique with bad timing and expect success. In that moment, I wanted timing more than any technique I have ever learned.

Running. Running. Now.

I executed a strike with the body of the Man Scythe, moving forward and dropping to one knee as I swung. Time slowed down, but I felt more than I saw the handle hit the runner. I'd intended the impact to occur above the kneecap on his trailing leg. I got more than I planned for. Goodie!

There was a cracking noise and the sensation of something moving past me in the air. I pivoted to face that direction just as Shawn rounded the corner, and allowed myself the luxury of snapping the scythe blade into place with a flick of my wrist.

A man lay on the ground about six feet away from me, arms flailing in the air. His eyes were huge, and his mouth gaped open in silent agony. I looked down and saw why he was unable to do more than wave his arms around. His right leg was bent in the wrong direction at the knee.

Then I saw the length of his fingernails. They were claws. Zombie. I moved again.

I covered the distance, put my foot on his shattered kneecap, and knelt down on my other knee. The scythe blade stopped one quarter of an inch inside his left nostril. All I had to do to make his afterlife a living Hell was shift my weight forward or backward.

"Good evening, you eavesdropping, cow-fucking, sad-ass excuse for a zombie with a sense of humor!"

He gasped, clearly unable to form words. It really wasn't a huge surprise, and I felt fairly thankful for it because I hate screaming. That is to say, I hate the sound of someone screaming in pain. Shawn's sister screaming in the throes of mad, valkyrie orgiastic pleasure is something I could tolerate. It is difficult to keep the mind on one thing when you've slid open the mental drawer on something else.

Shawn was standing at 9 o'clock to my 6 o'clock alongside the snoop. Jayashri and Baj approached from my 4 o'clock and stood quietly behind me. The zombie saw them and became very still, hands stretched out to his sides, claws sinking into the twilight dirt. I wasn't about to turn around to find out why.

I heard Baj clear his throat.

"Would you like to tell us why you were in my home, spying on us?" Baj's voice was incredibly calm, controlled, and civilized. If he wasn't already doing the genius thing, he would have made an incredible news anchorman.

Shawn added, "You'd better tell us if you were transmitting, or just planning to hightail it back with everything you heard."

"Oh, those are excellent questions!" I chortled, wishing I could clap my hands in glee for the extra effect. "I think, yes I do, you should answer every single one of them or I'll just cut the left side of your nose away. That would suck a lot!"

"I wasn't transmitting anything. I didn't have to," our snoop gasped.

"Nose!" I squealed, bugging my eyes out. I can't resist good over-the-top theatrics!

"Okay! Hightower already has surveillance equipment trained on your house. I was sent over to get context for the recordings. Personal observation. Would you please get off my knee? It's not like I can go anywhere like this."

"No." I answered him using the flattest tone of voice that I could muster, a phenomenally cold, lead doors-sealing-your-doom sort of voice. After all, I didn't want to get off his knee if it hurt. As a matter of fact, I probably would have enjoyed breaking the other one for a matched set.

"Gentlemen, if Hightower has been listening, he may not have any more information than we gave this one. On the other hand, if we are being watched, they are aware we have found the rat in our home." Jayashri made complete sense in a coldly calculating, yet delightfully musical way. It made me feel strangely warm inside as well as sent a torrent of images through the back of my brain.

For a moment, I was horrified that I'd imagined her using that voice in intimate situations. I needed to keep my brain on the moment. Zombie, scythe in nose, threatening, interrogation, we're all gonna die, until my brain showed me Shawn's sister and Jayashri in SS uniforms with riding crops. If my day kept going like that, I would need to teabag myself in ice water at the earliest convenience.

Jaya came over beside me and crouched down.

"Uh. My greatly adored daughter of the Ganges... Is that a Heckler and Koch MP5 in your hands, or are you just much scarier than I ever imagined?" H&K compact machine guns make women infinitely sexier...as long as they're not pointing the gun at me.

"Yes, my sweet hardware store proprietor and edged-weapons fetishist, it is an MP5."

I gulped. "I don't know why you used the word 'fetishist' in this instance."

"Darling friend of my husband and me, you are rough, cynical, big-hearted, and very easy to read."

"Shit," I responded, with quiet, yet intense feeling. "Should we be discussing this now, when this undead son of a bitch can hear us, or should we continue to interrogate him?"

"Indeed. So, let us take a rain check on those topics." She turned her eyes to him and stuffed the muzzle of the machine gun up his right nostril. "Tell me, little fucker, are we being seen as well as heard?"

"Eee," he said. The scythe nicked his nostril when he opened his mouth. It probably had something to do with the gun barrel shifting the blade over as the gun entered his other nostril. "I don't know for sure, but he's not stupid."

"Oh." Jaya sighed. "That means it does not matter in the

least if we end your pitiful existence now or later," she flipped off the safety on the gun, "unless you have many interesting things to tell us about his troop strength, strategy, and deployment. Do you?"

All listening to that exchange did for me was show me how desperately I needed to get laid. I'm sure the spy's experience of her gently ominous threat was entirely different than mine. I resolved, for the hundredth time, to sit down and have a deep conversation with myself about the funky things that got my motor running. I just needed peace, quiet, and time to do that in.

Yep. Not anytime soon.

Our captive zombie took a deep breath and closed his eyes. "Go ahead, finish me off. I don't have anything else to tell you."

Jaya turned to me, I could see out of the corner of my eye, and whispered quietly into my ear, "Finish that cut through his nose. Please."

Not before, or since, has an order to commit a violent act been issued to me in such a seductive way. I gasped just a little and the blade passed through the side of his nostril. His eyes flew open and he moaned like a tormented soul. There was very little blood, surprisingly enough.

"Listen to me very carefully. You are in an immensely delicate position. The virus that keeps you alive is degrading while you lie here, your knee is shattered, and you have two people beside you who would like to kill you where you lay." She spoke with that amazing, flat, matter-of-fact tone that Baj often used. "But you just lied to me. You do have quite a bit more to say than you have let on."

The zombie stiffened under us. He was either very tense about the situation or was about to throw us off and make a run for it.

"Don't you fucking move," I told him. "We might let you live through this, but if you try and fight back, she'll shoot you and the top of your head will come clean off. She can't miss."

His eyes bored into me like angry core drills.

Jayashri removed the barrel from his nose, stood up, and backed away. "Come away. Leave him there."

Not knowing quite what was going on, I stood up and backed away. The moment I was clear, I heard a pop and the sizzle of electricity. Baj had Tasered our prisoner, who obliged us by flopping around on the ground a lot.

No one spoke for a minute, then Baj and Shawn picked up our disoriented guest by the arms and started dragging him towards the back of the house. Jayashri put her hand on my arm as I was turning to go with them.

"I have to ask you to do things I cannot do myself. Shawn is too gentle and my husband is as well."

It was an interesting moment. I stood there, looking at her, and I had the distinct impression I knew what some of those unsavory acts might be. We needed information. We had a potential informant. Someone had to provide the motivation necessary to get him to speak... candidly.

"What is it they say about the female of the species?"

She smiled a little bit, "Oh, that we are much more fierce than the males when it comes to protecting our young."

I nodded and put her hand in mine, and we walked together to the basement door around the back of the house. A thought occurred to me before we entered the basement, "Do the two of you have anything, ah, more precise than the scythe? I might need to borrow it if you do."

"I will speak to Bajali."

Chapter 8

The guys were a marvel of instant efficiency and from the look of things, bondage as well. Our spy was lashed to a fold-out beach chair with lengths of Cat-6 Ethernet cable. They had even straightened out the leg with the shattered kneecap.

Probably wasn't comfortable. Sweet!

Jaya walked right over to her husband and said something to him in Hindi. I could see him go pale, even in the fluorescent light of the basement. He turned and swiftly went up the stairs into the house.

"Shawn," I said.

"Yeah, bud?"

"You're going to want a trash bag or can real soon," I told him.

"You know we butchered hogs when I was a kid."

"Yes, but you've never butchered something that looks and sounds like another human being. Just find a bag, or you'll probably want to leave the room. Better yet, keep Baj upstairs," I handed him my .45, "and make sure nothing happens to him."

I guess Shawn was mollified—being asked to do something important—because the look of annoyance on his face disappeared. He nodded, turned around, and went up the stairs. A moment or two later, Baj came down the stairs with a few things in his hands: a Swiss Army knife, a set of kabob skewers, a cleaver, and an 8-inch butcher knife.

The look on his face was... it wasn't good. I took the load

from him and laid them out in a line beside the beach chair. He looked green and I didn't want to push him any further, but there was one more thing I needed.

"Do you have a propane torch or one of those little butane torches for caramelizing sugar on crème brûlée?"

I don't know if it was me inferring there might be fire and burning or if mentioning the crème brûlée was what set him off. I watched him collapse, caught between fainting and vomiting. Instead of a dramatic explosion or falling over, his eyes rolled back in his head, vomit bubbled slowly from his mouth, and he just crumpled to the floor.

It was a wimpy but eloquent expression of his distaste for torture.

All I could really do was sigh. I did.

"Jaya, would you get him upstairs? I'll start on things here, but if you've got that butane torch... "

She turned a little green, scooted over to her husband, patted his face, and got him mobile. Sadly, when he stood up, the rest of dinner flowed down his face into an unsightly puddle on the floor. I watched them both look around frantically for cleaning supplies, and I knew they'd mop up the slop and polish the concrete until it was a uniform gray unless I stopped them.

"Guys! We don't need to worry about household chores. Both of you get upstairs, clean off, put in a loud DVD, and hang out with Shawn. I'll take care of things here, and I promise I won't notice the puddle at all."

I got blank looks, but they sped up the stairs. I'd be able to live without a torch, but it would have made things much tidier.

Turning around, I locked eyes with our spy, who had been watching everything that went down. There may or may not have been a trace of humor in his expression. Humor was fine with me; I'd rather have him laughing and telling me everything I needed to know, rather than put me in a position to inspire his replies to my questions.

"They're all too sweet to be in this," he said to me.

"You're telling me! I've known them all for a while and I'm still surprised they're alive." I walked over to the chair and stood over him, "I would be sorry about this, but you are the enemy. The most I can do, if you tell me what I want to know, is to splint your leg and let you go after all this is done."

"That's a nice gesture, but the virus die-off is starting. I'll be raving and insane before Hightower shows up."

I shook my head at him. "You guys call this 'living'?"

"I know you won't believe me," the expression on his face was deathly earnest, "but anything is better than the Dark. I've shot women, children, men, and insurgents, and I've had good friends blow up in front of me. All of that is better than the Dark. I ate my wife. That was better than the Dark."

"That's pretty profound for an undead snoop." I just shook my head.

"Yeah, and I used to write poetry and paint pictures of baby animals. Look, let's get to the point: I don't want to die again, here or anywhere else, and I'm not looking forward to torture. The knee's bad enough. Can we deal here?"

"Maybe. What do you have to tell me? Give me a little sample. Just a taste."

"Okay. This one is for free. There isn't any visual surveillance, except for our snipers watching your snipers."

I nodded. "That's a cherry piece of data. Thank you." He nodded as best he could from the awkward position he was in. "I would like location, troop strength, plan of attack, vehicle tally, secret weapons, super-powered sidekicks, and who I'd have to go through to get Hightower's head. Give me all that, and I will absolutely splint your knee and give you a free pass out of here... provided you don't go back to Hightower."

"Man," he said, "if I gave you a quarter of what you wanted, they would skin me alive and hang me out to dry. If I get out of this, going back there is not an option."

I made some understanding mumbles, knelt down in

front of the tool selection, and picked up a kabob skewer. His eyes were trying to track me and watch what I was doing, but he wasn't having very much luck with it. There wasn't much point in keeping this guy in the dark about what I was planning. He was probably a grunt soldier before all of this.

"Did you do time in the sand box?" I asked.

"Yeah, the Surge and a tour in Fallujah."

"That was some nasty shit."

"It was."

"I am contemplating my own nasty shit right now. See this kabob skewer?" I held it out for him to see. It was a long piece of 1/8-inch square steel bar with a loop in one end. "Your job is to start telling me what I want to know, or I will drive this into your shattered kneecap and pretend that I'm churning butter."

He didn't say a thing, but he did wet himself.

I looked down at him. He was sweating and a bit more than the expected amount of pale, so I said, "I didn't know that you all could still pee."

"Yeah. We just don't like to talk about it. Are you some kind of spook from one of those secret prisons?"

"No. You don't get to know who and what I am. Let's just stick with the abject terror we already have. Hmmm?"

"Okay," he said. "The primary staging area is the parking garage at the corner of Fairfax Drive and Glebe Road. We have one outpost at the corner of Route 29 and Glebe, in the old shopping center."

"That's an excellent start. By the way, what's your name?"

"Gordon. Jerry Gordon," he replied quietly.

"Jerry, I just want you to know that you're doing a fine job, and if you keep it up, you won't have to die here," I patted his left leg in a comforting way, "So, let's continue. Troop strength?"

"We've got about 30 guys from the unit I was in. Infantry. Demolitions. There are at least two guys with sniper training. There are about 300 or 400 civilian combatants." He took a deep breath and continued, "I think there are some spooks or black ops guys as well. Like, 12 or 13 of them. They don't really talk much, you know?"

"Yeah, I don't imagine they would. What kind of transportation or combat vehicles are we looking at?"

"How detailed do you want?"

I didn't like the derision that crept into his voice. Occasionally, when you interrogate people, they get little sparks of feeling ballsy. This usually happens if you don't follow through on a specific threat you've used to loosen their lips. Unfortunately for the interrogator, this means you've fucked up and let the drama lapse.

This situation can be corrected once, and only once, in a single-session, linear interview. Unfortunately for the subject being interrogated, the interrogator must now follow through on the aforementioned threat. Any threats after this correction must be executed without fail, unless the subject breaks entirely.

I stabbed downward with the skewer, lodging it about two inches into the rubble of his shattered knee.

He screamed and it was a good one. Long and high-pitched, and you might even say that it was "cleansing." I felt as though he had missed a possible career in professional yodeling.

I tapped the skewer with my finger and the entire beach chair danced on the concrete with the convulsion that ripped through his body. He stopped moving after a moment but was breathing like a bellows as he tried to keep the pain under control. If he had been a normal human being, I would have been worried about shock setting in, but I didn't see anything that looked like typical symptoms. I put that worry aside and kept right on going.

I looked down at him and called him a dickhead. His face turned beet red and he clenched his jaw so tightly I expected teeth fragments to explode upward.

"I didn't like doing that. I won't like anything else you

make me do. Your pain is your fault. All you have to do is answer honestly, and you won't feel anything worse than me pulling that skewer out before I splint your leg."

He started chanting "Fucker" at me in a very low voice. I could tolerate that, because it meant he was capable of being vocal and the skewer had done what I wanted: re-established the order of business.

"Vehicles?"

"Cars, one armored Bradley, a couple of SUVs, and seven Humvees. Three school buses."

"A Bradley? Nice. How about the plan to come and wipe us off the face of Arlington?"

He rolled his eyes, and I reached for the skewer. He stopped rolling his eyes.

I took a deep breath.

"There isn't a plan to wipe you all out. There's just a plan for a surgical strike to snatch and grab your friend and his wife. The rest of you aren't on our radar, unless you become food."

I nodded. It did sound reasonable from a tactical standpoint. A bunch of suburban sharecroppers is not much of a worry for even a semi-trained military; at least, that is what you would think if the world were remotely normal. All I could think about was Bugs Bunny saying, "Eh, he don't know us very well. Do he?"

Their poor intelligence about our little community was a possible saving grace in the midst of a steaming pile of gopher intestines. We had some interesting aces up our collective sleeves, in the form of our population and our products. For example, Gina Halperin, five houses over, makes nitroglycerin. On top of her skills, a few of our group have done extensive study of improvised explosive devices in the Middle East.

Don't ask what is in the bottom of the trash bin you pass on your way into the neighborhood from the Route 29 side. There are about 50 similar surprises around the major entry points into the community. I like it here.

"Do you think you could tell me where the strike will penetrate?"

"Before you grab that skewer or anything else, I can't. I just go where I'm told. The black ops guys have that job, not us."

Again, I nodded. Black ops personnel were trained to go into unknown situations and do nutty things, like extract people while keeping them alive in the process. I wasn't entirely sure that my boy was being completely on the up-and-up, but I also had to consider the possibility he didn't know anything beyond the general details of a mission he wasn't involved with. Sure, he was a veteran who came home in one piece, but he certainly wasn't trained for recon.

I decided to let it slide.

"For our next magical trick, I sense you want to tell me how many layers there are between your average Joe Zombie and Warren Hightower," I intoned with great gravitas and mysterious arm motions.

"You are one sick fucker. You're enjoying this!" His tone was both surprised and accusatory.

"In point of actual fact, Jerome, I am not enjoying myself. My idea of a good time is much like yours. I like to paint pictures of cute baby animals, but my real passion is flower arrangement. Now answer the question or I'll make butter inside your knee here."

"Four bodyguards, and he doesn't socialize with anyone but group commanders and team managers."

I wondered at the flat tone of voice he was using to tell me that. It wasn't quite bored, but it was questionable. In that quiet space, I found myself wishing I had a stun gun. A stun gun and a kabob skewer would make an impression.

"How many layers of people was that?" Asking a second time wouldn't hurt.

"I already told you, you've got managers, commanders and the other guys."

He was using a flat tone of voice, but it came off as just a little exasperated.

"Three layers, right?"

"Yes. Three layers."

"How many people in each layer to contend with?"

Jerry answered, "Three or four bodyguards. Three commanders. Something like nine group leaders," but he definitely sounded annoyed with the answer.

"That's three bodyguards?"

"Fuck! Yes! Three goddamned bodyguards!"

Butter time.

I admit, I stirred the wreckage of his kneecap around like sugar cubes in tea. I will also report that his screaming and cursing was some of the most intense that I've ever heard in either category. To repeat the cursing, just the cursing, would probably cause the Pope's eyebrows to spontaneously burst into flame.

"How many bodyguards? Really? Be honest, because you do not want me to escalate this. I've only got a Swiss Army knife, more skewers, and two kitchen knives to work with. My options are limited, but they all involve piercing or involuntary amputations." I leaned over, looked him dead in the eyes, and said, "Things would have gone much faster if they'd had a little cooking torch. Then I could have used the skewers to keep one of your eyes open while I roasted it in its socket."

I smiled. He went rigid, and from the look in his eyes I was fairly certain he understood the depth of shit that he was in.

Very quietly, he said, "There are four bodyguards. Three of them are ninjas. The fourth used to work for him when he owned his company. Vice President, or something."

"Ninjas? You're shitting me, Jer. Let me mix your knee a little... "

"NO!" He cut me off. "The guys say they're ninjas! They're always jumping around and balancing on strange shit like parking meters!"

There was a ring of truth to that. Ninjitsu is big on balance, especially in odd places and situations. You can't be

"Death from the Trees" if you can't walk around on a limb. In the urban jungle, a parking meter could be a reasonable tool to exercise with. As for the jumping around, even Silent Shadow-san likes to have a good time.

Ninjitsu is like Parkour, but with death.

"Thank you, Jerry. That's very helpful, and I mean that from the bottom of my heart. I *like* ninja; they're crunchy in milk."

"Fuck me," he said, and I just shook my head.

"Necrophilia is not on my list of joyful pastimes. There's also the small problem of you being a guy."

"Look, can you just keep asking me questions so we can be done with this and I can get out of here? You're fucking insane and it is really starting to freak me out!"

Got him.

"You guys got any superheroes or secret weapons over there?" I asked, grinning down into his face. I didn't want the psychological advantage to slip once we'd determined that I had it.

"Fuck no. Nobody's a super hero. No funky powers or shit like that."

"How many team leaders are there?" You always ask questions more than once. Remember that.

"I told you, there are nine. They've all got stupid-ass names like Team Fruit Fly and Team Crunchy Baguette."

"I guess this means that our boy Warren has a really odd sense of humor?"

"Hell yeah!" He seemed to forget that I was torturing him for a minute there, and I didn't mind. "He's had these strange parties where the team leads dress up in costumes they snagged from some kinky store somewhere and dance around. I've even heard he's got some kind of dominatrix or something up in his office."

"Dude, that's some sick shit!" I figured I'd keep him going a little bit. Besides, if you're the living dead and you're screwing your "food," you can't get much kinkier than that. Dominatrixes are small fry when compared to shagging, killing, and then eating people.

"The team leads always talk about her in really quiet voices. Like they're in awe of that shit."

"Damn. Where's the office? I got to see that shit for myself."

"Same building the parking garage is in. You know the one, there's a New York-style deli out front."

I nodded, still in his face, still smiling. "Jerry?"

"Yeah, man?"

"You weren't supposed to mention the location or the dominatrix, were you?"

"Oh, no." He was almost adorable in a zombie sort of way when he realized he'd given away more than he should have. His responses had been changing throughout the interrogation, and I didn't think it had everything to do with being invited to answer questions. The viral decay, which he'd mentioned earlier, was probably beginning to impair his cognitive functions.

"You were telling me about the interesting weapons cache you guys have, before you got on about the S&M. Remember?"

"Right! Yeah. We've got some shoulder-mounted rocket launchers, a few mortar launchers and this thing in a box that no one gets to touch." He was nodding while he listed those things, and just kept going. "Lots of machine guns and ammo. Um. Handguns. Three cases of fragmentation grenades and a whole shitload of flash bangs. Ninjas! Dude, did I tell you we've got some ninjas?"

Note to self: cognitive zombie impairment starts out with acting like you're stoned. I was betting if I didn't wrap it up soon, I'd find him entering the belligerent phase of My Brain is Melting.

"Jerry," I said and then got out of his face, "I just want to tell you you've done a great job and I'm really happy we got to work together on this."

"Dude! Me too! Me too! You're really good at this shit!"

"Hey. You're too kind. I'm going to take this skewer out

of your knee, and I want you to stay chill because it's not going to feel very good at all. Okay?"

"Sure! I'm a man. I can take it." He was nodding vigorously and it looked more like headbanging from where I was crouched.

"Count to three for me, and I'll pull it out on three. That work all right for you?"

"Yeah! Let's go! One."

I put my finger through the loop of the skewer and got a decent hold on it. He was looking far too eager to be sane.

"Two!"

Headbanging ratcheted up a notch or two. Interesting. I got ready to pull.

"THREEEEEE!"

I whipped it out. He convulsed, screaming, and tore his right arm loose. Before I knew it, his clawed fingernails had bitten into my left forearm. He had a death grip on me and was not about to let go.

I let out a yell of my own. Don't blame me. It hurt like Hell.

Jerry, on the other hand, was banging his head against the beach chair and denting the frame. That didn't bother me as much as the insane little laugh wheezing out of his mouth while he slammed his head back and forth.

"Got you now, you fucking piece of shit. Not gonna let you go either. Cut me loose or I'll tear your arm off." He didn't actually say it that quickly or coherently. It came out as bursts of words punctuated by the nasty, almost subvocal, laughter. I knew I couldn't let him go, even if I wanted to keep my promise.

Whether or not I liked it, I had to end him there, while I still had a chance. I had to get my arm back in one piece, and it was probably going to hurt like Hell to do that if I had to force his grip. Then I remembered the cleaver by my right knee.

"All right, I'll cut you loose!" I told him. "Just don't tear my arm off!"

"Heh. Good. Good. Good," he kept repeating it while denting the chair even further with his head.

I picked up the cleaver, tried to clear my head, and got a feel for the thing. A Chinese meat cleaver. Heavy blade. Good balance.

I swung and cut some of the Ethernet cable that bound his right leg to the chair. He cackled with glee and started chanting "More" as I pulled my arm back for another swing.

As you can imagine, I didn't swing at the cables, but at his right wrist. I fell into a roll across his arm when the hand parted from his wrist because I was so off balance between the grip on me and the force of my swing. I came back up into a crouch with the hand still attached to my arm, covered in my blood and the spray from his stump.

The whole beach chair was jumping around on the concrete with the force of his flailing. No human noises were coming from his mouth at this point. Whatever was left of Jerry the Soldier had been replaced by some kind of mindless, raging creature. Thank whichever God you want, I still had the scythe on my back.

I pulled it out, snapped the blade into place, reversed my grip, and put the spike right between his eyes. The thrashing stopped.

Then I did something I'd never done before because I didn't know if the structure of the weapon could take lateral torsion. I leaned my right knee into the body of the scythe and pushed. I half expected the pins and screws that held it together to pop out and go bouncing around the room, but they didn't. The spike twisted in the hole it had made going in, crushing things as it went. As long as I live, I never want to hear a noise like that again.

I pulled the weapon free, saw the brain matter on the spike, and decided I needed to sit down.

I put the Man Scythe on the floor. Then I sat down. The last thing I remember is the concrete floor impacting the back of my head as I passed out.

Chapter 9

There was darkness, and I think it was cold. Definitely not warm, like the kind of darkness you get from huddling under the blankets on a Sunday morning in the wintertime. This was a chilly darkness with a certain moistness. Lo, even a sense of things dripping.

Did I mention the dripping, cold darkness was soft and smelled exotic in some way? It was really soft. If I were pressed to describe the scent, I would have to use phrases like "warm spices" and "freshly washed girl."

Don't give me shit. There is a "freshly washed girl" aroma. I smelled it, spices, in a soft place that was drippy, moist, and dark. Overall, aside from the dark aspect of everything, it was pretty pleasant.

Then I opened my eyes.

"I'm blind!" I yelled and thrashed my head around, heaving myself up into a sitting position.

There was a cold compress flopped over on a big, bandaged sausage in my lap. Things weren't dark anymore, or soft, or cold and drippy. In fact, things were well lit, tastefully decorated, and two of my dear friends were composing their faces at the foot of the bed.

"You're awake now. That's splendid!" Bajali was smiling at me from the end of the bed, and Shawn clapped him on the shoulders, looking pretty pleased as well.

"Oh. How long was I out?" I looked around a little bit, but not very much because the back of my head hurt like a stone-cold son of a yak-buggering whore.

"About four hours," Shawn answered, looking a little bit green around the eyes and jaw.

"Ah. Knocked myself out on the floor. Is Jerry dead?"

"If you mean the zombie that you were interrogating, yes. I think that may have been related to the hole that your spike made in his forehead, and that his hand was still attached to your forearm." Bajali pointed to the big white sausage in my lap. I noticed the sausage started at my elbow and had a hand attached to the opposite end.

The fingers wriggled. I winced. It was my hand and arm, not a mutant bologna from Hell. I breathed a sigh of relief that it was there and functioning, if more than a bit painful.

"Hey? Is Jayashri all right?" I didn't see her and got a flash of serious paranoia that something had happened while I was out.

"Yes," I heard from behind me, "I'm fine. Thank you for being strong enough to do what I could not."

I scooted around on the bed, and discovered that the soft, spicy place where my head had been was her lap. She wasn't meeting my eyes, and that bothered me more than I could cope with at the time. I put my finger under her chin and lifted her face so that I could see she was all right. There were tears in her eyes and no small amount of embarrassment with them.

"I was very worried about you after we heard all the noise in the basement." She wiped her eyes.

Something about that statement perplexed me. "Which noise? Him screaming, or the breakdancing beach chair noise?"

"Dude, we didn't move until we heard you holler," Shawn piped up from behind me. That made a lot of sense, so I dropped the issue.

"I had to put some sutures in your arm, I hope you don't mind." Jaya gestured at the bandage-wrapped thing attached to my elbow.

"Do I want to know how bad it was?" I wanted to know how bad it was.

"Well, once we used the bolt cutters to remove the fingers," Baj mimed using a substantial bolt cutter, "it did look quite nasty. No major nerve damage that we could see, but he missed your artery by about a millimeter. It looked like Jaya put in… darling, was it three internal sutures and four external for each puncture?"

"Yes, my dear."

"Oh. No wonder it hurts."

"I would tell you not to use it seriously for at least a week," she said, looking at her own forearm, "but that may not be a realistic suggestion at the moment."

"No, I don't think we'll have that luxury." I shook my head, hoping to clear out some of the concrete-induced cobwebs, but all it did was make bright white starbursts behind my eyelids. "Nnng. Okay. Give me a minute and I'll try to lay it all out for you. We don't have a whole lot of time to waste."

Frankly, I'm not sure how long it took me to get my brains back together, but I was able to report everything I'd learned from Jerry the Zombie Grunt. My friends were a tough crowd, and I know it wasn't a performance they particularly wanted to be a part of. For my part, I was right there with them.

"All right. This is not a wonderful situation we're in, but we might be able to do something with it," Baj was doing his most thoughtful face. "We need to pull in our snipers before they get killed. They might be more useful elsewhere, or if we could keep them mobile at the very least."

"Not to put too fine a point on this, Baj," all I could do was wave my right hand around in a vague sort of way, the left hurt too much, "but what the fuck are we going to do?"

He sighed. "We are going to do what villages have done since people started gathering in groups. We are going to round up everyone we can find, have a meeting, and present the issues to everybody as we understand it." He looked really noble, standing there like a statesman, in the old sense of the word. "Then, the community will decide what we will do."

"Bajali and I can escape," Jaya said, "and that would take the brunt of any attack away from the community. It might not mean Hightower's plans are foiled, but it would give everyone we care about a little extra time to make their own plans."

"I'm gonna tell the two of you, right now, that you're spouting bullshit." Shawn was a plain speaker, no one would ever argue that point, but he had never delivered words with that much... I'm not even sure that there's a word for it. The closest I'd ever heard to his tone of voice came straight from movies.

Charlton Heston in "The Ten Commandments." Yul Brynner in "The King and I." If Shawn had suddenly intoned, "Pharaoh, let my people go," I would have sprung up from the bed and started looking for Hebrew slaves to free. As it was, I was glued to the mattress, and I could tell that Baj was just as stunned. Then again, he may have been thinking something like, "And who is this crazy, mountain of a redneck I have invited into this house? Is this moonshine I smell?" I doubted that, but it was a possibility.

"There is not a single man, woman, child, or even family fuckin' pet who would have the two of you run away if we could keep you safe." Shawn pointed one finger at Jayashri behind me and poked the other salami-size index finger at the end of Baj's nose. "Yeah, we'll have your meeting and tell everyone about what all is goin' down, but You. Are. Not. Running. Away. Have I made myself perfectly clear?"

All three of us answered with a quiet, "Yes, Sir." I don't know why I said it. I wasn't going anywhere.

"You," he said, moving the Jayashri finger to point at me, "Go make some space in the store so we can all talk about this and make some plans. If you've got a whiteboard and markers, set 'em up. We're gonna need 'em." He moved the finger back to Jayashri, and continued, "You two, round up our neighbors and anyone they see fit to bring along. They've got an hour before I come lookin' for 'em. Tell everybody to meet at the hardware store in 45 minutes. That's all. SCRAM!"

We scrammed.

Before I made it past him, he handed me back my .45. "Boy, you don't scram as hard as all that. You've had a shitty evenin'."

"Yes, Sir." I just nodded and made my way outside.

Chapter 10

Night had fallen all the way, and I wasn't even sure what time it was anymore. There were more stars in the sky since the world changed. The air was crisp, and I felt like I was really living in the moment. Even the sound of my shoes on the pavement was more real. Somewhere in the back of my head I remembered the sorts of poetry written by warriors who were about to go out and do battle with very little chance to return home alive.

You would get words that conjured up the transitory nature of being alive, how splendid it was to be in that moment, maybe even some yearning they felt would never be realized. I thought a bit while I walked and wished that I were a poet. Words were not my art, but every now and then I stretched myself in hopes I would find them in my heart, ready to be spoken.

The crisp autumn air shakes,
the falling leaves,
tumbling to Earth;

White burning stars light
a lonely path,
walking here alone;

A final moment grasping,
the dreams slumbering
between silent breaths;

I never banged Shawn's sister.

Those thoughts swirled around in my cramped brain, and I realized I needed to find another hobby. Failing that, I needed to find a tribe of suburban Virginia Amazons who would club me upside my head, drag me to their Ikea-furnished boudoir and make me father a whole new generation of busty womanhood.

"I could always take up drinking heavily," I thought to myself as I opened the store door. I paused for a moment, looked down at the crusty dreadlock head by my foot, and silently remarked that it felt like days since I had decapitated his sorry ass. Then I kicked it down the street like a soccer ball mating with an octopus.

Once inside I headed for the back room. I knew there was a whiteboard back there, and there was easily enough space to fit everyone who might show up. My portion of the event coordination was more of the Friendly Greeter and Concierge, rather than People Herder, at least until things got started.

I was not at all sure I'd be able to add anything of major intuitive thinking with this many brains crunching down on the subject. Then again, every idea counts, even if it is a bad one. For the moment, at least, I could breathe quietly and try to process how my day had gone.

The arm was sore. My head was still pretty achy, and I wasn't quite sure that all the beans in my maracas were shaking. I was even comparing my brains to South American noisemakers, and that didn't bode well at all. Instead of thinking about it too hard, I just walked back out to the front of the store, through the plumbing section. In a split second, I thought of 101 uses for PVC pipe.

While words have never been my art, building things is where my art expresses itself. You can tell me what you need to do, and I can figure out and build something that will help you with that job. In the world we're living in, that is an incredibly useful talent to have. Why do you think I set down roots in an abandoned hardware store? It isn't the ambiance or the foot traffic; let me tell you.

I got to the front of the store just as Grandmother Yan, Mister Yan's widow, appeared at the door. She came in, gave me a hug, and said, "You a silly boy. Don't let monster bite you arm. Meeting in back?"

"Yes, Grandmother." You learned very quickly not to call her anything other than Grandmother. She was tough as granite, wrinkled like a dried-up apple, and could move like lightning with a rice paddle.

She was another person I adored, and I would die to protect her.

If our community had a kind of strength, beyond the amazing set of skills available among us, it was the love we shared. I won't lie and say there weren't problems, but you expect problems in a tribe made up of so many different kinds of people. Think of it as a big blended family, and you'd probably not be far off. Those issues didn't stop the love, genuine affection, and loyalty.

Truth be told, it probably made everything stronger.

Gina "Explosivo" Halperin and her husband, Mark, showed up at a dead run, and I funneled them back to the meeting area. They were bickering about using broken glass or gravel in anti-personnel IEDs as they went. It would be difficult to call an argument about explosives and frangible material "cute" but they managed to do it in their unique, lanky geek sort of way.

I looked down the street. Hajj Siddig Muhammad and his family were jogging over. Jim and Darcy Smith rounded the corner, carrying gallon jugs in each hand. Darcy's cider was one of the best trading neighborhood products. No one knows why it is as good as it is.

Matt "Flower" Wilson was a bit further down the street and a more difficult to see in the all-black tactical gear that he was wearing. I never asked him where "Flower" came from. Matt is another one of those rugged guys, a former Ranger, and our primary sniper.

He had made intimations that his service didn't end when his enlistment was up. From the way he moved and how he kept to himself, I strongly suspected there was more to him than met the eye. I wasn't about to corner him and ask pointed questions. He never let any of us down, and that was enough for me.

I heard running from the other direction, turned my head, and saw our second sniper booking it toward the store. Nate Banks. I was willing to bet we wouldn't see his wife at the meeting, because she'd found herself in the role of community babysitter and elementary school educator. With all the adults at the meeting, someone had to...

The thought hit me like a ton of bricks to the nuts. They could go after the kids and force us to give up Baj and Jaya.

"Nate! Barbara! Go!" He heard his wife's name, pulled his weapon, and shot off in a different direction. I turned around. Flower had heard me and taken off at a run, too, in a slightly different direction.

I must have looked like I was about to go all the way crazy, because Siddig tapped me on the shoulder and told me that he'd organize things until I got back. Then I took off after Nate.

There's an alley across the street, between the shops and services that line Route 29 and our neighborhood. Nate's house was two blocks down the alley and one block in. Flower had taken off down Bajali's side yard, which would have him approaching from the front of the house, unless he jinked sideways. Knowing Nate, he'd go for the kitchen door.

That would mean if they were going to snatch and grab the kids, they would have to have a vehicle on Route 29, or no more than a block away. They'd have to move very fast, and distance was a killer if you're trying to keep a group of people under control. Failing that, they'd create a hostage situation right here.

Their other option, if the hostage taking didn't work, would be to just start blowing shit up. Kids. People.

Anything and everything that might make us want to hand our friends over.

Yes, we all shared a lot of love, but there are things that even a loving community can't suffer for the people that live in it. I imagine the faces of our dead children would motivate enough people to eject Baj and Jaya, even in the face of what Hightower would use him for.

I heard gunshots. One burst of three rounds, followed by a single shot. Then I got tackled by someone who had very bad breath. I couldn't help but yell when we landed on my bandaged arm and slid across the gravel and into the chain-link fence on the other side.

Black fatigues, goggles, helmet, black gloves with holes cut for claws, and a pistol rubbing into my right eye socket. Pretty full "utility belt."

"Don't fucking move." It was a hoarse whisper with fetid halitosis.

Two more bursts of gunfire. Four more single shots.

My attacker reached for the .45 holstered on my right hip. He shifted his balance to the right, and I helped him. The gun came away from my eye as he started to fall, and I turned my head towards the ground because I'd rather have a bullet graze my skull than take off an ear.

He hit the ground, and the gun didn't go off. Professional. We rolled in opposite directions; he went backward, but I went forward and to the right. Neither one of us was in a perfect position for a quick squeeze of the trigger. Of course, he had my gun, and I had nothing.

He started to sit up and bring both pistols to bear on me, and I had two choices. Stay still and get shot for sure, or move *anywhere* and gain a second or two. Easy choice, and I made it before I finished the thought. I moved straight for him, springing forward from my crouch.

Neither of the guns lined up fast enough, so I slapped his arms out as I cannoned into his midsection. I didn't follow him to the ground, but I did make a quick swipe at his utility belt as he fell.

Both guns went off when he hit the ground, and I turned around and ran like Hell towards Nate's house. I was too focused on running to hear if he got up, stayed down, or what. In fact, in that moment I only knew two things: I had to get away immediately, and I had the pin of a hand grenade in my right hand.

It seemed like an eternity of waiting to be shot before I heard a comforting explosion somewhere behind me. Not so comforting to be lifted off my feet, peppered with hot metal, and delivered onto asphalt on my left arm. Again.

It was dark, and then it was really dark. Twice in one day. That was a record I never wanted to break ever again.

Sometime later, the dark gave way to murky light and some very gummy noises, none of which made me eager to open my eyes any further. Something hurt a whole bunch, like someone was poking a pair of tweezers into an empty tooth socket. Very burny, very ouchy.

I may have groaned, because I got the tweezer feeling again, and I wanted someone to know I was immensely bothered by it. Given a choice, I'd prefer they'd stop. No such luck.

Maybe it wasn't tweezers? I suppose it could have been a bird with a sharp beak, reaching down and trying to pull out my nerve endings. Do nerve endings look like worms, or are they just bright and shiny enough to attract your average raven?

Great. There I was, laid flat out somewhere with strange noises, shitty lighting, and a sadistic bird pulling on my nerve endings. Maybe the grenade killed me, too? Seriously, if being in Hell is to be nibbled by birds for eternity, somebody got a huge fucking budget cutback! I rate a team of *quality* perdition engineers!

So, I decided to make my complaint to the customer service department. "Satan! You stinky ball of fudgy turd, I deserve a better damnation experience than this! One bird is not enough to make me regret anything! No wonder God threw you out! You suck!"

I was getting some kind of response, but it was thick and garbled. It did make a little bit of sense, but that could be because no one ever said demons would speak English. Then again, perhaps being dead meant I could speak their language? The soul is free from the body and all that past life historic crap is accessible to my unbound spirit.

Cool.

It never hurts to give things a try! I decided to express myself and let the language come to me naturally; after all, as a soul, it's all right there anyway.

"Aaaan! Ooo nkeee baaa uh geeee urd! Ooo uk! Ooo uk sa rd! Aiii omma ud ick ooo ass!"

That's when the raven went fucking bananas on me. I had gotten my point across in Satan's own tongue, and now I was going to get to see if my ass could be handed to me by a demonic bird in a low-rent section of Hell. No point screaming in English if they're not going to understand.

"Aaaan! Ow! At uckin urts! Ow! Uck ooo! Uck ooo! Eezus uvs ooo! Eezus! Eezus!" It made sense to call out for help to someone who would piss of His Demonic Lordship. Jesus loves me, this I know.

I sang it at the top of my lungs, in his own language. Kiss my ass! Yeah, baby! I got yer Man Scythe right here! If I'd been on my feet, instead of being held down by the bird, I would have done a touchdown dance full of slapping my own ass. The Prince of Darkness is a prideful old fucker, and it had to piss him off something fierce that someone as inconsequential as me could own him this hard.

YEAH!

Everything went black. Shit.

Chapter 11

An infinite amount of time later, my crusty eyelids ratcheted open. The light was brighter than when I was in Hell. Maybe I pissed Satan off so much that he vomited me out... somewhere else?

The raven on my back was gone. Maybe it got lunch breaks or went out for a smoke. I wasn't going to think about it too hard; I was having enough trouble with that activity to begin with. I thought I heard children, or maybe one child crying. I couldn't focus very well.

Then there were legs. Right in front of my face, wearing jeans. That was a nice, familiar sort of sight, and I wanted to reach out and touch one of the legs so I'd know if they were real legs or just some kind of demonic illusion meant to lull me into a false sense of security.

"Muh," I grunted and swung an arm at the closest leg. Swell! It was a real leg! I know because it jumped back after my arm hit it.

"Are you awake?" Somebody with a pleasant voice asked me, in English, no less.

"Is this," I coughed a little because my throat was dry and sore, "Hell? Raven on a lunch break?"

The person squatted down and I could see it was some cute African-American woman wearing glasses. She looked a lot like my friend Nate's wife, Barbara. I really hoped it wasn't Barb, because that would mean she was here in Hell, too.

"Oh, Honey! This isn't Hell. Let me run and get Jayashri.

You stay there, okay?"

"Not goin' anywhere."

She went away. Then sometime later, she came back with a second pair of legs. Wow! Two sets of legs! I wondered how she kept them coordinated when she walked.

Oh, it was another person. Silly me. This one squatted down, too, but she looked like Jayashri, not like Barbara.

"Good morning," she said. "Can you tell me your name? What is the last thing you remember?" She took my pulse.

I told her my name and explained about Satan, the Raven munching my nerve endings, and how I pissed him off so much he sent me back. And could I have some water?

Barbara-legs went to get me some water, and I wanted to remind myself to kiss her knees in gratitude when she got back. I told this woman who looked like Jayashri how I felt about Barbara-legs and their kindness to me in my peculiar situation.

"That is sweet of you. Now, I want you to try and focus, so I can tell you what really happened. Will you try to do that for me?"

"Sure. You look like the sweetest woman from India that I know. She's a doctor and has the nicest-smelling lap in the world!"

I got a very funny look.

"You were hit by shrapnel from a hand grenade. We brought you back here to your store. What you remember from 'Hell' is when you tried to regain consciousness during surgery. I had to remove as many of the fragments as I was able, as quickly as I could, because we have no blood to replace what you've lost. It was a very near thing."

"Oh." Barbara-legs came back and helped me sip some water. "What else happened?"

"We can talk more about that later. Right now, you need to rest. I have you on morphine at the moment, but I need you conscious and alert, so I will not be giving you more. You will start to feel very uncomfortable soon. I'm very sorry about that."

"Oh. Okay." I didn't really have much more to say about it than that, so I went back to sleep.

I learned that "very uncomfortable" is Doctor-Speak for intense pain. It woke me up with gentle aching when I tried to shift my position, so I decided to wake up all the way and sit up. The moment when the flat of my ass came face to face with the table I'd been lying on is one I am likely to remember for a good long time to come.

Some sort of strangled wail erupted from my mouth and I heaved my body into a standing position without a thought. Little Siddy, Siddig and Miryam's son, was scooting around the floor with a toy dump truck, and he yelped when I suddenly appeared in front of the toy. He picked up the truck, started to cry, and ran away.

There was a puddle on the linoleum.

Poor little guy!

"Honey, you probably shouldn't be standing up," Barbara said, somewhere behind me.

"I tried to sit, but it made me jump up," I replied, turning around to face her. We were in the meeting room at my store, which comforted me greatly.

"I'm not surprised. When Nate and Flower brought you in, the back side of your body was not a pretty sight, and your front wasn't looking all that great either."

"Yeah, I thought the explosion would make me that much more sexy. You know, suburban hero with an ass full of scars." Ow. "I'd shake my booty for you, but all my booty hurts."

She smiled, and it was one of the best things in the world that very moment. I smiled back and looked around for something to lean on, since sitting was not on the current menu. There wasn't anything tall enough to lean on, and I had a sinking suspicion I wouldn't be able to lean against a wall either. Having a friend smile at you is great, but when you hurt, sometimes sitting down is what you really crave.

"Barb? Is there a pillow around here, or something I could try to sit on? Or should I just lie down again?"

I watched her look around the room, tapping her bottom lip with a finger. Clearly, she didn't see comfortable objects either. "How about this, you lie down, and I'll go see what I can fix up? And I'll tell Shawn to come see you, now that you're up. Okay?"

What choice did I have? I nodded and climbed back onto the table, hissing when my left arm settled on the Formica. It was still bandaged like a well-wrapped baguette and seemed to hurt worse than before. I had been tossed into the air by an explosion and probably landed on it. More pain after something like that shouldn't be at all surprising, but I was a little taken aback by it.

Then my back and ass decided my forearm was getting too much attention.

Barbara came back with a pillow-like object that turned out to be a polar fleece blanket stuffed inside a pillowcase. Strung behind her like pearls on a necklace were all the neighborhood children: Juan and Julia, Yolanda's little ones; Nancy, Billy, and Matt Smith; Ezra, Rebekah, and David Klein; and Little Siddig, Junior, brought up the rear, and it looked like someone had changed his diaper.

Barb turned to the kids and said, "Now, what was it you all wanted to say?"

The kids looked at me with grave little eyes and did their best to say in unison, "Thank you very much for coming to save us! We hope your behind feels better!" They redefined "cute" in my internal Wikipedia, and I was caught between laughter and tears. Thankfully, none of them tried to hug me, or the tears would have been from pain, not emotional wobbliness.

They trooped back out of the room, and Barb helped me situate my rump on the makeshift pillow. It was a near thing, because the only parts of me she could touch without making me wince were my right arm and most of the front of my body.

I lamented to her that the heroes in movies never got banged up to the point of not being able to sit on their asses.

She reminded me some heroes *do* get that messed up in films, but just keep forcing themselves into superhuman tasks when they really should just lay still and let the bad guy get away. I had to admit she made an excellent point, and if Hollywood ever gets back to making movies, I want someone really hot and hung like a barnacle to play me.

"Why, in the name of God, would you want someone who has a penis like a barnacle's to play you?"

Fount of strange information that I am, I explained. "The common barnacle's manly equipment is four to five times the length of his body."

"You know, I love you to bits, but you are such an odd person." All she could do to follow up was shake her head.

"If I had more women who loved me like you do, they could make stew out of me with all the little love bits." I was forcing myself to be amusing to try and cope with the immense amount of pain I was feeling from the backs of my knees to the base of my skull. I think she knew I was trying to hide it.

"Well, Captain Barnacle Dick, I will be sure you get a good gumbo as your final resting place," she said and patted me on the cheek.

"Could I be some other captain? That one doesn't sound... hygienic."

"You just sit still. Shawn will be here soon, and you'll get a whole bunch of stuff to think about. That nasty mental image will be long gone."

She walked off to go do something, and I was left alone with my thoughts. The kids were safe, I knew, because I saw them with my own two eyes. Nate and Flower had brought me in, so it was a reasonable bet they were still alive. Even better, it didn't look like any of the kids were hurt. I allowed myself a sigh of relief over that.

I heard Shawn's footfalls and lifted my head. He was smiling.

"Brother, don't go scram like that when I tell you to scram. All right?"

"Yes, Sir, Captain Shawn, Sir." I saluted. "I will not scram in front of a grenade ever again, Sir."

"Better damned well not." He grabbed my hand and squeezed the jelly right out of it. If he had given me a hug, I would have wet my pants and screamed at the top of my lungs in a high-pitched girly octave. "Anybody tell you what all happened?"

"No, but the kids came by, so I know that they're okay."

"Yeah. I don't know how you figured that out, but you all got there in the nick of time. There were two goons in the house, the one you blew up, and a dude in a truck waiting on Route 29. The boys got the ones you didn't get. No casualties but you on our side."

"I'm really glad I'm all that got wounded."

"So are we! You're too ornery to die."

"Shawn, you're not telling me how long I've been out of commission. Why aren't you telling me that?"

"Because, if I tell you that, you'll probably pop some stitches and we'd really prefer to have you on the mend." He frowned in his own legendary way, and I knew it was bad.

"I need you to give it to me straight; don't be a pussy about it."

He heaved a massive sigh and told me, "You've been in and out of consciousness for the past three days. Yes, before you even ask, Baj agreed to go to Hightower and work on the project. Jayashri was allowed to remain here. This was the best we could do in the face of much superior firepower."

Surprisingly enough, I didn't explode when I heard all of that. I guess there was still enough morphine in my system to keep me calmer than I usually am when confronted with a situation that makes me want to piss nails. I found myself nodding, as though what Shawn said made sense or I could understand why Baj would do such a thing.

"Why?"

Shawn was doing an excellent job of not meeting my eyes. "It was the kids. No one expected they'd do that. No one but you. Problem is, you didn't even figure it out until it was almost too late."

"We were naive. We didn't want to think Hightower would stoop that low. FUCK! Not even his own spy thought he was watching us that hard!"

"Cool your jets. Nothin' we can do right now. People made decisions, and Bajali made the best deal he could to keep everybody safe. You know, as well as I do, he won't burn the midnight oil to get that nano-thing done. Hell, if he finds a way to fuck it up, you know he'll do it."

I went off the hook. The frustration, rage, and my own inability to do a damned thing about what happened while I was down climbed up my ass and throttled the Hell out of my brain. I don't remember what I said, but I got right up in my friend's face and poured shit out of my mouth...it might have been the drugs, or the stress, but I'll never know for sure.

The friendly, country boy exterior peeled off him like a snakeskin, and something much angrier was left in that place.

I didn't see the fist coming. Suddenly my face hurt, and I was on my back across the table. There were angry black spots in front of my eyes, and I was pretty sure I couldn't get up on my own.

"What the fuck is it with you, anyway? Are you so damned smart you can't imagine people making decisions without your input?" Even with black spots in front of me, more pain than I can ever remember, and the drug hangover, there was no way I could mistake how angry he was... how angry he had every right in the world to be. "Man, I don't give a fuckin' rat's ass what you think. You are not God. I will tell you, God as my witness, if you ever speak that way about people who saved your ass ever again, you had better leave town before I find you. If all you've got is that kind of bullshit: we don't need you."

I was wrong. I hated myself for it. Maybe I had over-stayed my welcome and really was better off leaving and finding someplace else to live.

I heard Shawn turn around, breathing like a freight train, and leave the room. I couldn't move.

The sound of your heart breaking is the voice of someone you care about telling you they don't want you or need you. Don't argue with me about that, because I know I'm right. I've been through it too many times, have too much data, and more scars than you.

Chapter 12

At some point, the world stopped looking like a bad acid experience and I knew I had to get off my back. That was a simple decision, really, because the pain was getting unbearable and sensations like that are enough to motivate even the most despairing of souls.

It did take a little time to roll over onto my right side without using my left arm or many of my other major muscle groups, but I did it. Time didn't really matter much. I wasn't sure about anything, other than the pain, and the growling of my stomach.

I guess I hadn't eaten anything in three days or so. I didn't really want to eat, but at least it would give me a purpose for a short time, and even a small challenge. Would I be able to get up the stairs to the loft where my food and water stash was?

Would I be able to get back down the stairs? Then again, it might not even matter if I couldn't get down the stairs again. I could stay up there, piss and shit into a bucket, dump it out the window, and never come down. If the food ran out, well, I could decide what to do then.

No time like the present to find out. Standing up again was a unique experience, and walking was just as interesting. Before long I was standing in front of the stairs to the loft. It used to be the store manager's office and looked out across the floor of the store. A great view.

I opened the door, once I made my slow and careful way up the stairs, and went inside. My sleeping bag and pillow were in the same place. The desk was still in the corner with the circa 1950s office chair, across from the racks of dry goods and bottled water. All I did was stand there because I didn't know what to do.

I couldn't sit in the chair and I couldn't get down to the sleeping bag and expect to get up again. The best I could do was use the desk for everything. There are worse fates. I gathered up some beef jerky and a bottle of water and lowered myself onto the desk.

At no other time in my life was I so aware of the location of my tailbone.

When I put the bottle and bag down on the top of the desk, I saw an envelope with my name on it. Careful block letters. Whoever wrote it wasn't rushed while they did it. Sharp corners on the letters. Probably written by a man. Not a love letter from Shawn's sister.

I'd always imagined that she'd have that rolly handwriting girls did when I was in high school. They'd make circles to dot the "i" and little hearts all over the place.

Love letters in school were the best! If the world hadn't changed, I bet I could have collected old love letters and turned them into some kind of Internet and coffee-table book phenomenon. Most of my dreams and ideas start out with "If the world hadn't changed."

Beef jerky and water aren't my favorite choices for a meal, but there was just very little likelihood enough energy remained in me to do anything more involved. The world looked very bleak through my eyes, having alienated myself from my people and knowing that a friend was risking mankind's future in an effort to give us more time to fight back.

Baj was going to get himself killed, infected, undead, or worse. God forbid he might succeed in one way or another.

Depression grabbed me like a piranha on the testicles of an Amazonian warrior. I couldn't tell where the pain was worse: my arm, my whole back, or my heart. The back, ass, and arm commanded a certain amount of care, whereas my feelings could be swung around without a care for their condition.

So, I danced with the piranha.

At some point the jerky was finished, and so was the water. The companion meat-eating fish in my heart were still gnawing on my gristle when I remembered the letter on the table beside me. I looked down at it and tried to resist the urge to read it. The Piranha Brothers were against me.

"Oyé, gringo. Read the letter, man. No, we mean it. Read the letter. Maaaan, read the goddamned letter!"

Persistent little fuckers, putting the Nom on my bits like that.

Of course, the letter was from Bajali.

My dear friend,

You have always given me the benefit of your friendship and honesty, and in this situation, I can do no less for you.
We were all duped, as you know. They have been watching us for some time, but we were foolish enough to believe the village we have made for ourselves would not be seen as a potential threat. So it goes, freedom and peace spoil the unwary.
As I write this, my wife is pulling shards of metal from your body, hoping you will not lose too much blood.
I think what I would like to say is something less rational than the words I used a moment ago. I hope if you are reading this, you will bear with me.
I am writing this letter to you as you are bleeding out across a table in a makeshift surgery. You may not live to read what I am writing. Jayashri is terribly worried, as are we all.
It is not our friends that concern me in this moment, but the terror that I will lose my friend — you, who had a flash of intuition that saved the children, whom we all hold dear, from capture or worse. Can I do less than my friend who is bleeding, as likely to die as to live, on that table? You will be furious beyond reason with me, and I dearly hope you will live to tell me so, but I know what I must do. Jayashri and I cannot flee. She is needed here and knows this better

than anyone. Wherever I go, our enemy will follow. Unless I go to him. Then, for the weeks and months it could take for me to complete the work he desires, my dear friends will be safe.

Should I choose to stay, and I think you would agree, Hightower will attack with all he has at his disposal in order to capture me or force my compliance. That is an unconscionable choice for me. I cannot let more of you be injured or killed so that I might be safe for another day.

I will go willingly. I will work and sabotage that work if at all possible. That is my duty to you and to each living soul I have come to love in this lifetime.

Pray, if you will, that we will succeed and meet again in this life. I will pray for that. Jayashri will pray for that. Nothing spoken in this world goes unheard; this, I believe.

Live.

Very sincerely,
Bajali

My chest hurt more than the rest of my body, and I couldn't help but collapse in on myself. Paralyzed and flooded, I tumbled to the floor. I am not even sure whether I wept or not, or even if I was able to form a coherent thought. The Piranha Brothers abandoned me without a single taunt to mark their exit.

All I had left was my breath, in and out. Everything else was disintegrating, and I was to blame for not thinking fast enough and for not holding my damned tongue. Even my breath, that last thing left in the shell of me, was too heavy to bear.

Chapter 13

Before I found this enclave of happiness a little over a year before that day, I'd been doing a lot of wandering. When the first stories about dead people coming back to life hit the news, I was in a pub in Duddingston, Scotland, soaking my tongue with sequential pints of 80 Shilling beer, dark, thick, malty stuff.

Duddingston is "over the hill" from Edinburgh. The hill is Arthur's Seat, and a decent little hike if you don't realize that the best way up is to just walk around to the other side and go right up the slope. Bing, you're at the top. Bong, you've just walked back down. It's a nice view.

Over the few weeks I'd been tramping around that countryside, the morning view across E-burg from the top of Arthur's Seat was my all-time favorite. I'd stop by Neal's Yard Cheese, grab a little something different, walk around the mini-mountain, up the slope, and chill out with the nibble. That day, it rained.

I jogged down, nearly killed myself slipping on the wet, mossy steps that lead into that Edinburgh suburb, and threw myself into the Sheep's Heid pub. I won't bore you with the history, but Bonnie Prince Charlie was said to have made war plans over a pint at the Heid. It's been around for quite some time.

Earlier in the week, I'd discovered that the bartender had a sister in Alexandria, Virginia, the city next to Arlington. Having come from that area myself, we had quite a lot to talk about. He was never one for keeping the telly on, except during important footie matches. That afternoon, on a lark, he turned it on.

I had three pints in me when the news came on about the dead rising from the grave in countries around the world. Within moments, everyone in the pub was crowded around the bar, and the volume on the TV was turned up all the way. We were a human chorus of incredulous murmurs.

Some hours later, in the wee half-light of the morning, I decided to head back to the little hotel that I'd been calling home for a few weeks. There was a scream from somewhere ahead of me on the cobbled path back to Edinburgh proper, followed by some thuds and wet noises.

While personal crime is lower in the UK than the US, there is still some to contend with. I figured I was merely going to witness a mugging, or a rape at worst. No such luck for me.

He was eating the girl by the time I made it close enough to see what was going on. I rushed in, and he threw me about 20 feet through the air. The landing made my teeth bounce around in my gums, but I was able to roll with it and come back up on my feet. I was surprised to find him directly in front of me when I completed the roll.

"I'm not interested in you, so if you stay out of my way," he growled, "you won't get hurt."

I've been menaced by thugs in the past, and I never really felt overwhelmed by it. My dad was to blame for that, having dropped me into the martial arts at a young age. I wasn't clear on his reasons for that, because he knew I didn't like it, even if I was surprisingly good at picking things up. Even my mother was unsure.

Deep down in the secret catacombs of my heart, I secretly suspected my father wanted to have this sort of conversation with people.

"Carl! Have I ever introduced you to my son? Carl, this is my son, Killing Machine. Killing Machine, this is Carl Businessman. Say hello, why don't you?"

"Grrr. Grrr. ARRRR. Grr. Mister ARRRRG."

"See? He's a great little kneebiter, isn't he? Carl? Where did you go?"

I left home well before I ever decided to ask him just what the Hell he was thinking. If you wanted to call my family "estranged" or "dysfunctional," I certainly wouldn't blame you for it, because they're really pieces of work, every single one of them. After all, they were the main reason I set off to wander the world for a while. I needed to get away from them and see who I was without their influence. The terror that gripped me occasionally came in the form of being afraid I was more like them than I wanted to be.

Although, at this particular moment in time, my angst came in the form of a homicidal, cannibalistic, acne-ravaged, blood-soaked, Scottish teenager. While he had informed me that the menu didn't include me, I got the distinct impression that roughing me up was part of his early-morning exercise plan. Unfortunately for me, I was not mistaken.

I slid backwards on instinct, and if I hadn't, he would have sunk his fingernails into my stomach instead of shredding my favorite windbreaker. Fortunately, he didn't get hung up on my zipper, which gave me time to move into him as he tried to come back with his other hand.

This time, I met his arm as he swung, caught it, and put him face on the ground in a classic Aikido arm lock. He was not happy. I also learned how insanely strong the undead are, because he was beginning to curl me over and down while I held him. Normal human beings don't do things like that from the sort of position we were in.

You are taught, in some martial arts, that the way to end a fight is to remove your opponent's desire to continue the altercation. I chose to try and communicate with my opponent by tightening my hold on his arm and dropping to my knees. Actions do speak louder than words.

I would have to say, my effort was successful. There was a loud pop, my opponent screamed, and I was flying through the air in the opposite direction. When I was able to raise my head, I could see him running away with one arm dangling like a noodle at his side. About the same time, I heard the distinct sound of police cars and saw the flashy blue lights through the trees.

There is an old rule of thumb that really should be passed down through the generations. If you are the only witness at the scene of a spectacularly violent crime, do not run from the police in whatever country you find yourself visiting. In this way, you go from being a witness to a suspect, and they will do their best to track you down in order to ask pointed questions. Depending on the country, the degree of unpleasantness you will experience when they find and interrogate you is variable.

In the UK, at least, you can expect some level of civilized behavior. With those things in mind, I stayed where I was, lying in the dew-wet grass, and slowly let my eyes close. They'd be here soon enough, and allowing myself the luxury of feeling as though I'd been tossed through the air twice wouldn't hurt me. A little acting never hurt, either.

"Uhhhhhhhhhhhhh... "

I heard the officer approach and crouch down beside me. "Lad? Are yeh right? Laddie," he nudged me gently, "can yeh open yer eyes?"

"Ow." I cracked my eyelids and didn't have to fake recoiling in horror when he flicked the flashlight on my face. "Gah!"

He spoke into the microphone that was clipped to his jacket. "We have one white male down, responsive. Contusions. Request ambulance for transport."

"Lad, I've got medics on the way. Stay still, and we'll get all this sorted out. Can yeh tell me what happened? Can yeh tell me yer name?"

I was faced with a moral choice. Continue to be the victimized witness or actually start interacting. The sooner I interacted, the less likely it would be drawn out later. Reasonable decision, I thought, so I told him my name.

"Izzat American or Canadian?"

"'merican," I slurred. It wasn't hard to act like I'd been hit by a truck. Impacting the ground at speed generally shakes up your bits.

"All right, now, can you tell me wha' happened here?"

"Uhhhh. Walking back to the hotel. Heard a woman scream an' ran to see." I followed up by trying to shift my position on the ground a little.

"No, lad, don't try to move around. Just be still. Can yeh tell me wha' yeh saw?"

"The guy was eating her. Blood everywhere. He threw me."

"Oh, aye. Go on."

"Got up, but he was right in front of me. Had big fingernails. Tried to gut me with them. Jacket all ripped up."

"Did yeh tussle wi' him? Defend yerself?"

"Yeah, got him in an arm lock. Think it broke. He threw me again."

The EMTs appeared at about that time and started checking me over. There was another set across the way where the girl was, but they weren't moving quickly at all. My set of law enforcement and health care professionals decided I needed to be taken to the hospital for X-rays and observation. I wasn't going to argue.

They were a competent duo, this ambulance crew, and I even complimented them on their sterling gurney technique. It got a few laughs. Then we heard a ruckus and two gunshots. The officer who interviewed me took off at a dead run, followed by one of my Dynamic Duo: the one who had the bag of medical goodies.

I wanted to get up and haul ass after them, but it wasn't in keeping with the image I was working on building. I heard my gurney driver get the order over his walkie-talkie to deposit me in the ambulance and come running right away. He wasted no time.

The ambulance door shut, locked, and he took off. I was left alone with my thoughts, which had only just started processing the day's events: people coming back from the dead to eat the living—not just a good news story but something that was actually happening.

I couldn't deny it, because I'd fought with one of them. What was the world coming to, and why?

The beer may have done it, or it could have been two major encounters with Mother Earth, but I nodded off in the ambulance. An indeterminate amount of time later, the EMTs came back, checked me over, and off to the hospital we did go.

"Hey," I said, giving the fellow who was riding in the back a tug on the sleeve of his jacket. "What happened back there with the gunshots?"

"Oh, you're awake then. I think I can tell you, you're not a suspect anymore, so you needn't worry about that."

"What do you mean by that?"

"The fella that did that girl tried to attack an officer who cornered him over by the Sheep's Heid. Our lad's partner shot the guy once in the leg, but he kept comin' and didn't listen when he was ordered to stop."

"So the partner shot him again?"

"Aye, right between the eyes."

Maybe I was a little more sideways than I thought I was, because that didn't seem to give them a reason to rule me out as a suspect. Not that I wasn't grateful, but I couldn't follow things and wanted very badly to be brought up to speed. "Why does that not make me a suspect?"

"It probably has somethin' to do with your clothes not being sopping wet with blood. You also didn't have the victim's cell phone and clutch purse in your possession. I'll also add that you don't have bits of her titties stuck between your teeth."

"Oh."

The rest of the trip to the hospital passed in silence. X-rays were taken, viewed, and the requisite prodding was accomplished. It was declared, in blunt Scottish fashion, "I don' see why they brought yeh here. Nothin' wrong wi' yeh tha' a cuppa tea will na fix. G' home."

Before I got terribly far, the officer who met me in the field walked up to me. I gave him my contact information, was assured that I was simply a witness in a case that will never see a courtroom, and exchanged pleasantries. He was entirely pleasant, but I could tell that we shared quite a bit of the same distress at having been a part of such a "singular event," as he put it.

I left the hospital, and it was near 7 am if my memory serves me correctly. There was the start of commuting madness, but it was a mere trickle in Morningside, compared to what it would be on the highways or deeper into the city. I noticed a Cafe Brutus on the corner of Falcon Road, and strolled over in hopes of a quad espresso that might keep me awake long enough to get back to my hotel over in Old Town.

The bell on the door rang when I opened it and I lumbered in. My brain was sending me feeble signals that something was a little off, so I looked at the people who were enjoying their morning beverages and snacks. They were all looking back at me with some form of alarm. That wasn't good.

There was an upright refrigerator, stocked with juice and whatnot, and I glanced at my reflection in the glass. Oh.

"Pardon me," I spoke in a tiny voice, "but is there a restroom? I'd like to splash my face before I have brekkie."

The girl behind the counter pointed across the room, and I scooted over as quickly, yet calmly, as I could.

My face was not a comforting sight; neither were the remains of my jacket. I ran wet fingers through my hair in an effort to get it to lay down, but it resisted, leaving me with "Sex Pistols" spikes. I couldn't do anything about my eyes.

I looked like I'd seen bad things, hadn't slept at all, and been roughed up badly. I didn't remove the hospital wristband, but I did take off the jacket. Hopefully, no one would call the police because this coffee shop was close enough to the hospital that you'd think accident victims would wander in periodically.

I tried to smile in the mirror. It wasn't convincing. At least I could be an example of truth in advertising if I did nothing else.

The television was on in the shop, and most of the locals had given up looking at me in favor of the news. Then I heard what was on the news, namely the events I'd been involved in.

The girl who had been killed was Lois Griffin of Leith, an 18-year-old university student. Her photo was plastered on the screen and looked so different from what I'd seen. Vibrant eyes, winning smile, a little stud in her nose, and lavender-colored hair.

Her killer was Marty Andrews, 21, also from Leith. They had been dating for two years before he was killed in a drunk-driving accident three weeks prior. His family had not reported that he had returned to the family home two days ago. They were just so happy he "had not really died" in the collision, even if they'd been the ones who identified his body at the morgue.

Police shot and killed Andrews after he resisted arrest, assaulted an officer, and attempted to flee.

The news nailed me to the floor, and it took a Herculean effort of will to turn around and order that quad espresso. I managed.

The barista spent a good amount of time giving me something approaching the "evil eye," and I didn't particularly feel as if I deserved it. I didn't know her. I certainly had never gone out with her and generally preferred women who didn't have enough piercings to be dangerous in thunderstorms. The young woman doing cashier duty was much friendlier, with a tasteful amount of metallic decoration, and someone I would have gone out with.

I sat down with my drink and did my best to put my brain back together. The caffeine and heat of the drink woke me up a little, but I couldn't really kick-start my thought processes or make sense of anything. There was a huge sense of the world going awry and not being able to do anything about it. From the looks on the faces of the other customers, they were feeling something very similar.

Twenty minutes later, I killed my first zombie.

My stomach started growling halfway though the drink, so I got back up, ordered one of their larger breakfast plates, and returned to my seat. A little bit later, my sausage and eggs showed up with an apology for only being able to give me a steak knife for the meat, rather than a normal table knife. It didn't bother me, I said so, and mere minutes later would be thanking God for the cafe's horrible dishwashing system.

The shop door opened, and a girl walked through it. I didn't pay much attention until I heard the conversation that started shortly thereafter.

"Mary! There you are! I knew I'd find you at work in this stinking little hole. Come here and give us a kiss, you whore." This came from the mouth of the girl who had walked in.

Metalface, who must've been Mary, screamed.

"Oh no, girly! Don't be screaming at me like that unless we're fucking," she said as she prowled into the shop. "Nice people like this lot don't want to hear your freaky little cum screams."

Mary joined in with, "Tess! Don't come any closer. You died, Tess! Last week! You overdosed. You're not really here!" There was the bright crystal twang of Mary's mind snapping.

"But, baby, I've come all the way back because I love you! You smell so good!"

Zombie Tess was about five feet away from me, which made her about fifteen feet away from the cowering barista and closing. I suppose my brain snapped, too. I got up from my chair and plowed into her.

We ended up on the floor, with me on top. Enjoyment in this was somewhat ruined by the set of long, thick fingernails buried in my side. Tess laughed at me and sunk her other fingernails into the flesh of my forearm. I screamed. You would have, too.

"What, boy? Did I make you so hot you wanted to do me here on the floor?"

It wouldn't have been so bad if she hadn't been gyrating underneath me. Her fingernails were acting like a food processor set on "sensual slow," twisting in my arm and side. I had the steak knife in my hand and I realized I had a decision to make before she decided to stop toying with me. If she was already dead, then it didn't matter what I did to motivate her to let me go.

She was making all kinds of really lewd noises when I plunged the steak knife into her left eye. I felt it go through the back of the socket and into her head. Her naughty monologue abruptly ceased and was replaced by a wail. Her hands pulled away from me and wrapped around my knife hand, but not before I was able to churn the blade around. Her arms flopped to the ground and she just stopped as if someone had flipped a switch.

Cafe Brutus was very quiet after that.

"Would someone call the police and an ambulance?" My voice was deafening in the silence of the coffee shop. I didn't move, just stared at my hand wrapped around the steak knife handle protruding from this woman's eye socket. There seemed to be an awful amount of blood on her.

It took me a very long moment to look at my arm, specifically where she had impaled it with her fingernails. Two of the holes were spraying in time with my heartbeat. I remember thinking, "Oh. I guess that means she punctured the artery in two places," before my gut instinct took over and I clamped my other hand over my arm. Put pressure on a wound. Pressure.

"Fuck." Again, a very loud word in the silence, but it wasn't alone for long. The police and an ambulance arrived. I rolled off Tess's body onto the floor as the cops and EMTs stormed the cafe.

With my luck, I had the same police officer as before. I

always appreciated consistency in law enforcement, and I told him so. He looked at me as though I'd lost my mind, but he rushed the EMTs over anyway. They might have even been the same guys from earlier, but I couldn't be sure.

I knew I was going into shock. Shock is one of those things you don't forget after the first time you feel it. If you're not stuck in panic mode when it happens, you'll feel the chills, a kind of existential claustrophobia, and how your thoughts get random and slow. I started to giggle gently, and then I just passed out.

Having your vision contract to blackness and your consciousness wink out like a light is another unforgettable human experience. It might be the closest we get to what a quiet death feels like, depending on how you go to sleep every night. For me, I've always fallen asleep in the middle of a thought or had sleep sneak up on me. Not the slow decent into blackness.

There weren't any dreams in that darkness, not even a near death experience, just a return to groggy wakefulness. I could smell the international aroma of hospital ward, so I knew where I was before I was completely able to see again. What surprised me was that I couldn't raise my hand to touch my face and move the oxygen mask around. There was something hard around my wrist.

Both of them, actually.

They'd cuffed me to the bed. That just didn't bode well for me. Then again, having been involved in two major crimes in less than 12 hours might make me interesting enough to handcuff to a hospital bed. I set those thoughts aside for a bit to let the rest of my mind come back online. It wasn't booting up at the usual speed.

I looked down, once I realized I wasn't flat on my back but actually a bit elevated, and confirmed the sets of handcuffs. My side was sore, and I noticed there was a substantial amount of bandage around my right forearm. That was good, especially since the bandages were white and not red or brown. They'd sewn me up at the very least.

Shifting in the bed, just a little bit, informed me there were sutures in my side too. I was hoping Tess hadn't punctured my kidney or anything like that, because that would certainly have made my life more complicated than it already was. I didn't see a tube snaking out from under the sheets or feel anything odd about my groin, which probably meant they hadn't slid a catheter up Mister Happy, and this added to my confidence that my kidney was okay.

Yes, kidneys okay. New problem: my bladder was also doing just fine. I was cuffed to a bed, an oxygen mask over my mouth and nose, and I needed to pee. GREAT!

"Yoohoo!" I called out from behind the silicone mask. "Yoooohoooo! I need a bedpan! Yooohooo!"

I heard her coming, bedpan clanking, before I actually saw her. I hadn't been aware that Scottish hospitals hired extras from Japanese monster movies. She was a... grand woman. In her younger days, I was fairly certain she'd been striking to behold. Striking, like a sledgehammer to your big toe. In a fair fight with an Angus bull, this nurse would have won.

"Well, which is it then? Number one or number two?" She croaked out the words as she flipped down the sheets on the bed and flipped up my hospital gown.

"EEE!" I really didn't have much to say other than that.

"Oh, aye. That sounds like a number one then," she snapped on a rubber glove from the table beside my bed and I experienced a sort of distress only prescription narcotics could have made disappear. Mister Happy, I'm guessing, saw what was coming and decided to hide as best he could.

No such luck. She reached down, yanked him out by his turtleneck, and bent him over the rim of the cold bedpan. "All right. Let 'er rip."

"I can't." I had no bravado left. Lady Scotzilla had me by the Happy Part and even my bladder was recoiling in revulsion.

"You called me over here to take a piss, and now you're tellin' me tha' you canna do it?"

"Um. Yes, ma'am."

"Well, that's for shite." She reached down with her other hand and leaned on my abdomen. To this day I'm surprised the urine didn't cut a hole in the bedpan like an industrial water jet machine.

The humiliation was complete when she gave it a shake, put down the bedpan, and carefully wiped me off with a tissue. She was kind, in her own way. Perhaps, even charming in that rough, plebian, We Neuter Livestock With Our Teeth sort of way. Nothing I thought along any of those lines made me feel the least bit better about the experience.

Mister Happy, for his part, pulled his turtleneck up and retreated behind Prostate Rock to meditate on the cruelty of human suffering.

The nurse trod off with the pan, whistling tunelessly to herself. I considered it great luck that the rest of the patients on my ward were asleep, comatose, or hiding beneath their blankets. God only knows to what sort of madness they had been subject in the days before I had arrived.

We were all captive together. There was a certain gemeinschaft that came from shared terror and equal subjugation under the rule of a Tyrant Kaiju. Or would that be "Bakemono"? Moreover, why was I suddenly remembering Sociology and Japanese in a bed in Scotland?

I'd been sedated. They had sewn me up, after all, and this probably meant that some sort of funky medication had been squirted into my IV. My father had erratic and unusual reactions to sedatives and drugs that ended in "-caine." Perhaps I'd inherited that quirk from him?

My thoughts continued to swirl around in happy little currents for what felt like quite a long time. I had closed my eyes and was humming to myself. It was delightful.

Nurse Kaiju returned without ceremony and stuffed an infrared thermometer in my ear. Obligingly, I squealed like a pig, a sound I'm sure she knew well, and she put one giant hand on my head to hold me still. It was over in one eternal instant of existential angst. She grunted to herself, noted my temperature on the chart, and slipped the oxygen mask off me.

"Can you tell me your name?" Oh, the litany of questions they use to see if you have any brain cells left! I smiled, because I could take that test and pass it.

"My name is... Bum Stroker. I wrote the bestselling novel... "

"Look, I know you're stoned from the drugs, but I'd prefer it if you didn't mess about with me on this. Am I makin' myself clear?"

Gulp. "Yes, Nurse," I strained to read her nametag, "Cruickshank."

"Good boy. Name, date of birth, place of birth, and age? Now."

I rattled them off, suddenly feeling very sober. She patted me on the shoulder with one of her giant hands. "That's a fine lad, then. Are you up to speaking with a police officer?"

"I guess," I answered her.

Pat. Pat. "Good. Inspector Andrews has been waiting for you to wake up. Good lad."

Nurse Cruickshank trundled off, thermometer gripped in her hand like she was expecting Klingons to appear from underneath the hospital beds. In my opinion, even if they had, she wouldn't have needed to worry about anything. They would have either immediately started crooning love poetry or just prostrated themselves in respect for a terrible and vengeful Goddess.

The double doors of the ward parted but did not dare hit her in the ass as she lurched through. Even the doors had learned their lesson.

A few moments later, the doors opened and admitted Inspector Andrews. He looked like Central Casting's version of a gumshoe detective. The only thing missing was the fedora, and the only extra element was the astounding handlebar mustache. He could have hidden a troop of lemurs in it.

He stopped at the foot of my bed and addressed me.

"Looks as though you've been having an eventful day. Hm?"

"It looks that way."

"Well, I do need to explain the customary caution to you before we continue our chat." He lifted his eyebrows and the wombat on his upper lip puffed up. "You do not have to say anything, but it may harm your defense if you fail to mention when questioned something which you later rely upon in court. Anything you do say will be given in evidence. If you do not have legal counsel, you will be appointed one free of charge. Do you understand this caution as I've explained it to you?"

"I do. I am willing to make my statement to you without benefit of a barrister present." I figured I might as well be as friendly as possible, since I had killed a dead person and was fairly sure the law hadn't caught up to such things.

"Very good. I've already spoken with Officer Randall regarding the incident you were involved with last night, and that you were released without being charged or retained as a person of interest. What happened after you left this hospital earlier this morning?"

I explained my day in detail, including my altercation with Zombie Tess. He nodded, asked for clarification on one or two points, and made copious notes.

"I am curious about something, Inspector Andrews."

"Go on."

"Am I actually under arrest?"

"Not as such, no. You are considered a person of interest in this situation." He looked a little uncomfortable when he said that.

"If I am not under arrest, you didn't have to caution me or handcuff me to the hospital bed. Why have I been detained in this manner?"

"As an inspector, I deemed it appropriate in light of the possibility that you would flee prior to being questioned." He actually puffed up his chest.

"And, let me guess. You cautioned me because you

weren't sure you wouldn't arrest me?"

"A fairly standard procedure. Yes."

"That girl was already dead."

"True. Apparently, she came back to life at some point before you put a steak knife through her eyeball."

"Please confirm for me, Inspector, that I have been detained, cautioned, and suspected in the self-defense killing of a woman who had predeceased the actual altercation."

"That is a... correct statement."

"Has the US Embassy been informed of these matters?"

"Not as yet, no."

"Because I am not under arrest at this time, I wish to contact the Embassy to obtain assistance in this 'singular' situation." I locked eyes with him and bored all the way to the rear of his skull. "Unless you are going to formally arrest me, I suggest you unlock. These. Handcuffs. Now." I paused. "Please."

Inspector Andrews was unhappy with me, because I was supposed to be wobbly from the drugs and not someone willing to fight back on the issue at hand. Truth be told, I was still loopy but an entirely different, ass-kicking, portion of my mind had been activated by his presence. Normally, I wouldn't have had the balls to confront a police officer on his turf like this.

Then again, how much could he possibly do? I'd killed a dead woman. There was no crime on the books anywhere for "re-manslaughter." It didn't even fit the parameters of "defilement of a corpse" because the corpse had been moving and fighting back at the time. If I hadn't popped her in the eye, she might have defiled *me*.

The mind recoils in horror.

The Lip Wombat moved silently, breathing, probably about to stomp down his face and start grazing on his bad tie. His eyes, thankfully, were not breathing, and stayed the same size. They were the absolute definition of a "flinty gaze" in color and expression of restrained frustration. This was not a pleased, Lip Wombat symbiote.

"Do I have to tell you, Mister Diplomat, that if you leave town before I am finished with you that I will personally order INTERPOL to arse rape you before they bring you back to me?"

"Fine. Just make sure they're French so I can lampoon them properly. Do I have to repeat my request to have these shackles off?"

Inspector Andrews had reached DEFCON Seethe. With a flushed face, angry Wombat, and depleted uranium gaze, he unlocked the cuffs. I stayed stock-still. It was a tense moment, full of the potential for me to have my blowhole violated in a Scottish jail cell. All my fabulous memories of the lovely country (sweet people, undead bisexuals from Cafe Brutus, smooth beer, and intense whisky) would be ruined by such an end.

After stowing the cuffs away in his trench coat, he flicked his card onto the bed between my knees. "I expect that you will be calling me if anything comes to mind, Mister Diplomat."

"I have no doubt I will see you many times before my stay in Scotland is at an end, Inspector 'I Can Strain Krill With My Upper Lip.'" The look I received for that remark, had I been free of narcotics, would have caused my large intestine to expel itself out my ass in order to escape prior to the messy death that was promised. As it stood, I simply gave him the "Mona Lisa Lime Juice Smile;" just a hint of mirth, a gallon of bitterness, and a dash of spite, mixed with contempt and served cold.

At that point, he spun on his heel and marched out of the room. The man had an impressive march. Decades before, if he had marched like that at a demonstration in Germany, there would have been applause, cries of "Ja! Ja! Ja!" and the SS would have adopted it as their Official Walk of Teutonic Overlordship.

Overall, I kinda liked him.

Three weeks, seven interviews with the police, a short fistfight, and six bottles of inexpensive Safeway Isla Whisky later, I was on a flight back to the US.

Jeffry "Wombat" Andrews and I stayed in touch for a while after that, until things really began to hit the fan a year later.

Chapter 14

I put down Baj's letter after reading and rereading it countless times, and the emptiness inside me did nothing but gape wider. I debated just getting down on the floor and giving up completely. There were enough weapons in easy reach, so it wouldn't have been at all difficult, except for the messy shit left behind.

Getting up from the desk was torture, but I didn't care. I deserved it. So much for the Bad-Ass Freelance Zombie Exterminator, brought down by the sad reality that he loves people and wants to be loved. With some effort, I got down to my sleeping bag, and I just stayed there.

At some point or another, I fell asleep, dreamed some things best not mentioned in the light of day, and woke up again. In between the cycles of sleeping and waking were hours and hours of feasting on the finest self-hatred to be found anywhere. After the first day, I stopped eating.

After the second day, I stopped getting up to use my bucket. There wasn't anything left in my system that needed to come out so urgently that it couldn't be ignored, or there just wasn't anything that needed an exit. I didn't much care either way. It was all I could do just to roll over and take the pressure off the shoulder I'd been lying on.

The day after that, there was a seriously large thunderstorm. Being on the top floor of a building with a metal roof is like being on the inside of a steel drum in the Caribbean, but without the rum and bikinis. Every time the sky cracked with a peal of thunder, I shivered.

It seemed like a very long storm. The noise came from everywhere and felt like it crept into my body like the beating of Poe's "Tell Tale Heart." Boom. Boom. Boom. The noise came in through my ears, flashed in my eyes, and shivered me with existential angst. I was still too cowardly to die, and I always have been.

During the storm, my arm and back started to itch. I'd always been told that the itchy feeling meant you were starting to heal up in earnest. Curiosity got the better of me, and I unwrapped my forearm as I lay there on the sleeping bag.

Pretty bruise colors. Neat sutures closed the claw holes, and I mused on the fact that I had scars in similar locations on the other arm. A matched set.

Jayashri kept so much of herself secret, it took months before I found out she was a surgeon before the world went to hell. Looking at the precision of the sutures, I could imagine her delicate hands looping around, pulling me back together with nylon thread and a sharply curved needle. She'd saved my life, and I'd failed to protect her and her husband.

There was more thunder and lightning and it gave me chills. I never noticed footfalls on the steps up to my space, or even the door opening over by the desk. Perhaps I didn't notice because I didn't want to believe anyone would bother with me after everything Shawn and I had said.

"Francis? Frank?"

My heart rate was already strange from the crashing and strobe light of the storm, but it went off the chart when I heard my full name. No one calls me "Francis" because I ask them not to use it.

I tried to roll around quickly but there was not an ounce of strength left in me. I wanted to see who it was, because there are only two people I allow to use my full name without glowering at them. In my mind, either one of those people appearing in my living space was astronomically unlikely. I hadn't seen or heard from my mother in well over a year, so that left only one person it could be.

"Go away, Jayashri."

"I have left you alone for the past four days. As a medical professional, that is an uncomfortable length of time to be out of touch with your patient." She knelt down at the far end of my sleeping bag. "Certain people suggested I let you come to your senses, and you would reappear soon enough."

"Four days?"

"Yes. Four days."

It hadn't felt like four days. Three at the most, at least that I could remember. "I'm sorry, I... " I couldn't finish my thought.

"Let me see your arm, now that you've taken the bandages off." I turned to her, completely mute, and offered her my arm.

"Grip my fingers. Good. Turn your forearm to the left. Good, now, to the right. Is there any pain?"

I shook my head no. My brain and voice were not working. I wasn't sure who could hate me more, myself or this wonderful person I had failed so completely.

"Now, please lie down on your stomach. I want to remove the bandages on your back and see how you are healing." She put her hands on my shoulders and helped me ease over onto my front. Her hands were warm and not unkind. "Good. I'm sorry about this, but you know how surgical tape feels when you remove it. I will do my best to be gentle."

I heard her snap on latex gloves. They had appeared out of nowhere, giving me just a bit more reason to believe she was magical. She was also honest; surgical tape is only one step removed from duct tape in how nasty it feels to have it pulled off your skin.

The bandages across my back must have been keeping me warm, because I got a serious case of the chills when she folded it back to inspect her work. She made quiet positive noises, so I wasn't as worried as I might have been otherwise. There was a moment of sharp pain that made me gasp and try to turn around.

Her hand on my shoulder checked my movement. "Don't worry. That was a piece of shrapnel I was not able to remove the other day. It was kind enough to work its way to the surface, and I just gave it a little assistance." She put pressure on that spot with her other hand and let my shoulder go.

"Here. Look at this," she reached around and dropped something in my hand.

It was a bloody curve of dark-colored metal.

I really couldn't do much more than nod. There simply weren't any words in me. My chest was tight and it felt as though there was an elephant trunk wrapped around my neck. Thinking about an untold number of these things slamming into me gave me a feeling of lightheadedness that was distinctly uncomfortable, as if I needed another set of sensations to process.

"I think you are going to have many interesting scars to go with your story. The good news is you appear to be healing very well; at least, your body is." She was silent for a moment and the elephant trunk tightened, as if it knew more words could come out of her mouth that would leave me helpless. "I want to apologize for something, if you can listen to that right now. Do you think you would be able to?"

Dumbstruck, I nodded yes.

"I had to shave your back in order to get the shrapnel out and put the sutures in."

"Noooooo."

"Yes. You are going to itch very badly when it starts to grow back."

"Ohhhhhhhhhhhhh noooooooooooo."

My voice was small and full of real horror at the thought of my skin trying to crawl off between itching from sutures and then from the regeneration of my Rear Man-Pelt. It had begun to look like the universe was quite clear on the karmic repercussions of my mistakes: suffering with the physical discomfort of the healing and hair regrowth processes.

Jayashri laughed and gave me a pat on the shoulder. "You know, Frank, if you had a girlfriend, I am sure you could persuade her to scratch your back."

"I don't think there are many prospects."

More laughter. "I think you sell yourself short. There are plenty of women who find a masculine zombie hunter, who happens to have a heart of gold, to be quite a catch."

That did it. There is a certain something about a person being kind to you when you're hurting so badly you can't even think straight. For all intents and purposes, she undid the tight wrapping I'd secured around my emotions. I wished, like many times before, that I were one of those people who wept silently. But I don't. I sob.

Somehow, she managed to get the bandage back up while I tried to contort myself into a fetal ball with my face buried in the pillow. I couldn't speak and was only barely able to breathe through the tsunami of my own emotions. She wrapped her arms around my shoulders and gently tilted me against her lap. Again, more kindness. Worse, it was compassion from the person who should hold the most against me.

It burned like magnesium, and the water running off my face didn't do a thing to put it out.

You lose track of time when your emotions are running roughshod over you. The magnesium burned out after a while, leaving me limp against Jayashri's leg, breathing hoarsely.

"I told Bajali not to give that letter to you, but he was not of a mind to listen to me. I have seen the friendship the two of you share and have been envious of it." She stroked my hair, in exactly the way my mother never had. "You bring out the best in one another. Do you know that? You may not be able to hear this with your heart right now, but I do not hate you, nor does anyone, for the decision my husband made."

"Shhhhh." It just hissed out of me.

"Why?"

"Because, I'll just start crying again if you keep that up." My voice was small again.

"My dear friend, one tear or hundreds more mean very little to a woman in damp pants." She patted my head again. "I heard about your argument with Shawn, and he told me he was sure you would feel as though everything was your fault. He is very worried for you, you should know."

I nodded. I was afraid I'd start spraying from my tear ducts if I actually spoke.

"We had the community meeting after I was sure you were out of danger. Bajali had already made his decision, and because it is my duty as his wife, I must support him. No one was able to change his mind."

With a heave, I flopped over onto my side, so I could see her face. I'm sure I looked like a human dog that was waiting to have his belly rubbed. Thankfully, she didn't rub my tummy. It would have been... very strange.

"He shouldn't have gone. I could have stopped him."

"No," she said, shaking her head, "you could not have. My husband must follow his path and do what he feels is best in order to defend what he loves. Do not think for a moment I am happy about any of this. I am simply aware that my feelings are my own and that Bajali must do as he sees fit."

"But—"

She waved her hand, silencing me.

"There is no point in stopping someone who believes and has faith that they are walking on the right path. Could anyone have prevented you from running to rescue the children? I think not."

She had a point, and it was a big one. I just wanted to argue so I could feel like I had some control over the world and the safety of people I care about. I imagined, as a doctor, she could understand that drive to protect people under her care. Then again, perhaps she had learned there were things that went beyond anyone's control and was more able to accept it.

"Jaya, I don't know what to do."

"The first thing you will do is something over which you have no control. You have to allow your body some time to heal. You are not a superhero, even if you wish you could be."

"That's not what I meant." I was stumbling over words that didn't want to make it from my brain to my mouth without turning into lumpy oatmeal. "I don't know if I should leave or not. I've cost all of you so much."

The gentle music of her voice did not change, but the look in her eyes did. It was like how copper is soft and malleable until you've worked it enough. Then it is hard and unbendable. Jayashri's eyes lost their softness.

"You have not cost us anything. We have given freely to you in return for what you have freely given us. I see your hurt has made you blind to the love around you, and that saddens me deeply." I decided in that moment I never wanted to see a frown on her face again. It was physically painful for me to see the soft curves of her face turn upside down. "Francis, in my eyes, you have cost me nothing. You have not listened to me, but to the voice inside yourself that says you are the cause of bad events. Bajali made a decision. We all have. Each one to their own beliefs. We come together because there are beliefs we share."

At the time, I could barely process what she was trying so hard to tell me. My pain was the only thing for which I was truly to blame. She was absolutely right; I couldn't see or hear because I was soaking in the hot water I had boiled for myself.

"I tell you that I love you. Bajali loves you. Shawn loves you. You are beloved of all of us and it would hurt to see you leave, but no one can stop you if that is your choice. When you arrived, you brought so much to our lives, and your intuition saved the lives of our children." She leaned down into my face, put the tip of her nose against the tip of mine, and said, "You are already the hero you wish you could be. I would ask you not to leave us, as a woman who needs a hero and a friend in this most distressing time."

My face must have been a sight to behold when she pulled back, because she laughed in that delightful way so unique to her. I knew my bloodshot eyes were as wide as they could get, but she shared with me sometime later that my mouth was open and I looked like a surprised fish.

"Now, my Hero Francis, I will leave you to rest. I suggest you do that, drink plenty of water, and I will have someone visit you every day to make sure you eat. When you are ready, come back to us." She got up, smoothed the lines of her pants, and started towards the door. "And," she said, "I will be back in two days to look at the sutures and remove the ones in your arm at the very least."

She left gracefully, much like everything else she does. No matter where I go or what I do, I judge what I see by my memories of her and how she seemed to flow when so many other people look like machines in comparison.

They talk about Geisha and how they walked as if they were floating. Their movements were precise, effortless, and designed to stir the heart even more than the desire of those who saw them. For me, Jayashri Sharma was what Geisha aspired to be, combined with an amazing mind and a depth of compassion for which I have never found a match.

Except in her husband, Bajali.

She left me with a spinning head and the fallout of my own emotions. I still had the dull gray curve of metal in my hand. It had very sharp points.

I fell asleep with that shard of steel in my hand. The thunderstorm was long over.

"Hola, Francisco!" I snapped awake when I heard her, but I was still a little too stiff to bounce to my feet.

"Yolanda. Mi amiga muy querida," I replied. My beloved friend.

"You are a flirt," she said and smiled at me. What Jayashri did for grace, Yolanda did with the art of smiling. She was five feet, two inches tall, with curly black hair, and she managed to smile with her whole body. Just, please, remember that I told you: do not ever get her angry.

I still believe I saw her levitate one afternoon when her husband accidentally ruined a batch of her cheese. My Spanish is nowhere near as good as it used to be, but what I understood of her rapid-fire screaming was enough to make me want to build a bunker and hide behind it.

Ómer, her husband, would stand in the face of her fury, smile, nod, and go about his business. I once asked him how he was able to control the urge to flee in those situations. He handed me a cold beer and replied, "You know, you had better know who you marry. Besides, her mother, much worse."

Yolanda sauntered over to me, a covered plate in one hand and a lidded Mason jar in the other. I smelled something alluring, tantalizing, and remarkably like her cooking. My stomach got the message and growled prodigiously.

She laughed like a waterfall. A serious force of nature, this lady.

She put the plate and jar down beside me, still laughing, and stood back up.

"Now, you listen to me, Francisco, you eat and heal up. Okay? Juanito and Julia miss you, and my husband needs to build a chicken house."

"Si, Mamacita. Voy a comer porque te amo mucho." Yes Mommy. I'll eat because I love you a whole lot.

"Ay! Me encanta ese hombre!" Oh! I love this man!

We bid one another fond farewells, and I pulled the cover off the plate. There, revealed unto me, were huevos rancheros, sausage, and a big block of her queso blanco. Of course, there was also the Mason jar of milk. This was the "Breakfast of Champions," no matter what the advertising executives said.

If Julia were older... Perish that thought before it starts. There's no way I could cope with a woman who learned to yell from Yolanda. Sticking to my fascination with Shawn's younger sister was probably the best bet. Yet there were still a few sticking points to that issue.

First of all, we'd never met. Second of all, I've never even seen a photo of her. Shawn had never described her to me. She might have been some sort of radioactive redneck princess with three eyes, two rows of nipples, and perverted desires to hit men with bunnies. Third of all... there wasn't a third reason. The first two were good enough. Regardless, I could keep up my adoration from afar without disturbing anyone too much. I hoped.

My only breakfast in days took longer to eat than I had imagined it would. I suppose a little fasting was enough to make my stomach shrink a tiny bit, so I just ate more slowly. Not a hardship in the least, because the flavors were worth rolling around on my tongue for as long as I could make them last.

In my experience, there are three situations where food tastes far too good to be believed: when you've not eaten in days, when the food has been cooked over a real campfire, and lastly, of course, when you think you're about to die in the immediate future. This meal fell into the first category. Shawn's BBQ fell into the second.

No opportunity at that juncture to comment on the third possibility. I suppose I should have felt lucky about that in some way, but I didn't.

The breakfast that morning in Scotland didn't taste any better, nor did my lunch in Kyoto a few months after that. Although, I have to say, the Japanese zombies are some of the wildest I've run into. It is almost as though you throw people from certain cultures into bizarre situations and they get an attitude of "Oh, well then. Might as well push it for all I can!" In other situations, people revert to their idea of what things "ought to be" rather than carve their own path through a new situation.

The Japanese zombies were a startling combination of both of those reactions. Deep down in the strange recesses of my heart, that afternoon will always be known as Day of the

Cosplay Zombie. Honestly, it still gives me the shivers.

My breakfast settled inside me and I quietly blessed whichever cow the milk came from. The inevitable happened: the digestive system issued a blanket order to the rest of my body. "Shut down non-essential systems. Restart post-grokking of groovy chow." My brain happily obliged, and I napped-out across the sleeping bag.

I dreamed of my mother. I saw her dancing with a former President at a social reception in the Oval Office. For some reason, it didn't strike me as odd that he would have a large swing band in the Oval Office, probably because of the other things he did with cigars and dresses. Regardless, there were canapés, champagne, heads of state, and Mom cutting a rug with the Prez.

They looked pretty good together, all things considered.

Zombie Jerry, looking swanky in a mauve tuxedo, offered me champagne from the tray he was carrying. We enjoyed some small talk, and he moved on to serve the head of the UN Security Council.

The dream went downhill quickly after Jerry bit off the guy's nose. It was all bloody mayhem. Out on the dance floor, my mom was grinding on the Prez from the Female Superior position while clawing out gobs of his chest. The man was a pitiful, pitiful screamer. Shawn appeared out of nowhere, clothed in nothing but a Speedo and sunburn, mowing down the guests with a giant machine gun.

His sister, or what I imagined his sister to look like, tapped me on the shoulder. In the dream, I turned around to take in her Country Amazon goodness, only to find her wearing nothing but some kind of harness and a distressing strap-on. It was black and looked just like H.R. Giger's Alien, if that critter had been a dildo.

She smiled and the dildo hissed at me, opened its mouth, and stuck out its fangy tongue. The mouth snapped at me. I screamed.

The scream woke me up. I looked over at the empty plate and Mason jar, and I silently cursed them for being psychoactive substances disguised as tasty cooking.

Abruptly, I needed to get out of my room. My bladder and bowels were speaking, but that wasn't the deeper motivation. I felt the need to see people and find out what day it was.

Getting down the stairs was not as awful as going up them was some days before, and I took that as a positive sign my body was deciding to heal up well. I could see sunlight through the shades on the store windows. A good thing, I thought.

I wandered the aisles a little because it was comforting and seemed to settle my mind. After a while, I went in the back to use the facilities for the first time in a couple of days. The less said about that unique experience, the better.

Strangely enough, it managed to ground me back into my body better than having breakfast did. That, in turn, lead me to wonder where my weapons of choice were hiding, because I'd not taken them upstairs with me. I was also ambushed by a surprising thought.

"Frank?"

"Yes, Brain?"

"You've been wearing the same clothes for the better part of a week and you have not bathed. Aren't you worried you will upset people when you encounter them?"

"Oh my!"

"Precisely!"

Chapter 15

I scooted off to the storeroom. I hoped there would be water left in the tub that wasn't supporting an algae-based ecosystem. There was no point in worrying about the temperature: it would be frigid unless I started a fire, scrubbed myself off, and then started soaking. I wasn't sure if I could deal with frigid, or if I was concerned enough to cope with tepid water.

Shortly after I appropriated the hardware store, I built something I'd always wanted. An ofuro: a Japanese-style bathtub. I even built a wood-burning water heater, a drain system, and a rainwater barrel. Immensely cool, even if I do say so myself.

Having basic handyman skills is the best way to survive the slow collapse of civilization. There's no point in going out if you can't end your final days with a good, hot soak. This is a fundamental tenet of my belief system.

I heard soft singing when I got to the door of the storeroom. Puzzling. There were also muted water noises. Apparently, my desire to rejoin the human race was linked inextricably to a Goldilocks situation.

There was someone in my ofuro. Unacceptable.

I was unarmed and wounded, which was also unacceptable. I was forced to ask myself which of these situations was the most traumatizing to my psyche. The answer, of course, was having someone taking a dip in My Precious without my informed consent. You just don't fuck with a man's bathtub.

All I could do was hope it wasn't a member of America's fastest growing social group: the Undead. A zombie would definitely finish off what the grenade had started, and I took that into consideration for about ten seconds. But my tub was more important. There are things a man simply must take a stand for, even at the expense of his own life.

Small children. Pregnant women. Really cute women. Women in general. Bath tubs. Good friends. Apple pie. Freedom. Beautiful weapons. Yolanda's cheese.

I slid the door open a tad, so I could peek. Luck was on my side, because the blond-haired head was facing away from me, still singing quietly. Female. Steam. Some foreign blond tart had fired up my heater and was enjoying the fruits of my labor! Unacceptable!

Just keep facing the other direction, missy. We'll settle this invasive behavior in just a moment.

Scooting through the smallest space I could quietly make between the door and the jamb proved to be intensely painful. I swallowed the yelp when the lock plate grazed some of the sutures in my back and did my best to control my breathing. There wasn't much I could do about the tears that sprung to my eyes, so I just kept moving forward.

The plan was a simple one. Get to the side of the tub, right behind her head. Reach over with my right arm and get her in a headlock across the wooden planks. Zombie or person, she'll grab my arm, which will tell me, by the length of her fingernails, what sort of shit I was in.

I glided across the floor like a ninja with Crisco on his booties. Silent and full of righteous power fueled by my indignation. Ready? Steady? Yeah.

In mere seconds I was in position to execute my plan of identifying and neutralizing the interloper. My arm was up, ready to move, and I was suddenly looking at a pair of green eyes, not the back of someone's head.

Oh. Damn.

"Um. Hey. I bet you're Frank. Right?" Even coming from behind the cedar planks of the tub, it was a pretty voice. I

James Crawford

really hoped I wouldn't have to kill her before we could discuss why someone had been in my tub and *was still there.*

"Nargle." Sure. It wasn't a suave way to begin an attack or interrogation, but that was what I had.

The eyes looked down and back up. "Yeah, you're definitely Frank. That arm must hurt with all those stitches. How's your back?"

"Perkin' squashem." I had no eloquence, menace, or ability to speak properly.

She laughed at me, and her eyes crinkled in a really merry sort of way. I really hoped she wasn't a zombie.

"Oh," she exclaimed abruptly, and put her hands up above the line of the wood. "I'm not a zombie, if you were wondering about that."

"Who?" A little better: I got a one-word question out.

"I am so sorry! No one told you I was stayin' here until you started moving around again?"

"Nope."

"Remind me to kick some ass." She arched one eyebrow in a particularly menacing manner, and I could tell someone was going to get it when she got out of my tub. Strangely enough, I wasn't all that disturbed about my squatter's rights at that moment.

Her right hand scooted up over the rim and sort of bent down as if to shake mine, so I shook it.

"I'm Charlie, Shawn's sister. Pleased to meet you!"

"Oh." Bollocks! So much for my quixotic tilting at the windmill of a woman I'd never met!

"Yeah, I'm really sorry we didn't get introduced properly. This really has to be a surprise, finding me in your tub like this. I hope you don't mind!"

Sweet cooties of Ganesha, I didn't mind at all! I was simply, astoundingly unprepared to see anyone, much less the woman I'd threatened to snog the stuffing out of.

All I could do in my unprepared, taken-aback state was throw up my hands, shake my head, and make non-specific negative noises. I could cope with taking a bath in... taking a bath in her... oh submerging... Woman. Water. It was surprisingly hot and humid in the storeroom.

"Tell you what? You were going to wash off before getting in, right? This is an ofuro after all," she said, poking her face up all the way over the rim and smiling at me.

I found myself thinking, "The cute. It BURNS!" Her nose was a gently upturned button relaxing above a set of full lips and surrounded by a gently rounded face. Topped, as I mentioned, with short, disheveled blond hair. Burns! My Quixote aimed his lance and I was vastly grateful for the loose-fitting jeans I was wearing. Even my Sancho Panzas were pleased they had room to move in. Nevermind.

"You've got your stool and washing kit over there, so why don't you do that, and I'll soak for a little while longer until you're ready. Then we'll switch up, and I'll go find us something for dinner. Work for you?"

"Ah, yar mmm-hmmm. Ah." It didn't occur to me I'd be naked in the same room with her until I was actually sitting on the stool, facing away from the tub, getting ready to sponge the Quixote.

He was gracious and retreated. I got an evil case of goosebumps instead.

In short order, my mind turned to other things, because the amount of crap I was washing off myself was just this side of nauseating. Jayashri may have put me back together, but she didn't do much in the way of cleaning off dried blood and other things. I can't imagine what I looked like after days of languishing in my own depressed filth.

I have never been vain. At least, I don't think I have been. I simply prefer to meet new people without a week's worth of beard, dried blood, crusty eyelashes, greasy hair, and body odor that would have made maggots barf.

It took a while to get my legs clean, because moving my back hurt too much, but I managed it. When I got to my face, I dug around for my razor, lathered up my face, and closed my eyes.

Shaving your face by touch alone was something I'd

started doing in college. There were post-party mornings when I didn't want to see what I looked like in a mirror and the best way to shave was to do it by feel. Once I got used to it, I found it to be a wonderful way to center my thoughts, almost meditative.

The meditation of shaving through the lawn that had appeared on my cheeks must have been extraordinary, because I didn't hear her get out of the tub. I put the razor down, and I felt a hand on my shoulder.

I squeaked, levitated, and, I'm ashamed to say, farted in surprise.

The next thing I knew, she was on the floor holding a towel around herself and laughing her ass off. I guess we'd managed to break the ice. I confess, I wasn't thinking about ice.

She wasn't tiny, but she wasn't a Country Amazon either. Words like "lush" and "ripe" were slipping in and out of the folds of my brain. The Sancho Panzas struck up a Gregorian chant that was surprisingly lewd.

I hadn't noticed that she sported shoulder and half-sleeve tattoos on each arm. They featured things like matched passionflowers, vines, leaves, and orchids. Whoever her artist was, he was a genius with a needle and color.

I suppose I was staring, because the next thing I knew, she was sitting there, looking back at me with a slightly serious expression on her face. Shit.

"Um. Um!" I tried to stammer out some sort of apology, but it really was not happening.

"Frank, you can't get into the tub with your back all bandaged up like that."

"Murfle?"

"No, really." She stood up, walked over, and put a hand on my shoulder. "All of this would get wet and just hang off you. I'm sure you're due to get this stuff changed anyhow. Let me help you get it off, and then we'll get you into the tub. Okay?"

"Okay." Damn me, and my terminal lack of suave!

"All right. Now, do you want it fast or slow?"

Señor, this is Quixote. Sancho #1, Sancho #2, and I would like to comment at this point in time. Thank you for your patience. It is our opinion that we want fast, slow, and anything else the Señorita might think of. Muchisimas gracias por su ayuda.

"Whatever. You. Think. Is. Best." I spoke, even if it was a little mechanical.

"Gotta say, Frank. I like hearing that from a man!" With those words, she spun me into a sharp moment of ripping agony. Quixote, Sancho, and Sancho fled back inside my abdomen and shut the door behind them. I was left making tiny "eeeeeeee!" noises.

"Oh my." I didn't like the sound of her voice when she said that.

"Nargle?"

"Jayashri and Shawn told me you dropped a grenade on a zombie and took off, but I had sorta thought you'd make it farther away before it went off. You sure you're alive?"

My voice came back and I asked her, "Is it really that bad?"

"You haven't even looked in a mirror?"

"No, I don't have one upstairs."

"Well, let me tell you. No, actually, I'm not going to tell you anything. Just be really happy that nothing is infected and you're still around to take a bath. How about that?"

"Oh dear."

"That's putting it lightly, believe me." She really sounded like she meant every word, which was more than a little unsettling to me. "I'm going to sponge your back down before you get in the water. I don't know how this is going to feel, but you just do whatever you need to do. All right?"

"Okay." I was not doing well in the witty patter department, and I was also a tad worried about how bad my injuries really were. My arm didn't look half bad, and there wasn't any pain when I moved the hand or wrist. It did look like the stitches were about ready to come out, and I still felt a little itching now and then.

Somewhere behind me I heard her fill a container with water from the tub. All my hindbrain wanted to do was talk to me about "Charlie Tea," while my forebrain was becoming progressively more nervous. Quixote and the Panza twins were giving my hindbrain a wide berth, and I was happy about that. The whole thing was embarrassing and vulnerable enough without adding another element on top of the Self-Consciousness Pie of Doom.

Splash. Splash. "Okay, I'm going to dab some water on you. That's all, no scrubbing. Just like a sponge bath, but with a washcloth instead. You doin' okay so far?"

"I think so."

Charlie made an affirmative noise and put the wet cloth on my shoulder. I couldn't help myself, I made little bliss noises... for about 5 seconds until the hot dripping water reached one of the stitched-up holes. I sucked in air between my teeth and tensed up in an effort to not make "meep" sounds.

"Looks like it feels a little intense. Am I right?"

"Yessssss," I answered.

"Is it the sort of intense you can cope with or should we find another way to handle this?" I had to admit, I liked her. She was cool under pressure but retained compassion, and I found that mighty impressive.

"Keep going. I'll adjust." My answer was partly due to my own bravado, because I didn't feel as if I'd made a good impression up to that point. Was it stupid of me? Yes.

She was gentle, firm, and let me make all the "meep" noises I needed in order to get the job done. I got a bit of information from her about why it hurt so much. Not only did I take a punch from the concussion of the grenade going off and a pile of puncture wounds from shrapnel, I also got burned. When Nate and Flower picked me up off the ground, ass over teakettle, the back of my shirt was roasted through. Flash-fried.

Charlie said it looked to her like a bad sunburn with

patches that looked like they'd been blisters a few days before.

Eventually, I did get used to the temperature and decided to give the tub a try. Charlie impressed me again, because she helped me up and got me into the water without making a single joke. That was kind, because I'd decided to give up on being worried that I was in the buff, and a joke would have made me tense up.

To put it as simply as possible, leaving all the hyperbole and prose out of it: "Water is good." My ofuro felt like what I imagined it must have been like to be a fetus floating around in the womb, minus the darkness and amniotic sac. Whether or not it was an accurate fantasy, I can say I felt restored by soaking in the tub.

Charlie kept me company, leaning on the tub wall on my left. It was like having a disembodied head resting on arms and hands, but this particular head was much more attractive, funny, and pleasant to be around. She actually reached over at one point and messed up my hair.

I looked back at her and she was smiling. It was radiant. That was the moment Shawn walked through the door.

Chapter 16

"Charlotte Marie Cooper! What the Hell are you doin' in a towel?" It certainly wasn't a yell. Shawn bellowed.

"I was takin' a bath, Knocker!"

"Damn it! I told you not to call me Knocker ever again! Please don't tell me you were BATHING with that pervert!"

"No, Knocker, I just gave him a sponge bath and put him in the tub. Ya big lazy shithead!"

"Um, 'pervert'?" I raised my hand just a little. Both of them yelled at me to shut up.

"Don't you 'No, Knocker' me, little sister! If you're gonna be a tattooed slut, there are other people around you can scratch your itch with. Don't you be pawin' all over him."

I heard her move and the sound of a penetrating slap before I was able to turn around in the water. When I got myself oriented in that direction, I saw Charlie's back, towel still in place, and Shawn holding the side of his face. Looks like Big Brother mouthed off just a hair too much. That had to have hurt.

"Listen to me, you overgrown hick. If I want to tear off this towel, jump in that tub, and fuck the shit out of that poor wounded man, it ain't none of your business." Charlie punctuated her tirade with meaningful finger stabbing in my direction.

Quixote and the Panza twins formed a Mariachi band. I managed not to smile like a buffoon, but there was definitely a party starting in the subaquatic environment.

"Charlie, don't say things like that! That's just nasty,

hun!"

"Shawn, you're my brother, not my gun-totin' chastity belt. I'm not 12 anymore."

"But. But. But. He's already told me he wants to bang you!" I had never heard Shawn whine before. It was, in a word, awful.

"Have you looked at his back?" She grabbed her brother by the hand, pulled him over to the side of the tub, and told me, "Would you turn around, please, and stand up if you can? This idiot needs to see for himself."

I did as I was asked. It really wasn't a good time to get saucy with her, I could tell.

"See that, you big goober? He couldn't bang *himself* right now, much less me! I'd kill him by accident!"

The Groin Mariachi Trio were caught in a maelstrom of despair at the truth in her words, but were immensely excited at the thought of a deadly roll in the hay. For myself, I just wanted to sit back down.

"Hey, man? Does this hurt?" Shawn gave me a poke somewhere around my right kidney. I howled and collapsed into the ofuro.

"Oh my God! Frank! Are you okay?" I gave the Big Man some credit for the sincerity in his voice, and then I ran the chances of me being able to strangle him in my current state. Nope.

I turned around in the water, crouched down as I was, and looked him dead in the face. He went pale. I said very quietly, "If you ever do something like that again," my brain ceased functioning for a moment, "I will marry your sister. I will have loud, fierce sex with her beneath your bedroom window every Thursday and Saturday night. She will bear my children, who will all look and act just like me. Have I made myself perfectly clear?"

His eyes were huge. Charlie was smothering laughter behind her hand.

"I will never do that again," he said solemnly.

"Thank you, Shawn." I nodded at Charlie, noted how she

restrained her mirth, nodded again, and turned back to my large, bleached-out friend. "Now that we have an understanding, I would like you to leave so I can finish this restorative bathing experience. I have no doubt I will see you again when my clothes are on, and we can catch up on things. That would be nice. Don't you think so? Besides, you make my water cold."

"Uh huh."

"Me too. See you later, then."

"Okay. Hope you feel better," he said, and then he slowly turned around and made his way out of the room, closing the door as he exited.

"What's 'Knocker?'" I asked the lovely lady still standing by the tub.

"Oh. We used to call him that when we were kids. He'd get scared or nervous and his knees would knock together."

"Got it."

"By the way, Frank?"

"Mmmhmm?"

"Did you really say you wanted to 'bang' me?"

Have you ever had a moment of complete social panic? You look around the room for anything to take the attention off the social gaffe you just made, hoping there is something more interesting than your embarrassment. I did precisely that. Tub. Water. Soap. Heater. Panic!

"Gosh! Charlotte Marie. That's a lovely name, and you're wearing a rather splendid towel. Wherever did you find such a high thread-count towel in this day and age?"

"I found it in the cabinet over there." She turned and pointed at my re-purposed plastic yard storage cabinet. She was smiling and crinkling her eyes at me. That was worse than the original question in a way I couldn't define. "And you, Mister Frank, are avoiding the question."

She didn't walk back to the tub. Charlie *strutted* back to the tub. Her hips rolled and swayed. This was a woman who knew her body and her mind and had decided to mess with me using the tools the Divine Powers had given her.

Quixote and the Panzas kept shouting unhelpful things like, "Arriba! Mira la rubia! RARRR!"

"SHUT UP!"

"What?"

"Sorry, Charlie. I was talking to someone else... erm."

"I have to say, Frank, you're a quirky guy." By that point, she was in my face, and she said, "Lucky for you, I like quirky men." Then she planted those lush lips on the end of my nose. It would have been a very chaste nose kiss if she hadn't used just a little bit of suction.

"Er." My mouth wasn't working properly.

She pulled back, looked me dead in the eyes, and had a belly laugh at my expense. When she finished laughing, she tousled my hair again. "Let's get you out of there before you turn into a prune full of stitches, all right?"

"Okay."

Chapter 17

Getting out was more difficult than getting in and I spent a little time holding onto the side of the tub, making sad groaning noises. Sancho Panza #1 got caught between the plank and my leg as we were trying to ease me up and over without annoying my back. Charlie didn't laugh. She got *so* many brownie points for that.

She got me a towel and suggested I get clean clothes from upstairs after I dried off. She'd handle finding food and Jayashri to look over my back and put new bandages all over me. I nodded mutely and started to dry myself off. By the time I looked up, she was half dressed.

"You didn't think I was going to run around in a towel, did you?" She was looking at me from over her shoulder while she pulled up her jeans. I looked away, in hopes of maintaining some sort of gentlemanly detachment while my brain catalogued every curve I saw and the back of her green lace panties.

"You never know. You might be a towel fetishist for all I know."

"Oh? Little Country Girl me, a freaky, tattooed, exhibitionistic, bath towel pervert?"

I tried to recover. "Hey! There's something out there for everyone!"

This got a laugh out of her while she pulled her t-shirt on over those colorful shoulders. Matching bra. Five catches in the band. Catalogued. There are times I hate my visual memory and other times when it comes in very, very handy.

Charlie got me to assure her I'd be fine while she was gone and that I wouldn't streak through the store on my way upstairs. I agreed that clean clothes were a must and promised her I wouldn't put on a shirt until Jayashri had a chance to look things over. She waved and then sauntered out the door.

Mmmm. Saunter.

True to my word, after putting out the smoldering wood in the water heater, I did not streak through the store. Streaking implies a sort of gleeful, body parts waving in the bright sunlight-type of jog. I did not streak. I ran very carefully in the nude across the store and up the stairs.

As I was opening the door to my space, I heard Charlie call out, "I bet that's a great ass when it doesn't have stitches in it, you big ol' pervert!"

I slammed the door behind me. Busted. Smiling, but busted.

Maybe half an hour later, I heard her at the bottom of the stairs, talking to someone else. She definitely had the sort of voice that carried, especially when she laughed. I was just counting my lucky stars that I had such a good-humored person looking after me, that she didn't want me dead for lewd comments made in her absence, and that she didn't make too much fun of me. My ego is a fragile thing to begin with.

I grew up as one of the geeky kids who didn't fit in. I was too smart and too socially awkward, and I had too many unusual hobbies to be a typical kid. My father had me chewing through martial arts classes, not back and forth to team sports. I liked to make things out of other things I'd just disassembled, like the washing machine. Dating and traditional mating behaviors were something that escaped me for much of my early life.

Jayashri might call me a hero, but I certainly didn't have the superpowers or harem of stunning women following me around that a studly Zombie Killer ought to have. It could be Zombie Killers didn't rate the same fringe benefits as

Vampire Executioners. Since there are no vampires to blow holes in, I will never find out.

Sigh.

Charlie knocked on the door. "Are you decent, Franken-ass?"

"I've got pants on and no shirt, Blond Passionflower! Come on in!"

She opened the door and walked in, followed by a smiling Jaya and her medical bag. That would have brightened my day all by itself, but it got even better when Jaya came over and gave me a kiss on my freshly shaved cheek.

"Charlotte tells me you're squeaky clean and I should have a look at your arm and your back. Are you in the mood for such treatment, Mister I Run Naked Through The Store?"

"Oh, fabulous! Now I get to have *two* snarky women gnawing on me in my own home," I said, tongue in cheek and with an improbable facial expression to take any sting out.

"Wait! Jaya, don't big studly heroes get piles of snarky and demanding women following them around?"

"Yes, Charlie, they do. Sadly, I am married to another man, so I can only be snarky and demanding as a guest. The rest of the harem is something you will have to organize," she said and turned to me. "Turn around, Captain Studly, and let me see your back."

There are moments in a man's life where he decides not to make smart remarks, and when a woman who controls your recovery makes a request of you that involves your progress toward being happy and healthy... that absolutely qualifies as one of those moments. What else could I do but turn around?

She made little affirmative noises, which I took to be a good thing. I heard the snap of rubber gloves and instantly tensed up, fearing the pain of being touched, even if it was in my best interest to let the medical professional do her job.

"Charlotte tells me you have not even looked in a mirror

to see what you have back here. I am surprised. You are usually much more curious than that."

"After you told me I got shaved and stitched and that one piece popped out of me, I wasn't really sure it was something I wanted to see. Charlie said I ought to feel lucky to be alive. That gave me a little pause."

Charlie didn't say anything, and I wouldn't have even known she was there if I hadn't been able to see her out of the corner of my eye. It seemed uncharacteristic of her (as if I could really have an accurate opinion of someone I'd known for less than two hours!) to be quiet when there was something that could be commented on.

"As I said when I last spoke to you, it was a very near thing. Does this hurt?" I felt a little pressure towards the center of my back, to the right of my spine.

"No. I do feel some pressure, but nothing painful. Shawn poked me lower down on that side, near my kidney. I thought I was going to die."

"Ah. That's not surprising. One of the fragments pierced your kidney, and it took a bit of finesse to remove it."

Charlie took that moment to ask, "Does 'finesse' mean you had to open him up like a fish, hunt for it really fast, and get him stitched up before he could bleed out?"

"Ah. That would be an accurate, if blunt, way of expressing it."

I may have gone a little pale at that thought.

"Oh, Charlotte! Would you do me a favor? I left dinner for the both of you on the counter in the kitchen at my house. Could you run over and get it while I finish up with Frank?"

"You bet!" Charlie paused before she left, touched my shoulder, and said, "You take your medicine and don't flirt with the pretty lady too much while I'm gone. Got it, Franken-ass?"

"I hear and obey, Delicate Flower of My Recovery."

Jayashri laughed. "I think you must have made an impression on our Frank. I have never heard him agree that quickly to anything!"

"It's just good ole Southern charm!" I turned around to see her share a grin with my friend's wife, and then she headed out the door and down the stairs.

Jayashri turned to me and commented, "She is so much like her brother, but also very different. Don't you think?"

"You took the words right out of my mouth. Shawn doesn't have hips like those."

She laughed and guided me over to the desk, turned me around gently, and helped me sit. I offered her my forearm for inspection, which she dutifully looked over and pronounced ready for suture removal.

"Have you had a fever or chills since I saw you last?"

"No, just a strange dream or two."

"That is not a surprise at all, but I am happy to hear you have not had a fever. I did not expect it, since none of the impact sites show any sign of infection." She looked up at me from assessing my arm. "I am concerned about one thing in particular, and I did not want to discuss it in front of Charlotte."

I had no idea what might be on her mind, since I wasn't being very active or spurting pus. "Okay. What's that?"

"Your back is healing quite quickly."

"That's a concern?"

"Yes. If you told me you had experienced a fever or chills over the past few days, I would assume you had been infected with the zombie virus."

I know I went pale when I heard that. "Oh. Fever and chills. Healing too fast."

"Yes. Also, considering how close we are to a den of those bastards, I would also have expected to find you dead, or recently revived. Luckily for all of us, you're still alive and apparently unchanged."

All I was able to do was nod in agreement. It wasn't a small pill I needed to swallow, even if I hadn't "changed." My brain wanted to shut down and try to form a spunky or brave response. I have never liked surprises or being afraid.

"What does this mean?"

"Frank, I do not know. I spent a large part of my residency in a trauma unit and had a number of patients die on the table who were not as badly wounded as you were. Experience tells me you should have died, but you have not." She shrugged expressively. "My experience also tells me you ought not to be able to walk or crack jokes this soon after major surgery. I would also have assumed, considering the lack of a proper sterile field for operating on you, that you would have had some sort of post-operative infection. You will note, as I have, that you did not."

"I'm at a loss here." I threw up my other hand, because she had a firm hold on my left arm. "I've always healed pretty fast, but not enough to make a big deal about it."

"Some people do heal very quickly. That much is true. Still, I did not want to discuss this openly, in case you had a secret you needed to share. There is not a secret you need to share, is there?"

I kept a straight face. "No. As far as I know I am not infected and have never been."

"Very well, in light of that information, I can only assume you're a naturally fast healer. You should be grateful for whichever side of your family provided genes like those! Now, let's attend to the sutures that ought to come out."

We did. The lady was precise, poised, and if it could be called a pleasure to watch someone take threads out of your skin, it was, if only to watch her work.

"I don't want to flog a dead horse, but is it possible the virus mutated somewhere along the line? There are some people who seem to be naturally immune to it." I hated asking questions, especially since we were discussing my personal health and well-being.

"Viruses do mutate to adapt themselves to different situations. The influenza virus is a sterling example of that. HIV is also amazing in that respect. I suppose it is possible changes have occurred as the zombie virus has passed between more hosts and different segments of the global population."

Her facial expression was deadly serious and lacked the warmth I was used to seeing. I already felt incredibly uncomfortable and Jayashri's icy countenance didn't do a single thing to improve my state of mind.

"Can I ask a favor of you?" I thought it was appropriate to be equally serious.

"Anything within my power."

"If I die, please make sure they cremate me right away. I don't want anybody to be at risk for me making a surprise reappearance."

"Consider it done." It was exactly what I wanted from her. All I could do was give her a hug. It didn't seem like the sort of moment in which you issue a grateful "Thank you," and then go about your business.

Chapter 18

Charlie returned with a tote bag over one shoulder and my Man Scythe in her hand. I confess that I was happier to see my weapon of choice than I was to see an attractive woman bringing me dinner in a bag.

"My baby!" I reached out both hands and made gimme gestures, Charlie looked puzzled. "The weapon. I mean, I wouldn't be upset if you decided you like m... um ... Yes, the weapon, please." I had nearly stumbled over some odd concepts, thought better of it, and tried to clarify matters as quickly as I could.

She handed it to me and, God help me, I hugged it. You can keep your teddy bears, stuffed rabbits, plush unicorns, and other cushy toys. Nothing in the world made me feel as secure as my Man Scythe.

"Well," Charlie said. "I've seen guys get misty about trucks, guns, and hunting dogs. I guess I shouldn't be surprised you'd be lovin' up on that, but if you kiss it, I'm going to go bunk out at Shawn's place."

"Don't worry. She's too sharp. I want to keep my tongue."

Jayashri turned to Shawn's dumbstruck sibling and explained, "You see, our Frank is special, much like an idiot savant or someone who has been touched by a god. His actions may not make sense. His words may confuse. His results, however, must not be ignored."

"You mean he's going to pull a 'Rain Man' any second?"

"If Rain Man had been a genius with weapons and

bloody mayhem, then I would have to say yes. Yet," Jaya patted me on the cheek, "for all his special qualities, he is a gentle, warm, loyal, and very silly boy."

"Is there a reason why you two are talking about me as though I'm not here?"

"Not really. I just want to make sure you're not going to pounce on me during the night and be all crazy." Charlie emphasized her point by making fists with both hands and cracking her knuckles.

Jayashri laughed at both of us and told Charlie she didn't need to worry at all about me. Then she told me to turn around so she could put new bandages on my back.

Truth be told, I don't remember a lot of what they discussed next. I made non-specific noises at appropriate places in the conversation, but my mind was elsewhere.

I was attempting to remember every time I'd been exposed to the bodily fluids of someone who had been infected. It would have been simpler to recall every time I'd slept with someone over the past two years or so. One. Her name was Allison, and I met her in Glasgow at a pub.

How many times had I been exposed to blood, sweat, or some other form of people juice that originated in an infected body? I couldn't come up with a number. All I could think of was "far too many times."

The most recent time was the little boy I decapitated over by the old McDonald's. I had his blood on my hands at the very least, in more ways than one. That instance alone would have been enough to infect me. It *should* have infected me, based on the information Bajali found on the web.

There should have been a fever, short but high. Chills. Sweats. That is what happened with Mister Yan. He'd simply smiled and said, "Oh, I have flu." Then the first critter came after him in his garden and got a hoe in the brain for his trouble.

I had at least two zombies tell me they weren't interested in eating me within a 24-hour period. The one I blew up was more interested in keeping me out of the fight than he was in eating me, or he would have done that right away.

If logic would hold the argument, I was clean, by virtue of experiential data on the subject. Jayashri also had a vital point: if I had been infected over the past several days, I would either be dead and starting to regenerate, or I would be up and undead already.

Cogito ergo illegitimus non carborundum, I was clean. Case closed. Not feeling vastly better about all of it, but case closed.

In the case of Mister Yan, the only infection cycle I'd witnessed personally, he went from "I have flu" to being attacked by hungry undead cannibals in 48 hours. Grandmother Yan told me he had traded cabbage for broccoli three days prior to the onset of symptoms. She never developed any symptoms, despite sharing the same bed as her husband.

Based on that timetable, you contract the contagion and are being chased down within five days. Again, if I'd been infected, I'd already be dead.

Still not feeling good about it.

Something in the back of my head told me I ought to emerge from my navel exploration, because it had been quiet for a while. I looked up and turned around. Charlie and Jayashri were watching me quietly. Time to cover my tracks.

"Oh. Sorry. I must have nodded off for a minute there."

"That's okay, Frank, you're healing up. That takes a lot of energy out of a person. Doesn't it, Jaya?"

"It most certainly does. As his physician of record, I recommend you both have dinner, drink plenty of water, and that he," she pointed at me with both hands, "go to bed shortly thereafter."

"I'll take care of it. Don't you worry. I think Frankie Rain Man and I have an understanding." Charlie looked incredibly smug when she said that. I couldn't fathom why.

"Ah. Frankie Rain Man is wondering who made you my babysitter."

They both looked at me and said in unison, "Everybody."

"Oh." What else could I do? I shut up and handed my fate into the hands of a woman I barely knew. The Groin Mariachi was quietly gleeful and wanted to know if she could use castanets with any skill. "Oye, Gringo. Preguntale la rubia si quiere bailar contigo." No. I'm not about to ask her if she wants to dance or click my halves together. Put a sock in it.

Jaya kissed me on the forehead, admonished me to take a walk out in the sun tomorrow, and turned to my Passionflower Babysitter and told her to make sure it happened. Charlie saluted and promised, and they shared a laughter-filled hug over it. My favorite doctor slung her bag over her shoulder and left us to our own devices.

"All right, Frankie Sack 'o' Nuts, let's do some food!"

"Are you going to keep doing strange things with my name, Charlotte Marie Cooper?"

"Mmm. Let me think." She actually put her finger to her lower lip, tapped it a few times, looked around, and then said, "Yes, I do believe I will. Got a problem with that?"

"It probably wouldn't do me any good to tell you if I did, would it?"

Charlie smiled at me. The Olympic Smile Judges gave her a 9.3. It was just that sweet and winning of a facial expression. Even my jaded and under-sexed heart was moved by it.

"Honestly, Francis, if it really bothered you, I would probably stop. Thing is, you just keep smiling. That doesn't look like annoyance to me. Should it?"

Busted. Owned. Bitch slapped. Bent over and filled with Cheez Whiz.

"Hey! What's for dinner?!"

"Anyone ever tell you you're slick, Mister Frank?" I would have been worried if she hadn't been smiling.

"Only when I've rolled in olive oil," I said, returning the smile.

We broke into the dinner bag simultaneously. Naan

bread, paneer tikka masala, from the smell of it, and a Tupperware bowl of something that made sloshing noises. Charlie wondered out loud about the contents of the bowl and was strangely timid about having a look inside.

"Oh! That's right, they don't have Indian food where you come from."

She was a little sheepish with her reply, "Well, not really. There was one Indian family in town, but they kept to themselves. The closest we got to ethnic cuisine was takeout Chinese."

I was agog. Aghast. Flummoxed! Growing up in Northern Virginia, ethnic food and communities were something you just took for granted. Before life started to fall apart, you could barely go three blocks without some kind of Asian or kabob restaurant. I took it upon myself to educate this delightful, but woefully under-educated lady.

We sat, we ate, and I told her about what she was tasting and funny stories about eating in unfamiliar bistros in my travels. The conversation was full of laughter, the way the best conversations are. She brought it around a bit when she asked what my first experience with zombies was.

I gave her the rundown on Scotland. My description of Inspector Andrews got her laughing, and I decided I really enjoyed the sound.

She returned the favor. Her first encounter with the living dead was a bit more personal. Her cousin's boyfriend came back from the dead.

Charlie and her cousin, Chloe, were driving around a shopping center parking lot after grabbing a pizza for dinner. She told it to me as if cruising the parking lot on a Friday night during summer break when you're home from college was the major form of local amusement. Small-town America.

They were stopped at the stop sign in front of the liquor store, when Chloe's boyfriend came out of the store and pulled her cousin out of the passenger window of the car. By the time Charlie got around to the other side of the car,

Chloe was dead and the boyfriend was slurping the blood out of a hole in the girl's neck.

Undead boyfriend took out four of the local high school football stars before someone pulled a shotgun off the rack in his pickup and took off the top of the zombie's head with a 20-gauge slug.

Chloe came back about 48 hours later. Charlie took off the top of her head with the closest thing she could find, a shovel. It was a closed-casket funeral, and no one talked about it.

"On the upside," Charlie said, "no one else in the family contracted the virus. We were a bit worried for our sister, Shelly, who is the youngest, but it turned out to be mono."

"Hey, what did you go to college for?"

"I was a Psych major with a minor in English Lit for undergrad. I was going for my Masters in Psychology when all this fun broke loose."

Attractive. Brainy. Snarky. Spunky. Plus, she had an addictive laugh. It looked like I had another marvelous person in my life, worth recovering for at the very least.

"What did you do with your life before things got all bent out of shape?"

I hadn't been expecting the question, even though it made sense she'd ask, and I had to give myself a few breaths to decide what I wanted to say and what I would rather not get into. Back then, there were a few topics I avoided at all costs.

"My family had money, thanks to the Internet boom. Dad got out of it before that bubble went bust, invested the money in other things, and pretty much set us all up for life."

"Sweet!"

"Not really. You get things given to you and you lose touch with the world. I went to college, tried Pre-Med. Flunked. Went to a different school and tried Fine Art. Didn't flunk. But I couldn't get a job with that degree, so I started wandering with some of my family money."

"Well, that's better than a lot of what I've seen when family money is involved. At least you got a clue that you needed to explore your identity and had the means to do it."

"I suppose you've got a point there." I rubbed my eyes. I think I was starting to feel tired, even in the face of good conversation with a delightful new friend.

"Yeah. I've seen that face before. You need to be asleep, so let's get you situated."

"I'm not going to disagree with you. Where are you going to sleep?"

"If I'm supposed to keep an eye on you, then I'll be sleeping right here." She pointed meaningfully at the sleeping bag.

"What? In here? With me? In the same room?"

"No, Frankie Stick-A-Butter, I'm going to hang from the pipes by my toes, fold my wings around me, and snore in your face all night. I'm going to sleep with you." Her face didn't really allow for argument, but I wasn't completely sure how comfortable I was with the idea. Large, angry Southern older brothers featured prominently in the results I imagined for such a sleeping arrangement.

"Er. Ah. Nargle?"

"Any funny stuff and I'll pinch your nipples so hard they'll feel it in Tibet. Do I make myself clear?"

"Crystal." I found that threat to be very clear, and I didn't doubt her ability to make it a reality. "But. Uh. The sleeping bag is not all that big."

"My friend, you are as 'special' as Jaya says. See those blankets folded in the corner cubbyhole, underneath your graphic novel collection? I have to say, you've got some of my favorites, by the way." Incandescent smile. "We'll unzip the bag and toss blankets on ourselves. If something happens, I'll be right there if you need me."

I admit, after the day I'd had, I was feeling a little bit more vulnerable than usual. There was a lot of appeal in having someone that close to me, even if I was less sure about what my larger plans ought to be. One night probably wouldn't make a world of difference in whether I stayed, left, tried to rescue Bajali, or just gave up entirely.

Beyond my special skills at mayhem, I was also incredibly good at cutting myself off from people who offered me some kind of comfort. Being close to people who might hurt you or be taken away from you by viruses or undead friends was a horrible risk. I'd learned the price of not being the kid my parents wanted me to be, and I paid it every day by letting myself be close to people and risking that I'm not who they want to have close to them.

This woman, the spunky little sister of my erstwhile friend, Shawn "Kidney Poker" Cooper, didn't seem to mind having me around. I didn't really care to think about it any more deeply than that. Instead, I watched her shift my den around to suit her idea of what our sleeping arrangements ought to look like. It was a bit like watching someone rearrange your kitchen.

Is this the sort of thing they talk about when someone says your life needs "a woman's touch"? It was creepy.

She helped me down onto the floor, and I started to make myself as comfortable as I'd likely be able to get.

"Frank?"

"Mmm?"

"Are you really telling me you're going to sleep in your mostly clean jeans?"

"Well, I didn't want to scandalize you," must think fast, "or anyone by assuming otherwise."

"Take off the jeans. You can keep your boxers on," and she stuck her hand out to receive my pants.

"How did you know about the... oh, you watched me get taped up again. Right." I handed her my pants and I had a moment of not-quite déjà vu.

I've had interactions with people where it doesn't feel as though I've done that very same thing before, but more like an alternate universe quietly slipped into that moment and I could see the other side. I saw her, older, smiling, and reaching for my hand. Smile lines on her face, twenty or thirty pounds more, and gravity working differently on her curves. Then the universe snapped back into place as she took my jeans, folded them, and draped them across the back of my chair.

She must have noticed I was watching her very intently and stuck her tongue out at me. Then she did something that caused me to focus much more tightly on her. She took her shirt off.

Then she took off her pants.

Matching green lacy stuff. Tasteful. It wasn't the decoration, but the form underneath that made me want to howl, pound my chest, and kill a woolly mammoth in hopes she would drag me back to her cave.

"Been a while, huh?" She was looking back at me with one hand on her hip in the classic country style, eyebrow raised, and the sort of smirk that could mean either a frying pan will meet your cranium shortly, or she was just amused. Thankfully, I had no frying pans in my living space.

Weapons? Yes. Frying pans? No. Why was I less afraid of clubs, bludgeons, knives, axes, swords, two naginata, my Man Scythe, and several handguns than I was of a frying pan upside the head? This woman was bending my outlook on the world! No fair!

"Quite."

"Well, remember two major things. I will turn your nipples into doilies if you get out of line, and you are in no physical condition to even consider foreplay with me, much less anything else."

"Bu—"

"Don't say a word." She cut me off like castrating a young bull: quickly, efficiently, and with the ease of lots of practice.

I didn't make a peep.

She got down onto the floor, rolled over onto the sleeping bag, and pulled the covers up to her neck. I was still sitting up after surrendering my jeans, and I couldn't take my eyes off her. Then I realized she was watching me.

"So, are you going to sleep sitting up, or are you gonna come down here?"

My brain locked up, along with my jaw and tongue. I gave up, and allowed the universe to do with me what it appeared to want to do. I scooted down as carefully as I could, pulled the blankets over myself and ended up looking her right in the eyes.

Sometime during dinner, the light outside had faded to darkness, but my eyes had adjusted and I could see pretty well in the quarter light of the room. I saw a new expression on her face, and it wasn't the brash one to which I'd started to become accustomed. This was more wary and sad.

"Frank, I want to ask a favor of you, and I really would like to keep it just between you and me. Are you okay with that, or should I not ask?"

"Charlie, I think I owe you. Whatever you need to ask won't go any further than me."

She took a deep breath. "I need someone to hold me for just a little while. That's all. I've been running hard for months now and I'm just about tapped out. If you can swing some really good 'Charlie's a great person' improv with the cuddle, I'd be really grateful for that, too."

What else was I going to do for someone who helped me take a bath?

I slipped my right arm under her head, and pulled all of her close to my chest. I felt tension in her body that I couldn't see, and I truly wished I'd studied massage in my travels.

I started the way she asked for it. "Charlie's a great person. I don't think I've ever been taken care of so well by anyone in my entire life." I held her a little more tightly, and I kept up my improv motivational speaking for a long time. Somewhere in between the giggles, a tickle or two, and tears, she relaxed and fell asleep.

I did the same.

Chapter 19

Sunlight was burning a hole in my eyelid. But what woke me up was someone quietly calling my name, or at least I thought that's what I was hearing.

"Frank. Frank. Wake up. I need talk to you." Something passed between the sunlight on my eyelid and the sun. Shadow. Movement.

I opened my eyes and looked down the room toward the window, which was open. Someone or something was crouching on the floor in the shadow underneath the beam of morning light. I was half naked and unarmed, and there was a voluptuous blonde pinning my other arm to the floor.

"You want to tell me who you are before I get up and kill you?"

"No, not kill me yet. Bajali send me." It was a slightly quavering voice. Everything in my head clicked, and my blood turned to ice.

"Mister Yan?"

"So. So. Yes. Sorry to visit you bedroom like this. Bajali find me, ask me to tell you."

"You're dead."

"Ay. Yes. I dead. Very sad. Very sorry. Frank, you always my favorite. Please not tell Chunhua I here. Okay?"

"I won't tell Grandmother Yan you were here." I was scanning the room to find the nearest weapon in case I had to move quickly. I didn't rate my chances very high for two reasons. Number one, he'd gotten the drop on me. Number two, he had been a lifelong practitioner of several different styles of Chinese martial arts. As a zombie, he would be even faster than he had been in the prime of his life.

"So. Thank you. You always my favorite. Bajali tell me to find you an say project goes very slow. Hightowah think of new plan. Maybe poison water supply. Also, they come try an kill all you soon. Think all you dangerous."

"When?"

"Maybe three, four day. Not good."

"No." Then I really had to ask, "Mister Yan, why did you come to see me for Baj?"

"Ay-yah. Frank, I dead. I do not like. I love all of you. I love Chunhua. I do not want you all hurt, dead, maybe like me. Baj find me in the crowd. We talk and make plans, then Baj tell me to see you."

"I've missed you." I never got to say anything to him before they took him from us. He was a sweet person and a good neighbor.

"Oh, I miss everybody so much! Maybe you tell Chunhua you know I love her?"

"Of course I will. Are you going to go back to them?"

"No. I go away. I not eat another person. I go now. Remember, you most favorite. Good man."

"Goodbye Mister Yan."

He went out the window and shut it behind himself. The soul of politeness, even as a zombie.

"Frank?"

"You were awake for that?"

"Yeah, from about the point when he told us we'd be attacked in three or four days." Charlie sat up, and blood started to flow back into my right arm. "You're not going to go after him, are you?"

"No. See? About two weeks after he was taken from us, we installed anti-personnel IEDs around the neighborhood. There are seven of them and four tripwire triggers," I was interrupted by a muffled explosion that shook the windows in my room, "between here and the road. I think he found one."

"Should we get up?"

"No. Someone else can handle picking up the unidentifiable pieces. I want to stay here and remember him for a little while before I have to face everyone."

My right arm came back to life, and we sat there in silence for a little bit. She looked a little uncomfortable, which wasn't surprising considering she didn't know Mister Yan or any of the history involved. I came to a conclusion. Either I had to start moving or I would end up sitting there all day and we'd lose precious time.

"Charlie, are you planning to stick around for a few days or are you going to head elsewhere in the next 24 hours or so?" The concept of her being more to me than a friend's sister seemed like it came out of the blue. "Because, if you stay, there are a few things I need to know."

"I'm not going to take that question the way it seemed to come out, because I am not a coward. I came here to live with my brother, and that's what I plan to do, come Hell or high water."

"All right." Hearing that cheered me up a lot, but I had to file the cheer away for later. "Have you had any professional combat experience or training? Any preference for weapons?"

"Second degree black belt in jujitsu. We all hunted with Dad from the moment we could hold a shotgun. So, shotguns, bolt-action rifles, Japanese swords, 1911-style pistols, chain, and a steel pipe." She looked thoughtful for a moment and added, "I also messed around with Mexican knife fighting with some of the migrant workers' kids when I was growing up."

The Libido Tabernacle Choir started a rendition of "I Can't Stop Falling In Love With You." Quixote, Sancho, and Sancho attacked them, beating them about the head and shoulders.

"Shiny. Next question: do you want the shower first or shall I?"

"That's a Hell of a cognitive shift there, Frank. I'll just

wipe myself off if you want to shower, or I can stand guard for you if you'll do the same for me."

I pointed to the chest of drawers by my desk. "Pistols and revolvers in the top drawer. There's ammo in the second drawer. Knives are in the third drawer. Unusual stuff lives in the bottom drawer. Go crazy. You can guard me first." I figured I might as well leer a little bit. "I'll guard your body while you're naked and wet."

"You are one sick puppy. Now you want me to fish around in your drawers for your gun. Should I be worried it's loaded?"

"My weapon is always loaded. Sometimes I pop the clip out just to look at my fresh rounds."

We started laughing and ended up having a hug. She got up, rooted around in my drawer, cooed with delight, and pulled out my Desert Eagle. It was a shade too big for her hands, so she put it back, but she found my matched set of Taurus Judge revolvers.

"Frankie Clip o' Rounds, do you have slugs for these?" Charlie asked that question with enough bedroom in her voice that the gang war in my loins ceased fire, perked up, signed a peace treaty, and broke out the popcorn.

"Yes, I do, Charlotte Sex Leprechaun—second drawer, left side, rear. Maybe 20 shells."

"Damn, boy! You say the sweetest things!"

"Mmmm. Caveman speak firearm. Caveman take metal stick." I shook the Man Scythe with meaning and prehistoric gravitas. The blade opened just slightly. I think it was eager. "You toss Caveman Glock, maybe?"

She did toss it. It made me infinitely grateful that I put the safety on before I store my guns.

We scrambled down the stairs, laughing like little kids. For a while I forgot how serious things were likely to get in the near future. I suspect the horsing around did the same for her, and I knew she needed it, if only because she came out here to be with her brother, not to find herself in the middle of a suburban gang war. Sometimes the universe has other things in store for you when you think you've made a safe choice.

I did notice something disturbing, but not about her. I was moving a lot more easily than I had the night before.

She gave me a funny look when I put my weapons on the concrete floor, and I motioned for her to do the same. She did. I looked her in the eye and asked for a two-part favor.

"Would you peel the bandages off, then look at my back and tell me if it looks better than it did yesterday?" I turned around.

"Oh, fuck me," she said once the bandages were off. I had a lot of opinions on that comment, but I let them go.

"I guess it looks better then?"

"Yeah. The bruising is gone. Completely gone. None of the skin is even pink, except around the stitches."

"All right. Favor, part two. Poke me where Shawn did yesterday, would you?"

She did. It felt like being poked, not being rammed with a red-hot iron rod.

"Life has now, officially, become more complex. I'm going to shower now, before I start to get worried enough that my brain shuts down. Still feel like guarding me, Charlie?"

"Yeah. I'm happy to." That's what she said, but there was almost no inflection in her voice.

I showered, dried off behind her back, and took over guard duty. She undressed behind my back, hopped in the shower, hopped back out, dried off, and threw her "greens" back on. I did not peek, or even consider it. There was too much on my mind.

Charlotte Marie Cooper, my new friend, babysitter, and sister of my favorite mechanical genius, probably had a few things on her mind as well.

We made speedy work out of slipping into new clothes and appropriate tactical rigging. It was easy to stand outside my accommodations while she changed, not a single word passed between us after we left the storage room I'd turned into my bathing chamber of delights. There was tension, but I had no way of knowing what the source of her backing away was, other than the possibility that the guy she spent the night with might be carrying an interesting viral package.

There had been enough touching to ensure that if it passed skin-to-skin, she'd be infected by now as well. It would have been easier to tell her I'd just given her a raging case of syphilis or the clap. How do you tell someone you're sorry for passing along an infection that might turn her into some kind of undead monster?

Worse, how could I cope with the fact that I seemed to be in possession of a life-changing microbe? I sure as Hell couldn't ignore it; I also couldn't figure out where I'd gotten it and why I'd never had a fever or my own personal Hunted by Zombies experience.

It didn't make sense.

"Frank." Charlie broke the silence, and that surprised me. "We need to find Jaya first and get her take on this. Then we figure out what the next steps need to be."

"I agree." Mission defined and decided upon, we went forth.

It was a nice day out, people were milling around. Gina and her husband were walking very carefully, carrying a green plastic trashcan between them. That was probably the replacement for the one Mister Yan set off.

"Frank!" Gina waved to us with her free hand.

Mark, holding the other side of the trashcan carefully, gritted his teeth, furrowed his brow, and said, "Sweetie, we really shouldn't jostle the can like this. REALLY."

"Mark, it's solid, electrically activated, and is not going to go 'FOOM' because I waved at someone. Relax before you give yourself kidney stones."

I imagine that in a normal world, we would have looked like two couples talking shop about recycling or making your own compost. The trashcan would not have been explosive, of that I'm sure.

"So! It's good to see you up and moving around, Mister Pull the Hand Grenade Pin!" Gina was one of those freakishly positive people. I often thought that R.E.M.'s "Shiny Happy People" song was written because Michael Stipe had met her at some point or another. "I'd hug you, but I bet your back hurts a lot!" She turned to Charlie, "So! You're Charlotte, Shawn's baby sister! That's so great! Nice to see you! I'd give you a big hug but... "

"You'd have to put the can down, and it would make Mark twitch," Charlie finished off with a smile.

"That's right! Wow! You're just as sharp as your brother!" The perky. It burns.

"Frank," her husband said, looking at me.

"Mark."

"Somebody stepped on one of the pressure plates."

"Yes. The explosion woke me up."

Mark nodded. "They already hosed down the wall."

"Good."

"Talk to you guys soon."

"Thanks, Mark. Gina, have a good day, and thanks for your excellent work!" I actually allowed a little perky to slip out.

"Aw! Thanks! Remind me to give you a big hug when you're all better!"

I nodded, and we quickly started walking toward Jayashri's house. Mark and Gina went the other way, slowly and carefully. Odd thoughts were vying for time inside my head. On one hand, I felt like Charlie and I should be walking arm in arm, shades of that moment of Alternate Universe from the night before. On the other hand, I was very wrapped up in being afraid I'd managed to get myself stuffed with a mutant, life-altering thingamajig.

"Is Gina always that perky?"

We stopped in the middle of Jaya and Baj's neighbor's lawn, and I thought about the question for a moment or two. "No. Not all the time."

"That's a relief! I don't know if I could stand it for more

than a few minutes without hunting for booze or a hypodermic full of Thorazine."

"Whatever you do, don't give her alcohol," I cautioned Charlie.

"What happens then?"

"The perkiness doesn't go away. It just gets faster, more intense, and she starts trying to make out with everyone. The making-out part usually happens after she's taken off all her clothes."

"God! That little gal is a self-contained party, isn't she?" Charlie had a look of astonishment on her face, and I could see the sort of stuff that was going on between her ears. It looked like it was probably a little lewd, and I made a mental note to ask her about it if any of us survived the coming week. More than that, I wondered if I was in there anywhere.

Jayashri must have heard us coming or seen us walking up the street, because she had already opened the front door by the time we got to the steps.

"Good morning, you two. Did you get some rest?" She ushered us into the house, and gave Charlie a little push to keep her moving toward the kitchen. "No, breakfast is served in the dining room. There will be time to lounge after our meal."

"Jaya, you don't have to keep feeding us like this!"

"Charlie, speak for yourself!" I added, with a smile on my face. "If Jaya is cooking, you do not ask questions. You sit down, eat it, fall head over heels in love with her, and never want to leave."

"Francis, did you not hear me tell your new friend that you are a silly boy?" Jaya cuffed me on the shoulder. Her eyes narrowed when I didn't flinch. "Speaking of you, silly boy. You appear to be moving more easily today than yesterday. Was your night that refreshing?"

"Ah. Busted before coffee. This always happens." I sat down at the table because I didn't want to get into the whole thing while standing up, in case my knees gave way in sheer terror. "Charlie knows what's going on, so we don't need to be cloak-and-dagger about it."

Jayashri did not stop moving; she simply came over to the chair I was in, pushed me over onto the tabletop, and pulled my shirt up in the back. I don't know what she said, but it was long, impassioned, and featured "Ganesh" in there somewhere.

"Please tell me you did not lie to me about the fever or chills."

"Jaya, God as my witness, I told you the truth."

"Oh, for your sake I do hope so. If you have passed that virus to this lovely woman in the action of your physical pleasure, I will... Oh! Your karma will never recover!"

"Hey! Wait a minute here. Did you just dance around assuming we had sex last night?" Charlie's voice was a strange combination of icy and amused.

"You did not?" The look on her face was pure incredulity.

"No, we didn't."

My dearest doctor stood there, looking back and forth at us as though we were having some kind of telepathic ping-pong game only she could see.

"Are you telling me, Charlotte, that as a woman, you did not see how he looked at you?"

"He's a guy. They all see the boobs and they stop."

Jaya said something containing "Shri Krishna" and shook her head. Then it was my turn.

"You are going to tell me you did not see her batting her eyes and moving in such a manner as to accentuate her physical charms?"

"Should I have noticed?"

"My goodness!" She put her hands on her hips and glared at both of us, one at a time.

"If the two of you were the last fertile people alive on the planet, the human race would die out. I tell you, if Americans understood the power of flirtation... Gracious! You children frustrate me so!"

She walked over to the doorway between the kitchen and the dining room and motioned for Charlie to come with her.

"The least I can do, before we give the barbarian his morning coffee, is teach you a little bit about the secret heart of men. That one," she pointed at me, "might be hopeless at his age, but you are not! Come on."

Everything was going right over my head. I had expected a little less sedate of a reaction to my apparent biological changes, and I really didn't think I'd start the day, instead, by having my mating rituals critiqued by my dearest female friend. It seemed to me life was continuing to bend further sideways while I was trying to walk along in a fairly straight line.

A short while later, they emerged from the kitchen bearing coffee mugs, cream, and a tray of yogurt and granola-filled bowls. Charlie was biting her lower lip, I guessed as a way to keep from laughing. Jaya simply looked perplexed.

"Now, we will eat and have your barbarian coffee, and afterward we will discuss these new developments." Jaya's tone of voice was very much not to be trifled with. "Discussions fraught with intense subjects and decisions should never be approached on an empty stomach."

I asked, "Is that part of the Vedic tradition?"

"No. That is from the tradition of Jayashri and Bajali's home. The Vedas would suggest I use the yogurt and give you a high colonic. Would you prefer that with or without the granola?"

"The barbarian will now shut up and drink his foul steaming beverage."

"See?" She tugged on Charlie's sleeve. "There may yet be hope for him."

Breakfast passed quietly, the humor and lightheartedness slowly gave way to the heavier concerns we were facing. We had not even spoken to Jaya about the morning visitor and his report on what we should expect in three or four days. For my own part, I couldn't decide which news was more life threatening or dire. One way or another, I knew I would stand beside these people and do my best to defend them, even if I had to leave to prevent spreading my version of the virus in the community.

It was bad enough that I could have passed it to Charlie already. Probably *had* passed it, if I was actually hosting some mutant strain of the zombie-maker. That led me straight down the path of wondering who else I might have given it to, over time.

"The silence is very pregnant at this table. Don't you think so?" I said as I looked up to find both of the women looking at me with various levels of intensity.

"Yeah, I'd agree with that," Charlie piped in.

"I'm not sure where to start," so I took another sip of coffee and a spoonful of yogurt.

"I will start. I had an interesting morning, much like the two of you did, I expect."

Charlie and I fixed our attention on her with the speed of a switch being flipped.

"There was a knock on the front door a little before sunrise," Jayashri continued, "and I expected it would be one of you or some sort of emergency with someone in the community. I can see you know who my visitor was." She smiled. "Bajali is well and being treated with respect, although he is under guard at all times. Mister Yan also explained that we would be attacked in a few days, and that he was specifically told to visit you as well. From the looks on your faces, I see that he did."

"Yes. He told us the same things he told you, and I think he deliberately found one of the IEDs on the way out." I really hated to say that, but it was probably true. Mister Yan was too honest and good a person to be swayed by the temptation of a second life at the expense of consuming the innocent.

"He asked me for advice on how to end his life after he shared all of the information he was sent to give us." Jayashri looked like I felt: hollow. "I gave him the location of the smallest IED between the store and the road. He wanted to limit the amount of damage he caused but also assure there would be no way for his spirit to return to the body."

Charlie just shook her head. "That poor man."

"No, I do not see him as someone to be pitied. He was strong, full of love, loyal, and could not bear the burden of life at the cost of other human lives. His choice was both the act of a noble man and a dear friend. When the end of this life comes to me, I pray I will make such a good end."

Jayashri's words seemed to echo in my head. I knew they touched me, because I felt the swell of emotions that rose up within me. No one had ever spoken, out loud, something I believed in so deeply and held so tightly in my heart.

That sort of love and nobility was something I had been searching for my entire life. I never saw it in my parents or siblings. I tried to travel the world to find it, as if it would be lurking in a flea market in Beijing, stuffed behind the red plastic dragons and counterfeit shoes. Sitting in the dining room, over coffee and breakfast, my friend showed me the most moving truth I have ever known.

The thing I sought all my life was already within me. All I had to do was act in accordance with what I hold dear.

I may have been looking at her through a veil of my own almost-shed tears, but Jayashri glowed as she sat there with an expression of ageless resolve and peace on her face.

Even Charlie, whom we barely knew, seemed like she was transfixed in the chair, feeling or seeing something she was unable to look away from. I hoped it was something she needed. Having known her for less than a day, but after learning some of her story and having held her when she needed support, I knew at least some of it was speaking to her.

"Zombies don't want to eat you, and you heal faster." Jaya was thinking out loud. "Frank, is there anything else you can do that's out of the ordinary?"

"I don't know. I didn't even notice the healing thing, much less anything else."

"That does make sense, from what we know about the primary virus," Jaya added. "The initial symptoms are similar to a 24-hour flu. The initial symptoms go away quickly, but then you are immediately set upon by zombies and killed. That is the trigger for the virus to go into overdrive and repair the host. Once the victim returns to life, they are more optimized for predatory behavior. Claws. Much faster reflexes. Greater than normal physical strength."

"Are you suggesting I might notice things because I *nearly* died?"

"That is a possibility, if there is some variety of infection present. One of the areas where there is almost no data is the impact of living with the virus for any extended period of time. The longest recorded span of time between infection and violent death I was able to find research data for was six months."

She told us it was a topic she'd been curious about from the beginning and had been actively researching since Bajali had stabilized the internet connection. From what she'd been able to discover, the six-month survivor was quite unique. Apparently, he had contracted the virus in Alice Springs on a supply run, and then he had returned to his home in the Outback, some 9-hour drive away. Very limited human contact.

Six months later, he returned to Alice Springs for supplies. Within ten minutes of his arrival, he was attacked and killed by no fewer than five recently revived zombies. He revived in four days and was shot by police in a local casino after attacking one of the card dealers.

"How long have you been killing zombies?" Charlie asked me.

"Maybe a few weeks shy of two years."

"Is it possible you've either been really lucky, or that you've just managed to kill all of the zombies who wanted to eat you?"

That was an excellent question, and I wasn't entirely sure

how to answer it. I couldn't remember any situation in which I'd actually been attacked. For the most part, I just seemed to be around when something awful was happening, and I dealt with it.

"I've killed them, yes, but I've never had any come after me as though I looked like a tasty snack."

Charlie looked puzzled. "Well, that kicks our theory in the face."

"I think, for the moment, we should observe you and record any data as we go." Jaya made a lot of sense, which was not at all surprising. "Charlotte, if you develop anything symptomatic of an infection, please tell me right away."

"Absolutely."

Jaya stood up, picked up the dishes, and told us, "We need to concentrate on the other major issue at hand: they're coming for us." Then she turned around and floated across the floor into the kitchen. Her voice drifted back into the dining room. "A certain barbarian could help the gentle housewife with the dishes and it would be appreciated!"

Charlie pointed at me, made the classic "shame on you" gesture, and stuck her tongue out at me. I received the intended message, grunted, and did a credible Caveman shamble into the kitchen. My performance rated a dainty round of applause from both of them.

My hostess smiled and suggested, "If we ever decide to do community theatre, I should hope you would audition for the 'Hunchback of Notre-Dame.' I think you would do a marvelous job in that role!"

"Rrrr! The Bells! The Bells! Where do you keep your scrubby pads for washing the dishes?"

Chapter 20

It never ceases to amaze me how much simple joy you can have when you're in the midst of fighting for your life or are about to embark on doing precisely that. Jayashri and I flicked water at one another, laughing like children. Not to be undone, she increased the stakes by upgrading her offensive weapon: a tea towel.

It was damp from drying coffee cups and yogurt bowls, and when she snapped it in my direction it packed a surprising amount of sting. I sucked air through clenched teeth when she tagged my nipple through my t-shirt. Something like that would have woken me up better than any coffee product in the world, but I wasn't willing to get cross-addicted to something that stung like that.

"Oh! Ho ho ho! I have brought the Mighty Hunchback to his knees!" She did a very dainty Bollywood touchdown dance in the middle of the kitchen. Charlie dissolved into moist-eyed laughter in the kitchen doorway. I even smirked while I tried to rub out the sting.

I turned to both of them, and the skin on my back developed a nasty prickling sensation that reached down to the curve of my butt. I wanted to grab a spatula, serving fork, or an angry cat and try to make the prickly itching stop. Instead, I danced around a little bit and tried to bend my arms backwards.

"What's happening?"

"Jaya... my back itches like crazy! Nasty prickles! EEEE!"

"Wait, wait. Stop moving, and let me see." She came over

and pulled my shirt up while I tried very hard to hold myself still. After a moment or two, I heard, "Oh my gracious."

"Great! What now?" ITCH!

"Frank, your body is rejecting the sutures." Her hand came around and there was a perfect, knotted loop of black nylon thread resting on her fingertip.

"AH! Maybe you could help it reject them a little faster? This is driving me crazy!"

"Charlotte, go upstairs into the first room on your left. Beside the large crash bag, there is a smaller first aid pouch. Please bring me that and a box of latex gloves from the stack near the bag. Would you please?"

Charlie must have nodded or something, because the next thing I heard were swift footfalls on the stairs. Moments later, she was back, box and bag in hand. I was standing in place, vibrating with the need to scratch my back.

"No time for modesty, Frank. Drop your pants."

Jaya didn't have to tell me twice. I unbuttoned the jeans and let them fall to the tile. The underside of my left buttock felt like I was being attacked by fleas wearing little spiked booties. It was all I could do to lean against the sink and hold myself still.

I heard her put on gloves and thanked my lucky stars that relief was in sight. There were periodic tugs and the sound of scissors clicking, and small areas stopped itching. Other areas stopped itching as well, but I knew they were nowhere near where Jayashri was pruning me.

Great. Another interesting development. I silently asked God to stop giving me "interesting" things. Of course, there was no overt reply, just more itching.

"Holy shit! What's that?" Something caught Charlie's attention.

"I don't know!" Jaya responded.

There was a sharp squeezing pain, a sense of relief, and something hit the tile floor with some force. I heard someone gasp and a muffled, "Eeew!"

"What happened back there?" I was a little panicked, because I didn't know what my body was going to do next.

"I think you may have done something else... unprecedented," Jaya answered. "A shard of metal was forced to the surface of your skin where it was... ejected. It is on the floor by Charlotte's foot. Could I get you to put on a pair of gloves and pick it up?" The last part was clearly not directed at me.

Once again, I heard the sound of rubber gloves.

"Oh. Oh. This is just so weird. Ick!"

"What?" I would have to apologize for the exasperation in my voice later on.

"Frank, it's still warm. Jaya? What do you want me to do with it, 'cause I really want to put it down?"

"Get a sterile gauze pad, open the package, and slide it into the package. Don't let it get more contaminated."

Shortly after that burst of excitement, I stopped itching completely. I knew the majority of the tiny nylon loops littering the kitchen floor were not there because they had been snipped out. Too many of them were intact, and there were many more of them than I'd even wanted to imagine. I was very grateful I never looked in a mirror.

I looked over my shoulder, saw that the ladies were consumed by the piece of shrapnel that had popped out of my ass, and took the opportunity to pull up my pants. Killing the undead was one thing, but exhibitionism was never part of my psychological bag of tricks. Of course, if the opportunity was right and the mood much lighter, I might have wiggled the booty upon request.

At that point in time, after making my debut as a medical miracle and looking down the barrel of a full-on assault from the tribe of revivified maniacs across town, booty maneuvers would have been gauche. Running around, screaming, and generally being unhelpful wouldn't have gone over much better, truth be told.

I broke the silence, "Well! I wonder what other things I'll shoot from random body parts!"

The audience of two stared back at me with flat expressions, not even quirking their lips in an expression of displeasure. I noted quickly that humor was not on the menu and that moving onto more serious topics was probably the safest way to go.

"All right. The mystery of me expelling things from my body can wait a while. We need to clean up the kitchen, and then drag everyone together for a meeting. Organize one for later, at the very least. Agreed?"

They nodded. I nodded back, and we started picking up the kitchen without a single word. Jaya appeared to be lost in thought. Charlie was new enough to me that I couldn't hazard a guess about what might have been going on in her head.

Jaya pulled out a bottle of something from under the sink that smelled like a hospital operating room and sprayed it all over the floor and the surface of the counter around the sink. She didn't wipe it up, which struck me as odd. I asked her about it.

"Oh, this is CaviCide. It kills almost everything on non-porous surfaces, but many people make the mistake of wiping it up as though it were window cleaner. This chemical, you let it dry, and then you might decide to go back and make things pleasantly shiny."

Charlie and I sounded like a pre-recorded crowd track, "Ah. Oh. Mmm. Uh! Ah. Ah-hah. Hmmm."

She looked at us and showed a small smile on her face. "It has been such an eventful and exciting morning I can hardly think straight. Wouldn't it be lovely to have tea, soak in a bathtub, and try to sort all of it out piece by piece?"

"I don't think I could agree with you more if I tried," Charlie replied, "but I think I'd swap out the tea for JD on the rocks or a bourbon and Coke."

"Nigori Junmai Dai Ginjo."

"Karate Judo Samurai, what?" Charlie asked, quirking her eyebrow at me.

"If you're going to soak in a bath and consume alcohol,

super-premium Nihonshu, sake, is the way to go." My inner hedonist was not going to let it pass without having a say in the matter.

"Oh."

"My friends, let us talk to our neighbors, and then we can debate the fine merits of hot baths and libations of choice. Shall we?"

My Star of India had a point. If we didn't start moving, the worry, fear, and intensity of the whole situation might just cause us to freeze up. We had the luxury of a few days to plan, and we needed to make the best of it. The last thing we needed was to panic, freeze, or wait until the last minute to prepare.

Thankfully, we also had some information to work with about the maximum number of bodies Hightower could bring to bear on us. Unfortunately, we also knew he had a Bradley armored vehicle, automatic weapons, mortar launchers, and shoulder-mounted rocket launchers.

They could hit us from a distance. We did not have that ability. But if we took the fight to them before they could organize, there might be a slim chance we all wouldn't die.

Another option we had to consider was packing up our lives and going elsewhere. It was certainly not a fantastic thing to consider, as we would end up leaving most of our resources behind. Then, we would also have to look at the issue of where to go. Unless, of course, each family had a reasonable place to which they could retreat.

Abandoning our neighborhood would destroy everything we'd built and fought for just as surely as attacking us with overwhelming forces would. If anything, I felt, it would be more demoralizing for us to run than to try to defend what was precious to us.

This was not my decision to make. We needed everyone to decide. To lose the support of one family would be enough to tilt the table toward flight, rather than fight. We needed everyone in, or we absolutely would not survive.

We were standing in the middle of the front yard when

Jayashri turned to me and said, "I have been very remiss! Charlotte is not the only new person in the community. I forgot you spent the better part of a week alone."

"New people?"

"Yes. Both Nate and Flower were gone for two days after Bajali left. They returned with people they knew from their days in the armed forces. A total of ten new people."

"Military or former military, then. They'll be good resources. I'll need to talk to all of them, because we need to know what skills they have that would be useful in a fight, besides being able to use guns."

We started walking again. By pheromones, non-verbal communication, or telepathy, we all decided to descend on Shawn's place. Like my hardware store, his garage was on the industrial side of the street, as opposed to Baj's house, which was one of the center showplaces on the residential side.

Charlie was about ten steps ahead of us and had already begun a friendly familial negotiation on the use of nicknames.

"Bullshit! I'll call you whatever I want to call you, you overgrown, lily-white—"

"Charlotte Marie Cooper, don't you fuckin' start that shit when I've got guests," Shawn retorted, just as we poked our heads into the first bay of the garage. Sure enough, there were four faces I'd never seen before.

"Dude! You're up and movin'!" Shawn had either forgotten our fight from a few days ago, or he had replaced those concerns with wondering what his baby sister and I had gotten into.

"I'm up and moving around, that is certainly true. Who are the new guys?"

"Hey, that's right, you've been incommunicado since the boys brought friends over." Shawn pointed a meaty finger at the first guy to my far right. "This is Jackson, Fitzgerald, Kim, and Buttons."

My curiosity was piqued, so I figured I might as well ask.

"Buttons, is there any reason they call you that?"

He was a compact guy, middle aged, high and tight, wearing always-fashionable tactical black. My question rated a smirk, and he replied, "I push buttons. You the guy who didn't run away from the grenade fast enough?"

"No, that's the other guy." Buttons pushed my Smart Ass button. "I'm the guy that flies through the air with the greatest of ease."

He looked at me sideways. "Daring young man on a flying trapeze?"

"Dropping on zombies, quick as you please." I gave him a shit-eating grin.

I shook hands with the other three guys. Solid grips, equally solid stances. "You guys Special Forces?"

Fitzgerald answered, "Yeah. How did you know? We're wearing civvies."

"I trained with some guys who stood just like the three of you do. Plus, if you know Nate, it was a decent guess." I turned back to Buttons. "I'm going to bet you and Flower know one another."

"Good guess." His posture changed slightly, as if he'd decided I was something worth noticing.

The testosterone must have been elevated to nearly poisonous levels, because the other three guys backed up, along with Charlie and Jayashri. Shawn just sat behind his precious M-50 and looked clueless. Something was happening and I had no idea what it was, other than that Buttons and I needed to have a talk.

"Buttons. Let's walk, you and me." I turned around and strolled down the street in the direction of the hardware store. I didn't have to wait long before he was walking right beside me.

"Francis Stewart."

"Yes."

"I know who you are."

"Somehow that doesn't surprise me. I don't know who you are, and I sort of expect that. You're a few notches higher up the chain from Flower, aren't you?"

"That is correct. You want to start by telling me why the little Asian zombie didn't blow up on the way *into* the community but took a deliberate header on the way out?"

"That little Asian zombie used to be one of us. I don't know how he managed to get in, but I do know why he chose to exit like he did."

"Care to enlighten me?"

"Not especially. Let's just say that, what do you guys call it, the 'sitrep' has changed a bit."

"Do tell, Mister Stewart."

"The nanomachine project has either stalled or is moving slower than they anticipated. Hightower is considering an alternate plan to infect the water supply. The third bit of information is that this community will be attacked, with intent to wipe us out, three or four days from now."

We stopped alongside the door to my store. He looked up at me with the flattest gray eyes I've ever seen and showed me far too many teeth for my comfort level.

"We know about the nanomachine project and why they've hit a wall. As for the water supply, that's already been tried several times around the world, and it doesn't work. As for wiping you all off the map," he ran his hands over his buzz cut, "that's just Warren Hightower being petty."

"Petty? He's willing to kill all of us because he's petty? What about his dream of herds of human cattle? I'm sure we'd make great pets."

"Facetious much?"

"Whenever I can muster the energy." We strolled into my store, and I was feeling less and less comfortable with this guy. Clearly, he worked for, or had worked for, one of the Initial Agencies.

In DC-area parlance, an "Initial Agency" is one that is most commonly referred to by initials, rather than the full name. Central Intelligence Agency: CIA. National Security Agency: NSA. You get the idea.

Although I've always wondered why no one calls the Secret Service by its initials. Too many awkward feelings about that, I suppose.

There was no polite way to ask this "Buttons" person more about his background or current loyalties, so I decided to ask him in my own unique way. I kicked him up against the counter, pulled the Man Scythe free, and snapped the blade open in the same motion. The edge was resting against his neck when I stopped moving. Unfortunately for me, he had pulled a gun from somewhere on his person and it was pointed right between my eyes.

At that range, if I twitched, I'd open his jugular, and he would have time to aim and fire before he lost consciousness. We'd both be dead.

"Nice moves. I didn't think that behemoth of yours could be deployed that fast." He actually smiled at me. Very straight, white teeth.

"The benefits of a lot of practice. Before we kill one another, I wouldn't mind knowing who you are and what your investment is in all this."

"You're familiar with Section 41 already," he said. I nodded, feeling a hole open up in my stomach. He continued, "I'm with Section 23. Now we both have a better idea of who we're dealing with. Want to put that chopper down?"

"You first." The gun vanished. He was just that fast. I moved my weapon, folded the blade down, and nudged it back into the plastic scabbard at my back.

"I'll give you credit, you've done a lot with an improbable weapon like that. A .45 loaded with the proper ammunition would be faster and easier. Even a sword."

I looked at him and tried to put my impressions together so I'd have some kind of clue about Section 23's purposes. From what I knew about the special groups, they were named by year of inception. Section 41 was started 5 years ago, which means 23 began about 18 years before that in the early 1980s.

The Cold War was still going on, and the US was touchy from the Iran hostage crisis. The Space Shuttle was a reality. They'd started messing around with the Strategic Defense Initiative, or SDI: space-based satellite and missile killers.

Shit.

Buttons. SDI. Cold War era.

"SDI." I didn't ask. I simply said the word.

He nodded, barely perceptible but there. "Your file was surprisingly accurate. Quick on the uptake."

"You're not here because Flower asked you. You got in touch with him. Am I right?"

He was actively smiling at me, like I was an apprentice who had done something truly interesting.

"Excellent guess, and dead on the money. Why didn't you join the Sections when they tried to recruit you?"

A hard topic. Yet, he already had the file on me, so saying the words wouldn't divulge anything he wasn't already aware of.

"Like you don't already know?"

"Of course I do, but it is always interesting to hear things firsthand."

"Right. Why are you bothering with this neighborhood? S-23 can't have an interest in saving our asses, and Hightower is S-41's problem."

"It's pretty simple. The parts of the government that are working are still invested in the safety of the living population as a whole. Turning large numbers of Americans into a food source is not in the interest of our country, whether we can emerge from the Emergency as a functioning nation or not. Right now, we still have 30 percent functioning infrastructure in urban areas." He cracked his knuckles, and leaned back against the counter. "We can't lose any more of that. Ideally, we'd like to rebuild it. Regardless, Hightower has become too big for his britches, and I'm here to help you stop him. Quietly."

"You want to play in my playground. We do it my way."

He laughed. "You've claimed this place and these people

as yours? Your playground? You aren't even a bit player in all this."

"I need to save them. I need to get Bajali back. I have to help defend them. It's just that simple."

"You are not a tactical genius."

"No, but I love these people and am willing to die to try and keep them safe. What I need is a tactical genius, because ours went over to try and buy us time."

"Well, you're in luck. I'm a tactical genius." He said it and looked confident about it, but I found it a hard pill to swallow.

"That's fantastic, but I don't know what your game is. I need someone who loves these people and would die for them if it came to that." His face lost every bit of human warmth as I spoke. In any other person, I would have expected a punch in the eye to accompany that expression.

"You should have joined the military. Then you would understand the oath every soldier takes the day they enlist. I took that oath when I was 18, and I've made even more binding commitments since then." He was not giving me a tongue-lashing. He was explaining the world as he knew it, albeit coldly, to someone he felt couldn't grasp it. "I came here to do my job. Protecting this functioning micro-society is essential to the success of that job. That being the case, I will protect them with my life and from every demon in Hell if we fail."

"They've got ravens in Hell that bite your nerve endings."

"What?"

"Don't worry about it. It's an inside joke." I got serious. "You realize I will do my best to kill you if you're lying, yes?"

"I imagined that would be the case. Are we good at this point?"

"As long as you don't tell them what you know about me. I won't tell them about you and your boys."

He nodded. "Let's go back to the kids."

Chapter 21

We walked back silently. Everyone was as relaxed as they could be, given the situation. Nate had appeared while Buttons and I were discussing things, and the gang was sorting through how to organize everyone for the next big discussion. Apparently, things were going to be held in my "conference room" after nightfall, but this time the kids would be with us.

Not a bad thought, considering what happened the last time. Barbara would probably be tasked to keep the youngsters under control. No one had the knack for it like she did.

They asked me to do it once. I gave it my best shot and it was a spectacular non-starter. Little Siddig Junior wouldn't speak to me for a month afterward.

I volunteered to go around to the neighbors and give them the meeting time and location, but Nate and Shawn shushed me. They felt I ought to get a little more rest before the meeting so I'd have enough energy to participate.

"Look, you've been blown up. If Jayashri weren't walking around with you, I'd put you over my shoulder and jog you back over there myself." Nate gave me his trademark evil eye. "But, with Jayashri and Charlotte here, I know you'll be just fine. Now, go rest up. We're gonna need you when the party starts in a few days."

Nate and his buddies made appropriate "Rarrr!" noises in the spirit of everyone banding together to beat the oily fudge out of a common enemy. Bless their hearts, but they sounded like a bunch of fraternity brothers before a night of binge drinking. I strongly suspected that Barbara wouldn't allow such behavior, unless these guys had brought their wives. Then she'd hang out with the girls and the boys could get as plowed as they pleased.

It made for some interesting mental documentary footage.

"Don't you worry, Nate. We'll drag him back to his place even if he's kicking and screaming." Charlie gave him a comradely punch to the shoulder. He laughed, messed up her hair, and backed up two steps when he noticed the look on her face.

"Okay. The females of the Cooper family are even fiercer than the males," he said.

"You got that right, Soldier Boy. In the sack, or out of the sack: you'll never go back." I realized, belatedly, that she was flirting with Nate. I felt vaguely uneasy about it, but couldn't put my finger on the reason.

Nate's comrades made appreciative "Ooo!" noises, and he grinned like an idiot. Shawn just blushed.

"All right, Nurse Cooper. Let us take our young charge back to his home." Jayashri waved her along and snagged me by the elbow.

Shortly, we were walking up the street together, and they stopped me as soon as they felt we were out of earshot of Shawn's shop.

"Okay, Frank. You want to tell us who that Buttons guy is and what he meant by mentioning he knows who you are?" Charlie was up in my face, asking me that. I suspect she was more interested in what might or might not be common knowledge about me than she was in Mister Buttons.

"First of all," I began carefully, because I didn't want to get into my background too much, "our friend Buttons is either part of or is the head honcho of a different secret division that is not happy with our friendly neighborhood zombie leader."

"So, he is not Section 41?" Jayashri asked.

"No, more like 23. That group started during the Cold War, while the Star Wars defense plan was the big thing on the minds of the people in power."

"Did he tell you what the Hell he wants with us?" For someone who had only appeared in the community days before, Charlie was sinking her loyalties in very fast. Then again, I'd seen stranger things than that.

"He told me he's got two reasons for being here. His orders are to eliminate Hightower as a threat and to protect our neighborhood at the same time. It sounds strange, but he seemed pretty sincere when he shared all of that with me."

Both of them looked thoughtful, and I was glad that the line of questioning was being steered away from me. I didn't like the fact that I needed to be less than forthcoming about my life story, but that's the way the cookie tends to crumble. Secrets and people you love are an incongruous combination, like Ken Watanabe dressed as Tinkerbell, singing the theme song from "The Love Boat."

People have told me that I'm "special." I prefer to think my mind works in mysterious ways. It must have shown on my face that I'd slipped away from the conversation, because Charlie gave me a vicious poke.

"What are you thinking, Frankie the Lips?" At that very second, I was thinking as quickly as I could.

"I was thinking Buttons being here was a little incongruous. If he's got access to interesting data or resources, then I'd expect he could take out Hightower without involving us at all." I felt it was a good save and yet very pertinent to the conversation. Not to mention, true. It did feel odd to me.

Buttons claimed to be from a black project group, ordered to both protect us and bring down our mutual problem child. I am the person who inferred what Section 23 was; all he did was nod at me and disarm me with a compliment. That added a bit of quicksand to the landscape.

I explained my train of thought. We started walking

again, sharing an uneasy silence, until Jayashri tapped me on the arm.

"Frank?" Jaya asked.

"Hm?"

"How long does it take for your Japanese soaking tub to heat up?"

"Ah. Two hours, give or take. Why?"

"I was not kidding in the least when I said that I wanted to soak, drink tea, and sort out all of the thoughts in my head. I was wondering if you would be so kind as to allow me that luxury."

"Jaya, not only will I heat the water for you, I will make you tea to sip while you relax!" I bowed and pointed the way to my store with a completely overdone flourish of my hands. "This way to your après-meeting afternoon Spa appointment, Madame!"

"I will be happy to show off my skills, if you're interested, Jayashri?" Charlie stretched her arms and wiggled her fingers.

"Dare I ask what those skills are?"

"I went to massage therapy school before I decided to go for my Masters in Psychology. It was a great way to pay my way through grad school. Do you like Swedish or deep tissue?"

"My goodness! Between the two of you, you're offering me the garden of earthly delights! What have I done to deserve this?" She actually looked surprised and sincere asking that. For my part, she deserved all that and more, and I suspect her humility was what caused me to want to feel that way.

Humble people who go out of their way for others have always been inspiring to me. Coming from a privileged family, humility wasn't something we saw on a daily basis, at home or otherwise. Certainly, Jaya and Baj were well off, but they managed to not let it get to them the way it often did with others. Then again, "well off" in a barely functioning economy that valued barter over cash was a relative thing.

Still, I'd seen her go out of her way for others. That quality was part of the nobility, for want of a better word, and grace that made her who she was. Heating up a giant bucket full of water was a simple thing to do. I would have slain dragons, skinned them, and made her shoes, luggage, and some hot form-fitting jumpsuits if she'd asked me.

"Hey, Frankie Tub o' Water, have you got a folding table in the store that would work as a massage table if we put blankets on it for a cushion?"

"Hey, Charlie Green Eyes, are you going to keep adding things to my name or are you going to settle on one thing and stick to it?"

"Hell! I don't know! It's way too much fun and you make the best faces when I find a good one!"

Charlotte Marie Cooper. Curvy. Tattooed. Psychologist. Massage therapist. Utterly frustrating combination of too many interesting attributes!

"Grr, I tell you. Grr." I tried to be angry and fierce, but it didn't quite work with her. "I do have just the table and memory foam padding that you can throw some sheets on. Am I not spiffy?"

"Wow! Keep that up and I might just fall in love with you! How did you get a hold of sheets and memory foam?"

"I was walking by a home store one afternoon and a bunch of zombies were liberating the contents." I couldn't help but grin like an idiot. "So, I liberated the contents from the zombies who suddenly didn't need household goods."

Her face screwed up in an expression of disgust. "I hope you didn't get any goo on the stuff."

"Hey!" I replied. "That's what's so great about new products that are still in their clean plastic wrappers! No muss. No fuss. No brains!"

We wandered into my store, and I told Charlie where to find what she was after and suggested that the all-natural hand salve on the endcap of Aisle 3 would probably be an excellent stand-in for massage lotion if it were warmed up.

While she was tracking down the body lubricant, I located the accessories and left them with Jayashri, before refilling the tub and coaxing the water heater into blissful operation. After that little spate of activity, I scooted up to my room to hang out while the Spa was occupied.

The first abdominal cramp hit me as I was going up the stairs to my living space. It felt like I'd swallowed the hand grenade that had blown me across the lawn and doubled me over onto the steps. I made it to the door with my eyes full of uncontrollable tears and my mouth hanging open, breathing like an opera diva in the middle of natural childbirth. The Lamaze was doing nothing for the contractions at all. They came in waves.

A cramp hit me like I was trying to push a 25-pound baby through my navel, and I rolled through the door and onto the floor in front of my desk. When I had a moment to think, all that went through my mind were images of Chest Bursters from the "Alien" movies, and that did not help my heart rate nor ease my panic.

I looked up and saw my old chair in front of my face, and something in my head told me that I needed to be much closer to it, and I crawled over to it and rested my face on the steel leg closest to me. The next cramp slapped my face against the metal and I tried to vomit, but all that came out was tons of saliva.

God, my cheekbone hurt!

What I really wanted was to close my eyes and die, but it wasn't working out that way. My eyes weren't even working properly, because all I could focus on was where my spit had landed on the chair leg. The liquid wasn't running down the metal; instead, it looked like it was pooling. Not long after that, it seemed as though my spit was moving back toward my face along the chair leg.

Super! Hallucinations! I really wanted to go back to the raven and nerve endings.

CRAMP!

My tongue was out, touching the metal of the chair, and I

was panting hard. I tasted the cold steel and there was something calming about it. The next cramp wasn't as bad as the one before it.

I nearly screamed when my spit started oozing back onto my tongue and slithering back toward my throat. Looking down, there was a gray worm on the chair leg that was stretching back into my face and doing a fine job of moving toward my uvula. I was paralyzed with revulsion and shattered by waves of cramps.

Centimeter by centimeter, the gray spit slug made a beeline for my throat. The chair leg behind it looked bright and abraded, as if my spit had scoured the metal and then polished the scratches. The cramping was horrible, and each contraction took my breath away. Also horrible was the overwhelming urge to swallow. But I did. I couldn't help it.

The cramps backed down into waves of full-body tremors. I kept swallowing until the gray mess was gone. A minute or two after the last swallow, the shaking stopped and I flopped over onto my back.

If you have ever been to a horror movie that was so intense that you left the theater unable to form complete thoughts, then you know what it was like to be in my head after that experience. I wasn't able to think over the storm of wordless emotions that were crashing inside my skull, but I didn't have to wait for long for some kind of quietude. I passed out, which was happening far too often for comfort.

When I woke up, it was like an electric shock. I sat straight up, alert and ready to go, as if nothing freaky had happened. There was also a sensation of knowing how long I'd been out of commission. I wanted to say 15 minutes, 44 seconds, and 33 milliseconds.

Blocks fell into place.

I wasn't infected with the zombie virus. I'd been nailed by nanotechnology. Mister Yan appears and less than an hour later, I'm rejecting foreign bodies and healing far too quickly to be human. Just a little while later, I'm doubled over, sliming furniture and slurping the slime back up.

Why? The little bastards want to replicate.

Mister Yan went to Jayashri's house also. Chances are, she'd been "gifted." Charlie was with me, and if the tech wasn't typed specifically for the two of us, it would be floating around in her system as well.

I felt a little relief at that thought. I would prefer to tell her something like, "Hey! That bug that turns you into the walking dead that I thought I gave you last night? I was wrong! You didn't get anything from me! It looks like the little Chinese man gave you nano-critters instead!"

Whether or not that would be better in the end, I couldn't say. All I knew was that my new inhabitants had cleared foreign material out of my body, repaired tissue damage, and made me feel completely horrible in order to vomit drool all over a steel chair leg, oh, and then have me consume the goo I'd ejected, along with whatever material had been scavenged from the chair. That could make metal detectors troublesome in the future.

"Gosh, sweetie! I infected you with the little wrigglers Bajali sent me! You'll have horrible morning sickness, and in nine months, you'll have a bouncing baby Cylon!"

Deliver me, Oh Lord, from my own imagination. Why can't I give someone something simple that requires two weeks of antibiotics?

Oh, that's right. I'm not living in a normal world.

Chapter 22

I stood up, brushed myself off, and made my way back down to the Spa to tell my friends about the latest development. I confess, I was feeling a tad frustrated by all of it.

When I slid the door aside, there was an interesting tableau in front of my eyes. Charlie was passed out on the floor with the heater vent pipe in her left hand and soot all over her face. Jayashri was thrusting her hips, vigorously, against the water pipe and licking gray drool as it slid back down toward her lips. It was made 1,000 times more erotic because she was naked and covered in pearls of bath water.

Crotch Quixote and the Panzas began a rousing Mariachi rendition of Aerosmith's "Walk This Way." My frontal lobes gave up the effort to keep the music down, poured a strong one, and sat back in their recliner.

The effect was only slightly ruined when Jaya passed out, slid off the water pipe, and flopped onto the floor in a curvaceous tan pile.

I decided it was a splendid time for a mantra. "It turns and walks out of the room and closes the door behind it. It puts the lotion in the basket." I repeated those lines over and over and over again. Then something in my head changed the disposition of the lotion, and I ran out of the room before it could alter my course of action.

Standing outside of the room, on the other side of a large sliding steel door, felt much safer even if the House Band was encouraging me to go back inside. I could wait for fifteen minutes and then make snarky comments when they wake back up! What a great idea! No.

There are some things that even the painfully horny should never risk, even if there are lovely little nanomachines that will heal you up in a pinch. Of course, there was no way to know precisely how powerful the little buggers could be without testing of some kind. It seemed a smarter course of action to simply forget that they were around, but be safety conscious and cautious, rather than walk up to an IED and hope to stand back up afterward.

That being said, if the little bastards could give me claws and coat my skeleton in some fantastical metal, as well as heal any and every injury known to man... Let's just say I wouldn't bitch about it in the least. Unless it hurt like Hell to do it. Then I would bitch loudly, cry, wail, complain, and go throw myself off a building and then get up and do it all again.

I never said I was sane. Most people aren't.

What I really wanted was some kind of explanation for why Baj decided to do this without even asking. Of course, he probably couldn't have asked considering the position of being under scrutiny and having to hand off the "goodies" to Mister Yan to deliver. But that didn't answer the primary "Why" of the problem.

Could it be as simple as he wanted to give us an advantage in terms of surviving the coming attack? Possible, I suppose. That would have to do until I could ask him in person.

My brain perked up. Someone was approaching the door from the other side. I knew that they were at a 45-degree angle to my position and approximately five feet away. At current speed, that person would have their hand on the door in 4.5 seconds. The door would slide, and in .12 seconds, I would be able to turn and attack if necessary.

I also had the impression something inside me was waiting for a decision as it was counting down the hundredths of a second before I could assess the target. New information showed up, a pheromone signature—it was Charlie behind the door. That strange part of my brain, the nanomachines, I assume, disappeared from the edge of my consciousness.

"Hi Charlie."

"Frank, what the fuck was that all about?"

I turned around to face her. She was still covered in soot, but the tears were fresh. All I could do was pull her into my arms and hold her. I don't know if she needed it, but I did.

"Jaya's husband, Bajali, sent us a gift," I whispered in her ear. "I didn't give you the virus, because I didn't have it. What we've got are nanomachines."

"When did this happen?"

"Mister Yan was probably the carrier. That's why my body started rejecting the stitches; at least, that's what I think is going on."

She let out the breath she was holding and sagged into me just a little bit. "Then what was the deal with the cramps and licking metal?"

"My best guess is that the nanos wanted to replicate enough to do whatever it is they're supposed to do. Baj wanted to give us the best chance he could to survive the attack, and this seems to be a way to do that."

Charlie lifted her head up from my chest, looked up into my eyes, and said, "If we get him back, can I punch him really hard and yell at him a whole bunch?"

"If Jayashri leaves anything for you to punch, sure."

"Okay." She looked a little confused for a moment. "Why do I think someone is about to walk around the door and then up behind me in under eight seconds?"

"Probably because someone is. I got the same sort of information before you even slid the door open."

Before she even came around the door, we heard Jaya say, "No one is allowed to beat my husband into a pulp but me. I cannot find a towel and am not going to reveal myself to the prying eyes of someone who is not my cursed spouse. Where can I find something to cover myself with?"

"The plastic cabinet," Charlie and I said in unison.

"Thank you. I will tell you when it is appropriate for you to come in."

I looked at Charlie and we smiled, doing our best not to laugh. She was still in my arms, and I liked it. She was curvy, warm, strong, and feminine. Unfortunately for me, my brain started playing back the memory of Jayashri and the water pipe, and my anatomy stood up to share an opinion on that recollection.

It seemed that Charlie could feel my... editorial, because both of her eyebrows shot straight up and her mouth formed an "O" shape. Any sane man would have expected what I did, that she'd extricate herself from my embrace and slap the crap out of me. We would have been distinctly wrong.

She smiled like a shark and started to gyrate against me in a distressingly erotic manner. I blushed. I could feel it.

"My, my, Mister Stewart. Is there something you'd like to share with me about how you're feeling right now?"

"Nargle!"

She dissolved into laughter at my expense, and I was entirely grateful for it. Then we heard Jayashri say, from the other side of the door, "Charlotte, what are you laughing at? Did Frank make a fool of himself in some way?"

Charlie replied, tears streaming down her face, "Oh, honey! No more than he usually does!"

The sad thing is that I was becoming adjusted to being spoken about in that way. I imagined I might find it worrisome if my gonads weren't having a karate tournament in my reptile brain. She felt really, really good against me, and I wasn't able to decide if that was a bad thing or not.

We wandered back into "Frank's Bath and Spa" (as it would later be called) to find our friend sitting on the bath stool, looking amused and thoughtful. I was able to think clearly enough to decide against mentioning that I saw her adventures with the water pipe. It also occurred to me that I should have installed security cameras in the bath area.

"Looks like the little Chinese zombie brought us tidings of comfort and joy," Charlie said.

"That seems to be the most logical assumption, given recent events. What I cannot decide for myself is whether I am happy that my husband gave this to us, or if I feel as though I have been poorly used by him."

"Baj, narg narg fwhew love love. Yah!" My frontal lobes were taking their own sweet time in getting up from in front of the widescreen TV. That had to be it. The only other possibility is that the machines stole my IQ when I wasn't paying attention.

"Should I even try to understand that gibberish?" Mental note: Jaya pronounces "gibberish" with a G sound, not a J sound.

"I think I flirted with him a bit too intensely for his over-stressed brain to cope with. He'll be back to his normal self in a few minutes." Charlie looked me over, seemed to assess something I couldn't quantify, and turned back to Jaya. "If his brain doesn't come back, then we'll just find something for him to do that doesn't require much thought."

"For example?"

"Paperweight."

"Charlotte, your brilliance is only matched by your lovely personality and physical beauty."

"Why, thank you! I'm going to take my bath now, I think. Maybe I'll have the Brainless One scrub my back. What do you think?"

"Are you sure that he would be capable of such a delicate task, reduced as he is to a barely sentient state?"

"I'm willing to take the chance."

Jayashri stood up in the towel, walked over to her clothes that were folded so neatly by the opposite wall, nodded to both of us, and started toward the door.

"Grnnah room wa arg!"

"Thank you, Frank. I think I will lounge in your room for a while. Perhaps, if you have some books, I might read for a while?"

"Books, ight elf. Iction, nd row."

"Splendid!" With characteristic grace, she floated from the room, pausing only to slide the door closed.

Chapter 23

Charlotte started to undress, and I was still in the room. There was something incredibly wrong about that, but my brain was not ticking over fast enough to do anything other than watch her move. Her back was turned, and she didn't seem to care I was in the room.

Her tattoos fought for my attention. They couldn't have been old, because the colors were too bright, almost too intense for words. The pinks, reds, and greens stood out against the pale canvas of her skin, highlighting the strong curves of her shoulders and the smooth play of muscles as she moved. The architecture of her back, waist, and hips was more perfect than any set of numbers that could have described it.

She was luminous. Color, lines, forms, and shapes that moved me more than any of the cathedrals I'd visited in Europe.

In my travels, I'd felt God in quiet places. I'd heard angels in Bach and Beethoven. Until then, I had never seen art made flesh.

Charlie sat down on the stool in front of the tap with the soap and bucket. I couldn't see anything more than the change in the play of light on her skin. All I could do was watch while she soaped and rinsed parts of herself that I couldn't see, and I would not have been anywhere else in the world if I could have been.

"Will you wash my back?" She asked quietly, almost too low to be heard, with vulnerability that I'd never heard before... except the night before, in my arms.

To my credit, I didn't stumble over, or collapse to my knees. For once in my life, I had a moment of physical grace in the face of overwhelming feelings. She offered me the loofah, and I took it.

She scooted the wash bucket around to her side so I could use it. My thought processes were a little dim and I was grateful I didn't have to make my mouth work in order to have access to the water. All I could reliably do was what she asked of me, not because I didn't have some ideas of my own, but because I was so incredibly unprepared for the situation.

I put my left hand on her shoulder to steady myself as I sunk to my knees behind her. Then I did what I was asked to do. I washed her back. It was the fastest eternity I've ever lived in.

My hand was still on her shoulder when I put the loofah in the bucket and I was about to stand back up when she tugged my wrist. Charlie pulled my hand from her shoulder and across her chest, which gave me little recourse but to move in behind her, my chest to her back. Then she reached around, found my other hand, and pulled it around her tummy. I was Frank, the Human Cape.

Smelling her skin is what sunk me. I rested my head on her shoulder with my lips touching the side of her neck, and it was the most natural place in the world to be. She sighed, and some sort of tension inside her evaporated.

I needed to speak. I wanted to say things. My guts were filled with poetry and my heart was eager to pump the words out of me, but my tongue felt lifeless.

"Say, Frank?"

"Mmm?"

"You kinda like me, don't you?"

"Very much," I said, and my eyes bugged out because I actually used words.

"That's nice. You don't think I come on too strong or that I'm too ballsy to be a girl, do you?"

"You're strong. Sweet. Beautiful. You're funny. Sharp, but kind." Words. Okay. A little on the simplistic side, but at least I was getting concepts across. I hoped that the Poetry Pump would kick into gear quickly.

"You think I'm beautiful?" She laughed a little and tried to cover up by throwing humor at it. "I guess this means that you're kinky for tattooed, muscular country girls who are pushing BBW. Frankie likes the chub."

I had wanted to kiss her neck. Between the thought and the action, my mouth opened and I found myself gently biting her instead.

She didn't sigh. She quivered and made a noise that should never be heard outside of a bedroom. I felt both of our hearts slam inside our chests.

Maybe some day I'll know why I needed to bite down harder, but I did. Charlie jerked in my arms and her breasts ended up resting on my arm. They had warmth and weight, and I knew I wanted to turn my hand over so I could cup the one closest to it.

I did.

"Frank. Frank, please bite me again."

I moved my mouth down to her shoulder, and for a moment it felt like I had unhinged my jaw to fit as much of her in my mouth as I could. My hand found the curve of her breast and the crinkled hardness of her nipple. I bit her, closing my mouth around the petals of passionflowers, and pinched the flesh under my fingers.

She didn't jerk in my arms, or moan. She heaved and the stool went skittering away on the wet concrete. There aren't perfect words to use to describe what came out of her mouth. To say anything would be like throwing a box of darts at a dartboard in the hope that you'll hit inside the center circle.

We ended up in a heap on the wet concrete, my teeth still in her shoulder, and my arms around her. She made me feel like growling.

I let go of her shoulder, and she turned over before I

could even think about suggesting caution. Her arms slipped around me, under my t-shirt, and held on.

"I don't want to sound all girly, but I'm going to." She looked into my eyes and I was pulled into the rings of color and flecks of brown in her green irises. "Do you believe in first kisses?"

"How?"

She smiled shyly. "I've always believed that your first kiss with someone would tell you about what you could be together. That you'd feel their soul before you could have a chance to put all your walls back up."

At that moment in time, I would have believed anything and everything she asked if I could see that look in her eyes every moment of every day until I closed mine forever.

I didn't kiss her. She didn't kiss me. We fell into the kiss together.

I believed in first kisses, because what we shared gave us no choice. It was a living and vibrant thing that we made together, and it was bigger than both of us. The beginning was gentle, full of exploration, and it felt like it could last forever.

As if it had a mind and a purpose all its own, the kiss swept us up into something else. Passion. Instead of warmth and restraint, we fed on each other's lips, battered our tongues together, and our teeth clicked as we attacked without the civilized veneer we had tried to maintain.

Do people keep time when they kiss? I know I could have, had I wanted such a thing, but I didn't. I wanted to live in the exquisite *now* of exploring Charlotte Marie Cooper.

The kiss showed us that the passion didn't fade over time, even if the feral madness subsided. We were slaves to it, riding between the ferocious and the sublime. The gentle touch of lips on lips returned, but our hearts did not slow a single beat.

If Charlie was right about first kisses showing you who the person in your arms was and what you could be together, then I learned enough in those moments to change my life. I never knew that I ached for someone, or that I could, like I did for her. Every switch I had ever identified in myself was flipped by this incredible, vivacious, and beautiful woman.

I would die for her. I would live for her. I felt a future in those lips. There was fun in it, as well as joy, confrontation, adoration, love, and a dance of intimacy that would last until I could not go any further... and then, it would breathe life into me again.

Somewhere in that infinite moment, the kiss let us go. We were left with sore mouths, wide eyes, and more feelings than could have been expressed in anything shorter than a lifetime. I could have summed those feelings up in three words, but I was afraid to say them on the off chance that she did not feel the same.

I guess that is what she meant. The walls around my heart rose up when the storm passed.

"Ah. Charlotte. Um."

She smiled and shifted her body in a devious and delightful way. "Pretty impressive, wasn't it?"

"I'm speechless." Certainly, there weren't many words in my head, but there were about four million naughty thoughts trying to hog time on the Sex-A-Tron widescreen in my mental Madison Square Gardens. My anatomy had distinct opinions about things, and I was trying like Hell not to listen to the running commentary or follow the explicit advice of Quixote and Los Panzas.

How her thigh ended up pressing against my Three-Course Gourmet Feast didn't matter to me as much as that it was making it entirely too difficult to form a complete sentence. I know I can't hide anything of import if my face is in on the game. My features are way too mobile to conceal certain kinds of information, and Charlie was far too good at paying attention to little details.

She giggled at me and shook her head. "You're attached to being a gentleman, aren't you?"

"Yeah."

"Tell me it isn't because I'm Shawn's sister. I don't want to back you into a corner, but I'd like to know." The giggles and smiles were replaced by a more serious expression like a light switch being flipped.

My brain was frozen solid. I wanted her. I liked her. I did not want to screw up the flow of possibilities centered around the presence of this exquisite woman in my life. Words were not forming, and when you have no words, all you have is action.

I returned the favor of her thigh pressed against me, but instead of pressing, I pushed her thighs apart and occupied the space between them. I mounted her and ground the zipper of my jeans against what I ached to touch. With my arms holding me in place, I let her feel what I couldn't form words to say, and I kissed her with every iota of lust I felt.

Her legs wrapped around my thighs and she made incoherent noises against my tongue. I hadn't planned to keep grinding the zipper-enabled Mariachi into her, but I couldn't help myself.

I managed to break the kiss and looked down into her slightly glassy eyes. While our bodies tried to disintegrate my blue jeans by sheer force of will and mad friction, I managed to find words.

"I do not care who your brother is. I don't care where you came from or why. All I know is that I want you right here, right now, and every moment I can have you from this moment forward." There was a growl in my voice, a feral authenticity I had never heard before, and I still had things I needed to say. "I don't want to be your gentleman, Charlie. I want you screaming my name as badly as I want to possess you."

I saw her breath catch and her eyes open to the size of saucers. The more she lifted her hips off the concrete, the less control I was keeping over my ache to make the zipper go away, but I was not about to lose a fight with myself until I was ready. Growling, I slammed my crotch into hers and pinned her to the floor, sandwiching her between hardnesses.

"I'm a liar, a cheat, and a killer. Another minute of your unbelievably erotic body underneath me and I won't be able to be the honest man I want to be for you. Give me a little time, Charlie; let me give you the man I want to be for you, and then I will take the woman you want to give me."

She moaned, inhaled, and twisted somehow. The next thing I knew, I was the one flat on my back on the concrete with her on top. Just as fast, her hand went between the front of my body and my jeans, and she gathered me into her grasp. My back arched and all that came out of my mouth was a groan that started at the back of my throat and punched itself between my teeth.

"Goddamn it, Frank. Promise me."

"Praaaahh?"

"Promise me you're not... Arg! Fuck, Frank! Promise me... " She was having trouble getting her words out, so I didn't feel quite so awful. Actually, I felt more than a little pleased, because that meant I wasn't the only person almost blind with lust.

"I promise!"

"Promise me you'll love me and possess me and fuck me like your very own girlfriend!"

"God! Yes! I promise! Please get your hand off my Quixote before I can't ask you to stop!"

"What the Hell is a Quixote?"

"Penis!" I still hate that the word came out as a lame little squeak.

"Oh? You mean, this one?" She squeezed, and I thought I was going to die or experience the rapture.

"God!"

"You can call me anything you want, Frankie the Girder, just don't make a fool out of me."

"No, Charlie. I want you too much. I didn't know I needed... " I tried to shut up before I made a fool out of myself.

"What do you need?" She let go of Quixote, much to his dismay and my existential relief, and draped herself over me so that our faces were a breath apart. "Tell me what you need. Please. I want to know, Frank. Please tell me."

"I didn't know I needed you."

She kissed me, and it was as much about love as the one before was about sex. "You didn't know it because you're a boy, sweetheart. I knew it. That's because I'm a girl."

"I'm really happy about that. A boy with breasts like those would take a lot of getting used to."

"Ooo! I'm gonna pinch you for that one!"

"How about you wash my back, and then we can use the spiffy tub and soak together?"

"Jesus, Frank! That is so close to genius I might just fall head over heels for you!"

"Promise?"

We got up off the floor. I shucked my clothes and assumed the position on the stool after I retrieved it. She laughed, and I turned around to find out what was funny. I didn't expect her to be standing there, bold as brass, with her hands on her hips and not bothering to cover anything. The first thing that went through my head was, "Oh! Creamy!"

Guys like to talk about women who have curves in the right places. Charlie had curves in not only the right places, but also in Locations Optimized for Amorous Deployment. "L.O.A.D." in government speak.

"I guess I should've warned you, but I thought Shawn would have said something about it."

"About what?"

She grinned, and I had a Robert Heinlein moment. "We were pretty much raised nudist."

"Do you know the kinds of mental images that gives me about your brother? I mean, I see him leaping and pirouetting through the wheat fields of your homeland. Julie Andrews is singing in the background. This is just not right!"

She covered her mouth with her hand and started

laughing like a loon. I just stared, because the view was That Good (trademark, copyright, marca registrada, etc.). After all, she's a L.O.A.D.

When the laughter let go of her, she sauntered over, knelt down, and proceeded to scrub my back.

"You know, I can barely see where the scars are."

"Really?"

"No kidding. These little nano-things did quite a bit of work beyond throwing stuff out of you. Feel this?" She traced a line under my left shoulder blade, toward the middle of my back.

"It feels like your finger. Why?"

"I just ran my finger over five places where you ought to have scars from shrapnel. There aren't any bumps or swelling, just a little discoloration."

I shuddered a little. Having an army of Tiny I Don't Know Whats running around inside me, regardless of the fact that they'd been doing good things, gave me a feeling of vulnerability I did not like at all. Jayashri and Charlie probably had their own set of feelings about this, or would, once their little friends started to do active things beyond making them slurp gray goo.

Come to think of it, why was I okay with having had to slurp metal-loaded saliva?

"Frank, are you okay there?"

"Yeah, I'm just having a lot of funky feelings about having things altering my body and forcing me to ingest... stuff."

"I'm trying not to think about it. Besides, there are other things I'd rather do." She leaned down and whispered a few of them in my ear. My shudders started again, but for very different reasons.

"Let's use the tub," I said. "If we don't do that, then we're going to end up doing other stuff before... oh dear."

"What?"

"Did you mean what you said just then? The bit about screaming while your mouth is full?"

"Uh huh."

"We need to start soaking right now."

Charlie laughed at me, sauntered over to the tub, and lifted her leg to get in, and I got a brief glimpse of the Holy Land. There was a dainty metal ring above the door to the Holy Land. It derailed my train of thought.

It was a good soak, full of quiet, peace, hot water, and our toes wrestling underneath the surface. We both stopped moving at the same moment. I knew there were three people with lower than normal body temperatures approaching the outside loading door to my store. That loading door is the same one that opens the Spa to the world.

Ten meters. Approximately 60 seconds to reach the door at their current speed. They were moving stealthily, slowly, and within range to hear any noise Charlie or I made. That gave us two choices: we could make no noise and ambush them from our watery alcove, or we could make enough noise that they'd want to approach in order to "surprise us."

Charlie winked at me. She'd made her decision.

"Oh my GOD, Frank! Oh, you are so hard! God! Mmmmm!" Hearing that would have been insanely stimulating if she hadn't been rolling her eyes and doing her best to sneak out of the tub at the same time.

My turn. "Charlie... oh, girl, you are so nasty. Yeah. Nasty! That's what I like. Yeah," I started creeping out of the tub while I did my best to ad-lib without sounding too trite. "Damn. Yeah."

"Oh baby! Oh baby! Spank it, please! I need you to spank it." She slapped her damp thigh and went on, "Oh, honey! That's what I like!" She pointed out the door, brought up three fingers, and headed toward her pants. She'd snagged my Taurus pistols earlier.

My Glock and scythe were right beside my shoes.

"Yeah, slut! I'm gonna spank it again. Yeah!" She obliged me by slapping her thigh about five times. "Take it. Yeah. I'm gonna give it to you in that tight little hole. Mmm, take that!" Five more slaps.

Three meters from the door, 20 degrees staggered, and approximately two meters between each target, lead target approaching the center of the door. I made it out of the tub, snagged my pistol, and was surprised to see Charlie on all fours, facing the door. The revolvers were on the floor in front of her.

She gestured for me to get behind her, then started moaning like a professional and grinding her ass against the air. It took me a minute, but I got it. I got down on my knees behind her, Glock in hand.

"Oh God! You are so nasty! Take my cock! Yeah! Nasty, tight bitch!"

"Ohhhhh! Ohhhhh! You're so mean, stuffing my ass with that! Spank me, you bastard!"

I smelled our targets. Zombies. Extra data point: they'd avoided the IEDs.

I tapped Charlie's left thigh, the one nearest to the center of the door, where the primary target would be coming through. She nodded, went flat to the floor, and had a gun in each hand.

"Yeah! I'll spank you, dirty bitch! Take it! Take it!"

"Ohhhhh! Ohhhhh! I'm gonna! I'm gonna!" She did a very, very credible faux-gasm, and the rolling door was flung open.

Target 1 moved into the room in a tactical crouch, AR-15 tracking from side to side. Pro. Targets 2 and 3 scampered in, sweeping the room as well. Then they saw us.

Door Zombie did not have time to acquire a target before Charlie put a slug between the lenses of his ultra-black shades. How she shot Target 3 with the same precision, at the same instant, I don't know.

Target 2 had just long enough to get a shot off at me before I gave him a classic Cranial Double Tap.

I will say this about modern body armor. Kevlar helmets do a great job at containing the spray of exploding skulls. I managed to get that thought out before I realized that Target 2 had actually shot me.

"That was a damned fine double tap," Charlie said as she rolled over, lightly freckled with bloody spatter, and looked up at me. "FRANK!"

"Yeah."

"You've been shot! Oh... oh, God."

Chapter 24

"What?" I had no idea what she was so upset about. I didn't really feel anything and was strangely unconcerned. If anything, I felt fabulous!

"That is so, so gross." She pointed at my right shoulder.

I looked down and got to see the bullet finish emerging from my skin and the few drops of blood on my chest dissolve in front of my eyes. It was, as she said, "gross."

We both gasped when the bullet dissolved and dribbled down my chest. The hole in my shoulder closed up, and I had a sudden craving for rare steak.

"I don't know about you, but I think the little bastards made my endorphins go squirty." I nodded at her and thought about the pretty colors and how the room was being all wavy and organic. I knew I was screwed and high on my own juices when I started to dance in a formless sort of way with a loaded gun in my hand.

"Frank," she made her guns go away, and that was utterly *cool* for a naked hottie with a ring in her hoohoo, "maybe you ought to sit down or something. You look a little glazed over."

"Yeaaaah." I was still dancing to my internal MP3 library. There was a kind of shuddering collision, and I noticed that I was flat on my back, still gyrating slightly.

"Frank, you might be high on your own juices, but don't make me kick you to the floor again. All right?"

"Yeaaaah." Concrete feels good when you writhe all over it. "This is like the best back scratcher in the world!"

"Great. Tell you what? You stay right there, and I'll go look over the dead bodies. Does that work for you?"

"Yeaaaah."

I continued to chill and let the self-made groove cocktail slosh through my body. Really, if this is what I could have for getting shot, then I'd need to rethink my desire to dodge projectiles. It was mellow, thick, rich, and as gooey as freshly baked chocolate chip cookies. Then again, like most instances of being high, it ended less pleasantly than it began.

The cramps came back.

It was a different feeling that curled me over into a fetal position on the floor and completely evaporated the endorphin high I'd been enjoying. I didn't hear Jayashri come back in the room, but I did vaguely process that Charlie was examining the corpses' gear in the buff. That was strangely erotic for about four seconds, before it was swept away by the next cramp.

Jayashri knelt down beside me, pulled down my eyelids, and checked my pupils. I would have made smart remarks about the pupils not being the source of my discomfort, but she waved a can of full-sugar cola in front of my face, and my attention rapidly changed focus. I reached up, grabbed it, popped the top, and chugged it.

The cramps started to subside almost instantly. When I put the can down on the floor, the paint had been stripped off of it in a perfect handprint. Apparently, my little friends wanted sugar and whatever was in the paint on the can. However, they didn't want whatever that bullet had been made out of; they'd just made it into easily disposable goo.

"Thanks. I think I needed that."

"It certainly looked like you did. I would have been here sooner, but I knew the two of you had handled the situation."

"Yeah. I think our little friends have some kind of sensor package, or they're processing our input in a way that we don't. The science is a little much for me right now."

"Hopefully, we will speak to my husband about all of it before too terribly long." She looked over at Charlie and asked, "What do the party crashers have to say for themselves?"

"Not a whole lot," she replied. "We do have a nice AR-15, a couple of grenades, three Beretta military-issue pistols, and a pile of combat knives to add to our collection. If I were going to hazard a guess, I'd say that these three were probably regular Army before they went over."

"What makes you say that?" I asked.

"Well, they're wearing urban camo BDUs, and they've got Army rank insignia in all the right places."

"Oh."

Charlie got a really strange look on her face, scooted across the room, and vaulted into the tub.

That's when I heard, "Hey guys! Y'all okay in there?" Shawn was not far away, and my mini-friends informed me that there were at least six other armed people with him. Our cavalry, just a little late.

"Yeah! We're good! Had some unfriendly visitors."

Shawn rounded the corner with Nate and four other people I wasn't sure I knew. They were armed, and three of their firearms had been discharged recently. It took me a moment to realize why Shawn's eyeballs were bugging out; I was still on the floor, naked, and my junk was looking right back at him. Nate and the others weren't as fazed by it.

"Oh, put your eyes back in their sockets! I know I'm a vision of manly beauty and all that, but, fuck, you were raised a nudist!" That got serious laughs from the rest of the guys and a chortle from inside the ofuro.

The trademark laugh caught Shawn's attention. He turned a few shades of pink, turned around, and swiftly walked away. Nate turned to watch him go, and the other guys started examining the bodies.

"Oh, fuck me," one of them said.

"What is it, Ramos?" Nate turned and walked over to where Ramos was examining a set of remains.

"Ah, I was in basic with this idiot. It's a shame to see this."

"I hate to interrupt," I said, "but some of your weapons have been fired recently. What all is going on?"

Nate stood up, walked over, and crouched down beside me. "I think we just got a small tactical assessment from our good friends across the way. We were walking back to my place and Boyle, over there, saw someone fiddling with the trigger on one of the IEDs. Boyle yelled, and the guy raised a weapon. We took exception to that."

"Did your target have any friends?"

"No. There was just the one. They definitely got intel on our perimeter from somewhere."

"Well," I said, "they have been watching. The morning zombie blew himself up while doing recon, and I would imagine that they had a sniper watching him all the while." That is what I wanted to think. The other option was that they'd squeezed information out of Bajali or had been observing every move he made.

Thinking about someone dear to me being tortured did nothing to improve my mood.

"I've got a thought," Nate said, smirking down at me.

"What's that?"

"You might want to put on some pants if you want to keep fighting zombies today."

I frowned a most foul frown. "Just how long have you been waiting to say that to someone?"

"Man!" Nate laughed and said, "I've been wanting to do that for at least two years," and then looked at me with a certain amount of gravitas. "But seriously, having your junk pointed at me like that... It's disturbing."

I know I blushed, I could feel the heat in my face, and Jayashri was snickering gently. Nate stood up, chuckling, and wandered back over to give the corpses his own once-over. Since I didn't really have any choice, I rolled over, stood up, and went in search of pants.

Jaya walked over to the tub and peered inside. I

overheard part of the conversation, at least the bits that weren't expressed in the secret language of feminine giggles. For the most part, it involved surprise that Charlie was so bold, that I was so bold, and yet greater surprise that I managed to avoid the "inevitable conclusion," and the way we enticed our opponents into opening the door. That chunk of the recitation garnered quite a few, "Oh! My! Oh my goodness!" and other such comments from Jayashri.

When I turned around from pulling my pants back on, I noticed a certain Dr. Sharma from across the street was looking at me with an unusual air of consideration. I just shrugged. I couldn't even imagine what was going through her head, but I realized it would chap my ass until I found time to ask about it. Considering that there were three bodies to deal with, that conversation would have to take a back burner to the pressing issues at hand.

Nate and his guys were stripping the zombies, and one of them was walking toward my ofuro with intent to rinse out a helmet in the convenient water source. Apparently he had been paying more attention to the corpses than anything else that had been happening around him.

"You! Lack of Hygiene Dude!" I pinned him in place with my Erect Finger of Doom like a butterfly on Styrofoam. "If you dunk that helmet in my Soaking Tub of Earthly Delights, one or two things will happen. Number one: a hot blond woman will rise up naked out of the water and slap the shit right out of you. Number two: the irate owner of the tub," pointing at my own chest, "will levitate over there on a column of blue flame and bitch slap you. Oh, and three: I will never let you use my tub. Ever."

The guy turned, looked at Nate for direction, and received the following response, "White, Frank does not joke about his tub. I'd find a hose if I were you."

White turned back toward me and offered, "Sorry, man. Is there a hose I can use?"

"Yes. Go out the door, turn right, and you can't miss it." Another thought trickled into the front of my head, and I found the nearest towels. "Charlie, do you want to get out of the tub or have you become a prune with gills?"

"Yeah, but there's the whole People I Don't Know thing going on out there," she replied from inside the tub.

"Didn't you tell me that you were a nudist?"

"Nudism doesn't have shit to do with modesty or exhibitionism. Now bring me a towel before I get fierce."

"Fierce. Fierce, she says!" I walked over to the tub, blocked the view with one towel, and handed her the other one. Somewhere between getting out of the water and wrapping herself in cotton goodness, she reached around and tweaked my nipple. "EEEEE!"

"Secret for you, Frankie Twin Peaks: never joke about a woman being fierce."

"Ma'am! Yes, Ma'am!"

"That's better." She sauntered off, picked up her clothes and guns, and scooted out of the room with Jayashri in tow. I swear there was more giggling involved.

"Frank?"

"Yes, Nate?"

"She's Shawn's sister?"

"Uh huh."

"She's got a shot-loaded leather set of nuts underneath that towel!"

"And a sap dangling between, let me tell you what."

"I hope she sticks around," Nate smiled in a way that showed extra teeth, "because I like that in a woman. Makes me wonder if I'd like her mom just as much."

"She's mine, you man ho." Nate and I always joked around like kids in the locker room. We often ended up doing neighborhood dirty work, and the ass-slapping humor did a lot to diffuse how uncomfortable it was to dispose of bodies or dig graves. "As for Mother Cooper, do you think you could handle a woman who raised a daughter like that?"

"Shit. I *am* the Dark Meat. Nothin' God made that I can't handle." He waved me over, "Now get your pasty white junk over here and help me strip these bodies."

That's what we did.

Zombie blood is strangely thick and doesn't quite coagulate properly over time. Once we had the uniforms off, I took them over to the laundry room beside the bathroom on the far side of the loading dock Spa. A little bleach, decent enzymatic detergent, and two cycles of washing would have most of the blood out.

In a barter economy, even if cash still exists and is used, never turn down the chance to clean and hold onto trade-worthy items. BDUs almost always come in handy for such things. The helmets and body armor were also something of a treat for the same reason.

It occurred to me there might be another use for the stuff. We could possibly infiltrate Hightower's camp in disguise. That was an idea worth discussing with tactically minded people at the upcoming meeting. We needed to find and leverage any possible edge we could get if we wanted to come out alive.

Once again, my little "riders" informed me that an armed human was approaching me from behind. I'd just transferred the BDU load into the dryer and turned around as one of the new guys, Ramos, was about to tap me on the shoulder. It gave him a bit of a start.

"Excuse me. Nate told me to come over and ask what we ought to do with these three bodies and the one we tagged earlier."

"Probably the best bet is the woodchipper over at Shawn's garage. I think we've got an empty 55-gallon drum around here someplace." I thought for a minute. "Yeah, that's probably at Shawn's too."

"We're going to run the bodies through the chipper?" Ramos looked a little green when he asked me that. "And what are we gonna do with the drum?"

"In answer to your first question, yes. In answer to your second question, you chip the corpses into the drum. Then you toss lime into it, cover it, and wait until it turns into compost. If that's not pleasant enough, pour some gasoline into the drum and light all the chipped-up shit on fire."

"Ah." He was really green under the gills and did not look at all comfortable talking to me about this. "Doesn't that smell really bad?"

"No worse than a BBQ, and then just like burning meat of any kind. It's over in about six hours, and you can use the zombie ashes as fertilizer or to fill holes in your yard. The tomatoes love the stuff." I scratched my head. "What did they do with zombie bodies where you were?"

Ramos turned a little green under the gills.

"Mass graves," he replied. "We bulldozed them into mass graves."

The discomfort was as evident on his face as the shine on a new penny. He turned around and walked back over to Nate, who looked back at me and nodded.

Ramos, Boyle, and White each grabbed the feet of a brainless body and started dragging them around the corner to Shawn's place. Nate waved, told me he'd see me in a little bit for the meeting, and headed off to oversee the disposal process.

That's all right. I enjoy doing laundry. It is much more peaceful and smells better than ZPD. Zombie-Processing Duty. The acronym just sounds more professional.

The washer pinged, and I slapped the BDUs back in for a second run. From the look of them, they didn't really need it, but it seemed like a reasonable idea to wash them a second time, even if it was slightly "woo-woo" of me. At least I wasn't hunting for sage or incense to burn; that would be far too spiritually committed for me to indulge in.

I turned around, looked at my splendid soaking tub and all the brains and goo on the floor, and was filled with a need to put things back into some sort of order. I had just started to mop the floor when my critters gave me a heads-up about someone approaching the delivery door, which was still open to the world. The incoming individual was human, and that was a bit of a relief. In all likelihood, it was

Shawn or someone wandering over to ask about something.

"Afternoon, Mister Stewart."

I looked up to see Buttons standing in the doorway and managed to keep my overwhelming joy at bay long enough to acknowledge him with a surly grunt. He waved me over, and that was curious enough to make me stroll in his direction.

"You're familiar with the fact that there are thousands of objects orbiting the planet, aren't you Frank?" Buttons had a particularly inscrutable expression plastered across his face.

"Yes. Why?"

He put his hands on my shoulders, turned me so I was facing the area where our enemies had set up shop. You can easily see the high-rise buildings from here, and he pointed to one in particular. "There's a sniper in the offices on the top floor of that building. The distance is a bit of a stretch, but he could nail almost anyone in this neighborhood if he wanted."

"Yes. That's probably true."

"Would you also say he's got a decent vantage point to observe anything you do here?"

I didn't quite see what he was getting at, but I agreed with him on that point as well.

He looked at his watch, a matte-black tactical number that sported more dials and widgets than I'd ever seen. "Watch the top of the building for the next 11 seconds. You might be pleased if you did. Perhaps a bit more at ease, at the very least."

I started to think about demanding he spill his beans, when the top four floors of the building in question became an expanding cloud of dust. A heartbeat later, there was a noise that sounded like the bastard child of a thunderclap and a tin whistle. The clouds in the sky above the building looked like they'd been shredded.

"What. The. Fuck?" No amount of eloquence could have covered the shock I was feeling at the time.

"That, Mister Frank Stewart, was an example of the

buttons I have at my disposal and my commitment to helping you all get out of this in one piece."

"That was... what?"

"A shot from a satellite that does not exist and cannot be detected. That satellite does not have an electromagnetic railgun, nor can it be moved into a different orbit as necessary. Did you know that it won't be in the exact same position in 23 hours, 58 minutes, and some odd seconds?"

"I am, well..." I tried to find something to say, but all I could do was turn back toward the building and watch the cloud of dust dissipate. There were bent girders where those four floors used to be and no windows left for six floors underneath. I wasn't able to process what I'd seen, even with the explanation. "I don't want to know what the other buttons are. Do I?"

"No, you very much do not want to know what the other buttons are." He gave me a cold but wry smile before he continued, "That is the button I have been granted use of in order to see my mission through to completion. I have access to other resources if that non-existent orbital weapon does not prove to be sufficient to the task. Those other resources are not as precise and will negatively impact your community if they are used."

"Why haven't these resources been put to use before now?"

"The intel we had on Warren Hightower and his plans did not merit this sort of action. We had no idea that Bajali Sharma was in country and accessible to the enemy. When it became clear that not only was he in the country but had been abducted, action was authorized."

"How come you haven't used those non-existent things to blow all of Hightower's little operation into dust?"

"We want Sharma alive. That's the first reason. The second reason is that we believe our opponent has at least one nuclear weapon. A similar strike to the one you just saw has a 99 percent chance of setting off that nuke. We are far too close to the government's interests and infrastructure to allow that."

"Thank you for coming clean on this stuff. How much of it can we explain to our people?"

"Friends in high places, but not details. Feel free to make up something," he waved his hands around, "about a missile, UAV, or something to explain the explosion. Nothing about who I am or why I'm here. They don't need to know anything more than they can guess."

I don't know if it was his dismissive tone of voice or the fact that I didn't like him, but rage flooded through me when he said that. I shoved my fingers into his armpits and slammed him up against the wall of my store. Not one to be treated in such a way, he brought his forearms down into the crook of my elbows on each side, causing me to bend forward to meet the solid blow of his forehead against the bridge of my nose. I felt it crunch.

I staggered backward, not even bothering to bring my hands up to my face, and it was a good thing that I didn't. I blocked the roundhouse kick that had been speeding toward the side of my head, which I would not have even seen if I'd been concerned about my nose. I used the force of the kick to spin me into a strike to the back of his thigh and tap the back of his other knee to collapse the leg. He went to the ground with a numb kicking leg, which he used to try and sweep my feet out from under me.

Nice move. Too bad it missed. He altered the momentum and took it into a roll, which brought him up a few feet away, facing in my direction.

I watched him lock eyes with me and freeze in place, and I knew precisely what he was looking at. My nose was reassembling right in front of him. I couldn't wait to tell him that he had my blood all over his face and then explain why my nose was doing fun things.

"Before I need to find food, there are a few things that I need to explain to you, Mister Buttons."

"Sharma did it. That bastard actually did it."

"If what you mean by 'it' is upgrade my hardware, then

you're right on the money. You just might, in my blood that is drying on your face, have the next best thing to the salvation of mankind. Then again, you might not."

For once, there was actually some life in this tool's eyes. I couldn't tell, and didn't care to know, whether it was straight avarice or some cracked version of fear.

"As far as that goes, I really hope you don't, because I don't like you. I know you're hiding more than you're telling me, and I want us to continue to be clear on one major issue."

The cramps arrived, but I held it in. I wasn't ready to let this guy go before I was finished, or succumb to whatever it was that my body and critters were craving.

"And what is that issue, Mister 'Stewart'?" He used air quotes. Gauche.

"If anything you do or say leads to injury or death for any of these good people, I will hunt you down and kill you wherever I find you. Thanks to Bajali, you can slow me down, but you can't stop me. I will get you." I was exaggerating, because I had no idea at all what the nano-buddies were capable of doing. Truth be told, I was more than slightly worried about how much they would be able to do in excess of what I'd already seen. It was clear they were forming tighter relationships with my senses and my body's ability to heal. They were settling in for the long haul. "Have I made myself perfectly clear?"

"Not very trusting are you?" He sneered, which did nothing to endear him to me. "I shouldn't be surprised, considering your family tree."

"That's the truth. Are we clear, or are you going to try to tell me more things I'm already well aware of?"

"Why do you care what happens to these people? Everything your family has ever done has been antithetical to the sort of life these people want to lead. Power. Privilege. More money than people could use in a dozen lifetimes. Do you really expect me to believe you care, or is it the curvy, country whore that has snagged your dick?"

Chapter 25

People talk about "seeing red," but until that moment, I'd never experienced it. At that moment, I really wanted the full Wolverine Makeover. All I could see in the red that was spread out in front of me was a vision of him in a puddle of his own innards. Strangling him with his own intestines seemed like a fantastic course of action.

I never got the chance to move forward. Charlie had heard what he said when she rounded the side of the building, and she put her hand on my shoulder from behind. I didn't see her, but I knew it was her hand.

"Buttons, I'm going to tell you this once, and only once. If it doesn't sink in, and you ever say something like that again, I'll beat Frank in the race to shove my hand down your throat." Her voice, the one I was coming to like very much, was an Arctic wind over my shoulder. If I'd found icicles on my earlobe, it wouldn't have surprised me. "Now then, I have never taken money or anything of material value for fucking anyone. Ever. As far as this good man goes, I intend to screw him until he is a dirty little nub on the floor, and we're going to exchange our hearts with one another as a durable investment on that interaction. You will never know how good I feel in his arms, or underneath him in the middle of the night."

The Arctic blast had a certain amount of heat in it, and I found the red receding from my vision.

Charlie continued, "I could not care less if you can make manna fall from Heaven or dry rivers fill with water. We don't need your fancy toys to win our way out of this mess. More than that, you can't protect people with all your heart and soul if all you feel for them is some kind of disdain."

She walked around me slowly, strolled over to Buttons, and got right in his face. "Make your choice. Be with us, protect us, and show us some respect, or keep pushing until one of us puts you through the woodchipper and feeds you to the roses."

I couldn't see his face, but I heard him agree to respect and protect. He stunned me by actually offering an apology on top of that.

"See? That wasn't so hard, Mister Buttons! Was it?" Charlie patted him on the shoulder, but I saw her leg start to move at the same time.

There was a noise, a meaty and almost moist thump, and her foot settled back on the dirt. She followed up the roundhouse kick with a twist of her hips, and a tidy backfist to his nose. Buttons was on the ground making insane, inarticulate noises and holding his groin for dear life with one hand and his bleeding nose with the other.

"So help me God, if you ever call me a whore again, even behind my back, I will cut those off and feed them to you on a bowl full of grits! Have I made myself clear, you greasy little Establishment ass-licker, or do I need to show my whup ass to you again?" I would like to say that she screamed it, but it wasn't that. Charlie used the up-in-arms, fed-up, and vastly pissed off Yell of the Common Man that drove countless Spartan men into bloody battle.

I was falling head over heels in love.

Charlie turned back to me, walked over, snagged my arm with hers, and led me back into the Spa.

"Close that door on the garbage outside, will you, Frank?" Between the cramps that I was still swallowing and my general feeling of awe toward her, I wasn't about to balk at the request or sass back in any way. I just closed the door.

My large intestine started to slap the crap out of my liver, and I know it showed on my face. She took one look at me, snagged my arm, and hauled me upstairs to my room and stash of food. With a tiny push I was deposited in my desk chair, and she started hunting through my larder.

After a few minutes of confusion on my part, she brought me a glass of water, a box of dried milk, and a bag of granola. My stomach felt like talking to her in a more direct manner than using my tongue and made a noise that sounded like a walrus farting inside a metal box. I knew if I didn't grab at least one of her offerings that I'd end up with my saliva rushing off to find precisely what it wanted, and then having it come back with whatever it had scavenged.

Granola.

After about two handfuls I could tell that they wanted the dry milk. Calcium. The little guys had leeched calcium from somewhere in my body in order to rebuild my nose, and now they were keen on putting back what they'd used. Clever.

I popped the box open and started pouring it into the glass of water, slowly, just for the sake of experimentation. I wanted to see if they'd tell me when to stop, or how much of whatever material was enough. Eventually, the glass of water looked like lumpy buttermilk, and I felt no inclination to pour in anything more than that. I did want to drink it, as horrible as it looked, so I did.

I knew Charlie was watching me while I did this, but she wasn't saying anything. Once I finished with my glass of white mud, I'd see what was up with her... beyond the tongue-lashing and nut massage she'd delivered outside.

"Dried milk mud is not tasty," I said, trying to gum around the gooey mass in my right cheek.

"No, I didn't think it would be either, but you seemed to know what you were doing."

"Bleh." I made faces as I got the bolus to actually go down my throat. "What did I miss with you two?"

She smiled a little and it brightened up the post-Buttons mood a little. "Jaya and I talked about a lot of things and passed around a couple of theories about how the little nano-dudes work. She thinks you can have some kind of control over how they work, because she and Baj had quite a few discussions about this sort of thing over the years."

"Control would be nice. I'd hate to think I gave that bag of shit his own set of critters."

"You probably didn't. That was one of the things Jaya felt was likely to be controllable, or at least limited. Bajali didn't want to make a nanotech virus that didn't have some sort of discrimination about where it went or with whom it started a symbiotic relationship." She held up a finger on each hand. "You've got two major possibilities. One, the nanotech spreads like wildfire. Two, either the nanos are targeted, or the person with whom they've set up shop has some sort of impact on how they move through a population."

"Isn't that three options?"

"No, ya goober. One is no control, and the other is some sort of control."

"Charlie, that's stretching it."

She stuck her tongue out at me. What else is a guy to do? I reached over and grabbed it. She said, "Mmmp?!"

"Sorry. It looked so good that I wanted to keep it for my very own." I let it go, and she smiled.

"Play your cards right, boy, and you never know what you might get to keep."

I had to grin right back at her. At that moment, I didn't want to think about nanotechnology or impending doom; all I wanted was her in my arms.

"Just let me know what I can do to stack the deck in my favor," I told her.

"I will do that."

"Damn. Why does romance have to happen when death is on the line?"

"Frank," she gave me a penetrating look, "when you think you might die, you look for things that make you feel alive. It's human behavior."

"We're not just 'human behavior,' Grandmother, are we?"

She reached out, cupped my unshaven cheek in her hand, smiled gently, and told me, "No. I think we're more than that, or that we're going to be more than that. We just have to keep ourselves alive long enough to see it for certain. That's my plan, anyhow."

"If I don't pull this conversation back around to nanotechnology, I'm going to end up getting seriously romantic at you, and we probably don't have time for it before the meeting."

"Doesn't it just fuck things right in the ass, when you've got stuff you want to do but there are plans you can't change?"

"Yes. No lube at all," I said, utterly frustrated that there was so much going on and I couldn't find a reasonable stopping point to really dig into the feelings we seemed to share. "You were saying Jaya feels as though we might have some control over these little guys? Do we just talk to them or leave notes on the fridge?"

"Brat. She says they respond to damage, but we'd need to run actual experiments to see what else they respond to. Bajali had talked about linking them to the endocrine system for transmission between hosts, white blood cell count and T-cell response, and some other something about the body's electrical system."

"That part about us being hosts sounds really sinister." Actually, the thought gave me chills. It sounded far too much like these little guys had minds of their own and I had nasty images of waking up some morning to find that I'd been given an overhaul while I slept.

"I said the exact same thing."

"Why the endocrine system? Are we supposed to get some kind of boost of adrenaline and start spewing nano-pollen all over the place?" I waved my hands in the air and swayed back and forth, singing, badly, "Oh, aren't I just a lovely daisy! Aren't I just a lovely daisy! Sniff me! Oh, sniff me!"

She fell on the floor laughing, covered her mouth, and

attempted not to make snorting noises when she tried to breathe between attacks of Ha Ha. I had to laugh along with her because her amusement was contagious. I made up my mind for the 20th time that, if anything happened to her, there would be a rubber room for me before or after my descent into bloody revenge.

We should have expected what happened next. You don't stir up a hornet's nest and not end up stung. That is one of the rules of nature that happens to apply to the human animal as well.

The explosion was muffled from where we were, but we heard it, and we knew it couldn't be far away. Charlie got off the floor, and we snagged our weapons and flew down the stairs. By the time we got to the cashier's counter in the middle of the store, there was another explosion somewhere closer that rattled my front windows.

We burst out the front door of the store into pandemonium. I could see the fire from where we stood and the shattered skeleton of Siddig and Miryam's home just down the street. Jayashri was in the driveway with Yolanda and Flower, and there were three wounded people they were working on like mad. Jim and Darcy were trying to douse part of the fire with garden hoses.

I took off running.

I hoped I wouldn't see what I thought I would, because if I did I would come unglued at someone. By the time I was about even with the corner of Shawn's place, a large hand came out, grabbed me, and pulled me into the shadow of the garage.

Shawn used his other hand to snag his sister and pull her to the side as well.

"All right, we got three down," he started in on the data with no preamble, and I was grateful for it. "Nate says it was a mortar, followed by a rocket-propelled grenade or small missile. That means we've got a straight line between them and us. They've got to be past the store on the other side of Route 29, or someplace with elevation to get over the buildings to hit inside our perimeter."

"Shawn. Where's my bag?"

"Where you left it the other day when you got here Charlie!"

She took off into the garage, leaving me with her brother.

"Anyone got a plan?"

"Nate says we either head out there and recon or wait until they lob something else in on us."

Shawn's timing was perfect. We heard the whistle and hit the ground. There was an explosion right in the middle of the road on the other side of the garage. If he hadn't pulled us around the corner when he did, it would have been us being blown to Hell instead of asphalt. It occurred to me they'd actually been aiming for us, but probably stopped direct observation to correct their geometry.

Straight line. They were somewhere over beyond my store, and as soon as I could get there, they'd be dead.

Charlie reappeared and was tricked out like Soldier of Fortune Magazine's idea of a modern valkyrie. Two wakizashi-length swords across her back, Kevlar vest, MOLLE pouches full of clips, and some kind of compact submachine gun that I'd never seen before. Shawn was less than pleased, but I had no time to enjoy the family argument, so I took off back down the street towards our uninvited guests.

Nanotechnology makes you cocky. It also does other things you don't expect, especially when you didn't get the instruction manual with your first dose. I was getting used to the extra sensory range and data that they were handing me, because it was so damned useful.

I knew where the mortar crew was by the time I cleared the far corner of the hardware store. I had four targets. Two M-4 machine guns, four Beretta 9mm pistols, a mortar launcher, and a box with six more mortars in it. They were on the roof of the gas station on the other side of Route 29. Fine with me.

You hurt my people, I'll take exception to that, and then I

will make you pay to the best of my ability.

They were firing at me by the time I got to my side of Route 29. Concrete and asphalt chunks were flying everywhere. I was shot twice, in the upper right thigh and two inches beneath my right clavicle. The bullets went clean through, and I did not even slow down.

Not only did I not slow down, I got the strangest urge to jump up to the top of the gas station, as if I could take a leap of about 12 feet upward. Snarling, half unhinged from the pain and the rage, I went ahead and jumped.

Nanotechnology will surprise you when you don't have a drop-down menu of options.

I landed in front of the nearest zombie, tore the machine gun out of his hands, reversed it, and shoved the barrel through his open mouth. I noted that the barrel continued all the way through the top of his helmet. He collapsed like a 200-lb bag of rice, bringing the barrel of the gun into a beautiful position to stitch Mortar Zombie from crown to crotch with bullets and flying brain bits.

Zombie 3 closed the distance with his 9mm and popped me twice in the abdomen from close range. I gave him my elbow to the bridge of his nose and tried not to collapse from the pain. The remaining undead soldier decided to pretend he was in a movie and put the barrel of his machine gun to my forehead. I wondered if he thought that threat would stop me.

Human beings have two hands for a reason. You can do something with one hand and do something entirely different with the other. I chose to grab the gun barrel and pull it off to the side of my head and pull the Man Scythe free with the other hand.

For Zombie 3, it probably looked like Zombie 4 was spinning me on the dance floor with the barrel of his gun while it was firing into the open air.

The blade clicked into position. I pivoted the barrel over my head as I spun into him. The move wasn't for dancing or looking cool, but to use the momentum for the blade to do the dirty work.

I had expected to sever his spine, not cut him completely in half at the waist. Zombies scream a lot.

By the time I dropped my dance partner's upper half to the top of the gas station, something very sharp and very fast took Number 3's hands off at the wrists. The 9mm, still in a proper two-handed grip, hit the roof, followed very shortly thereafter by his head. Charlie stopped moving, a sword in each hand, and did a very fast, formal-looking motion that snapped the remaining blood off the blades.

"God. You're hot!" It came out as more of a croak than my normal suave and debonair diction.

"You know it, Mister. Sorry I'm late. I needed to convince my bro that I could handle the prom without him."

"Well, I must say, you are the belle of the ball and I'm entirely happy to see you. I do think I need to sit down now."

"You hit?"

"Four. The first two don't even look like they're there. The last two were gut shots, and they really hurt. I think that I'm going to get the cramps any minute." I flopped down, right on top of the body that I'd bisected. At that point, I was less concerned with the organs and gore than I was with whether or not my nano-buddies were going to be able to fix the latest damage.

My personal Angel of Mercy tore my favorite shirt right down the middle. I didn't really have enough energy to complain about it, and the pain was getting to be quite distracting.

"Oh. Fuck."

"Sorry. I think that's out of the question right now." It felt good to be just a little flip about the situation, even if it got me a seriously stern expression for the effort. "Hey, I'm just waiting for the boys to go ahead and do their thing. A little humor makes everything go faster."

The Pearl of my Delight said unto me, "Oh, they've started working all right. I think I need to go throw up over the side of the building. Be right back." She did exactly what she said she needed to do. It sounded horrible from where I was reclining.

"Why, what's going on?" I tried to sit up and get a better look, but I couldn't. Whole muscle groups were not paying attention to my brain, and I couldn't help but feel as though that didn't bode very well at all. "What are the little bastards doing, and why can't I sit up?"

Charlie walked back over and looked down into my face, and it was utterly clear to me that she was making an effort to not look back down at whatever had made her toss her cookies.

"I think that the nanos are scavenging," she said, looking a little green under the chin. With her complexion, it was easy to see the difference. "And," a look of revulsion passed across that lovely face, followed by a full-body shiver, "they're carting it back to where you've been shot."

"Oh." There wasn't a whole lot I could say to that, but there were still unanswered questions that I needed to ask. "What, pray tell, are they scavenging?"

She closed her eyes and swallowed hard before she spoke. "The body that you're lying on top of."

"All right. Which parts?" I used to watch an anime called "Hitman Reborn." There was a character in it, a hitman no less, named Lambo. He was a 5-year-old little boy who looked like he was the product of crossbreeding with a cow. His trademark line was, "Must. Keep. Calm." I call it my Lambo Mantra, and I was making great use of it.

"Frank, if I tell you, I'm going to need to run to the side of the building again."

"Charlie, I wouldn't ask if I wasn't really freaked out by this myself. If they're grabbing bits that have viral material, I'm going to be fucked sideways. I need to know what they're doing, and I can't get up to see for myself."

"Oh God. I'll try." There was a definite air of girding her loins before she continued, in a very controlled monotone, "There is a gray stream of fluid flowing from the lower hole in your abdomen into the... subject's ear. There is a second stream of pinkish-gray material flowing from the subject's nostril, back up your body, and into the hole."

Must. Keep. Calm.

"What did you say, Frank?"

"Oh. Sorry. That was my out-loud voice. It sounds like they went for brains, not other organs. I might not come out of this with the virus on top of needing psychotherapy for the rest of my life." I thought about it again for a moment. "I bet my mother never expected I'd be happy to have gray matter on the menu. Mmmm. Brains!"

There was a wet burping noise, then she clapped both hands over her mouth and hurried over to the side of the building. If I had the opportunity, I would have liked to join her, because I was feeling incredibly nauseous about it all. What I didn't expect was a loud verbal complaint from over the side of the building, two gunshots, and Charlie flying backwards onto the roof beside me.

She hit with an explosive exhale and sprang back up into a crouch. After a quick patdown she determined that her vest had caught the bullets. She snarled down in her throat, and I will admit to a moment of genuine pity for whoever had shot at her. I got to watch her unsheathe both of her swords, stand back up, and then jump off the side of the building.

I heard disjointed curses and a few heartfelt screams of pain very shortly after she hit the ground. They probably didn't notice that she was wearing a vest or expect a snarling hottie to fall from the sky with a sword in each hand. What a unique way to die!

"What did you catch down there, my Luscious Partner in Mayhem?"

Laughter. "Two more. They're not going to be a problem now."

"Did anybody go after the dudes with the rocket-propelled grenades?"

There was a pause before she replied. "I think I just got

them."

"Oh? Why?"

"Because one of them had it strapped to his back, you goober!"

A positive gain in our group weapons stash, but the cost was mighty high.

"Do me a favor, I need to know what's going on. Is Siddig's house still on fire?"

"Looks like it," she yelled back, "but not fully involved."

"Who were they working on in the driveway?"

She didn't answer.

I didn't ask a second time because I was fairly sure what the answer was, and there was not a single thing I could do about it one way or another. Nanotechnology might let me jump around, heal wounds, and be able to tell you how close an enemy is, but it was not a time machine. Admitting to myself that I was powerless to do anything about the events unfolding in front of me was agony.

You're supposed to protect people you love and care about. People who love you are supposed to do the same. People you care about aren't supposed to die horrible deaths. Somewhere, sometime during my life, I started to believe those things and never really managed to grow into a more pragmatic and adult view of life. Consequently, powerlessness and loss didn't sit well with me at all.

All I could do was wait until I could move again.

"Charlie?" I had to shout because I had no idea where she was. The nano-buddies were so occupied that they weren't feeding me data. At least, I assumed that was the deal.

"Yes?" She sounded like she hadn't moved very far at all.

"You don't have to stick around. You could head back and I'll meet you when my little friends are finished."

"No. I'm not leaving you."

My heart thudded extra hard. Had the situation been different I would probably have started professing my undying affection right then and there, but it was hampered by the grayish-pink stream of goo that was moving into my body. As things stood, I was starting to feel like I'd be able to move in the not-too-distant future.

In the relative quiet of the gas station rooftop abattoir I started thinking about the likelihood that Hightower was not though with us for the day. A large force that could overwhelm us made some sense, but so did small guerrilla attacks like this one. We could be whittled down over the course of a few days, with a larger mop-up operation to follow.

There was a certain "bonus" to small attacks, from an opponent's point of view, and that was how demoralizing repetitive loss of life would be for our community. I didn't know if I would go back to the neighborhood to find we'd lost someone, or a few someones. That was frightening to contemplate, even if I was fairly sure it would be the case.

Siddig's home had been hit in the late afternoon. They were good Muslims and prayed five times a day in their living room. That room faced the road. There were three people being triaged in the driveway. It was very easy to see what there was to be afraid of, and how badly it would hurt to be right.

I wondered whether this might not have happened if Buttons hadn't decided to show off. I needed someone or something I could vent at, and he was a splendid target. Whether I was right or wrong about the railgun precipitating the attack, it was something I could hang my frustration and rage on. I could apologize later, if any of us were alive to bother with it.

Sometimes you have to give yourself permission to sink into darker emotions.

"Charlie," I shouted.

"Yes?"

"Would you hop up here? I think I'm almost able to move, and I want to get back across the street before anything else can happen." I shifted around a little but couldn't sit up yet. The muscle wall of my abdomen probably wasn't 100 percent finished being rebuilt with zombie brains. I wish I hadn't thought that.

Between one thought and another, my valkyrie landed on the roof and walked over to where I was wriggling uselessly.

"Need a hand?" With a smile, she offered me hers and I took it.

"Easy up, now. Don't strain anything." She tugged, and I came up on my feet. A bit wobbly, but stable.

"Er, that's a little uncomfortable, but at least I'm on my feet." I was able to look down and didn't appear to be trailing a tail of nano-technological goo. Unconsciously, my hands found the areas that should have had scars or bullet holes, but were met with tender new skin instead. Even the exit wounds were sealed over.

"I'm going to strip the weapons from these bodies. Will you be okay just standing there for a few minutes?"

"Yeah, I think so." I turned toward her and said what I felt, "Thank you for staying with me."

That led to a lifetime first for me. Up until that point, I had never been kissed on the roof of a garage with my feet in a pile of entrails. It was so passionate I forgot entirely about everything in my head and at my feet, just so I could enjoy the pure physical delight of that moment. When we pulled away from one another, we were both grinning like fools with flushed cheeks and giddy laughter. The only thing that spoiled the moment was Charlie looking down at her feet, noticing what she was stepping in.

"Aw, man. That's just nasty shit."

"It might be. That's half a bladder right there."

Standing right in front of me, she screwed up her face into a combination of Buddha with gas pains and an angry Maori. It was equal parts endearing and horrible. I guess she was at a loss for words and let her fingers do the talking by punching me in the shoulder. I said, "Ow," and she told me, in no uncertain terms, that I deserved it. Probably true.

After a few minutes, she'd collected all the arms and

ammo, and we'd hopped back down to ground level. I picked up the other stack of goodies, and we walked back across the street.

I could see Siddig's house from the sidewalk, and the fire had been reduced to smoldering wood. The bodies in the driveway were gone, and I had no clue what that meant or didn't mean. It didn't seem as though we'd been gone long enough for things to resolve this much.

"How long were you waiting for me before I asked you to come up and help me stand?"

"According to my little friends, I was waiting for one hour, forty-three minutes, and sixteen seconds."

"That's a lot longer than it felt. Were you watching things over here at all?"

"Yes."

"They got the fire under control, I see."

"They did," she told me, nodding gently.

"What happened to everyone in the driveway?" I had to know.

"Jaya and everyone else stopped working on the... victims... before I got Shawn to let me go."

Having a feeling that something bad has happened is no preparation for being told, directly, that what you were worried about is exactly what happened. It felt like my heart fell into my stomach, and it was filled with ice cubes.

"Siddig, Miryam, and their son?"

"Yes. I'm so sorry, Frank."

Must. Keep. Calm.

"Let's drop this stuff off in the store before we go anywhere else."

Staying calm is one of those things that, in certain situations, is much easier said than done. Walking into the store, I tried to keep my mind as blank as possible, which is another one of the litany of activities that is nearly impossible when your heart is in your throat.

While the store was my place, it was also a reliquary of every memory I had made in it. It contained them and defined them in a way that reminded me of what cathedrals, with all their art and imagery, did for the lives of the people who worshiped in them. Another comparison would be what someone's family home might mean for them.

I didn't have a family home that gave me those things. All I ever wanted was to get away from those places where we had lived, mostly because they had so little meaning. In that store, essentially where I'd taken up suburban squatting, I had found the feeling of home that I'd wandered around trying to find. I also understood the price of "home" for the first time.

The place that I felt was my home now had more memories of senseless loss attached to it.

Months ago, when the zombies came for Mister Yan and we'd lost all those people, I learned that those eight people didn't mean to me what Siddig and his family meant to me. Those eight people were fighting in a war for our community when they were killed and were part of a different faction in the neighborhood to begin with. I wasn't at all close to them, and they never made any effort to hold a hand out to me.

I'd bounced Siddig Junior on my knee. There were not a few summer nights when we had all been sprawled on their lawn, listening to Miryam sing. I don't think any of us spoke a lick of Arabic or Farsi, but it didn't matter. Siddig, himself, came from a long line of drummers and would often accompany his wife's gorgeous singing. I cared about these people.

Now. Memories.

Charlie nudged me forward. I didn't realize I'd been standing dead still in the middle of the store, but I had been. I made some sort of affirmative noise at her, and we kept moving towards the stairs in the back. Somehow, she must have realized I don't leave weapons out where any of the kids could get at them, because she was taking the lead. I just followed her and was grateful for it.

My room used to be the manager's office, and it stretched

across the back of the store, one floor above the shop itself. Desk, chair, sleeping stuff, and lots and lots of shelves. I lived according to an unwritten rule: If you're a trader, you're also a hoarder. My shelves looked that way, but I could always find an open one to start a new category of stuff.

Handguns in the dresser, slides racked, and any bullets "in the pipe" removed before storage. The clips are in a separate drawer with other ammunition, sorted by type of firearm. The mortars and mortar launcher went on a shelf of their own. The new grenade/rocket launcher thing was a tad long for a shelf, so we stowed it in the corner between sets of shelves.

The meeting would be happening soon, and there would be many decisions made that would alter the course of our lives. Worse come to worst, it could mean the ends of lives, not the preservation. Buttons doing his thing had cost us lives and choices, and whether or not it was reasonable of me or even if it was his fault in the first place, I wanted to flay him alive.

More than that, I really hoped that my moment of Sturm und Drang earlier in the day had not left him with a batch of nanotech cooties. It would be a waste to have someone that slimy, useful or not, get a prize for being a creeping example of intestinal effluvia. All I'd be able to do would be to flay him, feed his cooties a live zombie, rinse, and repeat until my rage went away.

My Partner in Completely Justified Reprisal and I turned back toward the door of my space at the same time. Male, at the foot of the stairs, armed, and not a member of the undead minority.

"Frank? Charlie? Any of you people up there?" Shawn, thank goodness. Had it been Buttons, I probably would have blown my own door off the hinges just to jump on him from the top of the stairs. It saved my door and a whole raft of mess.

"Yeah, we're up here," Charlie yelled.

"Everybody will be here for the meeting in about half an hour. Y'all good with that?"

"Yeah. We'll be fine. Come on up and see the new stuff."

The stairs creaked a little bit as he came up. The Shawn is not a tiny man, and even if he didn't have a little extra weight he still would have been a miniature giant. This is to say nothing of the muscles, of which there were many.

"I'm going to open the door. Everybody decent?"

"Knocker, the man wouldn't have invited you up here if we were getting busy!" There's no love like family love, and no annoyance like being cheesed-off at a sibling. I had lived through my share of that.

He came through the door, blushing, and looking somewhat strained around the edges.

"Sis, I've known you since you were born, and there is not one bit of strange shit I would put past you, if you put your mind to it. Hell, it was bad enough to know you two had been all naked in that tub!"

"Shawn, you've got a fuckin' dirty mind. No wonder Mama beat you so often," she said. Her voice was not at all congruent with her actions, because you don't reach out and hug someone that hard when it sounds like you'd prefer to see them kicked to death by drag queens.

Regardless, it was a really warm thing to watch, and I wanted to add my own squirt of amity to the proceedings, but I held myself in check. They broke the embrace, and she elbowed me aside so she could walk her brother down to see the mortar and grenade launcher. Family bonding over military ordinance—I wondered if that qualified as an American value.

"I'm going to change my shirt while you guys are poking around in my drawers." I set about trying to find another shirt, woefully consigning my favorite one to the Sack of Useful Rags.

"Frank."

I turned around, said "Shawn," and waggled my eyebrows.

"Your back has healed and there aren't even any scars." In less than a second, he'd thrown Charlie behind him, and his sidearm had cleared the holster with the barrel pointed right between my eyes. "What the Hell are you?"

Oh. Shit.

"Shawn, I'm Frank," I told him, raising my hands and pitching my voice as carefully as I could. "We were going to tell people about this at the meeting... "

"What the fuck are you?" He cut me clean off.

"Bajali sent us a nanotechnology early Christmas present with the zombie that blew up this morning. It was Mister Yan, all right? Now put the gun down. I don't know if I'd survive a bullet to the face."

"Mister Yan? Nanotechnology? How incredibly stupid do you think I am?"

"Brother, put the gun down. Frank is not lying. I was here when Mister Yan showed up." Charlie was using a voice much like mine, the sort of tone you'd use to talk to an upset child.

"Charlie, you keep your wide ass out of this. This fucker is going to answer my question, or I'll end him right now." Shawn was edging closer to yelling, and that did not seem like a good thing.

"Shawn James Cooper, you will put that gun down right now, or I will," I heard her pull the hammer back on one of her revolvers, "put a slug through you."

"Charlie," he escalated to full yelling, "I will not! You aren't going to shoot your own brother. You fucking will not do such a thing! Now, shut the Hell up until this shit is settled!"

I kept very quiet. It seemed like a smart way to approach this *awkward situation*. Ho, ho! I am so droll.

"You're right, I probably wouldn't shoot you." She dropped the calm voice and allowed herself to sound as distressed as she felt. "Brother, I love you so much, but if you kill the man I'm falling in love with before you hear us out, I will never speak to you again and I will leave our family forever."

Falling in love? Me? Charlie? Cherubs started to appear at the edge of my field of vision, and I wanted to get down to a serious jam session of harp plucking.

Important note: Do not let the flights of angels appear until *after* the close-to-murderous brother has chilled out. The harp music will only confuse him and make him angry.

My perturbed friend looked like someone had just shoved a live eel in his boxers, but his gun lowered. I was fine with anyone having an eel in his shorts, rather than be occupied with pointing a weapon between my eyes.

"Because you're my sister, I'll give you two minutes to explain before I put a hole through its head. I don't care if you're falling in love with *it* or not."

"Shawn, Frank's not an *it* and neither am I." She walked around him, effectively blocking a shot at me by standing between us. "Bajali sent Mister Yan to tell us Hightower is going to try and wipe us out in a few days. We found out Mister Yan didn't just bring information. Frank's body started to reject all the sutures this morning after breakfast with Jayashri."

He did not look like he believed a word she was saying.

Charlie went on, "Mister Yan went to see Jaya before he came here. He left her with a bundle of nanotechnology, and because I was here watching over Frank when he came over I got them too."

Having your friend put the barrel of his gun in the middle of your future main squeeze's chest is not something for which many people are prepared. I certainly wasn't. There weren't many choices available that didn't involve someone dying; in this case, it was likely to be Shawn. Charlie and I would probably survive, although I was doubtful about living through a bullet to the head. Nanotechnology rebuilding brain tissue did not seem like a reasonable thing to expect.

"Why have you pointed a loaded gun at me?" Charlie asked him that question, and I couldn't tell whether or not there were tears running down her face, but it certainly sounded like there ought to be.

"Because I don't know if you're my sister anymore."

"Yeah, I'm your sister and I always will be. I'm just a little more than that right now, and we've all got a lot to lose if we don't get this right. I need you to see something, and it is going to freak you the Hell out."

"What is it?" my mountainous friend asked, looking like someone told him they were about to eat their own vomit with a spoon.

"I'm going to ask Frank to hand me a sharp knife, and then I'm going to show you something a zombie can't do. I am not going to cut you or stab you. Can you watch before you decide you need to kill me or Frank?"

Shawn nodded in a vague sort of way, Charlie turned to me and nodded, and I tracked down a knife. For whatever reason, things were incredibly quiet and tense. Likely, it was the fabled calm before the storm, because the opportunity for a tornado of tragedy seemed to be in the forecast if things went the wrong way.

It only took me a minute to put my hands on a knife, a sharp lockback folding knife that had been sitting on my desk. I had some idea of what she was planning to do, and I probably would have done something similar if she hadn't put herself between me and her brother.

I had a mini-moment of Alternate Universe in which life was normal, and I saw how dramatic a family holiday dinner with these people could be. It was enough to give anyone pause.

The knife I'd handed to Charlie had a 3.5-inch blade. She held out her left arm and plunged the blade in, up to the handle.

"Ow! Holy Mother of God," she screamed it out and proceeded to hop around with her left arm out and her right hand over her eyes. "Jesus! Fuck this bad-ass heroine bullshit! No lube! Ouch! Fuck! Fuck!"

There wasn't much blood because she didn't pull the

blade out. I think it was bad enough, however, considering Shawn's delightful Aryan skin tone had gone white as a sheet with tints of green. This isn't to say that I was at all thrilled with the tableau, because I wasn't.

"God! Shawn, pull out my Dramatic Statement! Right now!"

He was on automaton mode, because he probably would have complained about it any other time. Instead, he reached over, grabbed the handle, and pulled it straight out. I watched his eyes change focus from Charlie to the knife in his hand. Half the blade was eaten away, and there was not a single drop of blood on it.

On one level, it was gruesome and disturbing as Hell, and on another, it was sickeningly funny. Shawn's eyes got huge. It was like looking at a hairy china plate with two green-brown spots on it.

I really, really hoped that he wouldn't spew all over my floor.

"Earth to Shawn!" Charlie waved at him from less than four feet away and managed to catch his attention. "Look at my arm. Stop looking at the knife and look at my arm. Arm. Here."

It took him a minute, but he looked. There wasn't a drop of blood or anything to be seen other than smooth skin. The hairy china plate of his face developed a small jaw-hitting-the-floor problem.

"That's the gift Bajali gave us. Frank healed, I can heal, and I bet Jaya can, too. I'm still your sister, and they're still your friends. Now put the gun away and give me a hug and a kiss."

With motion that would have been more typical of a remote control robot toy, Shawn put the gun back in the holster and his arms around his sister. She kissed him on the cheek with an odd look of concentration on her face. He relaxed a little bit and hugged her even harder.

They stepped back, smiled awkwardly, and I suddenly had a large country boy giving me a bear hug and patting me on the back hard enough to dislodge my lung on that side. Damn me for not paying better attention to my environment.

He finally let me go, looked at us both, and said, "I'm gonna go downstairs and puke. That okay with you guys?"

"Oh yeah, don't let us hold you up! We'll see you in a few minutes at the meeting," Charlie said, patted him on the back, and led him gently over to the door. He went through, and she closed it behind him. After a long count of 30, she walked over to me and put her arms around my waist.

"Uh, hi there. What was that about falling in love with me?"

"Shush, Frank. I just didn't want him to try and kill you. Seemed like the best thing I could say at the time."

"No," I retorted, poking the end of her upturned nose. "The best thing to say at the time would have been, 'Don't kill him, he's your best friend,' not tell him I'm the guy you're falling in love with. You're silly."

"What? You didn't like my solution to the problem?"

"No." I was all serious. "I liked it very much and I want it to be real."

"Oh. I see. Lucky for you, I'm just giving you shit about it."

She kissed me like she meant it. It was the sort of lip-lock that turns boys into men, launches a thousand ships, burns topless towers, and makes being alive completely worth the pain and hard work.

When our tongues finished their Judo tournament with four out of five falls going to me, we took a moment to catch our breath. I am a shameful man, because I couldn't stop watching her breathe, even with a bulletproof vest on. Some part of my brain wanted her dressed in an apron, with a plate full of warm cookies, a lewd expression on her face, and a long Saturday afternoon to enjoy that experience.

"Would you do me a favor?"

"Sure, baby," the Southern Hotness replied.

"Ask for an inexpensive knife next time. Please?"

"Don't worry your high and tight little head about it, Sugar Nuts. I am never, ever going to pull a stunt like that again. Never. Ever." She was shaking her head and smiling ruefully. I don't doubt that stabbing yourself like that has to be a seriously painful experience, and I certainly wasn't going to be macho and try it myself.

"So! Race you to the meeting?"

She didn't say a word, but she took off out the door and started down the steps. My macho took the form of jumping off the platform in front of my door, onto the floor below. It worked just fine, inhumanly so. For the moment, I shoved that to the back of my head and concentrated on the fact that I had won.

I got chased into the storeroom by a friendly, yet irate, blond woman.

Chapter 26

Grandmother Yan was already there, setting out coffee mugs and jugs of cider and water, and I went directly over to her because I had made a promise. She saw me coming and smiled with such happiness and warmth that I nearly froze solid. Periodically, you get to see flashes of just how much you mean to someone else, or a clear view of precisely how they feel about you. That qualified as one of those moments and all I could do was hug her.

I leaned down to her ear, the left one, because the right one didn't work quite as well as it used to work. "Grandmother, Chunhua, you know Mister Yan loved you very much. Don't you?"

"Yes. I always know this. He come visit you?" Chunhua Yan, looked up into my face and must have seen what I didn't say, because she simply nodded. "He was very ashamed to be zombie. I know he love me with all his heart."

"How did you know?" I had to ask.

"Ay-yah! Young people know nothing about love!" She gave me the Grandmother Yan trademark pat on the cheek and went on. "You see shadow on you wall before sun comes up, is maybe two thing: you have dirty person in neighborhood, or you zombie husband looking in on you. No dirty people here look at old Chinese lady, so is zombie husband."

All right. Her English was alternately good and bad, whenever she felt like it, but her brain was working just fine all the time. I couldn't see any point in not going for full disclosure.

"He set off one of the bombs after he came to see me."

"Ah. Not surprise for me. He was a good man, always." I got another cheek pat. "You much like him, a good man. Maybe you find good woman now? Tattoo girl, not much on tattoo, but look like good choice to Grandmother Yan."

"You are too wise for me, Grandmother."

She covered her mouth and giggled at me.

"No. No. I too old for you. She look healthy, fun in sack, make you strong baby. You know, you never stop thinking, you get old, then people tell you, 'Oh, you so wise. Grandmother.' Make me laugh!"

Fun in the sack and make strong baby for me. I tried not to sputter. Then I noticed something: she looked better and was moving more easily than usual.

"Grandmother? How is your arthritis?"

"You know, I feel very good today. Nothing hurts. Feel so good, I want to have," she made the classic sake, little cup drinking gesture, and grinned in a very evil way, "good wine and handsome old man." I got another pat on the cheek and she said, "So, you find handsome old man, you send to Grandmother! Now, you go kiss pretty girl and make me happy!"

I got turned around and shooed away.

What else could I do, I walked back over to Charlotte Marie "Fun in Sack, Make Strong Baby" Cooper and gave her a decent kiss. Grandmother clapped and whistled behind me.

"What was that about?" Charlie wondered.

"Well, I think her husband dropped some nano-pixie dust on her windowsill this morning before visiting Jaya and the two of us. Her arthritis has let up, her cheeks are pink, and she's interested in getting drunk and tripping up a cute old man."

"Oh my goodness," she laughed in an endearingly merry way, "I'm almost worried about what a Nanotechnology Grandmother could do!"

"I bet she could kick some ass. She's scary smart and sly. I'd be worried to find her an old guy to go drinking with. She'd give him a heart attack."

People began filtering in. Gina and Mark looked a little gray after the day's events, and I strongly suspected that most everyone would be similarly subdued. Nate and Flower came in together, with sidearms very apparent on their belts. The rest of Nate's crew tumbled in shortly after.

Buttons, an Asian guy I hadn't met, and another fellow who at least looked as though I'd seen him at some point or another, showed up with their own folding chairs. I was willing to give them a certain amount of props for that sort of forward thinking, but not much beyond that. I was still seething somewhere underneath my bemused exterior, and the thought of taking Buttons out back and giving him a messy final moment was percolating with increasing vigor.

Shawn and Jayashri arrived at the same time, followed very shortly by Yolanda and her husband. Before too long, the room was as full as it could be, and it was pretty clear that everyone was ready to get things moving forward.

Normally, Bajali would chair the meetings, but his absence made something of a hole. No one looked quite willing to fill it, so I did an unusual thing and stepped up to the plate.

"I'm glad you all could make it," I began with no small amount of nervousness, "but I'd really like to know that someone is looking after the kids right now."

Flower stood up and said, "Yes. Barbara is looking after them, as usual, but they're all here in the store," and sat back down.

"Okay. I was hoping someone would think to have them closer to hand than the last time we had a meeting." There were a few muffled affirmative noises in answer to my comment. "We have a few major things to discuss on the heels of today's events, not the least of which is some major information about what we can expect within the next two days, if not sooner."

I hated that I had to say all of this, but it looked like no one else was willing to do it. What else could I do but keep going?

"Bajali sent us a message early this morning, in the form of a visitor to our neighborhood who blew himself up on his way out. Warren Hightower will, within the next three days, attempt to wipe us off the map. I suspect today's attack was one of two things. Firstly, retaliation for our guest, Mister Buttons, who blew up the top of a building where Hightower's sniper was located. Secondly, today's tragic attack may well be the first shot in a continuing offensive designed to whittle us down before mopping us up in a few days."

The room erupted into noise, which I tuned out. Flower had turned around in his seat to face Buttons, and from the look on Mister B's face, something was about to go down.

"All y'all, shut the Hell up!" Shawn's voice boomed out into the room, silencing everything but the sound of people breathing heavily. He stood up and walked over to stand beside me. "What you have to say is important, don't get me wrong, but what we *do* from this moment forward is more important than anything else. They're coming to kill us all, just like they tried to do today, and we've got a serious choice on our hands. Do we stay and fight, or do we all just bug out and head for the hills? That's what we need to decide first."

Everyone had their eyes on him, and so did I. I went and sat down with Jayashri and Charlie. It seemed like a sound policy to let the man say what he needed to say.

"If anyone decides to escape this shit we've been handed, then I will say to them, 'God bless you, and I hope you find safety and happiness wherever you end up,' and that'll be the end of it. I am not going to ask someone to stand up beside me, and probably die with me, if that is not what they want to do." Shawn took a deep breath, wiped his forehead with the back of his hand, and kept right on going. "What I will do is tell you this: this is my home and you are my family. I will stay and defend what we have built together, because I choose to do that. Every one of you who stays gives us that much more of a chance that this will not be the last of us, and every one of you who goes will make us fight that much harder because you're not here to help."

Shawn ran his fingers through his hair and looked us all over as if he was making sure all the sheep were in the herd. I wasn't sure I could have done a better job saying what needed to be said than he was doing at the time. There are only so many ways to raise an army from a diverse group of people, even if a common foe has arrived on the scene at the proper time. My friend was working with a classic paradigm: I'm going to fight whether or not you do, and my unspoken challenge to you is for you to stand beside me.

"I've said my piece, but there is one small bit left. If you aren't going to stay, then you have other things you need to do that are more important than sitting here and listening to us plan. Go home, start getting your lives as mobile as you can make them, and please be safe out there when you go." He took a deep breath, shook out his shoulders, and plowed right in on the rest of it. "Everybody who is going to stay and fight, we've got some work to do."

No one moved. I didn't hear a chair scrape the floor nor a single ass wriggle where it sat. Shawn, my mountain man, brother in arms, bowed his head. I'm not sure anyone beyond the front row heard him say, "Thank you, God," under his breath. When his head came back up, he was a different person, more determined than I'd ever seen, and I was proud to have the chance to be with him.

"Looks to me like we're in this together. Thank you. Before we really get down into it, I'd like us to have a moment of silence for the loved ones we lost today. I would say a blessing for them, but I was raised Christian and don't know what's appropriate. If anyone has the right words, I'd appreciate your help."

Someone in the back of the room started speaking in Arabic, and I turned to see who it was.

The Asian man who had come in with Buttons finished reciting, and then he shared it with us in English. "Allah, forgive our living and our dead, those who are here with us and those who are not, our young and our old, our men and our women. Allah, forgive him and have mercy on him, honor the place where he settles and make his entrance wide; wash him with water and snow and hail, and cleanse him of sin as a white garment is cleansed of dirt. Allah, most merciful, admit him to Paradise and protect him from the torment of the grave and the torment of Hellfire." He looked up at the rest of us, nodded, and said, "That's all I remember."

There were mutters of gratitude, and then the room fell silent. In my head, I knew there were no words spoken for two minutes and eighteen seconds, but it felt like an eternity to my heart. Shawn spoke up and invited Jaya to speak to everyone.

She stood, turned to face all of us, and began, "The messenger who brought us the information this morning also brought a gift from my husband, as well as his love that I should share with all of you. As you know, he was to be working on nanotechnology for our enemy; however, things did not go as planned. What he was able to do before the project ground to a halt was create a series of nanomachines that would optimize the normal human body for the rigors of combat. That was the gift sent to me." She pointed at Charlie and me. "They were also recipients of the information I was given, as well as the same gift of technology. You are all aware of how close Frank came to dying, and he is here, without a single scar to show for what he endured as a result of saving the children."

No one said a thing. I couldn't tell if it was some general state of shock or disbelief, but I would have expected more reaction than none at all.

"My husband designed these machines to propagate within a community of emotionally involved individuals. Human beings who share bonds of affection secrete hormones and chemicals in response to those bonds. The nanotechnology spreads when those chemicals are present in the host, directly to other people within a four-meter range who are also secreting the same chemicals."

That got a bit of a reaction—everyone in the room gasped and rocked back in their chairs. Jayashri pulled me up and asked me to speak about it.

"All right, everyone, hear me out. There is a better than average chance that everyone in our community has become hosts to these little guys. If you have a bad set of cramps that cause you to crave and consume really odd things, like your silverware, it isn't a pregnancy. It's the nano-buddies. You may pass out after you eat whatever they want you to eat. Don't worry! You'll wake up!"

My neighbors and friends gave me some very funny looks.

I just kept going, explaining what I'd experienced, and how I'd already coped with being shot five times. That drew quite a few appreciative nods and a few questions I deliberately answered without discussing how the critters would scavenge available tissue in order to make battlefield repairs. Sometimes it is worth glossing over disturbing facts when you're presenting a group of people with something that was already challenging to absorb.

I told them about the dried milk ball instead. That got a laugh or two and some screwed-up expressions of disgust. Make 'em laugh and it will be easier to swallow than a wad of dried dairy products.

Shawn patted me on the shoulder and whispered in my ear. "Does that mean I got these damned things running around inside me?"

"I don't know. What happened after you came downstairs?"

"Well," he got an odd expression on his face, "I had this really fucked up urge to lick a shovel."

I had to smile at him. "Did you lick it like a good Knocker should?" Watch me tempt fate.

"Aw, man. Don't you start! Yeah, I licked the shovel and flopped over for about 10 minutes."

"In that case, you're the first giant country nanotechnology-enhanced male descendant of Southern freedom fighters! Congrats!"

There are places in the world where the sort of look he gave me would have been accompanied by everyone in the immediate vicinity holding up mystical gestures meant to ward off the evil eye. I just smiled back at him, because I still owed him for punching me when we argued and then giving my back a poke before all the technological fun began. A little snarky behavior would prime the pump for serious teasing at some later date.

"Although," I thought to myself, "if I manage to get really involved with Charlie, that might be revenge enough." My hindbrain chose that moment to mule-kick my frontal lobes. "Okay, yes, I will be getting as deeply involved in her as humanly possible. That will be splendid revenge as well as carnally satisfying. Fine! Just don't kick me like that again." The hindbrain snickered and retreated to the warm, dark place that it favored for moist contemplations.

Shawn grunted, turned to everyone, and called the meeting back to order.

"All right, since we're gonna fight, we need to break things down and start putting together our contingency plans. I need Nate, Barbara, Jim, Darcy, and Omér on the issue of keeping the kids safe. Mark, Gina, Barry, Katherine, and I will get into local defense strategy. I'd also like input from," he gestured at Nate's friends, "y'all on this. Flower, you pick whomever you want for offensive planning. Jaya, would you grab Yolanda and whomever else you need to arrange for triage and first aid?"

Everyone broke down into their respective teams, and my whiteboard was commandeered by Gina for planning nasty surprises. Buttons and his people meandered over to Flower and began some rather animated discussion about things exploding. Charlie and I looked over the groups and wondered where we belonged.

"What do we do?" I asked Charlie, as if she knew any better than I did. She shrugged and wandered over to her brother, leaving me standing in the middle of the floor, looking like an idiot.

"Stewart!" Buttons waved me over. Joy.

"Yes, Mister I'll Nuke Them From Space, Just To Be Sure?"

"You need to be on the offensive team if there's going to be one," he told me. Flower nodded emphatically. "Your skills are more than up to par for it, and you've got a good relationship with Bajali Sharma."

"That's certainly true, but why are we discussing attacking them instead of defending ourselves?"

Flower spoke up, "It's a little counterintuitive, yes, but it makes a lot of sense. If Hightower commits the bulk of his people here, there will be fewer zombies available there to resist a small team of well-equipped people. At most, we send over five to rescue Baj and destroy as much as possible on the way out."

I nodded. Whether or not I liked the idea of not being here to defend my home and my extended family, the thought of bringing Baj back and busting infrastructure at the same time certainly caught my interest. Not being a tactician, I couldn't say if having five fewer people on defense would make a huge difference. We needed every person, surely, but we also needed substantially more firepower.

"All right, let's say for the moment that I'm in. How are we going to compensate for five people *not* being here to watch the home fires?"

The Asian fellow who had prayed spoke up. "I'm Shoei Omura. No fancy nicknames. We have significant firepower available to us onsite, not to mention using the orbital resources that you've been told about. Assuming we have a few days to act in, that will give us six shots from orbit to destroy, distract, or delay the opposing force."

No nonsense. I could like this guy. "Okay, what sort of firepower are we talking about? I'm assuming you had to have brought it with you, because I don't know about it."

Flower chuckled quietly. "Frank, you don't know everything that goes on in the neighborhood. You do spend a lot of time whacking zombies, and sometimes you miss... ahem... the occasional delivery from interested parties."

"Ah. Would you be so kind as to speak clearly about this issue?" I wasn't annoyed, per se, but I was intensely curious about whatever it was that I wasn't, and had not been made, aware of.

"Haven't you ever wondered where Gina gets her chemicals? Or the frangible material she packs the anti-personnel IEDs with?" If he hadn't been twiddling his thumbs, I think he'd have patted me on my blind little skull. "We also have several crates of automatic weapons, ammunition, grenades, and other goodies in my basement. Buttons, Omura, and Channing have a few other interesting toys besides the orbital ones. Want to fill him in?"

The third mouse, I assume he was Channing, smiled and told me about the fun they had in boxes, waiting to be assembled. "It's a compact, multi-node, automated Active Area Denial System. We set it up, and nobody wants to be within 200 feet of the emitters."

"Dilithium crystal drain cleaner, what?" I had no clue what he was telling me, other than he looked really pleased with it.

"Did you never watch the news or read *Wired*?" He was a younger fellow than either Omura or Buttons, and had he not been wearing black fatigues, I'd have been willing to bet there would have been a pocket protector in his daily wardrobe.

"Not if I could help it in either case. Why?"

"The Active Area Denial System," his tone showed he was clearly offended I knew nothing about his Precious, "is the closest thing we have to an anti-personnel force field. They call it the Pain Ray. Anyone within range of the device is bombarded with non-lethal, but incredibly painful microwaves. No one, and I mean NO ONE, can bear to be anywhere near it."

"Gosh. Thank you, Mister Worf." Oh, the dirty look I got! If it had been like the thing he was describing, I would have been boiled alive. "So, if we set it up, it will keep zombies from physically entering an area?"

"Yes. This is a scaled-down version of the original. If we were to, say, put a node at every clear entry into this neighborhood, nothing with functioning nerve endings would be able to come through that point. They'd have to shoot into the area, disable the units, or spend time coming through booby-trapped buildings."

"Shiny, Mister Worf! Shiny! Doesn't do much for rockets or a Bradley armored vehicle, but it helps with being overrun by the Mostly Dead." This little prick really wanted to tear my head off, and if I'd been him, I would feel much the same. There was something about him that made me want to take pot shots at his ego. If I managed to live through all this, I would devote a whole half an hour to discovering why, or so I promised myself.

I'm such a liar.

Channing looked around as though he was expecting some sort of sympathy from the group. He didn't get any. Sad, in a way.

I looked around at everyone and they appeared to be looking back at me as though they were waiting for something, or I'd developed a goiter and was completely oblivious to the swelling.

"And the Peanut Gallery says?" I waved my hands for emphasis.

"All right Frank, the main issue is whether or not you'll be in on our rescue mission or not." Flower was not afraid of being blunt about anything, at least not in my experience. "Buttons tells me that your mere presence on a mission of this kind is vital, so it hinges on you. You in?"

"In. Charlie comes with me." I pointed behind me to

where she was engaged in vigorous conversation.

Omura looked her over and asked, "Why her in particular?"

"Good question, Sir, and politely phrased as well. The answer, Watson, is simple." I refrained from patting him on the head. "Jayashri is needed here for medical issues, and that is not open to debate. Charlie and Jayashri are the only other people with as much experience with their nano-upgrades as I am with mine. That, Watson, is why Charlotte Cooper is coming with me."

"Fair. Combat experience?" Omura was asking questions like he expected to be on the team, and they were reasonable things to ask one way or another.

"Yes. Based on today's adventures, she took down two in less than twenty seconds, after taking two bullets to the chest." I didn't mention the vest, not that it would have mattered a whole lot, but I wanted her with me. I suspect it was my way of attempting to control as much of the situation as I could.

"Okay. We've got Frank, Charlie, looks like you're volunteering, Omura," Flower nodded at him and got an answering nod in return, "and me. We should have at least one more who could bring up the rear without getting it shot off." He turned around and gestured at the knot of soldiers hanging around Nate, and said, "Nate's friend Jackson is a reasonable person to ask. Nate gave me the skinny on him not long after they showed up. Good record, stable, and can take an order. Anyone object before I sign him up?"

We didn't. My friendly neighborhood sniper got up and made his way over to that group of people. I turned back to Buttons and his little cadre of bookends, and brought up the issue.

"Well," I said, addressing Buttons, "have you handed anyone my life story since we spoke last?"

"Frank, whether you like me or not is immaterial, but you do need to trust me. Omura and Channing know nothing more than they need to know and are completely capable of *not* asking questions. You're on the rescue mission for reasons you and I know very well, and that is all that needs to be said, unless you feel the need to be forthcoming on the topics we have discussed." For someone that I'd assaulted and my future girlfriend had nutted, he was being immensely civilized. In the interest of furthering detente, I gave him half a Brownie point.

I grunted and might have said more if Flower hadn't returned with our Number Five and Charlie in tow. From that point, we got into substantial planning for our little stroll into town on the day of the big offensive. In a lot of ways it was quite a typical plan for an atypical situation.

During the heat of the fighting, our team would exit the neighborhood, commandeer a vehicle from the enemy, and drive it right back to the building where Warren Hightower set up shop. Depending on resistance, we would either make our entrance via the parking garage or one of the service doors on the ground floor.

Stealth was preferred, unless it was impractical to the situation. If we were discovered, or encountered large armed resistance, the general thought was to create as much bloody mayhem as possible, so that at least one or two of the team could proceed toward the goal.

Omura and Flower agreed the secondary goal should be to destroy WH's ability to continue his little zombie union and associated technological pursuits. I interjected that a goal of opportunity would be to assassinate WH, himself. No one disagreed. We had a general plan of action, and, for the moment, that was enough.

"Charlie, could you give us a rundown on what you learned regarding local defenses?" Flower asked her with an uncharacteristic smile. He wasn't one to smile, so the appearance of his teeth came as a bit of a surprise.

"Sure, Matt." Charlie filled us in on the revamped IED plans, proposed sniper positions, and defensive fallbacks. They had proposed two separate escape routes through the backside of the neighborhood, through other residential areas, with Yolanda's dairy supplier's farm in Winchester, Virginia, as the rendezvous point.

Buttons and Channing nodded and headed over to talk with the Defense Team about burning microwaves and useful things that orbital railguns could do for making our opponents' lives difficult. We hashed out a few other details and separated back into the other groups to share information and learn more about what other decisions were being made.

A certain pressure was building in my head, centered around the reality that I would most likely need to come clean on an issue or two before we headed out to rescue our friend. I'm sure they'd want to understand why the goal of opportunity was as important to me as getting Bajali back safe... perhaps more vital than I wanted to admit.

The meeting dissolved about three hours later. Shawn felt there was a halfway decent chance some of us might live through it, and I accused him of being insufficiently positive about our chances.

"The problem," he told me, "is that we've got no idea at all about the sort of tactics he's likely to use when they go all out on us."

"Honestly, they've only got so many guns to go around. This guy is likely to just overwhelm us with numbers if he can manage it."

"You think?" He didn't seem convinced.

"Look at it this way, unless things have changed a lot since I squeezed Jerry the Zombie, there are far fewer trained military people than there are Joe and Jane Average Zombie. Those trained soldiers have to operate weapons systems and order around the untrained flunkies." I stuck my hands out in mid-air and mimed the classic shambling walk of Frankenstein's monster. "Left. Right. Yell, 'BRAINS!' Beat nice people with sticks."

Shawn smiled and conceded I might have a reasonable point, since there was only so much recruiting that can be done in less than a week.

"If Hightower managed to get reinforcements from some other organized group, we might be screwed."

"You have a point there. We're lacking fundamental intelligence on what is going on over there. Did you see which way Buttons and his gang went? I'm going to ask him about any useful data he might be able to get for us."

"Flower said they're going back to his place to uncrate some weapons and check over the Pain Ray units."

"Stellar. I'm going to wander over to his place and ask some questions. Will you be around your house later?"

"Yep!"

I had a sudden urge to tell Charlie where I was going, marveled at the sensation for a few moments, and gently interrupted her conversation with Barbara about the disposition of the children. She told me I was sweet to think of mentioning it to her, pulled me down for a kiss on my cheek, and turned back to her conversation. Barbara, on the other hand, was still looking at me with wide eyes and a little pinched smile quirking her mouth. Not being an overly dense male, I took my leave.

After all, I wasn't absolutely sure I wanted to be there if they decided to dish about me. I mean, it isn't an issue of pride so much as abject... ahem... knowing when to not butt into the affairs of the females of our species.

Chapter 27

Night had fallen while we made our plans, but I never needed the sporadically functioning streetlamps to tell me where I was going. Electricity was more common here than in much of the country, largely due to the government nationalizing most of the local utilities in order to keep itself functioning. Now, if you decided to travel a bit and went over 50 miles in any direction, you wouldn't have the luxury of utilities quite the way we do.

Large swaths of the United States were doing their best to keep things running, because people, as a collective entity, don't like having their schedules and expectations of civilized life thrown into the hopper. Certainly, during the six months of enforced martial law, things got a tad hairy. There were riots, strikes, and all sorts of unrest, as one might expect.

Certain groups, who were more prepared for the economy of the globe to tank, switched over to local trade and barter. Using our community as an example, it worked quite well. Another segment of the population, with the government's assistance and approval, actually went back to their jobs. The theory was that small areas could have much of the civilized life they wanted, if they were actually willing to go back to work and not panic. Especially if they worked in manufacturing, utilities, services and transportation.

The medical professions never took a break. They couldn't.

Slowly, the economic ball began to roll again, albeit at a

very reduced level. You could still get your manufactured products, as long as you ordered them and were willing to wait for the next truck that would deliver them to someplace nearby. More and more people, even around DC, were learning that becoming producers of products they needed or wanted was a much more effective way of going about things.

After decades of the world becoming more global, the whip cracked, and we had all started becoming much more local, even tribal. There were very few large gatherings anymore, and what few there were looked like medical safety accessory conventions. Masks and gloves everywhere!

No one wanted to chance becoming infected. Not a huge surprise, because we'd all seen what happens, in personal detail, to people who caught the virus. If they were not ousted from their community, they were either sequestered in the hope that zombies wouldn't detect them, or isolated so they couldn't infect anyone else.

Sadly, isolating never quite worked. We found that out with Mister Yan.

Here, in this lovely grove of lovely people, we had a rather idyllic existence. No one wore masks or gloves, because we knew one another, and most of us appeared to be immune. It was a Hell of a luxury, let me tell you, but it also contributed to how twitchy we all were when it came to outsiders.

That was not a rational response, by any means, because the likelihood of an infected person living long enough to visit was vanishingly small. The local undead population has always been quite high, even before they started organizing. I suppose this is one of those evolutionary bio-psychological quirks about humans in tribes: outsiders equal danger to the troop.

We've had one raid, run by another community about 10 miles away, since I've been a part of this one. There were two adults and about eight teenagers who tried to snatch and grab anything that wasn't bolted down. It was sad, poorly executed, and wholly unsuccessful. Shawn caned the two adults, Singapore-style, and lectured the teenagers with great enthusiasm.

I probably shocked all of them when I brought over popcorn, some of Jim and Darcy's hard cider, and a lawn chair. The caning was spectacularly brutal, utterly controlled, and strangely evocative of happier days in Tuscany. Jayashri was kind enough to use surgical staples to repair their asses after Shawn was finished.

Jayashri didn't stay for the lecturing, but I did. Ridley Scott could not have directed a better verbal lambasting of a scabby-assed group of young people than the one Shawn delivered at the top of his lungs that night. I will remember the expressions on their faces, lit by our bonfire, until I die.

I turned at the corner, about two houses down from Bajali's, when my reverie got the better of me. The tree on the other side of the street had apparently decided to sprout ninja fruit when no one was paying attention. A throwing star suddenly appeared in my right shoulder and *that* garnered piles and piles of attention from me.

"OW! Fuck!" I didn't waste any time to pull it out and dove across the bushes in the front of Jim and Darcy's yard. I had half a second to realize that I didn't have a gun on my person. All I had was a knife, and the flat piece of sharpened metal that was stuck in my arm. It was my mistake, being that unprepared.

Pulling it out was a carnal delight, let me tell you, but I supposed it was small fry compared to being gut shot earlier in the day. The shuriken had no blood on it at all, so I was fairly confident that my onboard repair service was up and running, but I didn't get a bead on my attacker. That seemed a little strange.

"Francis." The tree across the street talked to me. Damned ninja. I can't abide ninja stealth shit.

"Yo, Mister Hide in Plain Sight."

The tree chuckled a little, not giving away anything other than general position across the street.

"They told me it was you, but I didn't believe them, so I thought I'd come and see for myself. Lo and behold, here you are!" Ninja trees are so fucking smug.

"That's dandy, Mister Tree! I'm so happy you found me! Why the Hell am I interesting to you?"

"You wound me. You don't even remember my voice?"

"Look, whoever you are, you're talking through a lot of leaves about twenty feet away from me. You could be Donald Duck and I wouldn't be able to tell." I was slightly frustrated, but at least my arm had healed. The shuriken wasn't too damaged, and I was entirely interested in giving it back to its owner.

"Excuses. You're always good at excuses."

No. Please, of all the people it could be. "Stu?"

"Been a while, huh?"

I squatted in the bushes, flabbergasted beyond the ability to speak, but fully capable of imagining bloody murder. I've always been one to recover my use of words quickly, especially when my heart is filled with feelings of indignation and anger, but not on that occasion...it took me a full four seconds to lever my tongue into action.

"You went over to them? Don't tell me you went over to them." It came out flat, instead of fueled by the roiling emotions causing my heart to batter my ribcage.

"Francis, it isn't as though you get much choice when you're one of the Resurrected. In all honesty, it doesn't matter whether you are or you're still farting around as a mere human, everyone looks for the best plan or the best leader to follow. In my case, I didn't have to look very far."

"The Resurrected? Is that your cute little way of justifying slaughtering innocent people, you insane little shit?" I was begging my nanotechnology buddies for data, any organ they wanted to take over, just for a clear shot at this guy.

"It isn't cute. It's just the truth. I died and I came back, just like so many others. Just like you will, once all the preparations are complete." He had the gall to laugh before he added, "Of course, you won't die quite so quickly when you're a cow, and you'll have to be a very good cow if we consent to bring you over."

"You... motherfucking, bastard excuse for a soggy cock-sling. You make it sound like you're doing people a favor! You're going to herd them, collect them, milk them, and trade them with your friends!" Please, dear Lord of Nanotech, give me a sign! "These are human beings, you egotistical bag of barnacle turds!"

"Nobody said life is fair, Francis."

PING! I got him. The critters gave me a heads-up on his location: twenty-four feet away, eight feet above ground level, and behind heavy foliage. No clear shots from my location. Fuck.

"Ah well. Time to go! I didn't come here to debate morality with you, only to see you with my own eyes before we grind you into the dirt." Again, that damned annoying laugh! "I'll make sure that we take you alive, just so you can be my personal cow. I'll enjoy that. Maybe I'll even use you as my personal fucktoy between milkings! That would be dandy!"

The leaves moved, and he did one of the classic ninja things: ran away from me in a straight line behind the trunk of the tree. No clear shot, and too fast for me to catch him. My target of opportunity list had grown by one.

Don't they say the best wars are fought brother against brother? It looked like I would get to find out the hard way. I should never have grabbed his first name for my assumed name; I'll have to remember him even after I've killed him. Bother.

Chapter 28

The rest of the walk to Flower's place was done in something of a haze. My life had just become more complicated than I'd even wanted to think about, and I think part of my brain was trying to rebel and just shut down. I did what I could to keep that part of me under control by using it to track the throwing star I was spinning around in my hand.

Flower owned a lovely home that sported a two-car garage. It had one of those fiberglass doors on it, much like the big one in my ofuro room, and I could see shadows moving around in the light of the garage. At least I knew people were home, and my own good judgment told me I ought to announce myself to the group of people who were unpacking firearms.

Before I could open my mouth, I heard, "Hey, Frank. Come on in!" My neighbor sounded quite cheerful from behind the door, and I wondered how he knew it was me. Then again, if he'd snagged his own nanotech from someone at the meeting, it would stand to reason he'd be developing some of the benefits by now. I still found it a tad disturbing to be identified so quickly.

I went over to the side door that opened into the garage and used it, rather than the big door. No sense in revealing everything to the world. I found myself face to face with a large, black SUV of a model that I didn't immediately recognize. The passenger doors were open, and I could see Buttons' back from where he was bent over something on the ground, and there were a few more small Pelican cases sitting on the seats.

"You want to see something interesting?" I heard from the other side of the vehicle, and I made my way around the seriously reinforced front end of the black monster. Omura was crouched down in front of an open case, moving the foam off of the gray thing packed inside. The object looked like a matte gray square with a grid etched into the face. "This is one of the Active Area Denial units."

"It looks very unimposing," I commented.

"Doesn't it, though? The original versions were mounted on the tops of military Humvees and measured about eight feet square. This little guy is a miracle of modern technology." Whether or not I believed him, Omura sounded like he had all the faith in the world in the little thing. "We've got twelve of these units, each with their own power source and independent sensor package. That will give our little friends some fun times."

"Sounds like it." I turned to Buttons, who was kneeling in front of a laptop that had a satellite antenna plugged into one side, and asked, "Do we have any more data about the size of the force we're going to be dealing with, or any way to get that sort of intel?"

He looked up at me, frowning, and gave me an affirmative nod. "That's what I've been researching for the past hour. The recent visual data doesn't look good."

"By not looking good, you mean," I waved my hands a bit, "what?"

"It looks like they've been doing a lot of recruiting since I looked in on them yesterday. Or, at the very least, their recruiting is finally proving to be successful." He scratched his head, moved his other fingers around on the laptop track pad, and grunted.

"What sort of recruits are we talking about?"

"Yesterday's satellite data feed gave me a headcount on the number of unique people moving in and out of that building of 314. That's about on par for the data you got from your zombie earlier this week." He stood up from kneeling down in front of his little electronic altar, shook his head, and turned to face me. "The count I just got was 803 unique bodies. I've got photos that show 20 military-style Humvees parked around the building and on the parking garage's top level. Our lives have become much more complicated."

There was something about seeing this presumptuous bastard actually looking worried about these turns of events. I felt less surprised about the sudden appearance of reinforcements than he seemed to be, and I can chalk that up to my basic cynical nature. Make no mistake, it changed the entire framework of the plans we had attempted to make about defending our homes. Other options would need to be pursued.

"Well, got a plan yet?" I asked him, probably a bit more sharply than absolutely necessary.

"Not entirely."

"I can give you one set of thoughts right off the top of my head. Care to hear?" He nodded listlessly, but I didn't let it stop me for long. "We need one of two things to happen in the very near future. The first, and my most preferably option, is for you to utilize some of your orbital toys to make their lives more interesting right *now*." I was emphatic, but some people call my emphatic voice "yelling," and it is really just a matter of degrees anyhow. "The second option is much more annoying for me. We do a guerrilla raid and take out as much as we possibly can, and then bug the fuck out of there."

Buttons shook his head and was about to say something, when Channing (whom I had failed to notice at all) spoke up. "Using the orbital weapon systems is not that simple. None of them are in geosynchronous orbit over the DC area. And the ones that could be moved are pointed the other way."

Channing's mouth shut with a clack when he saw the look on Buttons' face. It wasn't just angry. It was murderous.

Looks like Poindexter let something out of the bag that wasn't to be opened in the first place.

When in doubt, poke the incision until something comes out.

"Buttons, what does he mean about weapons pointing the other way? At other countries, or something else?"

The Face of Doom turned back to me, and I was sure I was not about to get an answer other than a fist to the jaw. Then, he surprised me completely.

"Pointing the other way, Frank, means exactly what it sounds like. Those devices are not pointed at the Earth." He deflated a little bit.

I thought I'd caught on to what he was saying, but it made no sense. "You mean, you've got guns pointed at the Final Frontier, not at enemy countries?"

"That's exactly what I mean."

"Whatever the fuck for?" I had to laugh because it was completely absurd. When I stopped laughing, I caught sight of how he was looking at me. It wasn't anger. It was a sort of compassionate, sad look.

"I can't tell you. You already know more than most people with clearances four levels above Top Secret, and I could kill you for that and only have paperwork to do afterward. You do not want to know, nor should you ever want to know, what I do." He took a solid breath, popped his back, and let some of the tension ooze away. "Getting back to the matter at hand, I could get us another ballistic satellite, but it would take about 12 hours to move it into range. By then, we'd only be a few hours away from the original being in firing position. Not much good."

"I have to beg to differ on that. You're telling me the new one would be more mobile, right?"

"Absolutely, otherwise we wouldn't be able to move it into position," Buttons said, giving me a look that would have been appropriate for a high school math teacher when explaining that 2 + 2 equals 4 to the class.

"Right. You can move it. But can you *park* it?" The

corners of his mouth turned up, and I rejoiced that I'd popped him with the +10 Clue Brick and that we might be able to develop a working plan. "I can tell you're following my line of thought. What kind of ammunition do they use, and how much do they carry?"

"They use a solid carbon slug encased in a superconductive jacket that burns away in the atmosphere. Think of it as a copper-coated diamond the size of your head."

Somewhere, Sophia Loren was batting her eyelashes, overcome by a flash of sudden lust. I wasn't that excited, but I was pretty interested. "And how many of those would we have at our disposal?"

"Standard load on that series of orbital gun is 30 slugs. The impact is also adjustable from what you saw before to sub-surface hardened bunker penetration." He continued to smile, even when his brows furrowed as the thought came to him. "Before we get too excited, let me check something."

He got back down to the laptop and started hitting keys in a way that made no sense to me at all. I also noticed something unusual about the keyboard. None of the keys had letters or numbers on them, just symbols or icons of some kind. I filed that information away for later processing. I hadn't even gotten around to teasing Flower about knowing his name, and that seemed like a much more approachable task for the time being.

"I think I may have something more interesting than the railgun available." There was a tone of satisfaction in his voice.

"Tell me a story, Mister Buttons!" It was late; I'd run into my brother and had a long day. I was getting cranky.

"One of these days, I will kick you in the teeth when you can't heal it right away." It was a snarl, not satisfaction this time. "There's a laser satellite that could be diverted. Not as much damage potential for structures, but high damage to soft tissue. It also allows for a bit more finesse in choosing targets."

"What sort of damage to soft tissue?"

Omura decided to answer this one, "Think about making popcorn."

"All right. That doesn't make any sense to me, but I'll bite."

"All the water in the tissue explodes into steam at the same time as all the fatty tissues flash fry. You go from human being to an exploding batch of moist pork rinds in about two-tenths of a second." He made a popping gesture with his hands.

There is an upside and a downside to having a very visual imagination. It was quite a mental image to process.

"How large is the target area?" I had to ask, because one body at a time didn't seem very efficient.

"Ah! Buttons? The last time I saw the specs, they said '10 meters.' Is that still the blast area?"

"No. The newer versions have a tighter area of effect. Closer to six meters at full capacity," Buttons coldly replied, "with a wide range of depth of penetration."

Eighteen feet of steaming human fat chips. The mind boggled, but not for long, because we heard the tell-tale sound of one of Gina's IEDs exploding down the street. No one bothered to look at anyone else because they were patting themselves down to make sure their firearms were in place.

"Flower! Gun! Now!" I hollered, as if they hadn't heard it too.

With the calm of too much experience, he ran into the house and returned only a few seconds later. He handed me a gun that looked like an H&K P90 and a knife in a sheath. It never hurts to have an extra blade. By that time, Omura had already hauled ass out the door and down the street.

"Go! We'll hold things down here, in case that was a distraction. Send Omura back if you need us."

I didn't need to hear it twice. I just got out the door and ran like Hell.

Down past the intersection, about a block from Shawn's

garage, there was an overturned Humvee on fire. That was not as bothersome as the school bus that was parked on Glebe Road behind the flaming Humvee. I heard several gunshots, but did not see anything of Omura.

It was hard to see much of anything over the knot of zombies that were trying to invade Shawn's place. None of them were wearing fatigues or BDUs. Only civilian clothing, matched with sticks and makeshift weapons. They had either sent cannon fodder or were creating a distraction for something else.

"Behind you!" I heard Charlie yell from the roof of the garage and assumed she was talking to me. I went to the ground, rolled, and came up facing the other way with the gun pointed. Sure enough, there were four of them behind me.

I didn't ask questions; I just started things by shooting one of them in the face. The other ones did something totally unexpected; they closed the distance. They were armed with military M4 rifles, and they proceeded to open fire on me from close range. I couldn't dodge, but I could move forward into their weapons.

Three bullets went directly through me. Shoulder. Stomach. Upper left thigh. It was the gut shot that sent me to the ground, but it was suddenly finding a net over the top of me that kept me there. It looked like some of the group from the garage assault had turned around during my fun and thrown a weighted net on top of me when I hit the ground.

One of my armed opponents had his knee down on my weapon, while another one had the barrel of his rifle resting on the center of my forehead. The third little devil was the one who shot me with a Taser. The electric shock hurt worse than the bullets did and I flailed underneath the net.

Then the bastard did it again.

I am unclear what happened in the few minutes after that because my vision went to Hell while I was twitching on the ground. I heard a horrible bellow and a huge amount of rapid machine gun fire. Lots of feet were pounding on the pavement, away from where I was being held. There were screams, yells, and all kinds of din.

The weight on my arm shifted and the gun barrel that was on my forehead moved. I was still pinned down and not really capable of any coordinated movement. There were a few yells, some bullets, and my world was suddenly covered in a lot of hot, copper-smelling wetness.

My gun arm was free, but it wasn't responding when I tried to move it. Nothing really was.

The rest of the world was still full of gunfire and screaming. My little chunk of it was filled with a lot of pain.

It was just loud. That was the only thing I was able to process, but I did hear something that made me smile inside. Charlie yelled, "Get the fuck away from my man, you undead dickless wonder!" I was her man! That just rocked!

The temperature was dropping somewhere, and I started shaking. I think my brain was moving slowly as well, or time was playing funny tricks on me because I wasn't able to see much more than blurs.

Something.

Just something.

Not quite right.

Then there was nothing at all.

No dreams about ravens and Hell. In fact, it was incredibly quiet and dark wherever my brain was, for however long it was there. Really, it was lovely and peaceful. I had no desire to be afraid and I wasn't. There wasn't even any physical pain to latch onto, just a sense of floating peacefully in a big sea of nothing.

It cracked open as if I had been inside a black egg. I fell out, wet and sticky, into a mixing bowl of gunfire and pandemonium. I didn't feel as though I was in my body, because I could see the back of my head, but I felt some vague attachment to what my body was doing. It was pretty horrible, but I couldn't seem to stir up the energy to care.

My mouth let out a bloodcurdling howl, and I thought I'd certainly pay for that with a week of sore vocal cords. I watched my shoulders hunch as my head swung from side to side, surveying the fleeing attackers. There was a feeling of a decision being made, and I took off after one runner in particular. A young, slightly chubby, zombie girl.

With a heave, the body I usually occupy launched itself onto the running woman and rode her to the ground. It seemed like an awfully sexual thing to do with someone I'd never even spoken to before, but it did seem as though it wasn't me making the decisions. For example, if I had been running the show, I wouldn't have bitten into the back of her neck like that. Really, going all the way through her vertebrae to suck out her cerebro-spinal fluid was a bit much. I am a tool-using mammal, and I could have done it much more neatly with a drill.

I wasn't really surprised when my body started smashing her head onto the pavement, or when it dug out her brain and ate it. Again, the whole thing could have been done with so much less mess if I'd been given a little say in this activity. Nope. I got tossed out of my own head and had to sit through the insanity from the penalty box.

There were four other undead, former attackers, who were paralyzed in fear, watching my body eat their companion's brains. I almost felt a little sad for them, because if they'd been running away, my body might not have caught them so quickly. Tsk, tsk, tsk. Next time, you have to run away!

Wow. No one has a lick of self-preservation anymore. Really! If someone has just pounced on your companion and you're not going try and save her, then run away. Honest! It is a much more sensible choice than standing there until the monster is done with her, because *you* might be next.

What is this world coming to?

My body froze in the middle of consuming the fifth brain, and I felt a darkness encroaching on me from all sides. In moments, as before, there was nothing more than the empty darkness where I was alone, quiet, and feeling peaceful.

I came back to consciousness slowly, almost as if my brain was running through all my body's systems one at a time to ensure optimum functionality for becoming a walking, talking human being once again. It wasn't clear where I was, but then again, my eyes weren't open. Damned slow start-up sequence, I tell you.

" ... He fucking ATE their BRAINS! Did you not see that shit? You tellin' me that I'm gonna eat brains if I get gut shot? What the fuck happens if someone shoots my balls off? Does that mean I'm gonna run out and eat two babies with ketchup and mustard?!"

"Shawn, calm down. We don't know anything about why Frank attacked the stragglers. He may have simply gone mad." Jayashri's voice, always a nice thing to wake up to, if you ask me. Hearing Shawn get uptight over things is not a super-duper way to return to consciousness.

However, from listening to that snippet of their discussion, it appeared that what I'd experienced was not some kind of dream. Five brains. Well, that's unprecedented!

Somewhere in the back of my head, something was telling me I ought to feel really upset about losing my shit and putting the chomp on a bunch of zombies. I didn't really agree I should be upset about it; after all, they'd attacked us and tried to capture me, and God only knows what else they were up to. All is fair in love, war, and survival.

My moral compass wanted to put up a huge argument about the issue, but I told it to have a coffee break and talk to me later.

"When we get Baj back, I want him to get these little devils out of me." Shawn was up in arms again. Take a chill pill, Mister Tighty Nads! "I don't want to run around killing things like that."

"Look, Jaya said this nanotechnology is designed to optimize people for combat. I already saw it scavenge brains earlier today when he got shot in the gut twice. It took him a while to heal up from that, too." Charlie was taking the more rational course in the discussion.

Ping! I could feel my little critters come back online the rest of the way. Six people, living humans, armed, ranging from three to 25 feet away from me. External temperature, 52 degrees. Internal temperature, 98.9 degrees.

Clearly, we were still outside. Jaya, Shawn, and Charlie were closest to me, and I found that comforting with a certain quiet wish they'd take the argument a little further away until I could finish returning to consciousness. I decided to ask them to do that, since you will never get what you never ask for.

"Nimitz! Annie Sprinkle in the oven with a crosscut saw. Preacher hang up monkey another time?"

"Frank! What did you say?" Charlie sounded really excited, but she really should have been able to hear me from only three feet or so away.

"Creamed corn! Johnny Depp ankle brace, skinny Buddha refried beans. Masculine lactation?"

"Baby, you're not making any sense." She put her hand on my forehead and asked me if I could open my eyes and look at her.

I don't know why she thought I wasn't making any sense, but I figured attempting to open my peepers wouldn't hurt anyone. They felt as though they ought to be working.

Open.

Dude!

Closed.

Apparently, there was still a little work going on in the system check and they hadn't quite reached the optic nerve. They all wanted to know why I closed my eyes so fast, and I truly had no idea if I could explain it in a way that would make sense to anyone who didn't have strobe lights, plasticine clay, and a letter-size sheet of blotter acid.

"Annie Sprinkle's numb tongue whole lot of massive cheese. I never want to see anything like that again, as long as I live!"

Shawn reached down and snagged me by the remains of my shirt. "Why the Hell did you eat their brains, man?! They were running away! You didn't have to chase them down one by one like that!"

I swatted uselessly at his arms, hoping he'd put me back down on the nice, cool ground so I could finish pulling myself back together without all the excess drama.

"Just put me back down. Okay?"

"No! Tell me why! Why aren't you even a little bit upset?" He was getting substantially shriller as he wound himself up. Charlie moved in from the side and forcibly turned his head to face her.

"Shawn, put Frank down. Put him down. Freaking out is not going to help anyone or get anything done." Her voice must have had redneck soothing properties, because he lowered me back down to the nice cold pavement and let my shirt go. "That's it, bro. Now, what are you so upset about?"

"He *ate* their brains!"

"Right. I got that part. I was watching it, just like you were."

My lumbering friend was pacing in such short lengths that he was almost walking in circles. I had seen my share of people coming unglued before, and it had begun to appear that a certain mini-giant of a Country Boy would be joining that category of my life experiences. The symptoms were classic, including the obsessive wringing of his hair.

Strange thoughts of aprons and chocolate chip cookies danced at the corners of my consciousness, but did not stick around for me to ask what they were doing there. About that time, it occurred to me I was also not thinking very clearly and I probably should investigate that issue before too terribly long.

The soon-to-flip out friend had a significant point about one thing, and I wasn't loathe to admit it as much as I was numb. I had attacked and killed (and consumed the brains of) five members of the crew sent to harass us. That was an incredibly wild and uncivilized thing to do, and I strongly doubted anyone would debate that issue with me. Sparing the issue of living person versus zombie, I had committed a number of acts of cannibalism.

The idea of eating human flesh is repugnant to me, and I would rationally believe there would be significant emotional backlash after an incident like this. Yet, there I was, flat on the asphalt, not really giving two squirrel shits about anything in particular. Indeed, I was quite relaxed.

"Jayashri?"

"Yes, Frank," she said and knelt down by my side. "How are you?"

"Shawn has a point and I want to run it by you before I get twisted up into knots about it." She nodded at me, so I continued. "After losing my mind and going cannibal, I feel as though I should be morally outraged and disgusted at my own behavior. I'm concerned because I feel too calm about all of this, when I really should be pinching loaves like Shawn is right now."

A thoughtful look crossed her face, and she asked me, "Did you experience any moral issues when your nanotech went scavenging earlier today?"

"No, come to think of it. I didn't even bat an eye."

She looked up at Shawn and Charlie, who were still doing the Dance of Sibling Pacification, and she said, "I think you both should listen to what I am about to say." They went to their neutral corners and paid attention. "We know that the machines are designed to optimize human beings for survival and combat situations. That much is certainly clear, even if we were making assumptions from our observations. It would make sense, then, if they also had some control of, or effect on, our neurochemistry."

We nodded. What else could we do?

"Frank is not experiencing a moral crisis," Jaya continued, "because having a moral crisis in the middle of a combat situation is fatal. His package of nanotechnology set out to rebuild him as quickly as possible and to make the psychological impact of what was necessary as gentle as possible. In short, Frank is high."

It made plenty of sense to me and made me feel much

better about the hallucinations of a few moments before. Shawn seemed calmer, and Charlie never looked ruffled to begin with. All seemed to be right in my world, except for a single niggling issue in the back of my head.

My brother had made an appearance. Less than 30 minutes later, we were attacked, and I was singled out to be subdued. Had I not been full of the Milk of Modern Technology I would have either been captured alive, albeit wounded, or killed outright. It looked very much like my dear Stewart had a plan to make things much more personal for me and was not at all bluffing about turning me into his fuck cow.

I pushed Jaya out of the way, rolled over, and threw up onto the pavement.

"Now! See that? That's what you're supposed to do when you find out you've turned into a fucking cannibal!" I didn't need to see Shawn's finger pointing at me or the air of righteous triumph surrounding him like a laurel wreath on any given Caesar; I knew, even if I didn't see.

Chapter 29

When I finished heaving my guts out, I rolled back over, and made a good effort at standing up. I walked right up to Shawn, brains and bile dripping down my chin, and explained matters to him.

"My brother is one of Hightower's ninja. He popped by for a visit as I was walking over to Flower's place." I got as close to Shawn as I could, so he could see and smell my disgust. "He had heard I was here and wanted to come tell me that he would be sure to capture me so I could be his personal cow and glory hole."

I knew he'd broken out into a cold sweat. My little critters made sure I knew his body temperature, pulse rate, pupil contraction and expansion, and that he smelled afraid.

"I understand my turn toward Long Pig is disturbing to you. At some point," I was trying to explain, but I think it was coming across more as verbal intimidation, "I may be very upset I attacked those poor zombies who were attacking us. Or, maybe I will never be bothered by it. What I can tell you is I would rather eat *you*," I told him, as I emphasized by poking him in the chest, "than be a snack cake and hole for my younger brother to amuse himself with."

Shawn looked away. I think I managed to make the point.

"Dude," he whispered, "that's harsh."

"What? Eating you or being dinner and a show for my brother?"

"C'mon, he's family. You've heard of kissing cousins, right?"

I was agog. Aghast. Abhorred. Absolutely stunned. I just stood there and stammered at him until I looked into his eyes and noticed that they had smile crinkles around them while the rest of his face was utterly blank. Omura had joined us during my soliloquy on cannibalism, and he joined Charlie, Jayashri, and Shawn in snickering at me.

"Shawn?"

"Yes, Frank?"

"That was a horrible way to break the tension. Really disgusting." I meant every word.

"You're really not on an even keel, are you? You haven't even threatened to impregnate my sister with your devil wrigglers yet. I feel... I feel slighted."

I reached up, pinched his cheeks like your favorite Auntie would, and explained thusly, "Don't worry, that's still the plan. We just haven't had time to get buck naked and bang the stuffing out of each other yet."

"I beg your pardon!" Charlie sounded a tad incensed. "We have had a number of opportunities to summon the devil wrigglers over the past couple of days, Mister. *You,*" she gave me a very stern finger pointing, "have evaded every one of them. Damned 'gentleman'! What a pain in my ass!"

Omura looked back and forth at all of us like a spectator at a tennis match, completely befuddled by all of it. "People, I realize I'm new here, but this seems like an incredibly strange conversation to be having in the aftermath of a zombie attack and cannibalistic healing, and while standing in the middle of the road surrounded by corpses. At night."

Jayashri put a companionable arm around his shoulder, smiled in her winning way, and said, "They are always like this when something awful happens. I do not understand it either, but I choose to see it as a mark of being touched by the Gods."

"Touched by the Gods? Like geniuses and artists?"

Omura looked like he was starting to get a solid grip on things.

"No, like the insane. They are lovable, but quite mad. You understand?"

"Oh." The poor guy deflated like a balloon with a slow leak.

"Now, cheer up!" Jayashri jollied him along. "Let us all make our neighborhood a cleaner place and drag these bodies to the street. Hm?"

For a moment, I didn't feel bad about being a madman. I saw I was not alone in my madness; we were all a good bit around the bend. How could we not be, in a world as insane as the one we lived in?

We followed Jaya's lead and started dragging bodies out to Glebe Road. Omura remarked that it seemed an odd thing to do, and Shawn explained he knew a guy who came by periodically and picked them up to grind into fertilizer. He continued to explain that all sorts of interesting kinds of work appear in the niches of life when it becomes clear there's a demand for some sort of service.

I don't know if Omura was convinced, reassured, or vaguely disquieted by the thought of a local body hauler. It took me a bit by surprise the first time I ran into the man and got a serious look at his bio-fuel garbage truck of doom.

He called himself "Rancid Sam." I would have to say his heart was definitely dedicated to truth in advertising, based on that alone. Yet, it wasn't the smell or the name that got to me, nor was it his jovial personality, which was several shades darker, yet distressingly perkier, than my own. Those sterling qualities were compounded by the fact that he was also a "fabulous, raging queer, tranny teddybear," by his own description. The resulting frothing frappé of fabulous, the quim de la quim of boyish good times, the concoction of ... You get the idea.

I had to stifle a giggle at the thought of our guest getting a serious eyeful of our local color. I had nearly died on the spot when Shawn first introduced us, and I could only imagine how Omura, who appeared to be quite straight-laced, would react to the luminous, flamboyant, Master of the Peppermint Garbage Truck.

Charlie shot me a concerned look from the other side of the body we were carrying, and I looked up at her to reassure her that I was fine. I told her I thought of something funny to share with her later. I looked back down to the ground in between the arms of the body that I was helping her carry.

This particular body was missing a cranium. I was able to stare down into the remains of the upper sinuses, and I was intensely grateful that it was dark outside. Even with the occasional patch of light from the remains of the gently burning Humvee and one or two sodium streetlights, the bloody bones, empty eye sockets, and parade of shredded tissue lost some of the Technicolor impact daylight would have provided.

I felt blessed I didn't have to face the visceral emotions that sight would have brought forth, had it been the middle of the day instead of the belly of the night.

Something, another tiny thought, clamored for my attention in the middle of my moment of gratitude for being spared a small horror at the end of my day. When I took a closer look at that wriggling tail of a thought, I realized that my memory contained every color of that broken and torn flesh, in pure Hollywood detail.

My eyes started burning when I realized that the last time I'd seen this particular corpse was when I had bashed its head open to get at the brains. This body had been someone, even after she'd been killed and come back to life.

I'd killed and eaten the brains of some poor, silly girl who got caught up in the wrong things with the wrong people... Me, and my family even before I'd brought her existence to a brutal end, since my little brother had set this little raid in motion. I couldn't even process what I hated more.

My survival high came to a screeching, gut-wrenching

end.

Charlie turned around when the top end of the corpse hit the ground and discovered that she was dragging the whole thing by herself. There were probably some interesting and sharp words lurking behind her lips, but they never had the chance to be expelled into the world.

She dropped the feet of the body, rushed to my side, and did her best to comfort me. I was sitting on the pavement, rocking back and forth in silence. I wasn't able to do much more than stare at the brown remains of the blood dried on my hands. Lady Macbeth would have been so proud of me.

When Charlie put her arms around me, I stopped rocking back and forth, but the emotions were so huge I wasn't able to make a noise or gesture to acknowledge her kindness. I also noticed I was unable to move because she was embracing me so tightly, but that held so little significance it was shoved away almost as soon as the thought arrived.

There weren't any words I could have said or thoughts I could have imagined that would have softened the rebound from all of the compounded shock, horror, adrenaline, and sheer emotional exhaustion. I doubt I could have formed a coherent thought, much less strung words together, in the grip of such an overwhelming experience. I just sat there, staring at my hands, wrapped in the arms of a woman for whom I was quickly coming to have large feelings.

Unlike so many other times in my life, I had someone who was willing and able to support me, and it didn't matter at all if I couldn't think or speak. There was someone else who would rise to the occasion instead of me if the situation required, and that glorious realization carved a bright line in the miasma of horror that froze my soul.

A second spark of hope joined the one that had illuminated me a moment before. I realized being alive meant having the opportunity to heal from what had hurt me. Not to be undone, the original spark reminded me I wasn't alone, and I had someone in my life to help me heal and move forward. I could breathe again, but an older issue lingered in the space where the calm was starting to spread.

"Thank you." I didn't have to force those words out of my mouth, but they had the strength of my whole being behind them. I doubt I would have been able to do anything with concepts and utterances that carried less meaning than those two words.

"You're welcome, sweetie. Are you okay to move? Maybe go back to the store and get you cleaned up?"

Masculine pride might be salvaged in that sort of situation if the man in question had been able to brush off her embrace or deny (loudly) that he needed any assistance of any kind. Then again, I could be mistaken, and all that would have done is throw my collapse into a brighter, less compassionate light. At that juncture, there wasn't any clarity to hold the thought up to, much less the will to do so.

She helped me to my feet and got me steady and ready to walk. Shawn was on his way back from depositing the last corpse he carried and saw the two of us about to head off. With no small amount of surprise on my part, the brute hugged me.

"Frank, I just wanted to say I'm very sad for all you went through today and that I feel very brotherly toward you." He stepped back, still holding me at arm's length, and looked into my eyes with no small amount of compassion showing in his own. "I also wanted to say that, unlike your biological brother, I will never, ever want your ass for anything... " Charlie and I stared at him, mouths gaping like unfortunate bigmouth bass at a sport fishing tournament. A sane man might have stopped where he was upon such a vision, but not Shawn. He continued with, "... unless we all got stuck on a desert island with no food. Then I might want your ass, but only after you were no longer with us and had no use for it. It'd be really small BBQ, but somebody would live one more day because of your buttocks."

He actually had water welling up in his eyes. I was moved, clubbed over the frontal lobes, but moved, and I gave him a hug in return. He mussed up my hair, told his sister to be nice to me, and nudged us along. I just wanted to wail.

As we walked, she leaned into me and gave me a little insight into that moment of surreal interpersonal interaction.

"Don't let it worry you too much. Shawn really sucks when it comes to expressing affection."

My emotions were still too far sideways to find that information at all comforting.

It seemed like it took forever to go back up the street to my store. Even more forever seemed to pass by as we walked down the lonely aisles toward the Spa in the back. Dimly, I remembered she was going to help me clean up, and a slow glance down at myself revealed how much I needed it. I was caked with remains.

Even in my hollow-minded state, I had enough presence about me to stop before I could begin to consider where all the dried effluvia came from. Nothing good could come of that exploration, especially if I wanted to return to some kind of reasonable state of mind. Besides, there was another pressing issue that needed to be handled.

It wouldn't wait any longer. If I was going to fall apart any further than I already had, this was certainly the time, because I couldn't have survived much more.

"Charlie. I need to tell you something."

She turned back from the Spa door and looked at me, still holding my hand. "Yes, hon?"

"My name isn't Frank Stewart."

"I know. Most everyone here knows that isn't your real name, but don't worry about it. Everyone really loves you here... "

"Charlie," I interrupted her because I didn't think I'd be able to say any of it if I had the chance to stop. "I want you to know who I am and I don't want to hide from you. I won't be able to, soon, anyway."

"All right. You can tell me anything you need to say."

"My name is Warren Francis Hightower, III."

Chapter 30

Charlie froze for a moment, took a really deep breath, and gave my hand a squeeze.

"I appreciate you needed to tell me that. I can also see how much it must have been weighing on you to hold that in for so long." She hugged me.

She actually hugged me.

I know I was back into bigmouth bass impression-mode, and that the noises I was making were very simple ones, almost pre-human vocalizations. "Duh," I said. I followed it up with, "dur?" and "muh?" My expectations for the End of the World did not come to pass, and that added immense confusion to the top of my Existential Horror Sundae.

She smiled. It was a tiny, wry, little quirk of the lips, and it did not give me enough information or hint at anything that I could build into the End that I was expecting to have.

"I guess you're wondering why you're not going through even more horrible stuff. Am I right?"

"Ur!"

She nodded. "Feel like you're going to bust a seal if I don't explain why I'm not screaming and flippin' out?"

"Ourg!"

"All right. It's like this. When I first showed up, and you were busy locking yourself away from the world because you thought Shawn hated you after busting you in the chops, my brother introduced me around to people." Charlie squeezed my hand again and seemed to change her mind about what to say next. "Tell you what! Standing here, full of crud, talking about this stuff, is not going to get us cleaned up. Let's do them both at the same time. Okay?"

"Merp." It wasn't my best of replies, but she nodded and led me into the Spa. She leaned me up against the wall like a human plank and started fiddling with the water heater. Once she got it started, she filled up a bucket and sat it on top of the heater to warm up.

Charlie came back, sat down on the floor, and gestured for me to join her, which I did.

"All right. Shawn introduced me to everyone, like I said, and I spent a couple of days helping out Jaya. After Baj left, she was a little shaken up."

The story she shared with me went a bit like this, with my elaboration, of course:

They were a study in contrasts, sitting in the lounge chairs on the sun deck. Jayashri Sharma, a slight, delicate woman with skin the color of roasted cinnamon cream and long black hair that fell in a dark river from the top of her head to almost the backs of her knees... Charlotte Marie Cooper, a curvy, almost quintessential American Girl who sported colorful half-sleeve tattoos on both arms, with a pale complexion that showed every blush or approaching storm of feelings... drinking tea.

For Jayashri, serving tea was central to hospitality, civilized behavior, and comfort, and gave her a familiar ritual to ground some of her anxiety. Only 24 hours had passed since she had nearly lost a dear friend to a hand grenade because of his own suicidal need to protect other people, and she had endured her husband's need to do what he considered the right thing. While she understood Bajali's reasons, as well as the logic behind them and even the feelings that ran so deeply within him, the simple fact was that his actions were potentially as suicidal as turning one's back on a live grenade.

Being without him was not a future she wanted to contemplate, much less be a part of.

Underneath the serenity of her face, lurked a secret wish

that they could have sent Frank instead. They could have pinned a note to the sutures that said, "Dear Warren, your senseless megalomania has nearly taken the life of your firstborn son. Please let us alone, and many sons and families will be spared the tragedy you nearly suffered by your own orders." Behind closed doors, she had said as much to her husband, as she tearfully beseeched him to choose a different path.

"My darling, such a thing would make no difference at all to this man. You would sacrifice the life of your friend and betray the trust I have placed in you by telling a secret that was not even mine to tell. That would be the horrible karma of my sin in telling you what I should never have mentioned in the first place." He shook his handsome head. "I would still... we would still be hunted for the knowledge I have. Frank would only die before his time."

While his voice was calm, the words were like acid on bare flesh. She knew he was right and resented that he was nobler than she was.

Charlotte spoke her name, and it made Jaya's attention shift from the painful reverie that threatened to pull her downward.

"Yes, Charlotte?"

"I am not going to lie to you. I am absolutely here to pry into your business." Jaya found the girl's direct approach to be endearingly fresh and utterly American.

"Why would you wish to do such a thing on a lovely afternoon when there is tea to be enjoyed and sunshine to warm our bodies?"

"Your husband has gone to do something beyond brave, and you're left here to wait and see if he will come home. Jayashri, you're so upset I can smell it, and you are changing the track of your thought patterns by a force of will. I can see it. Please, talk to me. I am here to help you if you let me."

More poison! More acid on the wound in her heart!

"How dare you invade my privacy when I have invited you into my home and shown you every hospitality?!"

"I hear you saying you feel as though I'm invading your privacy." Charlotte nodded, not even raising an eyebrow in the face of Jayashri's sudden outburst. "This is a situation within your power to change. You can ask me to leave, and I will, if you feel that is the solution to the pain you are feeling."

"You have no idea what I am feeling!"

"You're right. I don't have any idea what you are feeling. All I can do is tell you what I am observing. You, on the other hand, can tell me what you are feeling. If you are angry at me, I am willing to listen to that, too."

"I am feeling that you are prying into my life when I have not given you permission to do so. You are new here and I have no reason to trust you, or to unburden myself on you."

"Then you aren't angry at me?" Charlotte's voice was soothing, and her manner seemed both genuine and slightly remote. It was the sort of thing Jayashri had come to associate with deeply religious or spiritual people, like gurus and Buddhist priests in India.

"I am not angry at you. I am very frightened and upset." Those two simple admissions were enough to make the walls she built around her feelings slide out of place. Tears started to collect in the corners of her eyes, and she felt entirely humiliated that they would reveal her to be so weak in the presence of a stranger.

Charlotte's hand found hers where it was, wrapped around the handle of her tea cup, and simply rested there. It was enough to shatter the walls and leave her weeping freely.

"I wanted to escape with him," she whispered between the silent heaving breaths, "and leave this place, so that bastard would never find us again. Then his own son inspires Bajali by risking his life to save the children! How could Bajali think of doing anything less than risk his life as well? He was so inspired by the love of this madman's son!"

She clapped both hands to her mouth, realizing that she

had betrayed the trust placed in her a second time. From that moment on, she wept in silence, terrified there would be another moment when secrets would escape her.

In time, the tears slowed.

"Jayashri, will you listen to me?"

"You do not need the attention of someone as horrible as I am. I betray my own husband's trust and question the love in his heart. I am a heartless, selfish thing!"

Charlotte got up, walked around the table, and pulled her into a close embrace.

"Jayashri, I know you feel these things and it is all so huge. You are not any of those things. Just breathe with me. Slow. Easy. In. Out. Come on."

They breathed together, and Jayashri felt the woman's heart beating within her chest. It was something to focus on that was not the agony of her feelings. It gave her a measure of peace.

"I want you to keep breathing just like you are right now," Charlotte said, mere inches away. "When life brings you experiences that inspire fear that someone you love will leave us or die, it is so intense it can swallow you whole. If people feel powerless in situations like that, they often lash out at everyone and everything as a way of processing the agonizing things they are feeling. We tell ourselves stories to explain and justify our actions, because the honesty would be too much in combination with the pain that is already there." She stroked Jayashri's hair, like one might do with the sad daughter who came home from school in tears.

"We expect so much of ourselves when we love someone, and sometimes we try so hard to be perfect for them that we forget we are nothing more than human beings." Jaya felt Charlotte laugh silently. "We treat our men as if they were our little boys. Women, sweetie, do not like to be afraid when it comes to their men."

"No," Jayashri said, nearly sotto voce, "we do not like that at all."

Chapter 31

"I'm not going to tell you more about that conversation. I treat it as therapist-patient confidentiality." Charlie stood up and went to check the water heating across the room. "Now, shuck your duds, Frankie the Face, because I'm going to sponge you off."

I did what she asked, silently, because too many thoughts were flinging themselves around in my skull. A two-part question came to mind that I needed to voice.

"Baj has always known who I am? How did he find out?"

Charlie walked back over, bucket in hand, and smiled at me.

"Honey, Baj worked for your dad. Don't you think a businessman, no matter how bent, would have a family photo *somewhere* around his office?"

In reality, that thought had never crossed my mind. Dad never seemed to give a damn, even if he periodically had us get family portraits done. I guess there was more reason for doing that than I'd considered. A businessman has to keep up appearances, and a pleasant family photo on the desk or the wall couldn't hurt.

"I am... " I tried to say more than that, but everything crushed together back around my uvula and the resulting mess was too tight for other words to get through.

"You are a lot of things." She closed the distance between us, and despite the dried mess on both of us, hugged me. "You're a good man and absolutely not your father's son in all the ways that count. Now, we've got the bowing ball out of your ass, and it is time to get ourselves cleaned up while we can."

Belatedly, I realized that I was standing there naked and had just been given a full-body hug by an equally naked woman. If my brain had been capable of processing any more input, I probably would have been jumping for joy, but I was completely crispy from my jaw to the top of my skull. Even my Groin Mariachi Trio was silent on the matter.

In the end, I just sat on the stool and let her sponge me off. Two buckets of water later, she got me a towel and took care of her own sponging. I sat there and watched, feeling like something of a voyeur, but beyond that vague sensation I was operating with nothing more than a head full of static.

She started to dry herself off, turned to me, and said something so mundane it flipped my brain over.

"Baby, the next time you're out, we definitely need more soap."

My voice came back online, as did at least a portion of my brain. "Does this mean you're moving in?"

Her cheeks got very pink and she laughed. "That might be a little, I don't know, premature?" I love how her eyes sparkled when she said, "I guess you could say I'm hoping to spend a lot of time here, even if I'm living with my brother. Tonight, included, because you're way too unsteady to be alone."

This time, when she hugged me with only my towel separating us, I was very aware of the sensual gravity of her heavenly body. I hugged her back, and even with the static in my skull, I loved how she felt in my arms. She was a source of joy in my life I had hoped for and joked about, but never truly expected. There's a certain stasis that is hard to move past when you've decided you're always going to be alone.

We froze at the same time. Someone was in the store. Armed, and absolutely not human-temperature. My furry brain allowed one large thought to pass into my consciousness. I didn't care who it was that screwed up my romantic moment, but I was adamant they were going to die for it.

Charlie and I parted, slipped over to our respective piles of clothes, and snagged the closest available weapons. Unfortunately for the store, the firearms were semi-auto. There was a decent knife on my belt, but I wasn't completely sure I felt like attacking someone in the buff. Then again, Ancient Picts painted themselves with woad and trudged onto the battlefield wearing nothing but evil expressions.

I pulled the knife, waved Charlie back, and moved forward in a crouch. I did not miss the raised eyebrows or the "What the Hell?" expression on her face, and was really gratified when she just shrugged and brought her gun up to cover me. As I approached the door, I got a solid lock on the intruder's position and, based on my memory of the store layout, put them about even with the checkout counter.

There was enough potential cover between the Spa and their position that I could, if I stayed down, get behind them. Sounded like a plan, so I made a bunch of pantomimed gestures to indicate what I was about to do. Charlie nodded, and I proceeded to hunch down onto the floor with the knife between my teeth and scuttle out the door into the store.

Our intruder was moving toward the back of the store, and I was crouched one aisle away from them, right beside the household cleaning chemicals. Brilliant idea! Squirt them in the face with something nasty, disarm them, and then ask some significant questions. I snagged a squeeze bottle of toilet cleaner, quietly opened the stopper, and waited for my quarry to reach the end of the row before springing into action.

I hate to admit I was enjoying this experiment in naked confrontation. There are not many occasions in a fellow's life when he gets to really dig into the primal meat of fighting for his life while not wearing a stitch of clothing and armed only with a knife and toilet bowl cleaner. It was satisfying. It was a little more pure than tossing angry pellets of metal back and forth. Then again, I may be completely delusional.

The intruder rounded the end of the row and I sprang up, a naked, snarling, modern interpretation of da Vinci's X-Man drawing.

"AAAAARRRRRAAGH!"

My opponent levitated and spun around, shrieking. Instead of facing another burly male across the shop floor of battle, I was buck naked in front of Miss Teenage Undead who was wearing a suicide bomber vest packed with C-4.

"AAAARRRGH?" I was slightly taken aback by the turn of events. Thankfully, so was Miss Undead.

Charlie didn't give the little thing time to press her plunger before her little blond skull was ventilated. Unfortunately, I got the extra spray of bits in the face.

"Honey, I told you to put away that nasty trouser snake! You scared the poor little dead girl so bad her head exploded!"

I made little "ptooey" noises to clear the skull chunks out of my mouth.

"Yes, I know. My rod and staff are fearful weapons in the war against the undead." You could have eaten my facetiousness with a spoon, it was so thick and creamy.

"I think your staff is pretty nice. Maybe you'd like to help me clean up the body and we could discuss your hiking equipment more intimately?" She just blew a zombie's head to chunks and was interested in my outdoor gear. I guess love does come in all shapes and sizes.

"I dunno. I've had a hard day."

She tossed her head and laughed at me. The gun was still smoking a little bit from the single round that had turned another undead person into a "returned to deceased" person. I found myself standing there, limp in every sense of the word, and too exhausted to care that there was a body oozing on my floor.

I couldn't even get excited about the new supply of C-4.

Charlie ended up relieving the corpse of a small 9mm of indeterminate manufacture, the explosive vest (having removed the battery in the electrical trigger first), and some boy's high school ring she'd been wearing on a chain around her neck. She was pretty for the instant I saw her terrified face before the top part of it became an expanding red cloud.

In the middle of all the numb, exhausted, thwarted lust, I had one coal left in the fire. It was a particularly hot little number, and it burned for my father and my brother.

My father set a machine into motion that took pretty teen girls like this one, killed them, brought them back to life and turned them into attractive explosive devices. It looked like my brother was Hell-bent on assisting Dad, too. The only reason I had a little incandescent coal left was because it was burning on hate.

Those two fuckers, and everyone who followed them, needed to die. While I doubted my power to end every single one of them, I wanted to be absolutely sure Dad and Stu were on the list. As much as I loved and still love Baj, looking down at that bloody high school ring, my dear friend became a secondary goal.

Charlie didn't interrupt my thoughts or ask me to help with disposing of Dead Tammy. She simply grabbed the body by the fairly expensive shoes and deposited it outside the front door of the store. I was dimly aware this was happening while my Future Main Love Interest was stark naked.

Then again, according to my terribly accurate, technologically enhanced internal clock, it was 3:52 am. Anyone up at that hour, watching out for us, probably deserved a little show for the trouble. God knows, it certainly had been a gruesome day for me.

Of course, if my FMLI (nice acronym, no?) was being watched by a pack of undead frat boys, they were just getting a look at one of the people most likely to deliver them back into their graves. It wouldn't pay for them to try to mess with Charlotte Cooper, tattooed sex valkyrie.

That thought managed to make me smile, even in the light of my tiny hate coal.

She came back, and we walked back to the Spa in silence.

I washed myself off again and gave her a nod, and we gathered up our things. On our way upstairs, I remembered to snag the 9mm and the C-4 vest from where we'd left them on the floor.

The bloodstained concrete could wait for just a little while.

I was unloading the pistol and sorting the ammo into the drawer when she broke the silence.

"Tired?"

"Yeah."

"Want to talk about it?" She sounded genuinely concerned, and I was distantly grateful for that. I don't know that I would have reacted well to Therapy Voice at that moment.

I scratched my head and said, "No, mostly because I don't know what to say. Lately, the daily events have been so far beyond my wildest experiences that I don't know how to process them, much less talk about it."

"I think that will be a problem as time goes on. Not just for you or me, but for everyone who survives all this."

"Do you think anyone will?" I asked, surprised that such a dire question had been lurking around inside me without being noticed.

She walked over to me, put her arms around me, and snuggled as we stood there. I don't know what I felt like to her, but to me, she felt like the single real thing in a nightmarish tornado of events.

"I think people still have a future. I think love has a future. I know zombies do not have a future."

"Why do you say that?"

"What happens when the last living human dies, and all that is left to walk on two legs is a zombie?"

I told her I didn't know.

"Then they'll die out, with nothing left to keep them alive. Mother Nature will reclaim the world."

"That's... unbelievably sad." I meant it, too.

"Uh-huh. Why do you think I want to believe in love so

much? It gives me hope, inspiration, and a place to stand when everything else has gone to Hell."

She's a brilliant, brilliant woman, and after listening to what she said, I decided to believe in it, too. I needed someplace to stand. I wanted someone to stand with.

I had both, and all I really needed to do was open my eyes a little wider to see it. My heart was a little more at peace when we went to bed, and I was more grateful for that than I could express.

Charlie rolled over in my arms and kissed me. "I know you're beat and there's more on your mind than I want to even try to guess at. I suppose I have one or two things I need to say, if you're all right with listening to me for a minute."

"I'm pretty sure I'd listen to you for years at a time."

She smiled that radiant smile that lit up the darkness of my room and ran her fingers down my chest. It was enticing, and I felt reactions pushing through the dung that had collected around my libido. This gentle play of sensual touch came to an abrupt end when she sank her fingernails into my nipples. I wanted to surge out from under the covers, but I didn't want to leave my nipples behind.

"Frank, if you ever, ever, ever keep important things from me from this moment forward, you had better make damned sure the bodies are buried. Because if I fall in love with you and find out you have yet another false identity, I will pop these titties right off you and feed them to feral kittens. Do I make myself absolutely clear?"

"EEEEE!"

She nodded, and pinched even harder. I couldn't help but buck a little under the covers, because my body wanted to do something to cope with the new frontier of torment that was being explored.

"I'm glad you see things my way. The other thing I wanted to say is I really want us to go on a date where you spend all day complimenting me, and we get up to some mad frisky afterward." She let my man-nips go.

"Yes!" I was enthusiastic. How could I not be? Blood was flowing back into my nipples! It also appeared to me as though the girl of my dreams wanted me to be frisky with her. My geek heart was doing back flips and spinning kicks through the bamboo jungle of my soul.

"But right now, I'm fucking tired. That gets you off the hook for tonight... eh, this morning. Just hold me real tight, tell me you think I'm shiny, and we'll snooze."

"You're so shiny!" I gave her a serious squeeze.

"I like you. You do what you're told. That's pretty shiny, too, Frankie the Hiking Staff."

Sleep came easily with her warmth beside me. A simple thing, like having someone to whom you really have taken a shine in bed with you, is unbelievably comforting. I would call that another hash mark on the checklist of things we find easy to take for granted.

I woke up when she shifted a bit, raising herself up on her elbow, but it was so decadent to be lying there that I didn't move. She was humming to herself.

"Sunshine in my eyeballs burns my retinas," she sang softly, "Sunshine on my boyfriend makes me smile."

"You can still smile with fried retinas?" My ability to warp tender moments should go down in someone's history books. I cracked one eyelid and looked up at her sleep-tousled hair and silly grin. She was still ravishing, even with crusties in the corners of her eyes.

"I can smile with fried anything. Unless my lips are fried, too, and all you'd get then is a toothy grimace."

Wow. I think I'd skipped right over Love and plopped into the Tar Pits of Adoration!

"I'd kiss you but I have horrible morning breath, and no one deserves that." Of all the compromising positions she'd seen me in, the only ones I really itched to keep to myself were morning breath and farting.

"Does that mean you don't want to cut the cheese around me either?" DAMN! Foiled again!

"I have no idea what you mean." I turned my head away

so she wouldn't see me squish up my face in mortal frustration. Hopefully, Baj hadn't built in some sort of Bluetooth networking with the nano-buddies. That would make life quite touchy.

"So, you're fart-shy?"

"How in the world do we get on conversation topics like this when we could be attacked by zombies at any moment?!"

She giggled. I hadn't heard her giggle before, and it was infectious. She sat all the way up, showing me curves that would need a high-powered Italian sports car to explore properly, and I believe I started to salivate.

"Look at it this way. Sure, we could be ripped limb from limb at any moment, though it is more likely that we'll be blowing bodies to bits today, too... and that makes every moment of normal that much more precious. More reason to laugh, touch, and be silly every chance we get. At least that's how I feel."

I sighed. "Yet again, your brain is every bit as fantastic as you are beautiful. I am in awe."

Charlie giggled, stood up, stretched, and gave me even more reason to be happy to have an extra normal moment. I was grateful that I was lying on my side; otherwise, there would have been a "tent" apparent in the covers. She probably would have laughed, but I would have felt awkward about it.

"Frank, you're super!" She reached down, tore the covers off me, and said, "You should get up with me and shower... Well! Is that for me, or is it just morning wood?"

Chagrin. Blushing. Quixote Fiesta. Utter inability to speak. Doom!

"Mumble." I had my mouth mostly shut and was fighting this bizarre compulsion I had to answer her question.

"What was that?"

"Yumble." I was starting to lose control.

"Come on, Frank, louder! Don't make me squeeze the

grapes before it's time."

"You."

She actually danced around a little and clapped her hands. "That's so great! I win! Yay! His penis likes me! His penis likes me!"

Oyé, Jefe... Ese dama, ah... ¿Piensa que soy muy guapo? Yes, I think the lady feels you're handsome. My Quixote was smug and retired from the field of combat filled with confidence that his return would be greeted with warmth. Ahem.

Charlie frowned a little, but I assured her he'd be back and that cheered her up immensely. She grabbed me by the hand and pulled me downstairs so we could brush our teeth.

Hooray for normal moments! They wouldn't last for long.

The daily ablutions didn't take all that long and were filled with the sort of cheerful, madcap goofiness that only new lovers can keep up for more than an hour at a time. We made a quick breakfast of various things we scrounged off of my supply shelves, put on some clothes, armed ourselves, and sallied forth.

It really was a nice, cool, sunny morning. Of course, there was still the matter of the Miss Teen Zombie Bomber corpse on the asphalt in front of my store door. I offered to drag it out to the big pile from the night before, and Charlie gratefully accepted my assistance in the matter. We walked, side by side, corpse feet in my hands, over to the garage.

"I'm wearing yesterday's clothes, and the only other stuff I have is with Shawn. I'll get changed while you drag off the beauty queen, and then we can hunt and kill some coffee. How's that?" She was actually perky. I was dragging a body, but she was perky, and I managed to cope with it, seduced as I was by the promise of coffee.

"All right. I'll be back in a few. Tease your brother for me, okay?"

"Like I breathe air!" She kissed me, thoroughly, and bopped off toward Shawn's front door.

I still had a few blocks of dragging to do, so I set off to do it in reasonable time, without a huge rush. As I rounded the corner, I saw Channing hooking up one of the Hot-Hot-Ow-Ow Destructo Projectors, and I called out to him.

"Sexy dweeb! How's the boy today?"

He turned around, saw it was me, and just shook his head. Our rapport, clearly, had yet to fall into place. "I take it that means you don't feel the same connection for me that I feel for you?"

"I'm here because I was ordered to be here, not to become buddies with all of you. Especially people full of nano-machines that attack and cannibalize... " He shuddered with revulsion, and I didn't blame him at all.

"Channing, if I had a free hand at the moment, I would swear to God that I'm about as thrilled with that development as you are. Much like everything else in this fucked up world, all I've got is what I've got, and some of it can't be changed."

He looked at the body trailing behind me.

"Did you eat her brains, too?"

"Actually, no. She was wearing a vest rigged with C-4 and Charlie blew her brains out. Then we went to bed." Come to think of it, saying those things in such a matter-of-fact way felt really strange.

"I don't understand you."

I nodded as I walked under where he was perched, looked both ways at the alley mouth, and deposited my erstwhile night visitor on the pile of her compatriots.

"Frankly, my dear, I don't understand myself most of the time. At least you and I can share the mystery together." I looked up at the gray square, mounted on the side of the wall, and allowed myself a bit of curiosity.

"So, does this pain ray work?"

"Once I connect this USB cable and turn on the generator, yes."

"What does it feel like?" I was curious because it sounded completely unreal to me.

"It feels like the whole surface of your skin is being fried. I was part of the group trial for this model, so you can trust me on the description."

"Damn. Could I feel it?"

"Are you categorically insane, or do you just pretend to be crazy for fun? This is not friendly pain. It really, really hurts."

"Yes, I get that. I'm just curious. Could you turn it on and then turn it right back off? Just a little taste?" I suppose, somewhere in my hidden heart lies the twitching form of an adrenaline junkie-masochist with attention deficit disorder. Don't tell anyone—they probably spray for people like me.

"Are you sure?"

"Yeah!" I actually bounced up and down a little, excited that I was going to get to try out a figment of Science's Imagination.

Channing didn't bother to give me a count of three, or even tell me that he'd agreed to do it. He just turned it on. I shrieked, turned around, and ran across the street. I vaulted a parked car and hid behind it until he turned the damned thing off.

The feeling made the Tasers of the night before pale in comparison.

"Didn't I tell you?" He hollered at me from across the four-lane road.

"Yes! You did! I believe you!"

"You don't want to try it again, do you? I can just plug it back in."

"NO!"

From the way his shoulders were moving, I could tell he was laughing at me and I wasn't really bothered by it. Considering the sensations that Active Denial thing was capable of dishing out, I was incredibly grateful to have that technology on our side, as well as someone capable of installing the things. Anything that would keep busloads of zombies from overrunning us was A-OK in my book.

Chapter 32

We were one day closer to the window Mister Yan told us to be expecting the big attack. Whether or not we would see any small ones before then was not anything I could predict, but being ready for that sort of thing wouldn't be a bad idea at all. These pain ray units would come in very handy.

What I wouldn't give for something that would stop rocket-propelled grenades and shoulder-mounted missile attacks!

I looked both ways and crossed the street. I didn't vault the car on the way back.

"So, Channing, how many more of these are left to install?"

"This is the last one. I got started right after the busload last night and haven't been to sleep yet."

For someone who was just taking orders about being here, I was grateful for his dedication.

"Why don't you come down from that ladder, and we'll go find coffee?" I waved him down to ground level. He nodded, climbed down, and we folded up the ladder together.

I slung it over my shoulder, and we walked back to the garage. If anyone was likely to have coffee brewing, it would be Shawn. If they were still with us, I would have taken Channing over to see Siddig, who was the man who had changed my outlook on the beverage. Maybe, if we all didn't die in the next few days, I could boil up some Siddig-style mud in a cup for people.

It was a nice idea. Sad, but nice.

When we got to the garage, we discovered quite a coffee klatch was already underway. Nate and all of his people were there, as were Flower, Buttons, and Omura. There appeared to be a spirited discussion of favorite combat and survival knives going on. A surprising amount of name dropping and showing off of toys was happening as well.

Nate's pal Franklin was extolling the virtues of his favorite knife, a handmade, evil-looking thing from American Kami that looked as though it could disembowel a pack of Yetis. Shoei Omura sung the praises of his preferred blade, saying that Chris Reeves was the one and only master of the hard-use knife. I grinned like a fool and pulled the Man Scythe out of the rig with that trademark snap of Kydex plastic. As usual, it stopped conversation dead.

I handed it to Franklin, who gently opened the blade out about halfway. He smiled, and it was the blissed-out smile of a true edged-weapon fanatic. My baby was garnering the attention she deserved.

"Who made this?" Franklin asked, closed the blade, and handed it to Charlie. She was making little "gimme" noises.

"The blade steel was smelted by Mack Lee, forged out by Scott Lewis, and the frame was milled by a couple of auto mechanics out in Fairfax, Virginia. They also did the final assembly."

"That is way beyond hot." He admired it, coveting my Darling while Charlie caressed her gently. I just sighed.

"Y'all are some sick monkeys!" Shawn appeared with coffee cups for Channing and me. "I don't see how you can make sharp things sound like they're your favorite topless dancer."

The assembled group chuckled at us for our perverse ways. I sipped my coffee for a moment, then retorted.

"Shawn? M-50 machine gun, refitted with a water-cooled barrel, plum-brown finish, and a full magazine of 3/1 armor-piercing tracer rounds."

"Oh man... yeah. That would be one smokin' piece of steel!"

"I rest my case." Everyone got what I was saying, even Shawn. Vindication was mine, sayeth the zombie killer.

Flower got a strange look on his face and yelled, "INCOMING!" We all hit the floor as something exploded near the side of the road. Guns came out, and the professional soldiers fell into instant formations.

Nate headed forward on point, trailed by his group. They skirted the IEDs at the end of Shawn's driveway that connected to Glebe Road and peered out around that dumpster. I saw him hold up four fingers, indicating two left and two straight ahead. Flower grunted and leapt to the top of the garage.

Omura looked at me, "Shawn, you, Frank, Charlie and Channing, stay put and stay down. That was a mortar, and they're trying to range in. That means we're dealing with a less experienced crew than before. Flower may take them out before they can land something in here."

We nodded, and I looked over at Buttons. He was crouched down, cradling his cup of coffee, and I asked, "About when will your next orbital gift arrive, and what did you target it on?"

"Six minutes, and the target area is the section of Glebe Road that directly connects to the side street where the parking garage is. I estimate a soccer field-size crater that may be as much as 20 feet deep."

"Fuck! That's bigger than the last shot, isn't it?"

"Yes, by about 50 percent. There will also be a decent amount of collateral damage from the debris exploding outward from the point of impact. Low likelihood of civilian casualties, and it probably won't detonate any nuclear devices."

"You mean there's a possibility that it *might*?"

"Of course."

Before I could reply to that, there was a hail of gunfire near where Nate and his friends were observing our latest annoyance. Looking that way I could see that none of them were in the line of fire.

A single shot rang out from the roof of the garage. Almost immediately afterward a muffled explosion and screams could be heard from beyond the dumpster. Nate held up two fingers, gestured to the left, and Flower squeezed off four more shots. Nate gave the thumbs-up sign and then stood up.

"What did we miss?" I called out to him from the garage floor.

"Matt put a bullet into the pipe of the mortar launcher, into the nose cone of the mortar. It exploded real pretty. The other four shots were double taps for the other two who weren't using good cover." Nate gave Flower two thumbs up and then got out of the way when he jumped down from the roof.

"I have to say, I was real skeptical about these nanotech add-ons, but," he gestured up to the roof, "I really like being able to jump around like that." There was something strangely unsettling about seeing a sniper smile like that.

"Based on the fun we just had, does anyone else feel we need to alter our set of plans?" I was beginning to wonder if we didn't need to just go over there and kick some heads before they could really put something into motion for tomorrow or the next day. While it is certainly an advantage to know your enemy is going to attack you in X number of days, it is also nerve-wracking. The little piddly annoyance attacks were also starting to seriously piss me off.

"I think," Buttons responded, "we should hold out for a few minutes before deciding anything. Then we get a look at the results of the bombardment and make a decision based on that data."

Nate gave me a comradely punch on the shoulder. "Waiting for anything like an attack is hard. Your patience wears thin really fast, so just chill as much as possible. They're still going to try to whittle us down before tomorrow or the next day."

I nodded. What I needed, besides the rest of my cup of coffee, was something active to do. Preferably something that would somehow add to the effort in some way or another. "Who do we have on lookout duty?" That seemed like a completely reasonable thing to volunteer for if people were needed.

"Omér and Jack for the next hour or so. Jim and Gina on the next shift." Nate pulled out his ever-present notepad. "And I've got Barry and Shawn down for the shift after that. The guys and I are going to walk the perimeter a little bit and see if there are any holes that need to be addressed."

"Ah." No dice. I didn't want to leave for the day and not be here if something happened. I needed, flat-out needed, to go do something.

"I'm going to go scout the area a little."

No sooner than the words were out of my mouth than a certain whistling thunderclap arrived to punctuate my sentence. What we didn't expect was how loud the impact would be. It actually rattled our windows, over a mile away. I can only imagine what it must have done to the windows in the buildings next to that stretch of highway, including the one that my father occupied.

It didn't matter very much if the glass imploded into the buildings or were pulled out of their panes by the air pressure behind the slug; there would be a huge amount of it everywhere. I couldn't help but hope that some of the troop numbers had been reduced by the impact and debris. We wouldn't know a thing until the dust cloud cleared, unless someone was insane enough to go look.

My mad idea for keeping myself occupied had arrived.

Chapter 33

"I want to go have a look at that. I'll be back soon." I got quite a few funny looks, but no one went to the trouble of telling me it was a bad idea or that I shouldn't do it. That worked just fine for me, really. "Hold down the fort while I'm gone!" I turned on my heel and jogged back to the store.

Charlie followed me. We made it into the store before she caught up with me.

"Are you sure you want to do that? That's a Hell of a lot of danger, sticking your hand in the beehive." She sounded rational and not as concerned as I might have expected from her.

We were standing at the checkout counter, and I tried to explain myself in a manner that made sense. That's one of the challenges you get when you have a brain that processes images better than words.

"I need to get out and do something. The 'waiting around for the next blow to fall' is making me a little crazy. I'm pretty sure I can get over there and back in all this chaos." I shrugged. "Besides, we really could use some on-the-scene visual reporting."

I could tell she suspected something, but her mouth said, "All right, I imagine this is your way of getting a little time to yourself to process all the stuff that's been happening. Please, and I really mean this, come back to me." She followed that up by hugging me so hard I fell backward onto the counter. "I do not want to lose you to zombies, or to something else you haven't talked to me about."

Jefe, besa la rubia. Esta un buen tiempo para un momento del amor. (Quixote again. Boss, kiss the blonde. It's a good time for a moment of love.)

This time I agreed with him, and kissed her with every joule of emotion I felt for her. It was electric enough I think my heart stopped beating for a moment.

"Charlie, I'm coming back. You're here, and wherever you are is where I need to be. Right now, I have to move... find out what our enemies have arrayed against us. I know there's no turning my father back from the path that he's on." Yes, I speak Hero.

"I'm telling you now, I am not your sister. I don't like furry midgets either. You watched those movies way too much, didn't you?"

"Errrr! Yub! Yub! Chabookie ookie!"

"Oh God," she rolled her eyes and massaged her temples, "I'm falling for a zombie-hunting dweeb! Aren't I?"

"Wanna see my Sarlacc Pit?" I stuck out my tongue and snaked it around for extra effect.

"Don't make me puke, farm boy. Now go upstairs, strap on your blaster and your lightsaber, go do what you need to do, and then come back to your princess. Make it snappy. Princesses don't like waiting!" She patted me on the cheek and then strolled out the door.

She had a really great stroll. It took me a few minutes to tear my brain away from the memory of watching her walk away, but when I managed it I headed up to my quarters for a little equipment.

I wondered if a couple of clips would do, or if I needed to upgrade to the gun I was using before I went cannibal. At that point I realized the less I thought about losing my shit and eating brains, the better I'd feel about the whole issue. In fact, I wouldn't mind if that problem went away entirely but that did not seem likely at all.

You're wounded; you need to heal up. That's a very binary situation for a tiny machine that is trying to keep you in optimal fighting form or is trying to make sure you survive in the first place. Although there were enough of them floating around inside me that I had to wonder if, as a group, they could think or if they only monitored and reacted through a very limited set of programming.

Could you call a limited set of programming by a different word? Like "instinct"? I wondered if there would ever be a way, other than sticking an Ethernet cable up my nose, to communicate with these little guys and ask them to do specific things. Baj would get some requests from me in that department, I thought, if we managed to save his ass.

For example, I wouldn't mind a set of retractable claws that didn't hurt when they popped in and out. I stood in my room, looked around to make sure no one was watching, crouched down, spread my arms, and said, "Snikt!" Yes, I did snarl a little for extra effect, but quietly. It was a nice moment of fantasy before deciding on the machine gun and a katana as my larger weapons of the day.

If you think I left the scythe behind, you would be sadly mistaken. I would rather leave my eyeballs in a bowl on my desk than not take that with me wherever I went outside the neighborhood. It was an extension of me in a way that no other tool or weapon ever surpassed in my experience. That feeling isn't something you can ignore, and I don't think it matters whether or not it is a firearm, sword, or a kitchen knife.

Dress code for the day? Basic black. You can never go wrong with black. Handgun. Machine gun. Sword. Man Scythe. Insatiable curiosity for more data about our opponents, and a willingness to remove offending heads... All go!

I went out my back window and dropped to the ground below. Sure, it was over two stories, but the nano-critters seemed to be good at things like jumping and landing. There's nothing wrong with taking every advantage you can get and then doing slightly superhuman things with it.

Dodging the trips and triggers for the IEDs was simple, since I knew the positions of each little surprise. For example, the explosive at the very end of the alley was underneath a recycling bin filled with glass bottles. If you nudged the bin too far, or put any weight on it over 50 pounds, it would explode. That was the first "deterrent" in a series that became progressively nastier.

In fact, the one Mister Yan detonated was large enough and nasty enough to leave very little of him behind. That was one of Gina's "Number 4" explosives. Her husband let it slip one night that she was planning a "Number 8" based on either magnesium or thermite. I believe his drunken confession involved the words "flaming magnesium pellets."

They're an odd match, but at least she's still got all her body parts after a few years of being an improvised demolitions specialist.

Standing at the side of the road, looking across towards the gas station where Charlie and I had dealt with the mortar launcher the other day, I could see the cloud of dust from the orbital slug's impact slowly drifting towards us. That would probably give us some crap in terms of cleaning up the neighborhood, but then it would be nice to do something simple like sweep up dust instead of coping with the bodies of undead interlopers.

I watched for any oncoming vehicles, didn't notice any, and walked across the road. Then I realized it was early afternoon on Sunday, and that cut down the likelihood of car traffic quite a bit. People were not all that interested in leaving home unless they had jobs, and on some level I think that was beneficial to familial cohesiveness. Whether or not that was the case, it was a positive thing to wish for.

My family was not that warm, tight-knit place I often wished that it were. If I went to the trouble of breaking down my motivations for sticking around anywhere in my life as an adult, I strongly suspect it would be tied to creating a feeling of home and family for myself. That certainly rang true for our little enclave of survivors.

Route 66 is between our neighborhood and the Ballston

area of Arlington. The building where my dear Papa set up shop was in an office block on the other side of the bridge that crosses over 66, give or take half a mile. I strongly suspected the reason Buttons chose the section of Glebe Road in front of the office buildings for the latest railgun target was because that stretch of road leads right up to that bridge. It would limit the directions the attack could come from, unless they had a good way to get around the crater and onto the bridge.

If that were the case, it would be a straight shot for them to drive right on up to the corner, unload whatever, and try to lay waste to us.

We could have targeted that bridge instead, but 66 was still a major route for anything going into or leaving DC. The debris would fall directly onto the road below and probably block it solidly for quite a while before the Armed Forces could remove it all. To say nothing for the potential fatalities of anyone driving on that stretch of the road when the bridge collapses, of course.

The road right beyond the bridge provided a reasonable target to create annoyance and delay for the enemy without going too far. While I might not like the man, on a personal level, Buttons did seem to have his head squared away as far as tactical decisions were concerned. That merited my grudging respect, if nothing else.

Between the gas station and the bridge was another neighborhood that was mostly, as far as we knew, abandoned. Flower and Nate often used the bell tower of the Methodist Church as an observation and convenient sniping point. I ducked into the neighborhood as soon as I was able, because walking down a road in broad daylight seemed like an excellent excuse for someone to take potshots at me. Body shots didn't concern me too much, unless there were enough of them to overwhelm my advantages, but the risk of getting a round to my skull wasn't worth the shortcut. Having nice brick houses, shrubs, and trees around me for cover made a lot more sense than just exposing myself willy-nilly to the idiots.

My nano-buddies perked up after about three blocks. Male. Zombie. Armed. According to my critters, he was forty feet away, roughly at my 2 o'clock. I looked over that way and saw him standing, leaning really, on the front porch of one of the nearby houses. He was not looking my way and did not appear to have seen me. Thank goodness for little favors. I took cover and had a better look.

With no pings on my internal network about other bodies nearby and having no clue what the range was, I had to assume that this one was alone. A lookout? Why else would he be hanging around on someone's front porch? I suppose there was a slight chance that he was the original homeowner, but I had to wonder why we'd never encountered him before.

Also, the digital camo fatigues and AR-15 rifle didn't look all that typical for Tom Suburbanite.

Next question: Where are the rest of them, if this guy is a lookout? Unfortunately, I couldn't just run around and have a look and see if there were extras nearby, because I'd likely run into them in the process. My brother did the whole Ninja Death from the Trees thing; I was prodded into more direct martial arts. Stealth is not a strong suit of mine. Although, God knows, there are days that I wish I were better at silent scuttling and hiding in plain sight.

When you can't answer your second question, it would be well to consider asking someone who might have the answer. The only candidate for my proposed line of questioning was Tom "Leaning Sentry" Suburbanite. I was feeling a little more like taking a direct approach with this fellow, mostly because I didn't want to get into torturing someone. Instead, I decided to rely on my wit and charm. Sometimes you just have to make a change to keep your life interesting.

I stood up, started walking as though I'd been doing it for a while, and put my hands in my pockets. "Hey!" I called out to him from about thirty feet away. "What the Hell was that God-awful noise a while back?"

He became alert very quickly, and his AR-15 came up, pointing at the center of my body mass. "Stop where you are!"

"Okay. That's a really classic thing to say to someone, you know! Man, they sent me over here to relieve you!"

"I haven't seen you before. Who sent you?" He was not looking or sounding terribly convinced about any of this.

"Sarge. Big guy, looks like he could bench press that Bradley back at the office." I made vague gestures of height and broad shoulders, praying he wouldn't notice that my fingernails weren't Zombie Issue from thirty feet away.

"That's the Major. Sarge is smaller. You're not military." Great. Data, but backed by a certain amount of disbelief.

"I'm in Management," and I pronounced the capital letter very carefully.

"Oh, shit! Sir. Sorry, Sir!" He actually saluted. "Why did they send you up here to relieve me? You guys never come out to the front."

"Well, it boils down to this. If you never get out and meet people, how can you expect to manage them?" It sounded good to me!

"Yeah. You've got a point, Sir!"

I clasped my hands behind my back and started walking toward him. "So, you head back and I'll take over here until your scheduled relief shows up." He nodded, slung the machine gun over his shoulder, and looked positively pleased the shift had ended a little earlier than he planned.

"Sir, did you notice if they'd delivered the new bunch of cattle to the pen in the parking lot yet?"

"Which pen?" Chancy question to ask, perhaps, but I knew this would end with me killing him and it didn't matter terribly much if it was in a fight or some quieter option.

"There was one in the side lot of the church when I headed over here. Did they set up another one?" He didn't appear to be suspecting much of anything, judging by the tone of his voice, and wasn't reacting in an aggressive manner as I approached.

I turned and pointed, "They brought out a second one about two hours ago and set it up in the front lot."

He plunged a knife into my guts as I was turning back around to face him. God as my witness, that knife hurt more than all of the bullets I'd met over the previous couple of days. The intimacy of having this jackass halitosis-breathing zombie in my face, while he twisted the blade around in my innards, was even worse than the pain of being stabbed in the first place.

All he did was smile when I vomited blood all over the front of his uniform. "How stupid do you think I am, fucker? I'm the Sarge, you know."

"I don't know. All you undead bottom-feeding sons of bitches have been mighty stupid in my experience." I don't believe all of what I thought managed to make it out clearly between the blood and the strange groaning noises I was making.

"Doesn't matter much now, because I'm going to pull the knife out and watch you die."

Chapter 34

I have to say, having the knife pulled out at an angle, rather than straight back, was a really horrible coda to that experience. There wasn't any option other than collapsing, so that is precisely what I did. All of the muscles in my abdomen were in spasm, and I was fairly sure that some of my intestines were now squashed between my body and the ground.

Sarge did his best evil laugh. In my haze, I gave it a 5 on a scale of 1 to 10.

"Wait a minute!" He had the nerve, the bald-faced nerve, to sound chipper about something. "You're *that* guy, aren't you?" He reached down and I could feel him pull the Man Scythe out of the rig. If I had been able to kill him for touching my weapon, I would have, but I could barely manage an anemic growl. As it was, the tsuba of the katana was invading the hole in my gut and I was lucky to make any noise at all.

My beautiful baby was being violated by a resurrected grunt and there was nothing I could do to stop it. To call the feelings simple "frustration" could never, ever cover the rage that I felt. It got worse when he snapped the blade open and started swinging her around like the clueless arboreal chicken-shit bastard he was.

"Jesus! If I'd know you were the Sickle Guy, I'd have shot you first, and then used this to chop off your head!" Sarge crowed at his amazing stroke of luck. As for me, I wanted to be able to stand up and stroke his cranium with my rifle butt. "You know... you know, I could still cut your head off with it. Then again, you'd get to die way too easily for the amount of trouble you've caused. I got time. We can play Cut off Things until you're about to die. Then I can cut off your head!"

"Sickle Guy? Did you just call me 'Sickle Guy,' you misbegotten sack of creamy monkey turds?"

"What did you just say, soon-to-be-dead Sickle Guy?" He punctuated things by swinging Her around like a baboon with a broom. He didn't notice, because I was down on my front, that I was starting to heal. Apparently, wooden porches have something nano-critters can break down into useful raw material.

"I said I'm going to punch you in the balls so hard your granddaddy will feel it, you poly-orchid, seagull-raping, toe-jam licker."

That did it! He really started pacing and growling then, muttering obscene things about raping my mother and pissing on the face of my dead father. I started to laugh, because I actually liked the idea of someone pissing on Warren "The 'F' is for 'Fuck You'" Hightower. I got clear on one thing very quickly: Sarge didn't share my sense of the absurd.

My right hand was stretched out on the porch supporting me, and it suddenly had the blade of my scythe growing out of the back of the palm. I howled in pain; anyone would have done the same. It was especially nasty because the pain in my guts was starting to subside and I had room in my brain to process fresh sensations.

Looking on the bright side of life, the blade was lodged in the wood under my hand. Turning again to the Dark Horrible side of life, the bastard was wrenching the blade around, trying to get it to come free. Needless to say, my right hand was being mangled as he exorcised his frustration with being stuck in the porch.

Sometime during the wrenching I felt my consciousness push free of my skull and settle into Frank's mental backseat. If things hadn't felt so calm, I might have genuinely felt bad for Sarge having to face whatever horrible thing was about to occur. Instead, I watched events unfold with a certain distracted interest.

My left hand whipped up from underneath my body and backhanded Sarge in the family jewels. It must have been quite an impact, because he flew backward against the door of the house and the Man Scythe went with him. When he landed, sprawled like a discarded stuffed animal, I could see the front of his uniform pants were turning black over the camo pattern.

He didn't scream. He wailed, dropped my baby, and tried to comfort himself by putting his hands on his crotch. Then again, maybe he was just trying to see if he was intact or not. Regardless, the pain was so severe he couldn't touch himself to confirm anything at all. Poor little guy!

My body stood up, and I could feel my mouth open, even if I couldn't see it. My lungs filled with air, and it rushed back out, contorted by my vocal cords into a noise that I hope I never hear again. It was the jungle nightmare of some simian creature crossed with Satan, bellowing out the rage of every generation of bipedal creatures since they came down from the trees in the first place.

Sarge froze stiff and managed to go from a healthy undead gray pallor to dead white in a fraction of a second.

The body I no longer controlled surged forward with the sort of speed God reserved for venomous snakes, hummingbird wings, and the common cold. Both hands came down on the sides of Sarge's skull with a sharp cracking noise. My left hand pulled backward and then struck out, slamming two of my fingers into each of his eye sockets.

With a growl I twitched my hand and the top of Sarge's skull came free like peeling the apron off of a crab at your favorite seafood restaurant. I was lightly surprised, from my vantage point, that I didn't damage his eyeballs, just popped them out onto his cheeks. Oh! Well done, Body! Well done!

However, just popping his skull open wasn't enough to make my hindbrain happy. Barely a breath after levering his noggin off, my bleeding right hand snagged his nearest eyeball, flipped it back, and pointed it at his brain. I guess he could see, because he screamed and shat himself.

He didn't stop making noise until the first big scoop of brains came out.

Abstractly, I considered the situation and decided the whole thing would rank in my Top Three Most Horrible Ways to Die. As usual, my musings were cut short by the sound of a twig snapping somewhere close by. Company had arrived.

I wasn't able to keep track of how many of them there were because my eyes were taking snapshots of them, their positions, and their weapons far too quickly. I saw my hand had wrapped itself around the handle of the Man Scythe at the same moment they opened fire on me. Everything after that I perceived in jump cuts and strobe light flashes of movement, punctuated by the sounds of guns going off.

The conscious part of my mind that was observing all of it simply had enough and checked out. I don't blame myself for wanting to blank it all out, because I got to see the results after I regained consciousness. I didn't stop to count the bodies, parts of bodies, or piles of... remains. I just ran home.

Chapter 35

Having gone through two experiences in which my discerning consciousness had been pushed aside for survival purposes, I felt as if I had a little room to take a look at what went on. The first episode had been, I think, purely to obtain material for use in repairing my body. This most recent occasion was more than a little different.

The first time I attacked a bunch of zombies was brutal, calculating, and maybe even vicious, but it wasn't sadistic. Making Sarge look at his own brain, especially while I was scooping bits out, qualified as sadistic. What's more, that sadism and brutality remained after I'd consumed the tissue. Perhaps it was because a threat arrived before I could ramp back down into "normal" behavior?

I wanted to believe that was the case. The Wolverine makeover sounded fantastic in my little fantasy narrative, but to be actually ruthlessly savage was a lot for me to bear. I also noticed that, in this instance, I did not feel warm and fuzzy about things as I had the night I got Tasered repeatedly. If anything, I felt a lot of concern.

The nano-critters did not come with a convenient manual or active "Help" function. No one, maybe not even Bajali, knew what they were capable of doing. Optimizing an organism for battle and survival could mean an incredible range of things, from physical changes to neurological and psychological ones. In all seriousness, there would probably need to be changes in *all* of those areas to stack the deck for surviving combat situations.

I hoped Baj had answers. I hoped Baj had a clue about what the changes would be and if there was some kind of upper limit where no more alterations would take place. These were things every person in our community needed to know, especially the kids.

Children are walking, talking, Freudian Id. What in the name of God would you get by altering a child for combat in this way? If the world was normal, and these children had to go to school, would they be ending playground scuffles by decapitating the other kids?

Every gift is a double-edged sword. Maybe this is why my Japanese language teachers used to say that gratitude was expressed in shades of regret. Because every gift has a price you can't see until later?

It didn't seem long at all before I popped out of the neighborhood and arrived at the gas station across the street from our community. What surprised me was that there were at least a hundred undead, armed with "peasant weapons," groaning and howling as they tried to breach the Active Area Denial system's force field of Ouch. Thankfully, they weren't paying attention to me.

What they were doing looked something like a peasant rebellion crossed with a mosh pit. Periodically, the group would force one of their tribe forward into the Denial Area and watch that individual scream and flee back into the crowd. I couldn't tell if they were having fun with it or if it was some sort of tribal dominance display of tossing the weakest member into the dangerous situation to see if things had become safe or not.

I was deeply puzzled, grateful I wasn't noticed, and on the verge of laughing at them. Then one of them had a brilliant idea after noticing the field only worked in a rough hemisphere in front of the opening between the buildings. He tried to cut through the custom frame shop, rather than face the heat, so to speak. He walked right into the trap that Gina and her Homeland Defense Forces had set in every one of those empty shops.

The explosion was absolutely deafening. The front of the custom frame store exploded outward in a gigantic belch of flames, smoke, noise, and the strange "zzzzzzz!" of tiny objects shooting outward. From my vantage point it looked like three rows of nearby ruffians were mowed down like dandelions in a tornado. Everyone behind them began yelling and screaming almost instantly and began to flee.

They were running right at me. I was given a grace moment to decide what to do about the bum rush of panic-filled undead peasants, and I settled on flipping the safety off my machine gun. It seemed to me I had been given an opportunity to reduce the number of our enemies, almost as though someone had presented me with a barrel of trout and ordered me to go fishing.

I simply stood my ground and waved my gun across the oncoming rush as if I were watering my petunias. The gun clicked empty, and I slapped another clip in. Twice. When the rush was over I stood in the center of a broad fan of immobile bodies, and zombies on their way to dying a second time. There were some *almost* capable of running away but for the rounds that had taken them in the leg or hip. Those cried.

Walking in a small circle, I surveyed the carnage, marked where I heard the noises of those who had yet to shuffle off to the happy hereafter, and sighed. I needed to decide if I was capable of finishing off an opponent who was begging and pitiful, because I didn't want the Critically Wounded Tabernacle Choir wailing until they finally died at some point later on.

"Excuse me, all of you freaks of nature that are too wounded to run away," I caught their attention with my witty patter and gore-smeared countenance, "if any of you would like to be finished off right now to avoid the rush, please raise your working limb."

"Are you telling me you want to know if we want to die?" This question came to me from a fellow to my right who looked like he might have been an investment banker before he turned to a life of consuming the undefended. His intestines were everywhere.

"Yes. It seemed to be a polite thing to ask, considering you're still alive enough to answer."

"Fuck you. No, I don't want to die. I want to get up, pull my guts back in, and go find a not-blond woman to suck the blood out of. After that, I want to go screw EVERYBODY... then a blond woman. Then I fucking want to go to Fiji!"

I felt as though I heard sarcasm, so I asked about it. "Are you being sarcastic with me, by any chance?"

"Wow! How long did it take you to figure that out, Einstein? You didn't blow out any brain cells deducing that, I hope!" He actually propped himself up on his arms in order to harangue me that much better. "You, you sick bastard, shot me in the back. IN THE BACK! At close range! You blew my guts out all over the street! I can't feel my legs, which means you SEVERED MY GODDAMNED SPINAL CORD! Of course I want to DIE! Fuck you!"

He actually started chanting that short phrase. I put a .45 round through his forehead, and the chanting stopped.

"All right! Anyone else want to shorten your decline and request it a bit more politely? Just wave a functioning limb. Any limb!"

I saw three hands and one foot raised in the air. Only one of them really got to me. He looked up at me and smiled.

"You know, I'm scared to death about this. I don't want there to be nothing when I'm dead." I couldn't tell if the tears were from the pain he was in, or from the existential angst.

"It's possible, you know," I said as I crouched down beside him, "that the virus puts you into stasis after you die the first time. Maybe you never actually *die*, per se, as much as you just stop until the repairs are done." That was disturbing, because it was so close to the description of what happens when the nanotech army fixes my wounds.

"You mean there might actually be a God and a Heaven?" He looked both incredulous and a little hopeful.

"There might be. No one has ever come back with solid evidence on either side of the issue."

"In that case, I don't suppose there's a priest around?"

I hated to tell him that there wasn't, but there wasn't a priest for... I actually couldn't remember the last time I'd heard of one nearby. "No, there's not. What do you need one for?"

"I want to make a last confession before I'm done." I could tell he was completely serious. "So I guess I'm going to confess to you, if you don't mind taking the time."

"All right." I still don't know why I agreed.

"Ah. Bless me, Sickle Guy, for I have sinned. It has been eight years since my last confession." He, very literally, told me the story of his life for the previous years leading up to that moment, lying on the sidewalk with several bullet holes in his body.

While I was listening, I noticed Flower walking across the road with his sniper rifle slung across his back. About midway through Andrew the Zombie's confession, Flower knelt down beside me, made the sign of the cross, and started to listen. When Andrew drew his story to a close, it was clear he was starting to fade.

"Andrew, I want you to pray with me," Flower said, making the sign of the cross on the dying man's forehead. "Oh my God, I am heartily sorry for having offended thee, because I dread the loss of Heaven and the pains of Hell, but most of all because they offended thee... "

I listened to both of them, noting that Andrew's voice was getting weaker and his eyes were slowly losing focus. I picked back up as Flower was saying, "... with Mary, the Virgin Mother of God. Never has it been known that anyone who fled to her for comfort was turned away. I forgive you your sins, in the name of the Father, the Son, and the Holy Spirit. I commend you, in this final moment of your life, to join our Lord in Heaven, and to sit at the table of our Lord, Jesus Christ, at his right hand, until he comes again in Glory. Amen."

Andrew breathed his last about two minutes after Flower was done. I stood up, feeling as though I'd trespassed on something, because I had never been a believer in much of anything, at least as far as God went. My friend Matt, who had a side to him I'd never seen or expected, reached down and closed the zombie's eyes. Then he put a round through his forehead for good measure.

"I know you, Frank," he said as he stood up beside me. "You want to know what that was all about." He looked down at me, being a few inches taller than me, and gave me a wry half-smile. "Haven't you ever wondered why I'm not married at my age?"

"No. I'd never really thought about it."

"I was a priest and a chaplain in the Army. I lost my faith in Iraq and left the Church. The only thing I had after my tour was finished was the faith of the gun. I requested Special Forces training when I re-enlisted. I never bothered to look for a life partner, since things got a little busy over the past couple of years."

He turned and began to walk back toward the ruins of the custom framing store, and I stood there for a minute, trying to process what I'd heard.

I called out to him, "Did you find your faith again?"

He turned around, waved me over, and replied. "Yes. I found my faith again with these people, here. Siddig helped me, believe it or not. Never suggested I become a Muslim either." We walked through the wreckage of the store together, with nothing but the sight of our chosen home in front of us.

"I notice, Frank, you look like you've seen a little activity since you left earlier."

"Yeah. I never made it out to the overpass to have a good look at the damage. Our little friends have an advance position in the Methodist Church parking lot."

Flower grimaced, "That could be a problem for our rescue plans. We'd have to go quite a bit out of our way to get over 66 and then change our insertion point."

"I know." We were walking up the alley behind the store, and I could see Gina and her husband tinkering with an open wooden wine box. "Are they working on the replacement for the one that just blew up?"

"Yep. Did you like the cookie cutters?"

"Is that what the zinging things were?"

"Oh yes."

"They're pretty horrible." They were. I'd had a look at the bodies before Matt and I walked back through the smoking hole that used to be a store. There's a Cuban dish called "Ropa Vieja," or "old clothes," where the meat has been cooked for hours and then shredded. Something like pulled pork barbeque. That's what the bodies reminded me of.

"Indeed they are." We waved at Gina and Mark when we passed them. They nodded as they argued the finer points of appropriate remote triggering action. Ex-chaplains, explosives geeks, nanotechnology wizards... You never know who your neighbors are.

The better I got to know them, the more I was impressed. In one or two cases, the more I got to know some of them, the more surprised I became. Flower used to be a priest. That was easily the oddest revelation about one of my neighbors I'd been privy to in months. Anything could be next. Maybe Shawn was a Chippendale dancer prior to his career as a mechanic?

No, probably not. That was a mental image worth destroying entirely, but with my luck it would stay with me for a very long time.

Flower and I ended up standing around the bay of Shawn's garage, listening to some of the Home Defense planning. Channing, Buttons, Shawn, and the rest of that division were going over what they'd learned from the Denial System in action. They agreed it worked very well and made things difficult for a large group of potential invaders.

Buttons turned to me when the agreement noises

stopped and asked, "Well, what did you see while you were out there?" I gave everyone a quick summary of what I'd learned, at least as far as the church parking lot went. My shredded clothes and fabulous Alice Cooper makeup (consisting of dried blood, brains, and other bodily fluids) were eloquent testament to the resistance I'd faced.

"Well, while you were out getting your balls shot off, we got some decent satellite images of the damage from our last railgun shot." Buttons looked quite pleased with himself about that.

"Yeah, I wish I could have made it that far, but getting my bowels cut out ruined my attention span. How did we do with that shot?"

Buttons turned his laptop around to me and poked one of the symbol keys, and I got a slideshow of the sort of damage we'd done. The impact was just beyond the 66 overpass, and I'm pretty sure he'd been inaccurate when he estimated the hole would be about the size of a soccer field. Without actually going out there to the site, waving hello to the nice zombies, and standing on the rim of the crater, I could only estimate how big it really was. It was a city block long if it was an inch, and the impact must have crushed the pipes underneath the road, because the images showed it filling with water.

Chapter 36

I said "Wow!" under my breath. It was everything we could have hoped for and a little bit more. When I perused the photos in greater detail, my heart skipped a beat and I was filled with glee. On the far side of the crater from the bridge there was a wreck.

Apparently, our little gift crushed their Bradley Fighting Vehicle, as well as a huge amount of road surface. In the photos there were two long lines of zombies trying to drag the wreckage out of the hole using chains. The armor plate was flattened, and even in the photos I could see the ripples in the surface of the metal. The slug must have hit the front of the Bradley, or somewhere very close to it, because the metal was corrugated in concentric curves like the ripples in a pond after you've tossed a stone into the water.

That little toy of theirs was the one thing I was most afraid of, at least as far as a potential attack went. Certainly, if my father had a suitcase nuke hanging around, he could turn us all into charcoal, but that would be incredibly fast in comparison to being blown to bits by the guns of a Bradley. Then again, we might survive a fusillade from machine guns!

I thought about what sort of situation we'd be in if there were a dozen of us, reduced to our nano-critters running our bodies, while we scavenged for whatever they decided was necessary to fix us up. Icky. Very icky, indeed.

"The laser satellite will be in the proper orbit in about six hours." Buttons' mention of that retaliatory goodness popped me out of my reverie headfirst.

"Laser satellite? As in, 'zap, zap, zap'?" Shawn hadn't heard about that, or so it seemed.

"Yes. A tactical, space-based, solar-powered laser weapon." Buttons sounded as if he'd explained that several hundred times already and that one more time, just one more, would make his kidney stones start to pass. It was a cocktail of boredom, irritation, and surrender to the lowest common intellectual denominator. I decided to forgive him because he didn't know Shawn was a crazed mechanical genius, and I was still freakishly happy about the demise of the Bradley.

"Is there an upward limit of how many times we can fire it, or does it just keep going until you burn it out?" That question came from one of Nate's compatriots, Fitzgerald, I think.

"The batteries will give us six shots at high power, which is what we would want for something like this. They'll recharge completely in 24 hours, but we would be able to get one or two low-power activations before the full-charge mark."

"What would low power get us?" Fitzgerald was looking thoughtful. "How many low-power shots on a full charge?"

"Low power from orbit is the equivalent of fusing glass at ground zero. We could get as many as 40 on a full charge. Fairly rapid fire as well, but that wouldn't be fantastic for the local weather."

"Why is that?" I asked.

"You get channels of superheated air, water vapor, and atmospheric disturbances in very small areas. Depending on the weather, a grouping of five or six shots within a small target area will cause small, extremely intense thunderstorms when the cooler air causes the superheated air to cool. Serious lightning strikes." Buttons shook his head as if he had remembered something uncomfortable.

"I don't know about you all, but that sounds like a very interesting way to distract a large number of armed opponents at the same time." Fitzgerald was smiling. He did have a point, especially if the laser were used at night. Much cooler temperatures could make for some very impressive thunder and lightning.

"Sounds like an excellent reason to do a preemptive strike at niiiiii," I tried to finish the sentence, but someone had shoved an ice pick into the middle of my skull. The ground came up and hit me while I clutched at my head.

I could tell people were crowding around me, checking my eyes, pulse, and things like that, but I was too involved in the agony that was churning in between the hemispheres of my brain. There was a feeling of cognitive static, like little electrical charges popping on and off, and the pain started to let up. I was able to open my eyes and rapidly discovered my field of vision was occupied by a large redneck.

"Shawn, would you please give me some room to breathe. I can smell the chicken salad you had for lunch."

"Oh." He was kind enough to give me the space I asked for. "Are you all right?"

"Yeah. That was really nasty, whatever it was." I closed my eyes again and took a few deep breaths. I had a passing thought that I wish I knew where Charlie had gotten off to, and my internal point of view shifted.

There was a ghostly map in my head, filled with bright sparks. I could tell I was sitting in a patch of eight sparks, and there were other twinkling lights grouped all over the gossamer view of the entire neighborhood. A spark I seemed to know belonged to Charlie was sitting in the map's representation of Jayashri's living room with another spark telling me that it was Jayashri herself. The third spark in that group announced itself as Chunhua Yan.

"Oh. Wow."

"What is it, Frank?"

"I think that instant migraine was a new nano-tech goodie coming online. I know where everyone in the neighborhood is. Charlie, Grandmother Yan, and Jaya are sitting in Jaya's living room. Nate's wife is over in Barry's basement with almost all of the kids. This is so cool!"

I had a sudden urge to look at the Charlie spark, so I let the vision float up in my head. It was as though she was an icon on my computer screen, and I wanted to mouse over her or touch the icon. There was a desire to interact with the image, not in terms of moving it to a different place, as much as it was a sense that there was more data to be had. The funnier, or stranger, feeling was that Charlie was interacting with the spark that represented me.

"Frank?" I heard her voice and felt her presence inside me. My ears didn't register actual sounds.

"Oh. Jesus." I looked up at Shawn, and he gave me a quizzical look back. "I think I just got cellular service in my skull."

Charlie laughed. It was almost as clear to me as it would have been if she'd been standing beside Shawn. "Yeah, this little function showed up for us a little earlier today. Tell my brother and the rest of the gang that we need you over here. All right?"

"Okay." I didn't have much more than that to say, as shocked as I was. "Shawn, I just got pinged by Charlie. They need me over there. I'll be back in a bit." I got up, feeling extra shell-shocked, and headed over to Jaya and Baj's house. I walked over in a daze, looking like something that had been spewed out of a pet food factory.

I knocked on the front door and just let myself in; after all, they were expecting me. Charlie rushed over and gave me a huge hug, ignoring all the dried crap and the shredded shirt. Jayashri gave me a genteel wave, which I returned with gusto. There was a little Asian woman sitting on the floor who was not Grandmother Yan, because this woman was far too young and certainly more attractive. Mind you, Grandmother Yan was lovely for a woman in her 80s, but this woman should have been on the cover of magazines.

"Well, the nano-critters aren't right all the time. They told me Grandmother Yan was here with you two, but I don't believe I've met you before." I walked over, held out my hand, and got ready to be suave.

The woman covered her mouth with both hands and shook with laughter. Her laugh, even behind her hands, sounded like bells ringing. When she stopped, she looked up at me, grabbed my hand, and used it to pull herself up from the chair. I was a bit surprised when she hugged me.

"Frank, you are still my favorite! Why haven't you made big, strong babies with Charlie yet?"

Sputter!

"Chunhua dropped by about three hours ago," Jaya said, "and I can see you understand how surprised we were."

Extra sputter with pickle and special sauce.

The incredibly attractive Asian lady looked up at me, smiling, but didn't let me out of the hug.

"Last night, I had cravings for all sorts of food. I ate every dried berry I had been saving, a wheel of Yolanda's cheese, and three chickens. When I woke up this morning," she stepped back out of the hug and gestured up and down her body, "I looked like this, and my broken English wasn't broken anymore."

"Why? How? Huh?" My eloquence had decided to take a serious coffee break in favor of trying to be shocked and surprised at the same time.

"We spoke about that very issue. It appears that the nanotechnology reversed her cellular aging, repaired various kinds of physical damage," Jayashri did not look happy when she explained all this, "and slightly rewired Chunhua's brain. She is optimized for combat and survival in a somewhat more grand manner than we are."

"Frank, you probably want to sit down for the rest of this. We've got a theory that is a little unsettling."

I took Charlie at her word and simply plopped myself down on the carpet.

"Charlie, while he hasn't fallen to your charms, you certainly have trained him well!" Chunhua giggled and gave Charlie a high five.

"You know, all the training in the world is meaningless if

you don't have a good foundation to build on," Charlie was on the verge of laughing hysterically, "and my Frank is superb material for my training program."

"Are we going to get to the disturbing stuff now, or are you just going to put a harness on me and ride me into the sunset?"

The renovated Chunhua Yan broke into applause, and Charlie collapsed over a chair, laughing her ass off. Jayashri didn't laugh, but her eyes were bright and full of mirth over the whole situation. I remembered what Charlie and I had discussed about laughter and enjoying moments of normal life in the middle of our shared insanity, and allowed myself to share in the laughter. I needed it more than I realized, as is often the case.

"The disturbing thing that we've been talking about," Jaya began, "is the nanotechnology itself. Have you not noticed how similar it is to the zombie virus?"

I stopped laughing. "What do you mean?"

"The critters, as you call them, repair damage and improve the body's ability to survive extreme situations. You are also gently altered in such a manner that your innate martial abilities are enhanced. Those are also characteristics of what the virus does for the host."

"Yeah, but people have to die before the virus really kicks in on the combat improvements." I wanted to find a reason to support that they'd made a really odd connection, rather than believe it. "I don't think the virus heals people before they die, and it certainly doesn't afterward. There's something wrong with your theory."

"We do not know if it heals people prior to death. Very few infectees live long enough to study, but we do know the virus goes into overdrive when they die and rebuilds their body."

"Where are you going with this? I know you've got a point." I may have sounded a little harsher than I intended, but it was bothering me that I felt as though she was beating around the bush.

"What Jayashri is trying to say is that she is concerned that Baj built the nanotech along the same lines as the actual virus... A technological version of the biological problem." I wasn't entirely sure why Charlie took over the explanation, but I did notice that Jaya looked incredibly uncomfortable.

"All right, supposing that is what he did. What's the problem?"

"I am not going to call anything that has saved our lives a 'problem.' The source of my upset is that I know my husband did not create this technological wonder overnight. He worked on it for years, some of which were prior to the outbreak of the virus." She was jittering in her chair and pulled her feet up under herself as if they were cold. "How do you create a technological counter for a biological adaptation as perfect as this is?"

My feet grew cold and the hair on my arms tried to stand up and walk right off my body.

"You can't create effective opposition if you don't know the nature of the opponent." I was very glad to be sitting on the floor, because it decreased the possible distance I could fall. "You're saying my father had samples of the virus years before the outbreak, and Baj began work on the technological counter... no, not counter, really... the technological version of the virus... at about the same time."

My guts were churning, and the course of my thoughts was uncomfortable, to say the very least. I knew the question I needed to ask and it frightened me.

"Jaya, what happened to Siddig, Miryam, and Little Siddy's bodies?" I didn't want an answer. I truly did not, because it had the potential to turn every good thing about surviving completely sideways.

My lovely, gentle, fierce, and graceful friend bowed her head. I heard her answer, even though she said it under her breath. "We had to burn them."

"Why?" My voice was cold enough that Chunhua and Charlie recoiled in their chairs.

"Their wounds," Jaya looked up at me, weeping silently,

"were severe. Each of them... oh. Each of them had been hit in the head by debris. Their skulls were no longer intact, and neither were their brains."

"The critters tried to repair them. Didn't they?"

She didn't speak, just nodded.

"They weren't themselves?"

"No. They were feral machines that did not know us. Yolanda and I nearly died that night while we were doing our best to prepare their bodies to be buried."

"God." I couldn't do much more than just shake my head.

"If Yolanda were less skilled than she is, or if I were not as good with a firearm, we would be just what they were... machines hunting in order to repair themselves. We took their heads and burned the bodies and heads separately."

"What did Bajali turn us into?"

"The perfect weapon against our enemies." Jayashri's melodic voice was uncharacteristically flat, and tears were still rolling down her face.

I had asked the questions and received my answers. My father started this whole fucking ball rolling. We weren't any more human than the zombies, and I had a dear friend to thank for it. I may never be able to say whether that was the crowning moment to a day that was filled with confessions, absurd amounts of violence, and sadism that I could not remotely control. All I knew in that moment was that I wanted the little bastards out of my body, even if it meant the next bullet I took ended everything for me.

My "critters" felt like just another version of the enemy.

"Is this my karma for having been born to a crazy man who wants to turn people into cows? I get to be as horrible a canker as he is, but I get my better living through technology?" I wanted to rage, but I didn't have the energy. It felt as though the only thing left under my skin was high technology and rancid yogurt.

"I do not know if it is karma or a bizarre confluence of events. I just wanted to—" Jaya broke down all the way, and

Charlie had her arms around her before I could finish exhaling.

Chunhua sat back down in the chair and hugged herself tightly, as if she couldn't be sure more arms would be comforting for Jayashri or if they would be an intrusion. I just sat there, like some kind of trans-human horror show, blank on things to say or do.

Somewhere in the back of my head, a part of me wished I could wave a wand and smooth it all over. We were stuck together, an extended family of hybrid Terminators who refused to surrender to the Machine, and that is how we would have to stay until we completed the one quest that had never changed. We needed to bring Bajali home. He was ours, and he was the one lynchpin that held our shared fate together.

He would be able to do something, give us back our human birthright of pain, healing, and death, if anyone could. I begged a God to whom I didn't pray that what I hoped for would come true.

It took some time for Jayashri to cry it out and for me to find a little equilibrium in the morass of churning, half-formed thoughts in my skull. Chunhua was probably the most lost of everyone in the living room, sitting there in what amounted to a brand new body and not knowing where to turn.

"Chunhua," I said, "I don't think I can call you 'Grandmother' now and sound at all convincing." I was able to give her a shadow of a smile when I said it.

We all laughed a little at that description, and it dispelled a little of the angst in the room. I was a little taken aback when she kept talking about it.

"Really, I used to wonder why women who had plastic surgery wanted to show it off to everyone they know. Now I understand it much better! It was all I could do not to run around the neighborhood stark naked earlier today!" Chunhua stood, pulled up her shirt, and said, "I mean, look at these! They weren't this perky when I was 16 years old!"

She pulled it back down, took a deep breath, and continued. "I'm not sure if I care that I'm a technological marvel, because I'm young again, very good looking, and feeling very... passionate!"

A pin could have dropped on the plush carpet and it would have sounded like the noise that had accompanied the Big Bang. Charlie, Jayashri, and I just stared, completely flummoxed by the display of perkiness. The lovely woman who was the source of our boggled silence looked at all of us and laughed.

"You see? That was the perfect thing to do to break you all out of that horrible mood!"

"I must say; they are very nice breasts." Jaya smiled, and that seemed to give us all permission to breathe again. "Where did you learn your comedic timing?"

"Oh, well before you were born! I was part of a burlesque troop in Hong Kong. That's how I met my husband." She put her hands on her hips, did a little jig, bowed, and smiled with theatrical grandeur.

"It just goes to show," Charlie added, "you never know who your neighbors are, even after you've seen their titties."

We all started to laugh when our heads exploded with someone yelling "INCOMING!" Without even looking around, we all went flat to the floor. There was a muffled explosion not terribly far away, but the shock wave rattled us from above rather than from the side.

I beat everyone to the front door. Omura was in the middle of the street, being rained on by debris, sheltering his head behind his arms.

"What the Hell happened?" I shouted.

"I just shot a grenade or a mortar out of the air, and aside from the hot metal falling from the sky, I feel very impressed with myself." Omura stood up, brushed himself off, and walked over as if nothing odd had occurred.

"Good job! I'd feel pretty impressed if I'd done that," I gave him a comradely clap on the shoulder.

He looked me up and down with a critical eye. "Did you

fall into a cat food factory while you were out?"

"Something like that. What do we have out there?"

"I don't know. I think—" He stopped talking abruptly, pivoted on one foot, and fired his gun into the sky almost at the same moment that I heard the telltale noise of another projectile. "I think I just got another one."

Nodding, I took off from the front porch and made a running leap onto the roof of my store, landing in the gummy asphalt that had been used to waterproof that surface. I had barely looked up when I pinged on something airborne heading in my direction with a characteristic whistling noise.

I bellowed, "Fucking Hell! INCOMING!"

The unexpected seems to happen around me more often than what might be called "normal" does. Instead of diving for cover, I pulled my .45, hit the safety, and squeezed the trigger. There wasn't a conscious thought in my head, and I'm not sure that I aimed, but something exploded in the sky above my head and little hot things fell like hail all around.

"What the *fuck* was that?" Charlie's voice was so loud in my head that I winced. Another thing went onto my rolling list for Santa Baj if and when we managed to get him back—volume control.

"I think I just shot a rocket-propelled grenade out of the air."

"Damn!" She said and covered my sentiments with precision. "Is there anything else headed our way?"

"Not that I know of, but ping anybody who has the new iBrain upgrade and find out. Omura is standing on the front porch. Snag him if you need anything." I had always wanted to coin a new "i" product name. Charlie closed the connection in my skull, and it was another strange sensation to catalog and review after I found out what the latest news was.

When I looked down, I saw where the projectiles had come from. There was a topless Humvee on the corner by the gas station, and some zombie was reloading a shoulder-mounted weapon of some kind. There wasn't even a need to aim my weapon, because our side already had things well under control.

Nate and two of his comrades in arms descended on the Humvee and the occupants like a trio of homicidal cephalopods, all arms and weapons. They were fast, accurate, and brutally efficient. They also managed to take the Humvee without damaging it. Score!

However, they didn't seem to notice the five zombies approaching them from the shopping center on the opposite corner. I decided to give the mental address system another try, pulled up my map, slapped Nate's sparkle around, and hollered at it. "NATE! Watch your six!"

I took aim and did my absolute best to knock down the enemy's numbers a bit. From the look of things, I was a helpful distraction, but unnecessary. Nate and his chums moved like a greased killing machine and took all five of the opponents down from a hundred yards away.

"Thanks, Frank. Do me a favor, not so loud next time. I almost pissed myself."

"No problem, Nate!" I cut the connection, took one last look around, and dropped back down to the ground in front of my store. We needed to discuss eliminating our local infestation more than I needed to clean myself up. As things stood, I was still dressed for killing, and there wasn't any real reason to change if more wet work needed to be done.

Omura was walking over with the Three Ladies trailing behind him, and I gestured toward Shawn's garage. That seemed to be growing into the staging area of choice over the past day or so, and I didn't mind the chance to invade someone else's space instead of filling my own storage room with rowdy freedom fighters. It was also the most likely place for Nate and the guys to head with our newly appropriated vehicle. They'd probably have to shift an IED or two out of the way, but that was a better plan than leaving the thing on the street.

We got the vehicle, fair and square, by murdering our

enemies in cold blood. Simple. Direct. Eventually, if we didn't destroy the thing ourselves, another party might turn us into bloody cottage cheese, and then they could have our spoils of war. For a moment, I missed the days when satisfaction happened with a swipe of a credit card, rather than random acts of violence.

By the time I turned the corner, Nate was carefully moving the IED closest to the open bay of the garage. I think we all held our breaths a bit, even being aware that the man was a professional and may have actually placed that trap himself. We didn't need another shock, chorus of pained screaming from grievous wounds, shower of body parts, or funeral. In fact, after my day, I could have used a month-long break from any of those things.

The guys got the Hummer settled and the IED replaced with no hassle at all. High fives were passed around, and Buttons nodded with satisfaction at the day's catch. It didn't seem like ten seconds had passed before Shawn had the hood up, doors open, and every storage area bare to the work lights. I told myself that he was looking for explosives or booby traps, but I was pretty sure he was having a geek moment over examining our acquisition.

This isn't to say he wouldn't find any potential booby traps, because he certainly would. I know him well enough to be sure that his main motivation was curiosity, not whether or not something would likely blow up if it was disassembled.

Omura turned to Buttons and said, "Sir, I think we need to wipe these fuckers out before they mount the large assault. Unless, you think the larger attack is less likely now, due to the crater?"

"Unlikely. I've been hitting the refresh key on the satellite feed every thirty seconds since we dropped the baby. They're trying to put together a convoy." Buttons did not look pleased. "That presents a certain set of options. They're preparing to create a new staging area for the assault on this side of 66, or they're going to attempt to nail

James Crawford

us early. Alternately, they're going to change the location of their entire operation."

Flower and I chimed in together, harmoniously. "Is that likely?"

Buttons blinked a few times, and said, "No. There is too much materiel that would require delicate handling if it could be moved at all. Whether or not Hightower himself would change locations is open for debate. His dossier suggests he's capable of a number of different decision forks when he's up against opposition."

"You've got a dossier on the man?" Charlie looked a little surprised.

"Oh yes. I have one on every single one of you and access to the files on your families as well. Are your mother's pickles really made with cucumbers from Danielle Chalker's garden, three houses over? It must have bothered you when her daughter, Missy, stole your boyfriend and was crowned Homecoming Queen three days after that."

Charlie turned white. Shawn didn't hear it, or if he did, he was buried head first in the Humvee and didn't show it.

"Mister Buttons, I am fairly sure I dislike you." Charlie's tone of voice was surprisingly even, considering the ferocity in her eyes. "I just noticed something about you as well."

He looked up at her, cooler than Mrs. Chalker's cucumbers, "And what would that be?"

"Your nose has healed." She was right.

"So good of you to notice." His voice was oily and expressionless, but the smug little smile told a more complete story.

"We need to nail the convoy when they've got it complete," Nate broke the tension by pulling us back to the original topic by the scruffs of our necks. If I had taken an anonymous poll, I think 100 percent of the respondents would have said the next thing that would be broken wouldn't be the topic, but Buttons' nose for a second time.

"I agree. The railgun is not the best choice for this and is not in range again until tomorrow." Buttons shifted his

- 336 -

attention from Charlie to the laptop without even blinking. I cataloged it as another bit of odd behavior from an odd man. "We do have the laser weapon available, and we could target individual vehicles with excellent accuracy."

I brought up my encounter near the Methodist Church, which elicited a few groans of annoyance. Buttons made his fingers dance on the keyboard and made little thinking noises under his breath.

"We could take that position in one shot from orbit at high power," he announced. "That would give us several low power shots for the convoy. With any luck, destroying three or four vehicles would be a deterrent. I do not believe in luck."

Flower asked, "What sort of resistance is there at the church? Could a small team get in there, break it up, and get across the bridge on foot?"

"I count forty combatants, six people who appear to be in a corral or a pen, and one Humvee-sized vehicle. Nothing appears in these shots that indicate any kind of heavy-weapon emplacements. There is a small heat signature in the bell tower and, in all likelihood, that's a sniper.

Flower smiled in a very disturbing fashion for a former man of the cloth. "Partners in arms, I think I have a reasonable plan. Anyone interested in hearing it?"

There were universal nods and grunts of approval from the assembled lot of us. Flower stretched his arms, laced his fingers, and cracked his knuckles. "We are relying on one major environmental qualifier. We need to do this as a night raid."

"Step one, we take the church area as our staging area. Step two begins with Buttons and his fancy light show." Matt continued explaining how we would wait until after nightfall to proceed beyond taking the church back. Buttons would use laser strikes to create confusion and vehicle damage in and around the convoy, and our team would then infiltrate the area during the post-laser freak out.

"The vast majority of that plan is sound; however, there

is something you need to consider. If we strike the convoy in position, that liberates a large number of personnel to defend the area." Buttons pulled up a local map on the laptop screen, and we all craned around to see. "We need to allow the convoy to leave and disable or destroy it at least midway to their destination. That gives you a window of time to execute the rescue with fewer opponents and at least begin a return to our side before the convoy stragglers can return on foot."

If there had been a fly on the wall, watching us, it probably would have written a description much like this one. "Late afternoon, garage wall: gang of two-legged giant mammals making noise and nodding in unison like trained meerkats. Smaller mammal kneeling before a black box with bright colors. Perhaps this one is the Shaman and this is a religious ritual of some kind?"

There was one potential issue: communication across the distances involved. If the built-in communications system that our happy critters gave us had a distinct range, we would need to rely on flaky cellular phone service or some kind of series of human relay stations between the team and home.

Channing brought up the issue before I could, and Buttons suggested that he take a run to the edge of our neighborhood, which we generally felt was about nine blocks away. One of Nate's chums headed out with him for extra security and they both promised to call in to test the range.

While they were gone, we attempted to polish the plan and pick out a reasonable team to take back the church, and decide which of that larger team would continue on for the rescue and hopeful massive disruption of Hightower's group. In the end, we decided to stick with the original team for the rescue: Flower, Charlie, Omura, Franklin, and myself. We added Ramos and Fitzgerald to the mix for the church and to hold that position until we returned.

"Townhall, this is Ramos. Do you receive?" We all

looked up at the same time, hearing his voice in our heads.

"We read you, Chico," Nate replied, "pull it in. We have matters to discuss."

"I hate it when you call me Chico. You know that, right?"

"Yes. Your point would be what?"

There might have been a whiff of vulgarity as Ramos closed the connection, but it was garbled. Nate stood there, shaking his head and chuckling to himself. It didn't take long until he was back in deep consultation with Flower and Buttons over the satellite images of the church parking lot. Omura seemed to take it all in without comment.

Never having been a formal soldier, some of the terms went right over my head, flapping into the afternoon on little olive drab wings. The gist of the church operation boiled down to three approaching from the houses directly to the nearest side of the parking lot and the other four flanking to the right around the near side of the main building.

Fire Team Flash, the three-person unit, would be armed with one of the captured rocket-propelled grenade launchers. Fire Team Thunder would have two major tasks, the first being to remove the sniper from the bell tower. The second would be to lay down cover fire for Flash until they had destroyed the enemy vehicle and entered into hand-to-hand combat with the opposition.

"Let me get this straight." I wanted clarification. "Once the vehicle is done, it basically boils down to free-for-all murder?"

"That is how it is done, dude." Nate smiled and patted me on the head. "You guys are going into a situation where you're outnumbered 6-to-1, or more. Once the sniper is down and their transportation is out of commission, just lay waste to the fuckers." I got a second pat on the head and a cheerful, "Just don't get killed. That goes for everyone."

Charlie spoke up with the sensitive, yet unasked, question. "What do we do about the people in the pen?"

Buttons had a simple and forthright answer. "Euthanize

them." It wasn't a pretty answer, but it was likely the correct one. I know Charlie did not like it one bit.

No one had the nerve to look anyone in the face after those words dropped like lead bowling balls onto the concrete floor. I will admit to wishing it were different, but any infected individual would become Undead Take Out and would show up again in a matter of days as another opponent we'd have to deal with. At least we would be able to be as merciful as a single bullet to the brain will allow, followed by the messy necessity of cracking open their heads.

I have never been sure that straight decapitation was the most merciful way to do things. There had been occasions in the past when the eyes would actually watch me for some seconds after the body and the head parted company. I watched them lose focus and fade, almost wetting myself every time, until I bashed the skulls open and knew it was over.

Bullets, especially well-aimed ones, seemed faster and surer than blades. Regardless, I wasn't about to change my weapon of choice. It had served me far too well and was more an extension of me than any firearm I had ever used.

Ramos and Channing returned and were swiftly briefed on the plans up to that moment, and Flower assigned us to our teams. Flash consisted of Omura, Franklin, and me. Thunder was made up of Charlie, Flower, Ramos, and Fitzgerald.

" Flower? What's the rationale behind the team assignments? I'm curious," and I was.

"Simple. You and Omura are capable of impressive mayhem on your own. Franklin knows his way around projectile weapons." He pointed at the members of Thunder one by one. "Charlie is a good shot and is impressive in close quarters. Ramos is a superb marksman. Fitzgerald is, from what Nate has said, an almost career point man. Yours truly? I'll nail the sniper, back you up, and then squash the resistance."

I nodded. It made a lot of sense, for those reasons, and for the unspoken reason. Charlie is not on your team because you'd be too busy trying to protect her and would probably make a dangerous error, resulting in getting your head blown off. Frankly, I couldn't argue with that either.

"Buttons?"

"Yes, Frank."

"Are the laser beams in the visible spectrum or are they on one side or the other?" I'd had a thought.

"An excellent question. This particular satellite can be adjusted from visible to high UV. Why do you ask?"

The idea was cruel but it might make it significantly easier for us to get back alive and in one piece. "If we can get the zombies to a window, or out in the street by picking off a target, would it be possible to blind the lot of them with a second shot?" I was disturbed at the look of satisfaction on Buttons' face almost as much as my sudden turn towards practical maiming.

"I think we could do that with very little trouble." He described a plan to get their attention with three low-power shots into the crater pool, which would likely dazzle anyone nearby and attract the attention of anyone that was not actively watching. Then up to four shots near larger groups that would easily leave them blind, if not burned. "That would still allow for nearly thirty firings to disable or destroy the convoy. An excellent plan! You might even be able to enter through the lobby of the building instead of using the parking garage."

I felt ill.

Flower picked up the ball from that point, describing how we would proceed into the area across the overpass and duck into the condominium development between the road and our target building. Depending on the resistance, we could decide on the fly whether to use the garage entrance or the front door. If we encountered any sentries that weren't blind, we were to dispatch them while maintaining as much stealth as possible, i.e., no bullets.

Fitzgerald would take point, Flower directly behind him, followed by me, Charlie, and then Omura bringing up the rear. Flower explained that their job was to get us into the building as safely as possible so Charlie and I could rescue Baj, and Omura could set several packages of explosives designed to bring the building down shortly after our egress. He also added that Charlie and I should feel at liberty to take out any targets of opportunity that appeared, provided that they did not compromise the rescue mission.

"Frank, that means no heroics." He gave me an incredibly stern look. "Charlotte, no heroics either. If Baj is compromised or somehow unable to come with you, end him as gently as possible. I would rather, and I think he would agree with me, he go by the hand of someone who cares rather than be crushed when the building goes down."

Charlie opened her mouth as though she wanted to argue but closed it without commenting on what the situation might require one of us to do. I didn't like the idea either, but it made tactical sense, even if it didn't satisfy our hearts or remaining morality. After all, I was going into that fight with the intent of killing my own brother. My father as well, if he presented himself as a target.

At that point I had no moral high ground to stand on, much less an emotional reason to disagree with a reasonable plan. We didn't need our hearts. We simply needed the will to do what we had to do in order to avoid being wiped out, and in this case, it looked like we needed to take it to them before they could bring it to us.

For once in my life, I wanted to live. There were too many threads dangling from the helter-skelter quilt of my life for me to go to my grave quietly. Charlie. I won't lie and say she hadn't become a major motivator for me. I wanted to live long enough to be in love with her and whatever else might arise from that.

There were also the nano-critters and what could be done with them and about them, and discovering if we'd ever be free of them. That led me right to Baj and then to Jayashri.

After them, there was this big pile of people who had become my family of choice, and by extension, their kids. We all deserved to have whatever chance we could carve out for ourselves.

Life often comes at the price of death, whether we like it or not. I had sympathy and pity for the people who had been victimized and brought back to life against their will, but they had made the choice to align themselves with a man and an ideology that stood in opposition to the freedom of every living human being. That could not be allowed to continue.

"All right. It is 4:32 pm right now." Flower's voice sounded like lead blocks of imminent doom. "We need both Fire Teams here at 7 pm sharp. The operation will begin at 7:10. Between now and then, Shawn, you need to coordinate local defense issues and personnel with Nate. You need to be ready to rock when we leave. Fire Teams, weapons of choice, body armor, significant spare ammo. 7 pm, everybody. Go."

We went.

Chapter 37

I headed for the store, as one might expect. I still needed to get some of the crap off my skin and put on something that hadn't been diced by an excited undead Sarge. I didn't notice Charlie was behind me because I was too busy leafing though my mental catalog of weapons, updating it with the full-auto rifle hanging over my shoulder on a sling, and trying to decide what I needed and what I didn't.

Full-auto, check. Scythe, check. Desert Eagle or .45 cal? No. Go with matched 9mm pistols because we're not hunting boar. Combat knife or katana? Compromise on an o-tanto, since it has the length and mobility likely to be necessary. The scythe can take the place of a katana for large-scale several-on-one melee encounters.

Charlie was so close behind me, and I was so lost in my own skull, that I didn't notice she came in the door behind me while it was swinging shut. She called my name and I jumped six inches straight up in surprise.

"You didn't hear me," she asked, sounding surprised and amused.

"No, I was lost in trying to decide what equipment I wanted to have for the rescue mission, and I was planning my wardrobe."

"Wardrobe?"

"Absolutely." I explained while we walked toward the back of the store. "I'm worried that all black is too somber. I was thinking that something in a smashing red-violet with fabulous drape, fishnets, and Fuck Me Boots would be just the thing for a chaotic evening on the town." I vamped a bit on the Spa door for extra effect.

She was caught somewhere between wanting to laugh and being immensely disturbed.

"You are joking, right? I mean, if you're into crossdressing, that's okay. I'd just like to know that my clothes will always be mine."

"Charlotte Marie, are you telling me that you won't *share*?" I can only imagine what it must have looked like, saying such a thing with batting eyelashes and enough dried stuff on me to leave me looking like the kabuki version of Mad Max.

"I ... I... Oh dear." She really looked like I was beginning to cause her some distress.

"Charlie, really, I'm just playing. The tension is starting to get to me and I really want to get some of this stuff off me while we've got a little time. I feel like someone poured a bucket of blood on me and left me in the sun to dry."

"I'll get you for that one of these days," she visibly relaxed, "when you least expect it. As for the bucket of blood, that is about what you look like, so I understand. Can I hang out with you for a while?"

"As if you have to ask! Spending time with you is probably the best thing in my life right now."

She laughed and held out her hands for my weapons so I could take off my shirt. I thanked her profusely, drew a bucket of cold water for myself, and grabbed the nearest dark-colored towel.

"Don't you want to warm that up before you... " the sound of me splashing water across my face cut her off, but she rallied with,"... start cleaning yourself off like a crazy man?"

I kept scrubbing and answered, "I thought that cold water would help clear my head a little, since I don't have an ice-cold waterfall to meditate under."

"Can I ask you a silly question?"

"Sure, Oh Specimen of Womanly Lusciousness!"

"You're not interested in Chunhua now that she's not a prune, are you?"

I froze like a rabbit caught in a flashlight beam. She didn't think I wanted to indulge the Perky Passionate? Did she? Why?

"Charlie. Charlotte... "

"Oh, Hell, you're using my real name!" I could see her eyes getting moist, and that needed to stop.

"Charlotte, I do not want to help Chunhua with her revived libido. Not. No. Never." She looked like part of her brain didn't want to believe what I was saying. "I don't care if she's giving me a lap dance, I will never be able to see her as anyone other than Grandmother Yan." I cleaned more dried stuff off my arms while I thought about what to say next. "Don't get me wrong, I love her to bits, and she's a good friend, but that's all."

"Are you sure? I mean, she's way hot! Really! Those boobs? Wow!"

"Not to put too fine a point on it, but you could help her out if you wanted."

"Frank, I am *so* not bisexual. I'm not even boobie-sexual."

I confess feeling a frisson of disappointment when I heard her say that.

"All right." Mental note about Charlie's preference, recorded and filed. "In that case, we can both appreciate the aesthetic qualities of her youthful physique, while declining any free samples."

She cracked a smile and started laughing, fit to explode.

"What?"

"I just had images of her passing out boob-shaped dumplings in the nude!"

I had to laugh with her a little bit, because it was a pretty amusing thought. Although, I'd been imagining her licking egg rolls with a lascivious expression on her face, but I wasn't about to admit that to Charlie. I don't think I'll ever tell her how cute she looks when she's distressed, either.

She put my stuff down and held up the remains of my

shirt. "Is this one for the rag pile or the trash can?"

"Garbage, for sure." I turned around, grabbed a towel, and dried myself off. Her arms were around me before I could turn back around.

"I'm sorry for being silly about Chunhua, but I really, really like you. Losing out on what might be amazing scares me pretty badly." She nuzzled my back, and I wrapped my arms over hers.

"I'm pretty sure I'm falling for you, so you really don't have anything to worry about. I've never met anyone who makes me want the things I do when you're near me."

"Like what?" she asked, with a smile in her voice.

"Long afternoons with nothing in them but you. Waking up with you every morning and knowing that the incredible curves underneath my hands belong to you. The laughter. I'm addicted to laughing with you." She hugged me a little closer and I asked her to loosen her grip so I could hug her back. When we were in the proper hugging position, I lowered my head to her ear. "I want a place in your life. I've never wanted that with anyone like I do with you. It's almost as if we were designed as a set but only knew it when we saw one another."

"Yeah. What else do you want with me that you've never wanted before?"

"Woo," I took a deep breath, "that treads on some really personal and private stuff, Charles." The Charles got me a slap on the ass.

"Like what, Frankie the Frog?" Her eyes were back to being sparkly with humor and that made me really happy.

"You're not going to like it, but it is something Chunhua said to me, that I realized was true."

"This is gonna be good. Spill it, Mister."

Deep breathing. I wasn't at all kidding about the treading on private things, but then I tend to make jokes out of serious matters. I answered her with, "Strong babies."

She blinked a couple of times but said nothing, and I could feel the tension oozing down my legs as I tried to predict what was going through her head. I might have said too much, and that worried me.

"Strong babies, huh?"

"Um. Yes. Strong babies." At least she was speaking!

"How many?" Her facial expression was all seriousness, without a touch of the luminous humor I loved too much.

"Well, siblings are important, so two for sure. I could wrap my brain around more, but two for sure."

"I come from a pretty large family, you know," she said, very seriously. "Shawn, me, Jimmy, Sharon, Lisa, Gordon, and little Shelley."

"Wow. I never knew you guys had that many siblings." I had no idea where the conversation was going, but the only way to learn anything was to participate, so I did.

"Yeah. Sometimes, because our whole extended family lived in the same town, it felt like we ran the place."

"I bet so!"

That got her to crack a smile and some of the tension left my legs. At least her arms were still around me and didn't feel as though they were going anywhere. I had a measure of hope things weren't about to fall apart thanks to that contact.

"I would like to be married before the kids start showing up," she said, thoughtfully but with a measure of serious sincerity, "and you had better be prepared for a number like five."

"Five?"

"Yes. Five. I think the seven of us was a little much, but five might be just right for the modern, post-zombie apocalypse family. Stagger the births by two years, if we can, so the little one is mobile by the time their little brother or sister comes along."

I found myself nodding my head as if I was in agreement or that I felt what she was saying made sense. At that point in the conversation, I was lost enough in my own thoughts and feelings I wouldn't have noticed if some little gnome ran up and pierced my nipple. On second thought, I probably would notice something like that, so I'll amend it to a little gnome running up and nuzzling my behind.

"Have I lost you, Frank? You're looking a little dazed." Again, she looked at me with such a serious and probing expression I didn't know quite what to do with it.

"No, not really." I spoke slowly, deliberately, trying not to convey my sense of sloshing around in the unknown sea of fate. "I'm surprised with the candor of our conversation." That was certainly the case!

"I feel you ought to know where I'm coming from about all this since you brought up strong babies. Candor is pretty important, don't you think?"

"Oh, absolutely, yes!"

"I'm glad we agree. Can I be candid about something else?" Her eyes twinkled a little and more of my brain started to focus, probably because it didn't want to miss anything interesting she might say.

"I'd love to hear anything that you want to share with me." It was a true statement.

"I'm from the South, so bear with me. Some things are easier for us to say than others," she said, pulling my face down to hers. "Frank Hightower, I have wanted you from the moment I met you." Her voice dropped into a range that promised passion and intensity in honey-covered tones. "You've been a gentleman, and I love that about you, but it has felt like a long, slow, teasing kiss that has been driving me out of my mind. I don't just want you, Frank; you've made me need you." Charlie's hands slid up the back of my neck and laced themselves in my hair. "I want you to make love to me. I want you to fuck me blind. I need us to be together before we go out there and face something that might be a carnival of horror."

She kissed me and I felt every word she said echoing in the touch of her lips. We fought ourselves to keep composure for just a little longer before we would end up gnawing on one another with hungry abandon. I knew what I wanted and what she wanted, and I was absolutely willing to follow her lead. If there had been a doubt in my mind, she erased it with what she said next.

"Please, Frank?"

There is a passage in the Sexual Geneva Convention that defines that sort of question, issued in a seductive yet vulnerable tone of voice as a Weapon of Mass Wardrobe Destruction. There was no way an armistice could be negotiated or signed after such gauntlets were thrown down. She sank my battleship.

I answered her with the ferocious kiss we had denied ourselves moments before, growling against her lips and hearing her answer in wordless sounds. When we parted, gasping, she looked at me with a smile on her lips and asked, "Does that mean we're going to fuck first and make love later on?"

"Rrrrrrrrrryeah!"

"Race you upstairs?" She was laughing, but her nipples were so crinkled they were poking me in the chest.

"YAR!!!!" We took off. We took my room door off the hinges.

I backed her up against my desk and learned how just how strong nanotechnology can make you when you're eager to get your partner out of her clothes. Snarling, I tore her shirt, bra, and shoulder-holster rig apart with a single pull, leaving her gasping and bare from the waist up. She exploded toward me, kissing me and whispering things that I could barely register as I kissed and licked my way from her ear to her shoulder. Her teeth found my earlobe and I lost the war.

I groaned against the firm smoothness of her shoulder, my mouth open and wordless against her skin. There was a whisper in my ear, urging me to bite her, so I did. Days before, when I bit her shoulder, I was unprepared for her response. That wasn't the case this time, and I held her arms to her sides with every bit of strength I had while she gyrated madly against me.

So help me God, it wasn't enough! She was chanting, howling, moaning for me to take her, but I wanted more than that. Instead of giving in to that heat, I threw her to the desktop, climbed on top of her, and held her down. I bit her shoulders, neck, collarbone, and down the curves of her breasts. She was a feral creature underneath me, unselfconscious about the noises she made, demands she issued at the top of her lungs, or how hard she was thrusting her hips up to meet me.

When my lips found her nipple, she forced her arms out of my grip and wrapped them around my head, panting against the top of my skull. I bit, sucked, and found a fierce joy in the power of her reactions. My hands were free, and I ruined her jeans the same way I ruined her shirt and bra. She screamed out a ragged, "Oh my God!"

Snarling, I let go of her breast and pushed her back down on the desktop, and she gave me the universal look that said that she really wanted what was coming next. Her hips slid downward and she spread her legs, anticipating the disappearance of my pants. I looked and saw the flash of metal that I'd seen once before. The pants were going to wait... for as long as it would take.

I didn't just move fast; I struck like a rattlesnake on amphetamines, wrapping my arms around her legs from the bottom so that I could keep them open. My mouth greeted the flashing metal and I felt like a rook pecking at a glimmering treasure. Charlie screamed in a way that had nothing to do with pain and ground herself against my face.

She lost control, which was just what I wanted, and bucked against my tongue as she orgasmed. I didn't stop, and neither did she. It wasn't until I heard her saying things like "Please! Frank! Please! In!" that I remembered we both wanted something very specific. I let her up, and she stayed on her back for a few minutes, panting to catch her breath.

"You... weren't planning to kill me... but if you were, could you do it just like that?" She was laughing, and I couldn't help but do the same.

She got up from the desk and frowned mightily when she saw that my pants were still on. "That ain't right." She tore mine off, belt included, just as easily as I had hers.

"Good. Can I please have this now?" Her fingers closed around the length of me and I lost my voice. All I could do was nod like a mute idiot. "Good."

I followed her down onto my sleeping bags and she never lost her grip on me; if anything, she held on tighter. As if I could run away or even wanted to! She settled down, much like she had on my desk and tugged me to her.

We kissed, and we discovered the ferocity had changed to something else in the minute it had taken us to go from the desk to the floor.

"Do you really want me, Frank?" she asked me in a very quiet voice and was rewarded with a quiver that rattled me from head to toe.

Her hand loosened enough that I could move away without leaving it behind, and I lifted my other leg so that I was between hers. I kissed her, told her I wanted her, and then I proved it.

Somewhere in the aching, soaring pleasure, I thanked God for her. We both cried out, and she lost control underneath me. Her arms pulled me tight against her as her lower half danced to a tune of its own. I heard every noise, every iota of gratitude to the Almighty, and every single time she told me that she loved me.

"Do you really want me?" I don't know where the question came from, or why I asked it, buried inside her as I was, but I did.

She blinked, and then she shrieked, "Oh, God! Yes, Frank, please! So much! Yes!"

I lost my control, feeling the push that was as old as time. You know, the one that sends your civilized behavior over the brink, leaving behind nothing but an animal in the throes of ecstasy? I wasn't alone. Charlie was there, making inarticulate noises underneath me, and meeting every single thrust until I lay shattered and spent in her arms.

Charlie and I were cuddling and periodically giggling. I learned that her floating ribs are insanely ticklish. She suggested I stop tickling her by poking one of my testicles. I stopped.

"You know," said a voice from my open doorway, "if I had known I would get a show, I would have brought a chair and some munchies!"

We squeaked like frightened mice and tried to pull the sleeping bag around ourselves from the opposite directions. Charlie caught on first and changed the direction that she was pulling in, managing to cover herself but leaving me buck naked on the other side.

I looked up, covered my three-piece set with both hands, and tried to look demure and defenseless.

"How long have you been standing there?" Charlie asked, squeaking from underneath the sleeping bag.

"Oh, a little while now," Chunhua said, grinning from ear to ear. "All I was expecting was a hug for bringing you both some dumplings for dinner," she lifted up the stacked steel containers that she was holding, "but I got a very hot show instead!"

"I am so embarrassed!" Charlie was blushing from the top of her shoulders to the roots of her hair. I just sat there, feeling very, very exposed.

"Don't be! Do you know how long it has been since I've seen any porn?" Chunhua put the container down on my desk, carefully stepping over the door on the floor to do so. "That was very hot, let me tell you! Woo!" She fanned herself with both hands. "I know you won't let me borrow him, but if you find out that he has a brother who isn't a zombie, let me know! Woo!"

"Oh my God. I'm gonna die." Charlie slipped behind the sleeping bag all the way.

"By the way, did you guys forget to use a condom, or did you have other things on your mind?" Her eyes were sparkling with something, it might have been mirth or it might have been a certain amount of sadistic glee, but she blew us a kiss and hopped back down the stairs.

We just sat there, looking at one another, wondering just

how much we'd jumped the gun on starting a family.

Chapter 38

"I think, really," Charlie began, ducking her head slightly, "I'm going to put that issue aside for the time being, for two major... No, three major reasons. Number one: I need to pee. Number two: we need to gear up. Number three: we are so going to eat those dumplings."

"But...," I tried to say something responsible and appropriately macho, but she shushed me.

"I'm serious, Frank. We can worry about that," she struggled for a word that fit, "possible consequence if we come back alive tonight. Even better, we can worry tomorrow morning, after we've come back alive, fucked like the Devil, and slept tangled together all night. Don't disagree with me, now. I feel really strongly about this." She took a pose that looked like the figurehead on a particularly busty sailing vessel.

"I'm not going to argue with you."

"Good man. Good man."

"Let's go pee." I gestured toward the open doorway.

"Together? Aw, Frank! That's so kinky! You didn't tell me that you're all perverted!" She stood up, gave me a hand, and grinned at me. I think she was joking. I hoped she was joking.

"Nah. I'm practical, not a pervert."

"Shucks!" She snapped her fingers in mock disappointment, crossed her eyes, and fled down the stairs.

"Wait up! What's wrong?" I hurried after her.

"A Southern girl won't tell! Gotta pee!" She disappeared

into the ladies room.

"I didn't think a Southern girl would admit she has to pee in the first place!" I called out to the closed door, stirring the pot a little bit.

"I'm a modern Southern woman. Don't sass me, Frank the Love Machine! Get your peeing done!"

Modern conveniences were utilized, a wee bit of readjusting was done, and I snagged some clothes that I'd dried but hadn't put away. Charlie pawed through the pile of clothes, gave me some grief about destroying her bra, and found some clothes that looked like they'd do for the time being. We scooted back up the stairs and threw our clothes on.

I thought she looked particularly saucy with no bra, but I was gently lectured about how inappropriate it would be to go into a firefight with bouncing titties. She was kind enough to listen to my theory that mobile mammary glands would be a superb tool for distracting any heterosexual male opponents. It got me a raised eyebrow and a smirk.

"Dude, I think you're a little biased here."

"Well, don't you think I ought to be? After all, we just had incredibly hot sex... in front of one of our neighbors."

"Oh, please do not remind me. Okay? I'm still beside myself about that."

"You're beside yourself? I'm the one who was flashing my butt and nuts at her." The memory made me shudder.

"Frank, you're right. Absolutely right, in fact. You should be horrified you were pointing your furry exit at a hot woman like that! Shit! You really are kinky!" She took one look at the horrified expression on my face and laughed herself sick at my expense. When she was done, we attacked Chunhua's cooking with terrible vengeance.

We were a hot zombie-killing couple, dressed in black-on-black, with shiny black weapons, ferociously devouring dumplings that were not black. The clock was starting to tick, but we were alert, tucking away some chow, and enjoying our Normal before things became Crazy again.

"I think we've got about ten minutes before we need to head over there. Shall we go, Milady?"

"Zounds, Sir Knight! Let us be on our way!"

We grabbed the last of our gear, snagged our vests, and headed to the garage.

Chapter 39

Being early was the rule of the evening, or so it seemed. Members of both teams converged on the garage from all directions; there were a few high fives and one or two friendly headbutts. Omura was the only seriously solitary member of the crew, walking along with a loaded rucksack that probably contained more explosives than it was amusing to contemplate.

Charlie ducked back into the more homely side of Shawn's place when we arrived, I suspect to quickly throw on a bra since I'd pulled the other one apart in my late afternoon zest for life. I had a momentary flash of potential parent paranoia and did my absolute best to drive it, kicking and screaming, into a lock box inside my skull. It quieted down when she reappeared and was promptly replaced by determination that the both of us come back alive.

"All right people, here's the rest of the plan. In three minutes, we load up into our appropriated Humvee." Flower gave us educational finger-pointing to go along with the lecture. "Ramos is our wheelman. We will enter the neighborhood around the church approximately 50 yards from our target, hard cover, break into teams and proceed on foot using appropriate stealth. The high sign to commence the mission is my rifle firing. You know the rest. Questions?"

"Do we get to sing road songs on the way there?" Franklin asked, bouncing up and down like an idiot.

"If you sing anything while we're moving, I will pop you

in the jaw with my rifle butt. Clear?" Flower was smiling but was also dead serious.

"Clear, Sir!"

"All right people, saddle up." Like we would have balked at that order.

"Frank," Charlie snagged my arm and whispered to me. "I think I love you, and that was really hot earlier!"

"I know." I grinned at her and she punched me in the shoulder. "I love you, too. Let's go rip it up, Chuck!"

Seven people and associated equipment were a bit of a snug fit, even in a top-down military Humvee. Franklin and I found ourselves standing in the cargo area, holding onto the roll bar. He had a tight grip on his weapon, which was, as he informed me, a Light Anti-Tank Weapon. He pointed at the box on the floor between us and suggested that I not step on it.

"Why?"

"It isn't a reinforced ammo container. You don't want to dislodge a warhead on an anti-tank missile. Trust me on that."

That was all the conversation we had time for, because we started to move.

It was a very quiet, nearly eternal trip. I had never been in a military version of a Humvee before and I was pretty surprised at how quiet they were on normal roads. That did not hold true for the occasional pothole.

The irony was not lost on me when we pulled up to the yard I had visited earlier in the day. From a visual standpoint, it was better in the dark, except for how white disjointed bones look in the moonlight. The smell, sadly, was also several hours more ripe. Zombies were not as attentive to burying their comrades as I might have hoped, or even wished, they might be.

We broke into our teams and I watched Charlie head away with her group. I had to swallow the worry and resign myself to the fact that I could help her best by doing the best for my team as I possibly could. Truth be told, the three of us were going straight down the throat of the enemy and were probably in a shitload more danger than she would be in a flanking position.

Omura took point, I was the middleman, and Franklin was bringing up the rear, lugging the anti-tank weapon over one shoulder and the unstable box of projectiles under his other arm. We halted at the corner of Sarge's house, as I referred to it in my head, and Omura poked his head around the corner. He gave me the high sign and pointed to the far corner of the neighboring house. I took the direction and moved.

I looked left, then right, somewhat surprised to find a sentry standing beside the residence's heat pump. The critters hadn't given me an advance warning about him, I assume because his body temperature was nearly the same as the surroundings. Cool or not, he needed to be dealt with. I gave a single finger sign followed by pointing right and then the closed fist for "stop." This one was mine.

The knife on my belt was situated for a right cross draw, much like a samurai sword would be, but edge down rather than edge up. I drew it with my left hand, giving me the classic "ice pick" grip, and moved toward my target. There wasn't a reaction I could see as I got closer. So much the better for me, because approaching someone from their side or from anywhere in their peripheral vision is a chancy matter. Any little flicker could cause a startle reaction and the encounter would begin ahead of time, rather than on your terms and timetable.

This sentry was either asleep, dead, or a mannequin. No reaction, not even a sigh, gave me a clue he even knew I was there. Something was up, and I was barely eight feet away from him. Generally, someone with a blade can cover eight feet before a gun can be drawn, aimed, and fired. Time for a risk.

"Dude," I whispered, "your fly is down!"

Dude snorted, startled out of whatever reverie he was enjoying, and looked down at his crotch. I was beside him, blade in motion, as he turned his head to look at me. The tanto in my hand cut his throat back to the spine, causing a spray of cool, gummy blood, but not a single noise. The sentry started to collapse, and I reversed the blade in mid-air, turned with him, and used my hips to make the second cut before he hit the ground. I caught his head while the rest of his body hit the dirt.

The third strike put the point of the blade through the head's eye and into the backside of the skull. I pulled the head off the knife, swished the blade through the air to get the majority of the blood off, and resheathed it. My skull pinged, and I heard a single word from Omura. "Clean."

I smirked and we moved on.

There weren't any other sentries between the one I dispatched and the row of broken-down cars at the far edge of the church parking lot. I may never be sure whether we arrived precisely at the best time or the most unfortunate. It was feeding time.

The noises the poor souls in that pen were making were some of the most pitiful and hideous I've heard up to that point or since. I had to hold myself down to keep from rushing in there and heating the barrel of my gun to bright red with flying bullets. Watching people die, even ones you could never keep from their fate, can fill you with an oozing bitterness unlike anything else you will ever experience.

This was what the poor, brave little kid at the wrecked McDonalds missed out on. Dying while I talked to him was a mercy compared to this. I wanted to kill them all, and the rage at having to be silent and hold myself in check was nearly as awful as the tableau unfolding in front of me.

Flower took his shot and I rose up from behind that car with a roar that was drowned out by the rifle in my hands spewing lead across the parking lot. Franklin tossed his rage through the launcher on his shoulder and turned their Humvee into flaming origami.

While my shots were nearly indiscriminate, Omura's were measured, precise, and unerringly accurate. Between him, Thunder flanking them, and my volume of fire, we dropped half of them in the first few seconds. The rest of the zombies took exception to our flashy entrance and returned fire.

They had enough cover that we couldn't simply keep firing and hope to force them out. I hollered at Omura and Franklin, "Cover me!" I snapped the Man Scythe out, took a bullet in stride, and headed for the nearest hard cover.

The zombie that was using that cement planter as cover took some exception to my sudden appearance. On the bright side, she dropped her shotgun and screamed when she saw my baby. I made sure it was the last thing she ever needed to scream about.

Her partner attempted to get the drop on me, but someone pumped him full of lead before he got a good bead on me. I spun on the ball of my foot and made a beeline for the nearest parked car. In my combat-juiced state, I vaulted over the little SUV. Charlie was on the other side, calmly wiping blood and brains off one of her short swords.

"RRRRRRRR!" I growled.

"RAAAAR!" She growled back. It was ferocious, bloody, absolutely full of love, and gave me something wonderful to counter the violence as I headed towards the next target, bracketed by a wall of gunfire.

The next three targets I encountered were either dead or about to go, so I simply took their heads and left their skulls open for the squirrels to snack on. The fourth was ready for me when I came across the top of the car he was hiding behind, and he planted the bayonet of his rifle between my ribs on the left side. It hurt, and if I hadn't been upgraded, I would have been dead the moment he pulled the blade out because it felt like he'd pierced my heart.

When the blade came free and blood sprayed everywhere, it was clear he'd done precisely that. I looked up at him and tried to keep the blackness from eating away at my vision. He was looking incredibly proud of himself for having done me in. I hoped I could ruin his day in a moment or two.

"Ow."

"What?" he asked over the din of weapons rattling all around us.

"That bayonet hurt." I had dropped the scythe and was clutching at my chest with both hands. He couldn't see that I had two fingers jammed into the wound. It kept some of the blood in, or so I hoped, and it gave me some sort of clue as to whether or not my critters were repairing the damage.

Things inside my chest were moving, and it wasn't just the muscles of my heart. It felt like nothing I could possibly describe without using words like "vibrator" and "hot Jell-O." The fellow who stabbed me might have found it completely vile if I had been able to vomit all over him, but I regretted I wasn't able, for that extra "Oh! I'm dying!" effect. The feeling of things moving around certainly inspired me to barf up the contents of my tummy, but the body disagreed.

"I'm glad it hurt, you murderous bastard! Do you know how many of my friends you've butchered?"

Let him argue. The longer he raved, the more time I'd have to heal, and then I would feed him every word.

"Let me guess," I coughed up some blood for effect, "two or three?"

"You killed Sarge and seven of my friends today!" I couldn't believe he put down the rifle and grabbed me by the ballistic vest I was wearing. "You didn't just kill them, you dismembered them and tore their brains out!"

"Oh... them. I didn't tear their brains out."

"Bullshit!" He was right up in my face, nasty breath and all. I almost thanked him for closing the distance, but I settled for giving him a Hell of a headbutt.

I fell flat on my ass, and so did he. By that point, my chest was forcing the fingers back out of the hole, and I wasn't dead, so it was time for more mayhem. My tackle caught him by surprise, but smashing his head against the side of the nearest car shouldn't have. I disliked how satisfying it was to feel his skull collapse, but I didn't have any time to reflect on it in a meaningful way. There were more zombies that needed mortification... or some variation on the theme of being killed.

Instead of vaulting over cars with appropriate barbarian cries of triumph, I decided to scoot carefully along and find my next target. I held up for a moment when my skull pinged with Charlie angrily commenting to me, "That little fucker actually bit my boob! I want to kill him a third time!"

"Don't worry about the dead guy with the oral fixation. Take care of my favorite breast! They're much more important."

"You don't even know which boob it is, so how can you say that it's your favorite?"

"They're fraternal twins, and I love them both equally. Therefore, as a set, they are my favorite breast." I felt a little smug about how well I handled that and managed to creep around the minivan in a seriously stealthy way.

"Baby, you are so full of shit!" Charlie signed off, but I think she was smiling when she did. I was gratified.

I remained gratified until the gunman on the right saw me, yelled, and tried to shoot around the side of the minivan from entirely the wrong angle. There was a certain something in the air under the gunpowder scent, and it reminded me of gasoline. My favorite critters informed me, without any words, that it was gasoline.

They took over my legs.

I had half a second to bellow, "Fire in the hole!" before my legs had carried me across the parking lot to "our" side. Either I dodged every bullet that was shot at me, or my body accepted each love tap or puncture without slowing down. I had barely stopped running when the minivan exploded in a ball of smelly flames.

"Fire Teams! Check in!" Flower broadcast his urgency through my skull and I waited for the responses, much as he was waiting, before I said anything.

Franklin checked in by swearing loudly. Ramos rattled

off a string of Spanish that was so beyond what I knew that he could have been speaking Martian. Omura reported that he was in the process of healing a severed femoral artery but was otherwise fine. I chimed in and was followed by Charlie, who sounded relieved.

"Fitz? Report!" Flower didn't sound happy.

"Flower, I see him," Charlie sent back to all of us. "I think he'll respond when he finishes... what he's eating."

While I couldn't hear everyone else say "Oh," I certainly felt it.

Flower spoke up again, "I mark four unfriendlies, three people in the pen still moving, and nothing else. Ramos, you and Franklin mop up those four. Frank, go and cope with the pen. Charlie, watch over Fitz. I'm pulling in to check on Omura. Go."

Frank. Cope. With. The. Pen. Fuck. Me. I didn't want to follow my orders, but I did. The pen was littered with the remains of at least three people who had been food, and three victims who were still, for some value of the word, alive. They were not, I assure you, the least bit happy to see me. I wanted to say something comforting but I couldn't think of anything that fit or wouldn't sound like some kind of mortality consolation prize.

I stood there beside the pen and did not have one word to say, flippant or otherwise. The living ones stared at me, crouched together on the other side of the pen, as far away from me as they could get. To be completely honest, I didn't blame them. There was no way in creation they could have thought I was there for any reason other than to kill them.

I imagined I could see it in their faces.

"I am so sorry." It was the only thing to say, and the only thing that would come out of my mouth. The poor soul on the left, who had a rough rope tying off the flow of blood to her gaping forearm, nodded at me but said nothing.

The only thing I could really do by way of mercy was to stop delaying and take the fastest and most fatal action I could. I drew my pistol and fired three shots from right to left, and another three from left to right. The first bullets were sure and final, but I added the second shots for an extra measure of terminal security.

Turning around, I surveyed the Methodist Church parking lot of Hell. Bodies and parts of bodies were all over the place, and two vehicles were still burning the last of their rubber and petroleum away into the night. The only people moving were the ones I had arrived with, and they all looked like animated blood-soaked ragdolls. It wouldn't be a stretch to assume I looked at least as adorable as they did.

"Frank?" I hadn't even noticed Charlie was walking in my direction, much less that she'd arrived.

"Yes?"

"Honey, you do not look... well." It took her a moment to end that statement, and I'll admit it was spot-on accurate. I didn't feel anything remotely close to "well."

"I don't feel well. I don't feel well at all. Let's finish this insanity and go home." I started walking toward Flower and Omura, who were standing together in the middle of the lot. I heard Charlie fall in behind me and was a little comforted by her presence.

It was 7:31 pm.

When I got to Flower and Omura, I had only one thing to say: "What's next?"

"Ramos goes back to the Hummer, Fitz stays here as a relay, and we head in when we get word the convoy has left and Buttons has executed his side of the plan." He looked me over like a head of lettuce in the produce aisle. "You need to eat something right now. You're looking gray."

"I didn't bring anything to eat," I explained, and dropped straight down onto my ass on the pavement, "and none of these poor idiots looked appetizing."

Omura opened up a Velcro pocket on the leg of his tactical pants and handed me a foil-wrapped rectangle.

"They didn't create these with good taste in mind. Think of it like one of those sports drinks that tastes like shit unless your body needs it and then it tastes really good." I gave the package the evil eye.

They were probably talking sense, so I opened the package and was enticed by the aroma of pure bliss that wafted from the broached foil. Tentatively, because nothing that smelled that good could taste that good, I licked it. Then I stuffed the whole bar into my mouth sideways. Buddha had nothing on my bliss.

"Gee, Flower, it looks like he needed something in his mouth," Omura snarked and cracked a rare smile.

"Damn. I have something he could have used for that!" Charlie piped up from right behind me.

"Both of you," Flower pointed at both of them, "stow it. You're making me ill." They laughed at him, but did stow the snark as he ordered.

The outer skin of the thing in my mouth started to slough away and I was content to sit there and let it dissolve into mush. Ramos headed back to the Hummer, and Fitzgerald found himself an easily defensible area to dig himself into. Before too long we had our Cranium Townhall relay set up and ready to go.

Fitz called out to us, "Buttons says the convoy has started to move. He estimates a ten-minute window before he can start the light show."

"Roger." Flower answered for all of us. I probably wouldn't have been able to answer if I had wanted.

My darling, blood-covered Charlotte sat down beside me and gave me the once-over. "What happened to the front of your vest?"

"Mmmrrr nnnnnnn mmmm," I replied, saying something that sounded a whole lot like a man who had a mouth full of goop.

"If you swallowed some of that instead of sitting there like a demented, homicidal squirrel, you could answer the question." I detected a bit of annoyance in her voice, so I did as she suggested.

"Ah got staabud in a ches wi a baynet." I swallowed a little more, because it didn't come out as clear as I might have preferred. "I got stabbed in the chest with a bayonet."

She looked shocked, reached over, and stuck her hand in the hole. "Frank, did he get you in the heart?"

"Yes."

"You didn't die?!" I was a little surprised she'd ask, considering the upgrade package.

"No. It hurt a whole lot and feeling the hole close up was really disgusting, but it didn't kill me."

"Damn." She shook her head. "I'm pretty sure I don't want to go through that, but I'd prefer not to die. Guess I'll just have to suck it up, huh?"

"Probably. How's your boob?"

"Fine. He didn't even dent the vest. I was just startled as Hell he thought to do it." She shook her head ruefully and added, "I'm really happy I had the vest on, though. I don't want to watch my body grow a new nipple."

I just nodded because I had no idea what to say to something like that.

Thankfully, the need to reply to her statement was taken from me by the nano-critters. All of us hit the dirt at the same time, faces down with our hands covering our eyes. I had to assume that my onboard posse was aware of something that I wasn't, like the impending laser show.

Charlie got up first. "What the Hell was that about?"

"Fitz, ping Ramos and have him ask Buttons what the Hell that was." Matt issued the order calmly but looked slightly rattled. "I don't know, Charlie, but we're going to find out."

We stood there, looking around as if we expected something to land on us. Eventually, Fitzgerald got back to us with an answer. Buttons saw a civilian helicopter land on the roof of our target building and took the opportunity to take it out on the off chance that someone interesting was about to make a break for it. Matt sent back a brief message of thanks that included a pointed request that we be informed before such actions were taken.

Fitz also relayed that the convoy was moving quite

quickly for such a large number of vehicles, and that the rescue team should start moving toward the overpass. Armed with that information, Matt rounded us all up and had us check and reload any weapons that were low. We were good to go in less than 60 seconds.

"All right. We've got about half a mile to cover on foot. The plan is to stick to the right side of the paved road with Franklin on point. We will take cover as necessary to avoid the light show. Clear?" Matt locked eyes with each of us until we gave him an affirmative. "All right. After the light show, we will cross the overpass on the right, as quickly as possible. If we have no incidents, we will then duck into the condo community, take out any sentries, and assess which entrance to the building will function best. Clear?"

We were clear. It was simple and direct. Things would likely become messy once we made our entrance into the building itself, but the degree of trouble would depend on things we were not able to predict. The collateral damage from the laser strikes being one of those things, the other unknown being the exact number of opponents we were going to have to face.

Franklin gave us the high sign and we started walking. I'm grateful, and I'm sure the others were as well, that it was a quiet and uneventful slog. There were no cars and not a peep on our "radar" that had anything to do with enemies. We stopped at the end of the overpass and got the ping from Fitzgerald that we had 15 seconds to get cover and get something over our eyes.

It was a long 15 seconds, facedown in the dirt with my hands wrapped around my face. Fitz came across on the Townhall channel to let us know that the strikes on the crater area were about to start. A moment after that it sounded like the sky squealed.

I didn't hear the following shots, even as far away as we were, because there were too many other noises. Booming sounds and screams carried across the road, and I felt sick to think that the idea I had come up with was as brutally effective as it sounded.

"Rescue, Fitzgerald here. Relay says you are good to proceed to target. Visual indicates successful strike, and B is moving to target the convoy. Godspeed."

Flower looked us over and pointed to the other side without a single comment. Franklin took point, and we scrambled over there, hoping to make good use of the confusion.

Hieronymus Bosch would have painted the scene we set our eyes on as we ducked into the elegant, but slightly damaged, brick condominium community on the other side of the overpass. It was Hell after the lights are turned out.

The laser strikes into the water-filled crater did three things we were sure of, even with a quick glance at the tableau. One of the beams melted the water pipe closed. The other shots dazzled or blinded quite a few of the observers instantly. Those near the crater rim, and for some distance beyond it, didn't fare as well as those that were blinded.

The heat caused the entire pool of water to explode into super-heated steam. There were dozens of bodies that had been steamed to death instantly. Still more looked like boiled lobsters, contorted on the bubbling asphalt.

If I live forever, I will pray I never hear a noise like the screaming of the poor bastards who were still alive. I will also hope that if there is a God, that forgiveness is possible, because I brought that suffering about. It didn't matter if they were murderous undead things; they still looked and experienced agony just like people.

Not even the most foul, genocidal, child-raping sociopath deserved to have half of their body cooked to the bone and still be conscious to feel the horrible burning that would kill them... not right away, but over hours. What was being human without some kind of mercy, even in the face of an abomination that masqueraded as a person?

God help me.

I didn't see the sentry until he tried to kill me. Omura took him out, deftly, with an almost graceful motion that sent the head into the air as the body hit the ground. Absentmindedly, it occurred to me I didn't know a garrote could do that, but I kept it to myself. The only thing that came out of my mouth was air, because Flower shoved me up against the nearest wall.

"Save the morality for later," he hissed at me, "you do not have time for it now. Do you want to rescue Bajali? Then fucking get back on the program or I will leave you here. Understand?"

Looking into the hardness of his eyes, for one second or a hundred, I was frightened enough that I remembered who I was and what I had come to do. The realization was tempered with the almost-sure reality that by the time the night was finished I would have seen more horror to lose sleep over for the rest of my life.

My brother and my father were here, somewhere, and they could not be allowed to escape or end the day alive.

"Thank you, Matt. Let's go."

He nodded, and we kept moving.

The view from our vantage point showed more activity toward the parking garage, and much less towards the front of the building. There was not a single intact pane of glass on that side and little to no movement to be seen.

What few guards that were at all apparent were clustered near the door into the building from the upper garage deck. We counted six other figures moving around on that deck and the one below it.

There was so little movement on the other side that it was actually suspicious.

Franklin turned back to the group and said exactly what I had been thinking. "There's too little motion at the front. No triage, no nothing. They rigged something in there."

"Franklin, move up to the near corner of the building. Hard cover if you can take it, soft if you can get it." Flower's orders were clear, and he seemed to have formulated an approach in mere moments. "I'll take out the guard closest to the door. Franklin, you double tap the middle one, and I'll take the third in the confusion. Frank, Charlie, and Omura, you three move up and take that door. We'll follow, depending on resistance. Got it?"

We got it. Franklin slipped across the street like a greased weasel, fast and fluid. Flower chambered a round in his absurdly long sniper rifle and waited for a signal from our point man. It could not have been three full breaths before Flower stopped breathing and his finger tightened on the trigger.

Crack! He didn't miss, but there was no way I would have expected him to miss. The guard closest to the door was the victim of a magic trick that made everything from his collar upwards disappear.

Franklin reacted as soon as he heard the shot and the second guard's head exploded into wet fireworks. The third dropped out of sight in a spray of blood shortly thereafter.

"Go." Flower's order was nearly a whisper, but all three of us heard it and moved.

We got the high sign from Franklin as we passed him, scurrying onto the top deck of the parking garage. The only thing there to meet us were the bodies of the three guards, and the cyclopean gaze of a security camera that we weren't able to see from our original position. The body of the camera sported a red "On" light, and in my imagination, the lens blinked at me.

I broadcast to our team, "They've got a camera. Probably know we're here, if the exploding heads weren't a clue."

Flower fired back a quick response. "Take out the lens." I raised my rifle and cracked it with the stock. The red light went out. "You three," he followed up after watching me disable the camera, "get in there, split up, and make shit happen. I'll follow in 60 seconds. Franklin will hold the exit."

"Sir, I pinged Fitz. Relay says we've got about eight minutes before the convoy stragglers enter the theater," Franklin sent to the whole team.

"You three, I'm giving you five. No more. No less.

Scram!"

Chapter 40

We went through the door in a single-file line. Omura mimed tipping his hat to us and scrambled down the open stairway. Charlie and I moved up to the door leading to the lobby and she poked her nose to the window, gave me a thumbs up, and we let ourselves in.

It was a fairly standard corporate lobby, tasteful marble tile, slap-dash colorful art on the walls, and you could almost hear the Muzak that would have been playing on any given normal work day. Unfortunately, it wasn't a normal workday. There was shattered glass all over the tile and enough dried blood spatters to make Jackson Pollock nauseous. We also learned that Franklin's intuition about the front door was spot on.

Someone had lined the area with trip wires, caltrops, and no fewer than five Claymore anti-personnel mines. It was, to my eye, inexpertly done, but it would have stopped us long enough for a team of defenders to pick us off like baby seals on an ice floe. The question became, "Then where are the defenders?"

"They were going to box us in and pick us off," Charlie whispered, clearly on the same mental page as I was.

"Yeah, that's my guess."

"So where are they?" She took the words right out of my mouth.

"Potty break, feeding time at the slaughterhouse, or they're waiting for us somewhere." I looked around, noting the elevators and the empty reception desk. "We don't have time to wonder too much. Stairs or elevator?"

"Stairs."

Charlie and I turned around and headed in the door towards the stairwell that Omura had used to make his disappearance into the structure of the building. His nefarious purposes were clear: blow it up. We had one clear objective, and a few that flew under the banner of "Gosh! It would be great if... "

The second floor was dead quiet, just offices with open doors into a central free area, and nothing much to speak of beyond that. We elected to not bother poking around and scurried up to the next level.

We were greeted with garbage and six people chained to the walls. They were all on their way to meet whatever Maker they believed in, and it was just a matter of time before they got there. I knew I smelled gangrene somewhere nearby, and a closer look at one of the poor saps confirmed that his hand from the leather belt at his wrist down to his fingers was turning distressing colors.

He wasn't even able to lock eyes with me. They just rolled around in their sockets. I didn't have time to look each of these people over, but this man moved me to take action. I slung the rifle over my shoulder and pulled the Man Scythe free as quietly as possible.

I caressed the inside of his naked thigh with the curve of the blade, and he didn't make a noise; none of them did, and he simply started to bleed out on the floor. When I turned around, Charlie wasn't behind me.

That's when I heard her yell, "Hey, Frank! Who's the asshole in the pajamas?"

I took off down the hallway and into the boardroom at the end of the hall. Charlie stood against the far wall, surrounded by a small crowd of zombies carrying clubs and machetes. Both of her wakizashi were glinting in the light of the daylight-corrected fluorescent light bulbs.

I looked to my left and saw someone I really would have preferred not to see. Unfortunately, I didn't have much choice in the matter.

"Charlie, meet Stewart. Stewart, meet Charlie. He's my younger brother."

She looked thoughtful, a wakizashi in each hand, surrounded by no fewer than eight zombies, and asked me, "Well, does that mean you're going to kill him or let him make a deal and we'll get him later?"

I looked at my smug, undead younger brother. His ninja jammies were pressed, he didn't smell bad, and his claws had been shaved down to long, clean tapers. I couldn't have been more disgusted if Josef Mengele had popped over to bugger one of the poor bastards who were chained to the wall in the foyer. There was enough blood on Stewart's hands to merit an eternity of nasty reincarnations.

"If you don't mind, m'dear, I think I'll kill him now."

Stewart "I'm a zombie and I don't smell" Hightower actually had the nerve to look surprised!

"Frank! I'm still your brother! What do you want to kill me for? Join us! Besides, you'll make a fabulous cow and fucktoy for me and my associates."

I couldn't believe he used Dad's oily, salesman voice on me. All things considered, I probably shouldn't have been surprised—Stu was a fucking nudge as a child.

Stewart and I closed the distance on one another and I snapped the blade of my weapon of choice into a low guard position. He drew his sword, the "classic" ninja chokuto. I was also willing to bet there was something in the hand he kept out of sight behind his leg. Shuriken?

In the quarter of a second I had to think about it, it seemed less likely he'd have a distance weapon, even an annoying one in here. My brother was a sneak. I didn't think more training, dying, and coming back to life would have changed a single thing. Instincts told me it was either a weighted chain, or something equally compact.

I tuned out the noise coming from Charlie's direction, because something bloody had begun. None of it sounded like her. A few clubs, claws, and teeth against someone who was comfortable using two blades wouldn't do much good unless they rushed her. Even then I'd put my money on her.

That moment of considering my environment nearly cost me my life. Stewart flew forward and put a foot on the Man Scythe, which slammed it to the floor but not out of my grip. His sword came down, and I let him bury it into my shoulder. It hurt like Hell.

The look on his face when he realized he'd not only landed a hit on me, but that he'd actually tried to kill a flesh-and-blood relative, was almost delightful enough to make me forget that my shoulder was on fire and that I truly wanted to vomit. Instead, I smiled at him.

"Hey, Stu," I said. "Why don't you pull that out of my shoulder and take a good look at it, you festering excuse for an ass boil?"

With a snarl, he obliged me, and I dropped to my knees. The snarl cut off rather abruptly, because it was a bit of a shock to see how little of his sword blade remained. The section that had cut into my shoulder had a lovely crescent of metal missing, leaving only a pencil-width of steel holding the blade in one piece. I guess my little friends needed to make more playmates, and I was deeply grateful for their sense of dramatic timing.

He took a step back from me and looked at me as if I were the one who ate people for fun. When he shifted his weight off the business end of my weapon it became instantly clear that a moment of truth had arrived.

I don't feel any guilt for taking advantage of his surprise or for killing him. He was already dead once, and the second time didn't matter.

A flick of the wrist turned the Man Scythe upward and sent it slamming into his body. I think it entered behind his testicles and continued for all 20 inches of the blade until it popped out under his sternum.

He froze solid, gasping. I stood up, reversed my grip on the handle, and pivoted with my hips. The blade pulled free, cutting through his pelvic bone, and opening his abdominal cavity to the world. My brother was too shocked to scream and didn't even attempt to pull his guts back in. All I got from him was a blank stare and a spray of bloody entrails.

I pulled my pistol from the holster and put the barrel to his forehead.

"This is a shame, Stu. I love you, but I'm not the least bit sorry." I fired once. There was no way to miss.

When I turned around, Charlie was watching me with a very sad expression on her face. The crew that would have done her harm was strewn around the floor in various states of decapitation and dismemberment. It didn't look like any of them had managed to lay a finger on her.

"We'll talk about it later. We've got to get Baj and get out of here." I waved her out the door and followed her.

There was a certain silence between us that I didn't quite understand, but I also knew we had very little time to deal with the rescue. Whatever was happening between us needed to wait until we got the job done, because it wouldn't matter at all if we died in the attempt. For all I knew, she'd take it up with me in the afterlife, if such a thing existed.

She had stopped in the foyer and was surveying the five remaining people attached to the walls. I tapped her on the shoulder and raised my eyebrow when she turned to face me. Her voice appeared in my head, and she told me she had to do something. I nodded and told her I'd meet her on the next floor.

I turned to go and headed up to the next floor. I had no clue what she was planning; all I knew was that I didn't hear any noises as I hauled ass up the next flight of stairs.

The fire door was dented and the reinforced glass was cracked, but it was typical in every other way. I eased it open, and stuck my head into the room, followed by the rest of my body. My baby was still open in my hand, and I remembered to shift my grip at the last moment before it could have made a racket against the steel door.

Another lobby, but it was neater and a lot closer to high

tech than the floor below. When I turned my head, I saw something that I had been loathing to see but was an important indicator I was in the right place. The logo of my father's company was on the far wall for all to see, looking sharp and angular in brushed stainless steel.

What I didn't know was simple: was this the nerve center or just the first of the floors that he controlled?

Charlie appeared beside me, having accomplished whatever it was she felt compelled to do for those sad people. She indicated left and right and then forward, so we split to opposite sides of the hallway and explored ahead in tandem.

She found the lab on her side. I didn't find anything or anyone.

To laypersons such as us nothing in the lab looked all that unusual. Computers were set up all over, as were microscopes, beakers, and several industrial refrigerators. It wasn't as simple as finding something with a sign next to it that said, "Steal me!" We looked at one another and made the decision to move up another floor, and quickly.

This time we were not disappointed. The nano-critters pinged at us, so we knew there were smelly people nearby and girded our loins before we pushed open the door.

Surprisingly enough, they appeared quite ready to receive visitors. In fact, it looked like they knew we were coming. A cup of coffee and Danishes would not have surprised me at all. What surprised me was my mother.

I stood there with Charlie by my side and gaped like a bigmouth bass. My own estranged maternal organ stood in front of us, backed up by a flock of exotic perverts from Central Casting. The woman I had known all my life was utterly transformed and I could barely process it. Denying it wasn't even possible. You don't forget your mother's face, hair, eyes, or the big diamond ring that cut your lip open when you were 12.

The last time I saw her, barely two years ago, her style was much more Christian Dior dress, tasteful diamonds, and flute of champagne than leather and lace. My mom never would have worn black leather underbust corsets and chainmail skirts. I won't even mention the silicone appendage that protruded from a hole in the front of the skirt.

I don't know which was longer, the bullwhip in her hand or the beastly monster that the skirt couldn't contain. What happened to my giggly mother who knitted and collected Coach handbags?

"Baby! I knew you were coming and I didn't bake a cake." She strutted over to me, working curves that no son should ever be aware that his mother has. "I've missed you so much! You've been a bad little motherfucker."

She hauled back with one hand and slapped me with all her might. The claws on the ends of her fingers dug into my cheek, ripping away ribbons of my face as she swung. I didn't give her the satisfaction of reacting. Charlie did it for me by closing the distance and laying the barrel of her pistol right between my mother's eyes.

"Don't you ever hit him again." She looked my mom up and down. "What the Hell are you supposed to be, the Undead Leather Cougar of the Year?"

Mom laughed, standing still with the gun between her eyes. It was the same old musical laugh she always had, but the look on her face was not anything I had ever seen in the whole of my life.

"I'm a dominatrix. I used to beat his daddy before I decided to marry him and make babies. Now I discipline everyone, my wayward son included." Mom leered at me. "He's come to kill his daddy, but now his mommy gets to fuck him up. I should have named him Oedipus."

I couldn't tell whether Charlie was more disgusted than I was or not. I knew that people who came back from the grave returned with certain bits missing, like their internal editor, but to hear things like that... I felt ill.

"Then again, I could have the executive staff fuck you both up now," my mother continued, "and that might be an amusing little scene to watch."

Standing and lounging behind her were seven men and women dressed in leather harnesses, shiny metal buckles, plates, as well as clips and clamps that would have made wonderful accessories in an operating room. They had not even moved since we came in the door, but they all started to chuckle in unison after my erstwhile parent's comment.

It was a creepy effect, but it came off as being staged rather than a natural communal response. I was vaguely queasy about all of it, but I certainly wasn't frightened.

"We don't have time to fuck with your friends, Mom. We came to get Bajali. Kindly save us the trouble and tell us where he is."

"Warren, that's so dominant of you. Mommy just got drippy for you, you disloyal little worm." She tossed her curly hair over her shoulder, stuck out her tongue, and squeezed her nipples.

Seeing my own mother, even as a zombie, doing things like that...Why is there never a trashcan handy when you need to regurgitate your last 20 meals?

I made my intentions clear to Charlie with my in-skull telephone. She agreed to keep my mother occupied while I took out the Leather Belt Manufacturers Convention behind her. We started to move at the same time thanks to that little bit of communication; I went left to skirt my mother's reach, and Charlie changed her aim.

My mother shrieked when my girlfriend put a bullet in her kneecap.

Charlie yelped when my mom's whip snapped out and curled around her neck. I wanted to pay attention, but we were outnumbered and something needed to be done about Mistress' entourage. I had faith in Charlie, and I had faith in scary marvels of technology.

I found myself in a kung fu movie full of yelling executives wielding expensive sex toys instead of guns. They had claws, teeth, silicone appliances, leather straps, paddles, and oodles of bad attitude. I had a deadline.

"Excuse me, I don't have time for you PowerPoint-pushing shits right now. I'm here to rescue a friend, not expand my repertoire." I got that out of my mouth and one of the enterprising bastards broke a hardwood paddle across my skull. The world went very gray.

When I squirmed my way back to full consciousness, I noticed that someone was trying to stick something up my ass. Not having consented to such treatment, I got ready to take issue with their idea of fun and discovered that the morons had not disarmed me before taking a break to plunder my rectum. I let them have a second to indulge their fantasy of successful ravishment.

Charlie and my mother were still involved in their first meeting. I couldn't have been in limbo long because the whip was still around Charlie's neck. My mother's penis was two-thirds shorter, thanks to the bare blade in my girl's hand.

I was about to yell, "Just shoot my mom," when the prodding at my exit got serious. I whipped the Man Scythe behind me at random, figuring it would either hit someone or stop them from rummaging in my basement.

Someone screamed and my ass was free. I scrambled to my feet, annoyed that my belt was gone, my delicate parts were uncovered, and my pants were around my knees. That didn't do much for my ability to move around. Seeing my lack of composure as an opportunity, some of them tried to get the weapon out of my hands and others set about beating me with dildos.

Having zombies try to rape me was one thing, but hitting me with phallic objects... that was the straw that broke the camel's back.

I bellowed at them with the rage of ten thousand suffering prudes, dropped to my knees, and swung the blade in an arc around my right side. Three of my opponents were suddenly much shorter. Two of the remaining kinky undead dropped their plastic dicks and fled.

Upper Echelon Executive Latex Man shot me in the chest

with my own pistol. Unfortunately for him, it hit an area where my vest was intact. All I got for his trouble was bruised and very annoyed.

"Unacceptable." I spat in his face and lopped off the hand that was holding my gun. He fell to the floor squealing, adding just that much more to the wailing in the room.

Over all the moaning and weeping in pain, I heard a Charlie yell, "When you get to Hell, tell them your future daughter-in-law sent you!" I didn't look. I simply stood up, pulled up my pants with one hand, and calmly decapitated the last of the entourage.

I felt lucky, standing there holding my pants up, that my Best Charlie had a background in psychology, because I was really starting to resent Bajali for all of this gore-encrusted bullshit. With a deep sigh, I put the scythe down, tracked down my belt, and reassembled my wardrobe. The weapons were easier to locate than my belt.

"Charlie, if you didn't take her head, you really ought to." The words came out of my mouth as flat as glass, but much less reflective.

"I hear you. We need to go." I knew something was coming because she started to stammer a little. "Is there anything you need right now?"

"I need to find Bajali and then I need to get out of here alive with you. Let's go."

We went out the door we came in and scurried up the stairs to the next floor. Charlie was on point and went through the door low while I took the high position. Nothing.

Same boring floor plan, similar cheesy pastel art on the walls, except for the places where they were redecorated with arterial spray. We didn't hear any noise or detect any movement with our little high-tech friends, so we moved up another floor.

It was a solid six floors before we even got a chirp. It was a Hell of a chirp.

Crouched behind the door, we knew that there was a human being not too far away from us on the other side. Near that human were four readings of abnormally low body temperatures, gunpowder, and something that the critters didn't like but we had no reference for. Unless they had taken someone other than Baj at one point or another, our friend was behind that door.

"Frank, will any of the ammo in these guns make it through this door with any accuracy?" Charlie asked me over the private channel.

"Probably not. If they get through at all, I'm guessing that they'd end up changing direction from deflecting on the steel. We'll have to go in there if we want to find out anything."

"The human in there doesn't read as having critters. No spark or anything."

That raised a little curiosity in my head. Baj would have nanos. It simply stood to reason that he would have exposed himself to them first.

"Charlie, I have no idea, but we need to find out and we need to do it now. You go high, I'll go low. Count of three."

My Luscious Commando and I went through the door with our guns already aimed. Our targets fired at the same time we did, but our aim was better. They were out of the conflict, permanently. Charlie and I took hits to our vests and probably one or two flesh wounds.

The impacts slammed us back into the door we'd just come through, but I did look up and see Bajali tied to a chair. My skull was ringing, but I was feeling like the end was almost in sight. We had him and we could get him out.

"Warren Hightower!"

Someone called that name from down at the end of the hall, and I turned my head to see who yelled. My father and some dude in a suit were at the end of the hall.

Bajali screamed, "Frank, duck!"

I shifted my eyes and caught a flash of light at the end of the hall. I didn't understand why my head was moving or why Baj looked so distraught.

The last thought I had was that my father had shot me in the head.

Chapter 41

It is accurate to say I didn't have a conscious thought for quite some time after taking a 9mm round to the middle of my forehead. I don't think it would be accurate to say there was no one or nothing functioning from my neck up, because my body kept moving.

Unlike the instances in the past where my consciousness observed things from outside my body and commented as things unfolded, even having the choice to shut off rather than to observe, this time there was no choice. Everything I was went along with my body, but there were no comments or functions that spoke of me being a product of modern civilization. Warren Francis Hightower, the third, was gone.

Calling that creature "me" unsettles me, even after the fact. My soul, values, love, and humor were gone. All that was left running my flesh was nanotechnology that unlocked millions of years of evolution and threw the gears into reverse. It wasn't *me*. It was a beast that I had become.

The thing that was using my body bounced back off of Charlie's thigh, screaming wordless noises full of indignation and rage, and sped down the long hallway. Hot, stinging things hit it and tried to knock it down or deter it; that was simply not going to occur. There was a very simple instinct that forced breath through my body and each muscle that pumped power into the legs that propelled the thing I'd become down the corridor: You hurt me; now you will pay.

The upright animal in the gray skins interposed itself

between my rushing body and my father. Animals don't have words for concepts like "unacceptable" or "this is a thing that shouldn't be." The only thing my body knew was that Gray Skins was in the way.

I learned much later that my father's bodyguard was none other than Ronnie Bianco, the most efficient hitter the Rhode Island Mafia had ever produced. But none of the skills he had learned or the experience of dying and coming back to feed on the living prepared him for what that round to my brain had created.

With a drywall-shaking bellow, all that was left of me challenged Gray Skins and did not bother waiting for an answering call. Our bodies plowed together with the wet pop of breaking bones, the front of my forehead crushing Gray Skins' lower jaw.

Now the opponent had one less weapon. That was a satisfactory exchange for the pain that flooded my wounded skull and made sight difficult.

The former Mafia hitman noticed that the impact caused me to gray out for a moment and knew he had to press that advantage or not live long enough to recover from a broken jaw. The quarters were too close for him to pull his gun, but he did have access to the switchblade in his coat pocket and the claws that arced out over his fingertips. Somehow, without words or gestures, I knew he decided that a blade was for killing a man, but claws were for killing animals. As for me, this guy with a hole in his head, it certainly looked like I had left "human" far behind.

He grabbed me by the hair, pulled back my head, and tore my throat out with a single pass of his sharpened claws. While my body was operating on nano-critters and primeval rage, it couldn't ignore the shame it felt when it hit the floor. Ronnie "Black and White" Bianco stood up. The gray suit was ruined, but there would be other gray suits.

Warren Hightower, my father, tapped him on the shoulder. Ronnie turned around and looked into eyeballs that had grown to the size of floodlights, and then followed the pointing finger to the floor.

The animal that remained after the bullet washed me away was crouched there, staring at them both. The ruined larynx and esophagus twitched and writhed underneath the horrible expression on my face. With something like pissing-terror, they heard my lungs inhale through the shredded meat that dangled and squirmed above the top of the bulletproof vest.

With an intact windpipe the noise that erupted from the Frank-Animal's chest and caused the tattered flesh to swell would have been enough to terrify any creature into submission. Instead, Ronnie and my father were covered in spraying blood, accompanied by a sound like teatime at the slaughterhouse.

My rage-filled animal self lunged, dropping Ronnie like a bag of lawn clippings and, in the same motion, breaking Warren Hightower's left knee with a single twitch of a foot. Mister Hightower, my dear old dad, collapsed onto the bloody industrial carpet, which put him face to face with the last moments of his employee's life. He wasn't even able to retreat or shrink back when the top of Ronnie's skull landed in front of his nose.

All he could do was lay there, transfixed by something. It might have been the eyes of his own son that never left his face, even while the son ate the warm brain of the man he had just killed, or it might have been abject horror that left him crumpled there on the floor. In retrospect, I am fairly sure it wasn't guilt.

In the back of his head I know he was screaming and fighting to move his limbs so that he might avoid being next. It didn't do him any good.

He watched the creature that had taken over my body start to heal. My skull was closing, and my ruined throat had become whole enough to swallow gobbets of Ronnie's brain. Whatever I was, he knew I was not his son. More than that, he knew he was next.

The thing that had been me grabbed him by the throat

and slowly pounded his head against the poorly cushioned concrete floor. My father didn't want to die without saying something, but then again, he didn't want to die at all, I'm sure. This was supposed to be the next step in human evolution, managed, planned, and directed by Warren Hightower who would live forever, enshrined, hallowed, and worshipped.

It was his ego that fought back and forced a scream of defiance out of his mouth, I think. His pride surged and issued an undeniable command to fight back, which he tried to do. The claws on the ends of his fingers tore into my Kevlar vest and snagged in the fibers.

Instead of fighting back he made it even more impossible to flee. His son, or at least the animated body of his son, the one rhythmically slamming his head against the floor, made a noise. It was a single bark of condescending laughter, and the last thing he ever heard.

From the moment I rebounded off of Charlie's leg, probably from the instant the bullet entered my head, I ceased being human. I pieced together memories of those few minutes from the vivid images and emotions that were left behind, as well as from what Bajali and Charlie saw. I suppose it should surprise me that their memories are crystal clear about those events. Especially Bajali's recollections, I would think, because he encountered something he hadn't planned on.

The moment he was given access to the lab, he took the work he'd started years before, made a few alterations about how the nanotechnology would propagate between hosts, and tweaked the integration and host repair systems. The original nano-critter was incapable of being spread and nowhere near as efficient at keeping people alive.

As soon as it was functional and the few computer models he ran it on said it would fulfill the criteria of "keep the host alive in urban combat conditions" and give that person a leg up on healing damage, Baj started looking for a way to get it from the lab to us. Whether it was the grace of

God or good luck, he didn't have to wait long at all.

It seems as though my father's bright idea to motivate Baj by using Mister Yan as his pet scientist's caretaker backfired. According to our friend, Hightower, Senior, had been told that one of the "flock" had been a resident of our neighborhood and, believing that any "reborn" was loyal to him, offered our old neighbor a job. Mister Yan was not stupid and accepted.

That bit of poor judgment on my parent's part is what allowed Bajali to set his plan in motion. He thought we'd thank our lucky stars, take the gift we'd been given, and escape. Mister Yan tried to explain it was more likely that we would turn and fight so that we could "make family whole again," but Baj was not listening.

He believed, or wanted to believe, that we would leave him to his karma and save ourselves, because he would likely be killed for failing to produce what my father demanded. It had become very clear during those four days that the nanotechnology would not have assisted the spread of the virus at all.

Bajali spent hours explaining things like particle size versus viral size, transmission rates, natural immunity, allergic reactions, and payload delivery. If the nanomachines were the virus, he told my father, then we could pick and choose who is infected and who is not. To have that sort of control with a biological infection, they would have to compromise the immune system of our entire species first, and then allow the machines to make the decision over who is infected and who is not.

"What happens after that, Mister Hightower? Simple. Mass fatalities begin over simple things like a sinus infection or pricking oneself with a rose thorn," he told my father. "There is no way to turn the immune system back on, on a global scale, at the same instant, everywhere. I cannot even predict how many people, or your cattle, would die before some sort of reset could be introduced into the environment."

Frustrated, my father sent him upstairs to have his attitude adjusted by my mother and her executive motivation team. It was the first of many such appointments over the space of a few days. Baj's attitude didn't change, but they decided to keep him alive while they pursued other methods that would allow the Great Plan to be set into motion.

First, they decided our little local resistance would have to be dealt with and then they could properly plan how to use Bajali Sharma for their own benefit. Ultimately, that decision set everything else in motion, culminating in using him as a distraction so that my dear Pops would have a clear shot at my head.

Things turned out a wee bit differently than planned.

They told me Flower showed up just as I was throttling my father to death. I didn't crack open his skull and eat his brain. I tore his head clean off and stomped on it until it was an unrecognizable mess.

"Frank!" Charlie called to me from down the hall, and enough of me remained that I lifted my head and looked at her. I don't know that I knew who she was, but I had some clue that she wasn't a threat. "Come with me, all right? Omura says we've got two minutes. Come with me!"

She waved me over and I went to her, following her directions like some kind of overgrown mutant terrier.

There was a vague sense that I knew these other upright animals, so it didn't bother me that we clumped into a group and hauled ass down quite a few sets of stairs. A short time later, we opened a door to the outside and were greeted by another animal I knew. He was caked with blood and baring his teeth in a pleased sort of way.

"Frank, you look like Hell. Did you do everything you came to do?" I just stared at the smiling creature. It was Omura, of course, but I didn't have a name for him or any context beyond recognition that he wasn't a threat or a challenger.

"Omura, Frank took a bullet to the front of his head. He's

I recall meeting two other people in a place where there were objects still burning, and an uneventful ride to another place where there were more people who were excited about something. Charlie moved me away from the hubbub as quickly as she could manage without being impolite. Omura followed us into a dark building that had lots of objects stacked on things that kept them organized.

"Charlie, I need to talk to you," Omura said when he caught up to us.

"I'm a little busy right now. Can we do it later?" Her voice was cracking and her hand was trembling, which set me on edge.

"No, it can't, and Frank needs to hear it."

She turned on him, almost wrenching my arm out of the socket. "Hear it? Omura, he can't understand a fucking word any of us are saying! Frank... oh God... He's not in there anymore." Tears were streaming down her face, and I was concerned because something was bothering my person.

Logic dictated that the smaller animal was upsetting my person, so I started to take a more aggressive stance. It was simple: he would go away and my person would be fine. I knew I could make him go away, but Charlie knew what was happening and squeezed my hand.

"Relax, he's one of us. It's okay." She said it loudly enough that I could hear it, and with enough authenticity, despite her tears, that I took her meaning.

"Charlie, you're wrong. He does need to hear it, because he's going to remember it. He's going to remember everything." Omura's tone of voice was absolutely serious, as was the expression on his face.

"He got shot in the brain. That shit doesn't heal, Omura!"

"In his case, it might. That goes for all of us who got Sharma's tech. I'll tell you why." He kept his hands at his sides as he spoke, as if he understood that large movements would trigger me. "Buttons is not in charge of our group. I am. Have you heard about CIA agents having a 'handler'?"

"Yes, but what does that have to do with this?"

"I'm Buttons' handler. The reason I'm his handler is because he suffered traumatic brain injuries in the Second Gulf War and was recruited for experimental treatment by the medical side of DARPA." He sighed deeply and continued, "Without going into painful detail, Buttons received injections of nanotechnology that are ten generations more primitive than what we've been given. Between that, and a solid year of retraining, he became functional enough to resume most of his former duties."

Charlie was squeezing my hand very tightly, but I couldn't read her emotional state beyond how intensely she was listening to the noises that Omura was making. Barring any other direction, I held my place and endured the discomfort of my hand being squashed.

"There were problems with his behavior and changes to his skill strengths and weaknesses," Omura went on. "Think of him as a high-functioning autistic with Attention Deficit Disorder. His control of emotions is weak, but he can hold a huge number of cognitive balls in the air at once and can process varieties of data that normal humans cannot. Really, honestly *cannot* process. My job is to keep him doing his job, without losing his focus or composure."

"Are you telling me that Frank is going to heal?"

"If Buttons can come back to what he is now from losing function in most of his right hemisphere on antiquated technology... I'd have to say Frank will do much better than that, but," Omura held up a cautioning finger, "he's going to come back different and he will need a handler until we know more."

"Don't worry. I'd take that job even if he didn't pick me."

"Yeah, I wasn't worried about that for some reason," Omura smiled, and it looked to be a very genuine one. "Once things calm down a little more, I have to talk to everyone about what all of these things mean for your community and for me, since I got Sharma's critters along with the rest of you. Life is going to change dramatically."

About the Author

James Crawford is an artist, graphic designer, amateur bladesmith and subversive suburbanite when no one else is looking. He lives in the Washington, DC area with his wife, pursues hobbies that pay off in cuts, burns, tendonitis, full sketchbooks, and the occasional freaky idea. Once in a while, those freaky ideas refuse to die and shamble off to create lives of their own.

The author would like to thank friends and family for their support as this project evolved over time. In particular he would like to thank Rachael Fink for her editing, commentary, and extensive understanding of the Southern female psyche.

To you: if you like *Blood Soaked and Contagious*, recommend it to your friends via your favorite social media outlets and in person.

Credit for the cover image design goes to Karen Fletcher at Karen Fletcher Design.

Connect with me online:

My blog: http://www.bloodsoakedandwriting.com
Twitter: Crawford4033

14
BY PETER CLINES

Padlocked doors. Strange light fixtures. Mutant cockroaches. There are some odd things about Nate's new apartment. Every room in this old brownstone has a mystery. Mysteries that stretch back over a hundred years. Some of them are in plain sight. Some are behind locked doors. And all together these mysteries could mean the end of Nate and his friends. Or the end of everything...

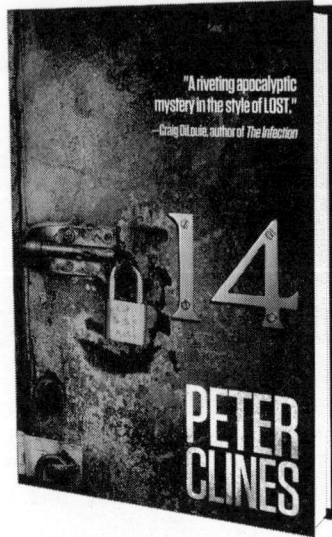

"A riveting apocalyptic mystery in the style of LOST."
—Craig DiLouie, author of The Infection

14

PETER CLINES

PERMUTEDPRESS.COM

THE FLU
BY JACQUELINE DRUGA

Throughout history there have been several thousand different strains of influenza. Each year hundreds are active. Chances are, this year, you will catch one of those strains. You will cough, sneeze, and your body will ache. Without a second thought, you'll take a double dose of green liquid, go to bed, and swear you'll feel better in the morning. Not this time.

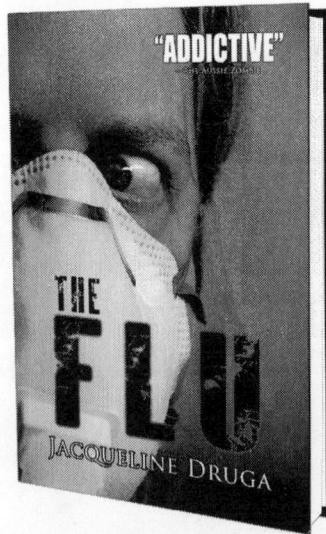

"ADDICTIVE"
THE AUSSIE ZOMBIE

THE FLU

JACQUELINE DRUGA

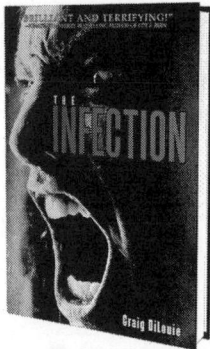

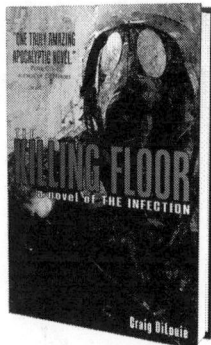

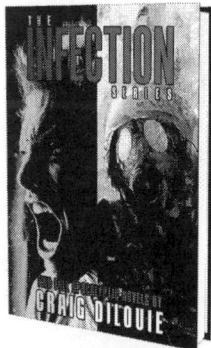

DOMAIN OF THE DEAD
BY IAIN MCKINNON

The world is dead, devoured by a plague of reanimated corpses. Barricaded inside a warehouse with dwindling food, a group of survivors faces two possible deaths: creeping starvation, or the undead outside. In their darkest hour hope appears in the form of a helicopter approaching the city... but is it the salvation the survivors have been waiting for?

"SURPRISED ME...A QUICK, VIOLENT AND EXCITING ADVENTURE."
—DAVID MOODY, AUTHOR OF *HATER*

IAIN MCKINNON
DOMAIN OF THE DEAD

REMAINS OF THE DEAD
BY IAIN MCKINNON

The world is dead. Cahz and his squad of veteran soldiers are tasked with flying into abandoned cities and retrieving zombies for scientific study. Then the unbelievable happens. After years of encountering nothing but the undead, the team discovers a handful of survivors in a fortified warehouse with dwindling supplies.

"ABSOLUTELY SUPERB."
—JOE MCKINNEY, AUTHOR OF *DEAD CITY*

IAIN MCKINNON
REMAINS OF THE DEAD

AMONG THE LIVING
BY TIMOTHY W. LONG

The dead walk. Now the real battle for Seattle has begun. Lester has a new clientele, the kind that requires him to deal lead instead of drugs. Mike suspects a conspiracy lies behind the chaos. Kate has a dark secret: she's a budding young serial killer. These survivors, along with others, are drawn together in their quest to find the truth behind the spreading apocalypse.

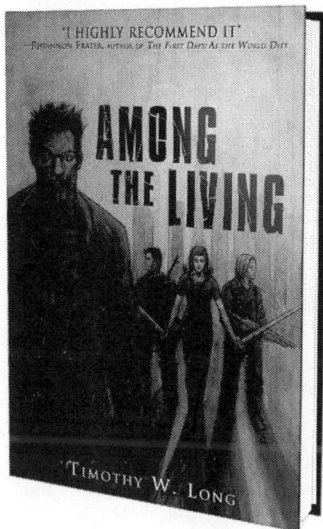

PERMUTEDPRESS.COM

AMONG THE DEAD
BY TIMOTHY W. LONG

Seattle is under siege by masses of living dead, and the military struggles to prevent the virus from spreading outside the city. Kate is tired of sitting around. When she learns that a rescue mission is heading back into the chaos, she jumps at the chance to tag along and put her unique skill set and, more importantly, swords to use.

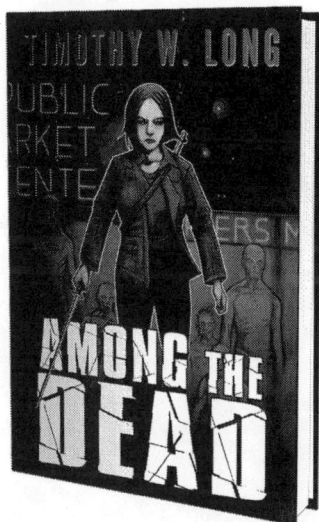

ROADS LESS TRAVELED: THE PLAN
BY C. DULANEY

Ask yourself this: If the dead rise tomorrow, are you ready? Do you have a plan? Kasey, a strong-willed loner, has something she calls The Zombie Plan. But every plan has its weaknesses, and a freight train of tragedy is bearing down on Kasey and her friends. In the darkness that follows, Kasey's Plan slowly unravels: friends lost, family taken, their stronghold reduced to ashes.

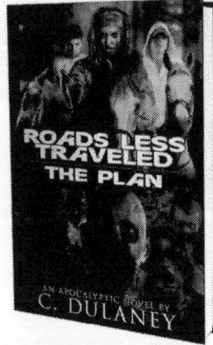

MURPHY'S LAW
(ROADS LESS TRAVELED BOOK 2)
BY C. DULANEY

Kasey and the gang were held together by a set of rules, their Zombie Plan. It kept them alive through the beginning of the End. But when the chaos faded, they became careless, and Murphy's Law decided to pay a long-overdue visit. Now the group is broken and scattered with no refuge in sight. Those remaining must make their way across West Virginia in search of those who were stolen from them.

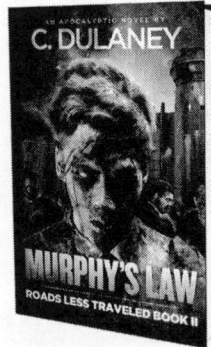

SHADES OF GRAY
(ROADS LESS TRAVELED BOOK 3)
BY C. DULANEY

Kasey and the gang have come full circle through the crumbling world. Working for the National Guard, they realize old friends and fellow survivors are disappearing. When the missing start to reappear as walking corpses, the group sets out on another journey to discover the truth. Their answers wait in the West Virginia Command Center.

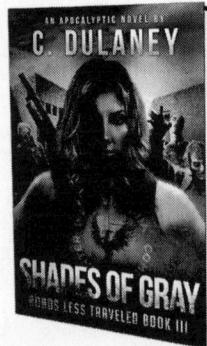

not himself," Charlie explained, and then his smile vanished as though it were never there.

"All right. We'll deal with that if we live. Let's get over into that condo development. We've got... Fuck, just run!"

Everyone ran and I ran too; it seemed like the reasonable thing to do at the time, even if I didn't know why we were running. I stopped when they stopped and let Charlie pull me behind a wall and into cover.

The noise of the muffled explosions was nothing in comparison to the wall of overwhelming sound that heralded the office building collapsing into rubble, floor by floor. I think I would have run if Charlie hadn't held onto me so tightly. Instead, I weathered the cacophony with her.

In minutes, we were coated in brick dust and God only knows what else. When our huddled pack of humans separated, the only areas that weren't covered in powdered detritus were the places where our bodies touched. Everyone looked around and laughed at themselves; I didn't understand and remained silent.

Charlie looked at me and saw I wasn't catching anything about what was going on. The gray dust around her eyes became darker and she swallowed very hard. "Frank, I want you to take my hand. We're going to meet the rest of our people and then go home. Okay?"

She held out her hand and I took it. I didn't understand a word she was saying, but my instincts told me she was someone worth listening to and following. I suppose I decided she was my person, like some breeds of dogs pick one individual in the family to be the one they always listen to or defend.

The pack wanted to run more, so I ran with them, keeping pace with my person and never letting her hand go.

No one could tell me what "home" was, and I couldn't ask. Language was well out of my reach, wherever I was or whatever was left of me. What I did know is that my person was going somewhere and if she were there with me, then "home" would be fine.

NEW ZED ORDER: SURVIVE
BY TODD SPRAGUE

The dead have risen, and they are hungry. In Vermont, John Mason and his beautiful young wife Sara believe that family can survive anything. When the apocalypse arrives they pack food, clothing, and weapons, then hit the road seeking refuge in the mountains of John's youth. There they, together with family, friends, and neighbors, build a stronghold against the encroaching mass of the dead.

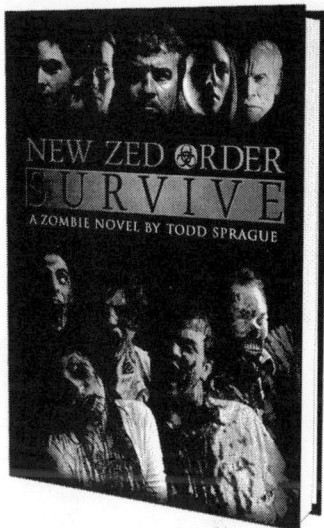

PERMUTEDPRESS.COM

THE JUNKIE QUATRAIN
BY PETER CLINES

Six months ago, the world ended. The Baugh Contagion swept across the planet. Its victims were left twitching, adrenalized cannibals that quickly became know as Junkies. THE JUNKIE QUATRAIN is four tales of survival, and four types of post-apocalypse story. Because the end of the world means different things for different people. Loss. Opportunity. Hope. Or maybe just another day on the job.

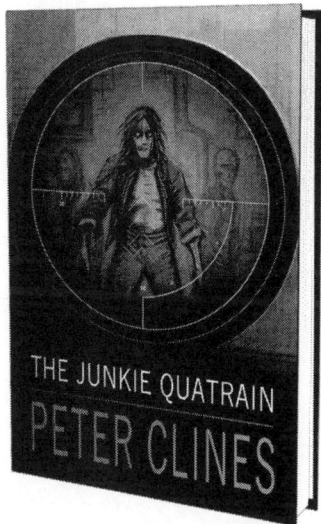

THE UNDEAD SITUATION
BY ELOISE J. KNAPP

The dead are rising. People are dying. Civilization is collapsing. But Cyrus V. Sinclair couldn't care less; he's a sociopath. Amidst the chaos, Cyrus sits with little more emotion than one of the walking corpses... until he meets up with other inconvenient survivors who cramp his style and force him to re-evaluate his outlook on life. It's Armageddon, and things will definitely get messy.

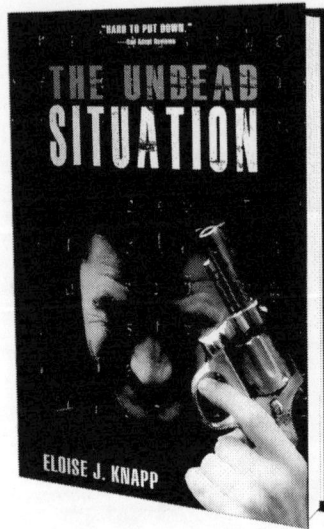

PERMUTEDPRESS.COM

THE UNDEAD HAZE
(THE UNDEAD SITUATION BOOK 2)
BY ELOISE J. KNAPP

When remorse drives Cyrus to abandon his hidden compound he doesn't realize what new dangers lurk in the undead world. He knows he must wade through the vilest remains of humanity and hordes of zombies to settle scores and find the one person who might understand him. But this time, it won't be so easy. Zombies and unpleasant survivors aren't the only thing Cyrus has to worry about.

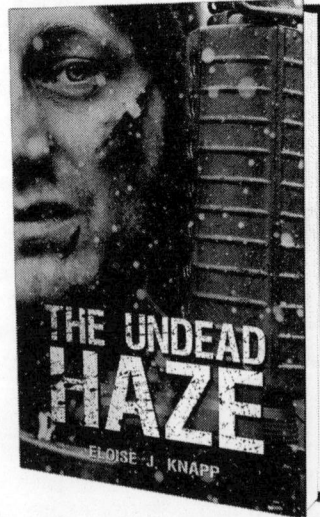

DEAD LIVING
BY GLENN BULLION

It didn't take long for the world to die. And it didn't take long, either, for the dead to rise. Aaron was born on the day the world ended. Kept in seclusion, his family teaches him the basics. How to read and write. How to survive. Then Aaron makes a shocking discovery. The undead, who desire nothing but flesh, ignore him. It's as if he's invisible to them.

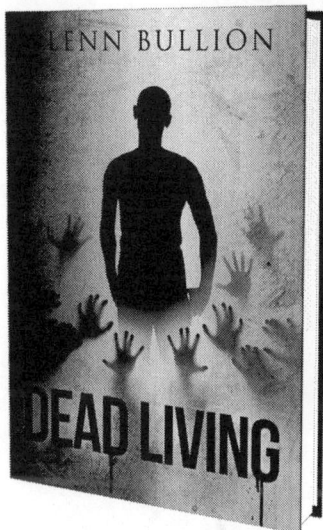

AUTOBIOGRAPHY of a WEREWOLF HUNTER
BY BRIAN P. EASTON

After his mother is butchered by a werewolf, Sylvester James is taken in by a Cheyenne mystic. The boy trains to be a werewolf hunter, learning to block out pain, stalk, fight, and kill. As Sylvester sacrifices himself to the hunt, his hatred has become a monster all its own. As he follows his vendetta into the outlands of the occult, he learns it takes more than silver bullets to kill a werewolf.

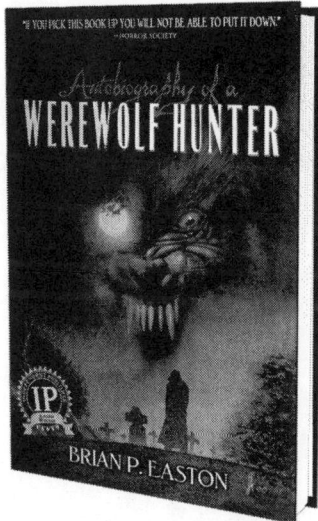

INFECTION:
ALASKAN UNDEAD APOCALYPSE
BY SEAN SCHUBERT

Anchorage, Alaska: gateway to serene wilderness of The Last Frontier. No stranger to struggle, the city on the edge of the world is about to become even more isolated. When a plague strikes, Anchorage becomes a deadly trap for its citizens. The only two land routes out of the city are cut, forcing people to fight or die as the infection spreads.

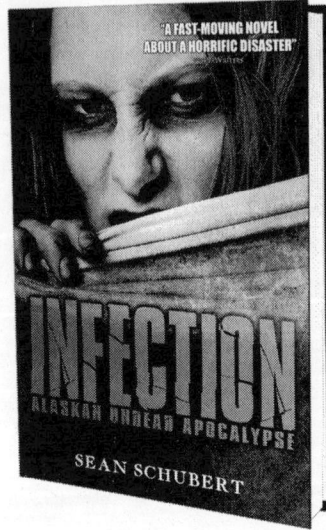

"A FAST-MOVING NOVEL ABOUT A HORRIFIC DISASTER"
– J. Walters

INFECTION
ALASKAN UNDEAD APOCALYPSE

SEAN SCHUBERT

— PERMUTEDPRESS.COM —

CONTAINMENT
(ALASKAN UNDEAD APOCALYPSE BOOK 2)
BY SEAN SCHUBERT

Running. Hiding. Surviving. Anchorage, once Alaska's largest city, has fallen. Now a threatening maze of death, the city is firmly in the cold grip of a growing zombie horde. Neil Jordan and Dr. Caldwell lead a small band of desperate survivors through the maelstrom. The group has one last hope: that this nightmare has been contained, and there still exists a sane world free of infection.

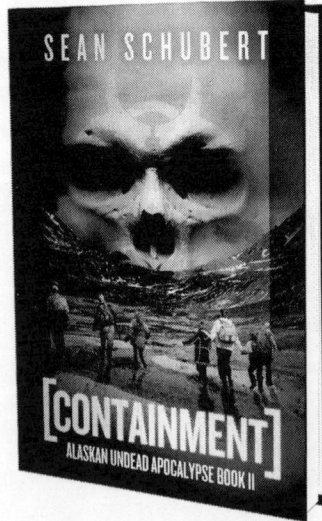

SEAN SCHUBERT

[CONTAINMENT]
ALASKAN UNDEAD APOCALYPSE BOOK II

MAD SWINE: THE BEGINNING
BY STEVEN PAJAK

People refer to the infected as "zombies," but that's not what they really are. Zombie implies the infected have died and reanimated. The thing is, they didn't die. They're just not human anymore. As the infection spreads and crazed hordes--dubbed "Mad Swine"--take over the cities, the residents of Randall Oaks find themselves locked in a desperate struggle to survive in the new world.

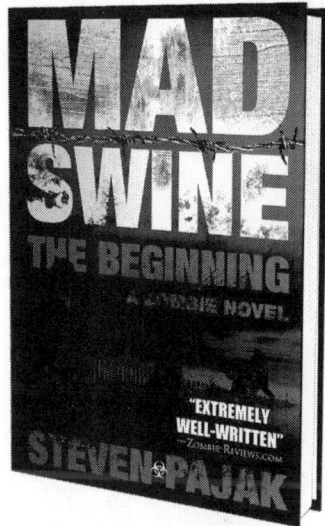

MAD SWINE: DEAD WINTER
BY STEVEN PAJAK

Three months after the beginning of the Mad Swine outbreak, the residents of Randall Oaks have reached their breaking point. After surviving the initial outbreak and a war waged with their neighboring community, Providence, their supplies are severely close to depletion. With hostile neighbors at their flanks and hordes of infected outside their walls, they have become prisoners within their own community.

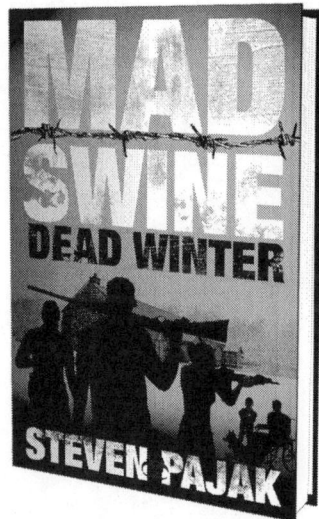

DEAD TIDE
BY STEPHEN A. NORTH

THE WORLD IS ENDING. BUT THERE ARE SURVIVORS. Nick Talaski is a hard-bitten, angry cop. Graham is a newly divorced cab driver. Bronte is a Gulf War veteran hunting his brother's killer. Janicea is a woman consumed by unflinching hate. Trish is a gentleman's club dancer. Morgan is a morgue janitor. The dead have risen and the citizens of St. Petersburg and Pinellas Park are trapped. The survivors are scattered, and options are few. And not all monsters are created by a bite. Some still have a mind of their own…

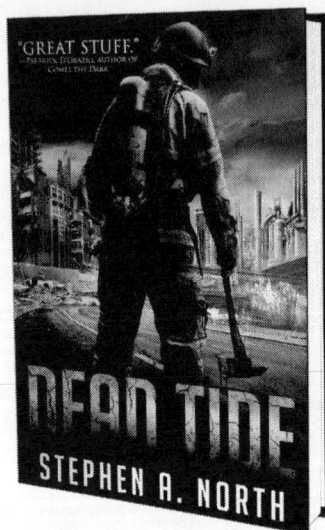

"GREAT STUFF."
—PATRICK D'ORAZIO, AUTHOR OF
COMES THE DARK

DEAD TIDE
STEPHEN A. NORTH

DEAD TIDE RISING
BY STEPHEN A. NORTH

The sequel to Dead Tide continues the carnage in Pinellas Park near St. Pete, Florida. Follow all of the characters from the first book, Dead Tide, as they fight for survival in a world destroyed by the zombie apocalypse.

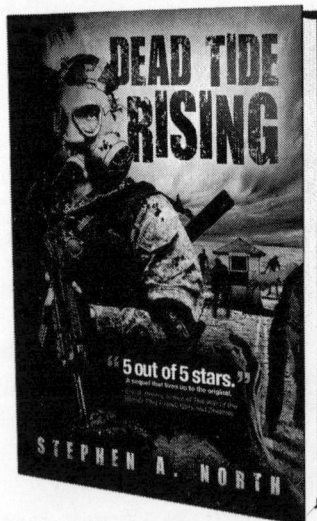

DEAD TIDE RISING

"5 out of 5 stars."

STEPHEN A. NORTH

RISE
BY GARETH WOOD

Within hours of succumbing to a plague, millions of dead rise to attack the living. Brian Williams flees the city with his sister Sarah. Banded with other survivors, the group remains desperately outnumbered and under-armed. With no food and little fuel, they must fight their way to safety. RISE is the story of the extreme measures a family will take to survive a trek across a country gone mad.

PERMUTEDPRESS.COM

AGE OF THE DEAD
BY GARETH WOOD

A year has passed since the dead rose, and the citizens of Cold Lake are out of hope. Food and weapons are nearly impossible to find, and the dead are everywhere. In desperation Brian Williams leads a salvage team into the mountains. But outside the small safe zones the world is a foreign place. Williams and his team must use all of their skills to survive in the wilderness ruled by the dead.

DEAD MEAT
BY PATRICK & CHRIS WILLIAMS

The city of River's Edge has been quarantined due to a rodent borne rabies outbreak. But it quickly becomes clear to the citizens that the infection is something much, much worse than rabies... The townsfolk are attacked and fed upon by packs of the living dead. Gavin and Benny attempt to survive the chaos in River's Edge while making their way north in search of sanctuary.

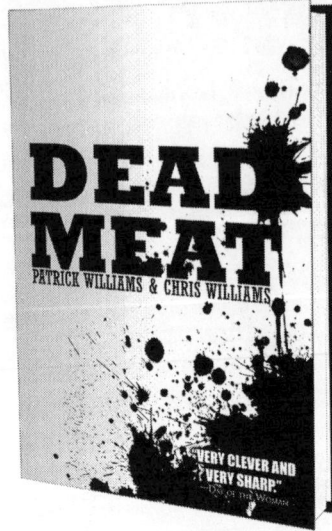

DEAD MEAT
PATRICK WILLIAMS & CHRIS WILLIAMS

"VERY CLEVER AND VERY SHARP."

PERMUTEDPRESS.COM

ROTTER WORLD
BY SCOTT M. BAKER

Eight months ago vampires released the Revenant Virus on humanity. Both species were nearly wiped out. The creator of the virus claims there is a vaccine that will make humans and vampires immune to the virus, but it's located in a secure underground facility five hundred miles away. To retrieve the vaccine, a raiding party of humans and vampires must travel down the devastated East Coast.

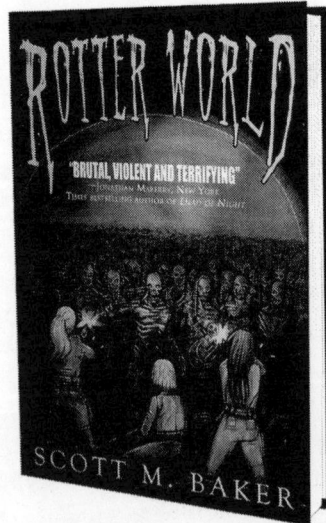

ROTTER WORLD

"BRUTAL, VIOLENT AND TERRIFYING"
—Jonathan Maberry, New York Times best-selling author of Dust & Decay

SCOTT M. BAKER

THE BECOMING
BY JESSICA MEIGS

The Michaluk Virus has escaped the CDC, and its effects are widespread and devastating. Most of the population of the southeastern United States have become homicidal cannibals. As society rapidly crumbles under the hordes of infected, three people--Ethan, a Memphis police officer; Cade, his best friend; and Brandt, a lieutenant in the US Marines--band together against the oncoming crush of death.

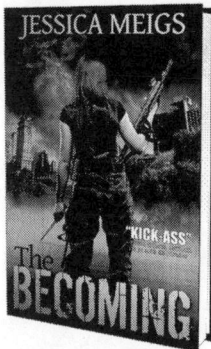

THE BECOMING:
GROUND ZERO (BOOK 2)
BY JESSICA MEIGS

After the Michaluk Virus decimated the southeast, Ethan and his companions became like family. But the arrival of a mysterious woman forces them to flee from the infected, and the cohesion the group cultivated is shattered. As members of the group succumb to the escalating dangers on their path, new alliances form, new loves develop, and old friendships crumble.

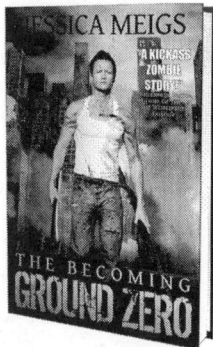

THE BECOMING:
REVELATIONS (BOOK 3)
BY JESSICA MEIGS

In a world ruled by the dead, Brandt Evans is floundering. Leadership of their dysfunctional group wasn't something he asked for or wanted. Their problems are numerous: Remy Angellette is grief-stricken and suicidal, Gray Carter is distant and reclusive, and Cade Alton is near death. And things only get worse.

PAVLOV'S DOGS
BY D.L. SNELL & THOM BRANNAN

WEREWOLVES Dr. Crispin has engineered the saviors of mankind: soldiers capable of transforming into beasts. ZOMBIES Ken and Jorge get caught in a traffic jam on their way home from work. It's the first sign of a major outbreak. ARMAGEDDON Should Dr. Crisping send the Dogs out into the zombie apocalypse to rescue survivors? Or should they hoard their resources and post the Dogs as island guards?

PERMUTEDPRESS.COM

THE OMEGA DOG
BY D.L. SNELL & THOM BRANNAN

Twisting and turning through hordes of zombies, cartel territory, Mayan ruins, and the things that now inhabit them, a group of survivors must travel to save one man's family from a nightmarish third world gone to hell. But this time, even best friends have deadly secrets, and even allies can't be trusted - as a father's only hope of getting his kids out alive is the very thing that's hunting him down.

Made in the USA
Charleston, SC
07 September 2013